Oh for a Ha'porth of Tar

Oh for a Ha'porth of Tar

Lucidus Smith

Dedication

To Mallipeg

Mallipeg is young and old, it loves to dance, it jumps for joy;
It can swim and bounce and ride a horse, it kicks and throws a ball up high.
Mallipeg can draw and paint; it puzzles, games and tends its pets;
It helps at school and in the home and never shoes or lunch forgets.
Mallipeg is good and kind and loves to wear a smiley face,
It brings such joy to these old eyes;
My Matthew, Luis, Lilly, Poppy, Emily and Grace.

31st December 2010   LS

Table of Contents

Introduction 1
Chapter 1 - And One for his Nob! 3
Chapter 2 - Something Shiny 13
Chapter 3 - Mikesh Palk 25
Chapter 4 - Calcutta Return 42
Chapter 5 - The Boer War 55
Chapter 6 - 'El Burro Volando' 67
Chapter 7 - Trouble in Lagos 81
Chapter 8 - The Iquique Massacre 95
Chapter 9 - A New Life 114
Chapter 10 - The Great War 126
Chapter 11 - The Big Fish 141
Chapter 12 - A Modern Form of Transport 160
Chapter 13 - Stormy Weather 175
Chapter 14 - So who are you now? 190
Chapter 15 - You Owe Me One 215
Chapter 16 - An Interesting Place 232
Chapter 17 - Comings and Goings 244
Chapter 18 - Three's a Committee 260
Chapter 19 - Family Problems 278
Chapter 20 - Here we go again 294
Chapter 21 - Red Rabbit 314
Chapter 22 - A Cargo of Farm Machinery 334
Chapter 23 - White Faced Chickens 354
Chapter 24 - El Burro to the Rescue 372
Chapter 25 - New Beginnings 390
Epilogue 411

Introduction

It is April1885 and the 'Long Depression', triggered by the 'Panic of 1873' still has a few years to run in Great Britain.

Robert Bannister the third, who is the only child of Alice and Robert Bannister, is celebrating his sixth birthday with his parents, grandparents and Great Uncle Harry. Since both his father and grandfather are also called Robert and they all live in the same house in Gravesend, England; Robert Bannister the third was called Bertie, right from the very start of his life.

Bertie is destined to work with his father and grandfather on their Thames Barge in and around London, but fate intervenes to give him an opportunity to attend a naval college and start him on a career that will not only take him all over the world, but also involve him in most of the world's major events over the next sixty years.

Some people are born heroes, some have heroism thrust upon them and others simply do their best wherever they are and whatever situation they find themselves in. Bertie is just an ordinary man whose professional approach to life and dedication to duty are an inspiration and example to everyone who meets him.

BLOSSOM
Blossom in good times and blossom in bad,
Blossom when happy and when you are sad.
For the world's sometimes gloomy and the path often
grey,
But the blossom within you can brighten your day.

Chapter 1
And One for his Nob!

"No, no, no, no, no Bertie! How many times have I told you? Fifteen two - fifteen four - a pair's six and one for his Nob is seven! Why do you always forget about the extra one? Crib is not a hard game, you just have to concentrate and remember the rules."

"Sorry uncle Harry," said Bertie, "I do try and remember, honest I do."

Neither of the players had noticed Bertie's Gran come into the room while all this was going on. "Bertie, love, it's nearly tea time. Go and wash your hands and tell your mum that tea will be ready in ten minutes and ask her to give me a hand please."

"Right'o' Gran. I'll beat you next time uncle and then you will have to give me my own Cribbage Board, remember?"

"Go on son, looks like your Gran wants a word with me," Great Uncle Harry said dubiously.

"What on earth is wrong with you Harry? The boy is six and it's his birthday and you are going on at him like he was one of your workmates you were playing cards with! You should be ashamed of yourself shouting at him like that, today of all days."

"Look, I just forget he is so young OK. He plays so well most of the time that I honestly forget he is only a young boy. Anyway, I didn't shout at him."

"Harry Noble, I was in the back yard getting the washing and I could hear every word you said to him. Even when you were his age, mum used to send me out in the street to tell you to stop shouting, "That boy will wake the dead", she used to say and nothing has changed. Go and wash your hands in the scullery and don't touch the food, you hear."

"Good grief Aggie, will you never stop bossing me about? I am thirty six and am quite capable of deciding if my hands need washing, thank you very much!"

With which he got up from the table and went through to the scullery and washed his hands and was about to try one of the homemade biscuits, when he heard his sister cough very loudly and wondered how on earth she could have known what he was about to do.

When he went back into the dining room he found Bertie's mum Alice, busily helping her mother-in-law, lay the table for tea.

"Uncle Harry, how are you today?" said Alice, as she gave him a kiss on the cheek.

"Alice you tease, how many times have I told you not to call me uncle. I am only ten years older than you, whereas my big sister here is twelve years older than me, you are just trying to make me feel ancient, like her."

"I heard that. No birthday cake for you today," said his sister.

Just then Bertie his dad Robert and his Granddad Bob came into the room and they all sat down at the big oval table to share Bertie's birthday tea.

They had soup to start with followed by fish and chips and then some rhubarb pie for desert, ending up with homemade biscuits and of course, the birthday cake, all washed down with tea for the ladies, ginger beer for Bertie and ale for the men.

"Did you get to see the England v Scotland football match the other Saturday, Harry?" asked his brother-in-law Bob.

"I certainly did, although the Oval is not my favourite place to go on a Saturday. It wasn't a bad game, one apiece, in the end; Bambridge scored for us and Lindsay for them. The only problem was that I found myself standing in the middle of the Scottish supporters, so I had to be very careful what I said."

"Bertie, it's time to cut the cake and make a wish," said his mother, "but you have to keep it to yourself if you want it to come true. I'll help you; hold the knife steady - and now cut down all the way to the bottom. Well done."

"What did you wish for Bertie?" asked his uncle.

"Don't you tell him son," said his dad, "he's just teasing you."

"Why don't you men go through to the parlour and take your drinks with you, while Alice and I clear the table," said Bertie's Gran.

The men and boy went through to the parlour and continued to talk about football and to tease Bertie, while the ladies cleared the table and retrieved a couple of packages from the dresser and then went through to the front parlour, where the fire, which had been lit an hour earlier, was roaring in the grate.

"Well young Bertie," said Harry, "I have a confession to make about the last time we played cards. Do you remember it?"

"Yes uncle, you only beat me by one point, it was the closest I have ever come to winning," replied Bertie.

"Yes, well actually, you did win. During the play, you twice forgot to count 'One for his Nob', which would have given you two extra points, so technically, you beat me."

"Harry, I don't believe it," said Aggie, "you cheated a five year old boy at a game of cards! I know you like winning, but that is terrible, you should be ashamed of yourself."

"I did not cheat Aggie. It is up to each player to count their own score, I just didn't point out his error. Anyway, I am a man of his word and as we all know that 'A man is only as good as his word', so here is the Cribbage Board I promised you and a tanner for some sweets." With which he handed over a brown paper parcel tied with string and sealing wax and a bright new shiny sixpence.

"Wow, thanks uncle," said Bertie, as he untied the knots and used his father's knife to cut through the wax, before he carefully undid the paper. "I can't believe I finally beat you at last. Here mum, can you mind the sixpence for me please, until I get upstairs."

"Thanks Harry, that's very generous of you," said Robert, "does anyone else want another bottle of ale, I'll get some up from the cellar?"

"Hold on a moment Robert, your mum and I have also got something for Bertie," said Alice, as she passed another parcel to her son.

He quickly untied the string and took out a new coat that his mother had only finished making that afternoon, while he was downstairs playing cards.

"Ah mum, its great and my old one was getting really tight, thanks ever-so," with which he gave her a hug and big wet kiss.

"Here you are Bertie, just one more for you," said his Gran as she passed another parcel across to him.

This parcel turned out to be a new pair of short trousers to go with the coat and a top for him to play with in the back yard.

"Now promise me you won't play with it in the street Bertie," said his Granddad, "I don't want you trampled by one of those delivery horses, do you hear?"

"I promise Granddad, anyway, my mate Dave got one for his birthday, so we will be able to compete with each other in his back yard."

"Thank your Gran, Bertie and give her a kiss and say goodnight to everyone as it's past your bed-time."

"Ah mum! Thanks Gran and Granddad for my presents, goodnight everyone. Are you going to read to me mum?"

"You get ready for bed and I will be up to tuck you in shortly," she replied.

While Alice was reading Bertie a short story and tucking him in, the men were chatting about the boat and Aggie was washing the dishes. When she finally came back downstairs, she had the accounts ledger for the boat business and a small bag of money. She gave the book and money to her father-in-law and sat down next to her husband.

Bob cleared his throat and turned towards her and started to speak-

"Thank you Alice for doing that for me and I assume the correct amount is in the bag?" She nodded and he turned to Harry and continued, "As you know Harry, we have now had the boat for just over six years and as agreed we have repaid your loan at the rate of two guineas a month since then. According to Alice's figures we have now repaid you one hundred and twenty two guineas and we still owe you a further eighteen guineas, do you agree?"

"What is this Bob? I don't keep count, I trust you, you know that," Harry responded. "If Alice says that is the figure then I am sure she is correct."

"I know you do Harry, anyway, we have been putting a little extra away each month, as a nest egg, just in case we had a bad month and couldn't pay you, but as it turns out, we have only had to draw on it once, so I am delighted to give you this, (handing over the bag containing eighteen guineas) as a final payment against your very generous loan to us."

"Are you sure it is not going to leave you short?" asked Harry.

"Absolutely sure," said Bob, "oh, would you mind initialing the ledger item please, or Alice will be on my case."

Harry put the bag into his pocket and signed his name against the entry in the ledger. "Do you have any idea what the boat is worth now?" he asked.

"One just like it went at auction a week ago, for two hundred and sixty five guineas and a couple of the sails were in a poor state of repair, so we think ours is worth more than that," replied Robert. "We were really lucky in buying the Florin, just at the end of the 'Panic of 1873', while prices were still depressed and of course we could not have done it without your help Harry."

"You know I was delighted to help and after the way you all helped me to nurse Sadie and supported me after her death, well what are families for eh?"

Aggie got up and gave her brother a hug and held him close while he composed himself again.

"Let's not forget that you also came up with the idea for the name of the boat," she interjected, "if it had been down to these two, it would have been called Two Bobs; what an awful name that would have been. Florin has a much posher sound to it."

"I have just had an awful thought," said Harry, "I have come here now, once a month for the last five years to collect my two guineas and stay the night and recently, play cards with Bertie. Does this mean I cannot come any more?"

The look on his sister's face said it all, "I was joking Aggie, I was just joking, put that poker down immediately."

Father and son were up and away just before dawn the next day, to walk down to the river where the Florin was moored. They turned the small boat over and put it into the water and Robert rowed his father to the Thames sailing barge, anchored twenty yards away, that was their pride and joy. They clambered aboard and tied the rowing boat to the anchor buoy and then hoisted the sails on the barge, untied its rope from the buoy and set off for Tilbury. Alice had secured a new contract with a newly licensed Wine Importer and they were to pick up a couple of dozen barrels of best Spanish wine and take them up to Harwich where they were to pick up a return cargo of hay the next day. This was to be brought down to London for the horses of the London General Omnibus Company, or LGOC as it was called. A contract that Harry had helped them secure, since this was the company that he worked for as a driver.

They arrived at the dock at Tilbury and Bob stayed with the boat while Robert went off to find the office of the Wine Merchant. The manager was expecting them and once the paperwork had been completed the barrels were put aboard the barge and covered with tarpaulins and securely tied down. Once all the dockers had left, the manager walked down the pier and stepped onto the boat. He had a small cask under his arm and handed it to Robert.

"This is the extra package I mentioned to you Mr. Bannister. Just hide it away under the tarpaulins and make sure you only hand it over to a Mr. Grover Wulters once all the barrels have been unloaded. My agent in Harwich is not to be told about this, do you understand?"

"Most certainly I do. Am I to collect any payment for it?"

"No payment as such, but he may just give you a box of cigars, which I would be obliged if you could let me have some time, at your convenience of course."

The manager left the boat and Bob turned on his son, "And what was that all about Robert? Are we carrying contraband? You know my views on that, it's just not worth the risk these days?"

"I know dad and as far as I am concerned it is just a gift from one businessman to another, nothing more. Anyway, when was the last time we were stopped and searched, stop worrying. We are being well paid for the wine and the return cargo is all profit, Alice has done well to get us this new contract. Come on, let's get going, we have a long way to go."

The trip was uneventful and they made good time as the boat was not unduly weighed down and they tied up in Harwich at about ten minutes to four. The agent was expecting them and the cargo was unloaded and safely stored in his warehouse before five o'clock. Bob went off to book a room in the inn and to make contact with the Feed Merchant whose cargo they were taking back to London and Robert stayed with the Florin to tidy things up.

He was busy coiling the ropes and folding the tarpaulins when a gentleman with a top hat and a cane, closely followed by a servant approached the boat.

"I say there, are you in charge of this vessel?" he enquired.

"I am that, sir," replied Robert.

"My name is Mr. Grover Wulters, I believe you have something for me."

"Ah yes sir, I have it here," with which he retrieved the cask from its place of concealment and handed it down to the servant who had stepped up to receive it.

"Now this is for my good friend at Tilbury," he said, passing a box of cigars to Robert. "Tell him I had to test a couple myself and they are truly excellent, a good choice and here is something for your trouble," with which he passed him a crown, smiled benignly and turned and walked away.

Robert finished his chores on the boat and then walked down to the inn where he found his father having a drink with the Feed Merchant's manager.

"Your father was just telling me Robert that you had a good trip up today and that you brought wine with you, well done, a profitable trip for you both this time. I can see I will have to negotiate a discount with your good wife in the future."

"I wish you luck there Mr. Jones, my wife knows to the penny what all the cargo rates are these days and with the water trade picking up now, we are fully booked for the next three weeks, she was telling me last night."

"Well if anyone deserves to succeed it's you two, let me get you a drink my friend."

They ate a good meal at the inn and were up early the next day and settled their bill before heading for the pier. When they got there, they were surprised to see several men on the boat, searching it.

"Hey, what the heck do you think you lot are doing? Get off my boat," yelled Bob.

The men stopped searching and walked across to the edge of the boat.

"We are Excise Officers and we will get off your boat when we are good and ready and you will stay there until we are finished, understood?" said the officer in charge.

They searched for another ten minutes and then joined Bob and Robert on the pier.

"Don't think you have gotten away with it, you two. We know you have smuggled cognac and we will be watching you both very closely from now on. Be warned."

Just as they were leaving the dockers arrived with the hay which was piled high and then covered and tied down, the necessary paperwork completed and they prepared to set sail for home.

"That was close son, where did you put the cigars?"

"The usual place in the bows, they could search all day and not find it. Still we will need to be a bit more careful in future. Hold on a bit dad, I used the crown that we were given to buy some potatoes and other vegetables, these two lads with barrows are probably bringing them now."

The vegetables were taken on board and the barge set sail shortly afterwards. The trip home was a lot slower but as the hay was expected that night they kept going into London where the LGOC had its own wharf and the dockers were still there and waiting for them. One young lad noticed the potatoes and mentioned that his family had not eaten for a couple of days, so Robert gave him half a sack of potatoes, but told him not to tell the others.

Although it was late by the time they got home, they carried what they could to the house and then Robert and Alice went back to the boat with the barrow for the rest of the vegetables, which they then stored in the cellar, after dropping off two sacks of potatoes and some of the other vegetables at the corner grocer's shop.

As they sat upstairs in their parlour drinking a cup of tea and Robert smoked a cigar, Alice commented, "Well that means the grocer owes us again now. We had just about used up all our credit from the ham and chutney you gave him last time. What was your dad talking about earlier, excise officers or something, are we in trouble?"

"No, I don't think so; anyway, you let me worry about that," he replied quickly, "you just keep getting us these lucrative contracts."

Chapter 2
Something Shiny

"Wake up Bertie, your dad is going down to the boat to sweep it out, he says you can go with him now you are six, if you want to, that is."

"Ah mum, what day is it, is it raining?" yawned Bertie.

"It's Sunday and its dry. You have to get up now if you want to go with him, he won't wait for you love. Gran has some porridge on the stove, so get dressed quickly and come downstairs."

Five minutes later, Bertie was downstairs consuming a large bowl of porridge at the kitchen table. His dad was polishing off some kippers and eggs and looked at his son approvingly across the table as he said,

"There was quite a lot of hay left in the boat last night Bertie and I was wondering if Old Mr. Bromsgrove might want some for his rabbits, pop down and ask him for me please. You can go out the back gate and down the alley, he will be in his backyard or shed if he is up and about."

Bertie finished his breakfast and went to put on his new coat but was promptly handed his old one by his mother,

"This will do fine today Bertie, I don't want your new one all messed up, just yet, thank you."

He went out into the yard, ducked under the clothes lines, which had some tarpaulins drying on them and out through the back gate, closing it behind him. His Gran could get very upset if a stray dog came into the backyard. Old Mr. Bromsgrove lived three doors down and shared the house with his son, the original Mr. Bromsgrove, who had a wife and three children, all of whom were a lot older than Bertie.

He could see the old man pottering around in the shed, so he went through the back gate and into the shed to speak to him.

"Excuse me Mr. Bromsgrove, but my dad said do you want some hay?"

The old man jumped at the un-expected visitor's question and turned round to face Bertie while holding a young rabbit in his arms.

"Hello Bertie, I didn't hear you come in, what was that you said son?"

"Dad said, do you want some hay for your rabbits. He had a load on the boat yesterday and we are going down to sweep up and I could bring you some back if you want."

"Well that's very kind of you son, I never refuse fresh hay; look, you can find some sacks under that end hutch, I will be happy to take all that you can manage and thank your dad for asking, for me."

Bertie walked towards the old man and looked at the young rabbit he was holding, "What's his name?" he asked.

"I don't give them names any more Bertie. This is about the two hundred and sixty second rabbit that I have had, at some time you just run out of ideas for new names for them. You can stroke him if you want, but don't keep your dad waiting though."

Bertie stroked the rabbit and then bent down and picked up the sacks and after saying goodbye to the old man, went back down the alley and met his dad who was coming out of the gate carrying a large broom and a shovel.

"Mr. Bromsgrove would like some hay and has given me these sacks. Is Granddad coming with us?"

"No, Granddad has someone to see this morning, so it's just you and me," replied Robert.

It was only a ten minute walk down to the river bank where the boat was moored and Bertie and his dad just enjoyed the fresh air and the chance to have each other to themselves for once.

"Now Bertie, the mud here is really deep and very dangerous, so you make sure you walk exactly where I do, you understand?"

"Yes dad, I know, you always say the same thing every time we come here."

"And I will continue to say it until I am sure you have remembered and any more cheek and I will box your ears my lad."

They got into the rowing boat with the sacks, broom and shovel and Robert rowed them to the Florin.

"I didn't understand what I heard Gran say to Mum yesterday about why the boat was called Florin. Can you explain it to me?" said Bertie, breaking the silence between them.

"Well your Granddad and I are both called Robert, as of course you are too; so to know which one of us is being spoken to, we each have a different nickname, that people named Robert are sometimes called. So, your Granddad is called Bob, I am called Robert or Robby and you are called Bertie. When we bought the boat, just before you were born, there were just two Roberts or 'Two Bobs', which is what we thought of calling the boat. Now 'two bob', as you probably know, is slang for 'two shillings' and the posh name for 'two shillings' is a 'florin'. So that is why the boat is called Florin, understand?"

"So if you had bought it after I was born, what would you have called it then?"

"Good question, but we didn't, so let's not worry about it, eh. You climb aboard while I hold the two boats steady. Now put the broom and things down on the deck and tie the painter round that pin there. Good boy."

It took them well over an hour to sweep up all the hay and they had enough to just fill three sacks and all the dust and stuff went over the side. Robert lowered his son into the rowing boat and passed down the equipment and sacks to him and then got in himself. The tide had gone out a bit further now, so Robert rowed to where a narrow, single plank jetty went out across the mud. He got out himself and walked a few paces up the jetty pulling the boat through the mud after him.

"Sorry Bertie, you will have to get out and walk, just take your time and be careful."

Bertie gingerly got out of the boat and stepped onto the plank. He put his arms out sideways and slowly walked towards his dad. He was fine for a few paces and then a big dog started barking on the shore and he turned to look at it and lost his footing and slipped on the wet wood and ended up with one arm and leg in the mud, but the rest of him stayed on the plank. His dad was over to him in an instant and took hold of the arm on the plank and held him firm.

"Just stay still a moment son, don't panic, don't even wriggle, just slowly pull yourself over onto the plank, just like you would roll over in bed. Understand?"

The boy nodded and did as he was told and then kneeled on the plank, staring out across the mud. He seemed completely un-phased by what had just happened.

"What's that over there dad?" he asked, pointing to a spot in the mud about five feet away. "It's something shiny. I noticed it as I was falling over just now. If you could pull the boat up next to the plank I could climb in and reach it I think.

His father decided that if his son was not frightened by what had happened, then he should not make a big thing of it himself, so he pulled the rowing boat up beside his son and carefully lifted him in.

"Now be careful Bertie, we don't want you falling into the mud again, you hear me?"

"It's caught on a bit of wood, dad, I can get it, just hold the side of the boat steady for me. It's a watch with a chain, dad, it isn't going though, yep, I've got it, hey, look at this!" he said, holding up the watch, "I'll put it in my pocket until we get ashore."

Robert pulled the boat, with the boy and its contents ashore and after emptying it, turned it over with the oars underneath.

"Let me see the watch Bertie," he said, holding his hand out to his son.

"Here it is, can we keep it? Mum would have been livid if I had worn that new coat, wouldn't she?"

"She most certainly would have, and we need to be careful what we tell her about your falling in the mud, as well. This is a gold half hunter watch Bertie, we certainly can't keep it son, but put in back in your pocket for now and we can go home by the police station and hand it in, if you don't mind walking around a bit muddy, that is."

Father and son with the tools and three sacks of hay, slowly walked to the police station, the mud drying on Bertie's clothes, which made him walk with one leg and arm almost straight. When they reached the police station they went in through the front door and found Constable Hughes standing behind the desk, on duty.

He knew Robert from of old and winked at him as they stood at the desk,

"I'm sorry sir, but we don't take in lost muddy animals here, you will have to take him with you or to the pound, I'm afraid."

"Constable Hughes, nice to see you again," said Robert. "Well you are partly correct but it is not a muddy animal I wish to hand in, but a muddy pocket watch, which young Bertie here, found lying in the mud down by the old Morrison's jetty, you know, near where we tie up the Florin. Give the constable the watch Bertie."

The watch was duly handed over and an entry made in the Police Station Lost Property Book with the credit of the find going to Bertie Bannister aged 6 of Raphael Road, Gravesend.

"No-one has reported it missing yet," said the Constable, "but we will send it to the jewelers in Bath Street for cleaning and perhaps they will know who it belongs to. Anyway, check here again in three months time and if no-one has claimed it, it is yours my lad."

As they walked home, they discussed what they were going to say to Bertie's mum and Gran and Robert suggested that Bertie take the sacks of hay along to Mr. Bromsgrove, while he informed the two ladies of what had happened. By the time Bertie got home after delivering the hay, stroking a few more rabbits and chatting with the old man about the morning's adventure, his mother and Gran had come down from the ceiling, where the news had sent them, and had agreed that they would remain calm and not fuss too much when Bertie came in.

No sooner was the poor lad through the door than he was grabbed by his mother, who removed all his clothes and stood him in the big sink in the scullery and then proceeded to scrub all the dirt off him with vigour, while telling him he must never go near the river again, while Robert slinked through to the parlour to chat with his dad.

The two men were interrupted in their conversation when Alice brought Bertie into the room, dressed in some clean clothes, crying loudly.

He ran across to his Granddad and sat on his knee and continued to sniffle, "It's not fair Granddad, she won't let me have a dog and now she won't even let me have a rabbit!"

"Who's she, the cat's mother shouted Alice," who turned and left the room, obviously still upset about the morning's misadventure.

"I didn't know you wanted a rabbit Bertie," said his Granddad, "tell your dad and me all about it."

"Mr. Bromsgrove said he had a young boy rabbit that he didn't need and that he would give it to me in exchange for the hay, if I wanted it. I told him yes, but mum said no."

"Well mum's a bit upset at the moment Bertie and rabbits do of course need somewhere to live and they do need special food and they have to drink and someone will have to look after it and clean it out, there's a lot to it you know."

"It's called a hutch Granddad and Mr. Bromsgrove said he has an old one I can use if I want to and they eat hay and oats and cabbage leaves and carrots and dandelions and blackberry leaves sometimes and drink water and he just cleans them once a week and said he would show me what to do. Please can I have one - please!"

"Your dad and I will talk to your mum and see what we can do, but no promises d'you hear, now tell me about the watch you found down by the boat."

Robert and Bob carried the hutch down on the following Friday night and put it up on some bricks in the yard against the fence so it was about a foot off the ground. Old Mr. Bromsgrove brought the rabbit down on Saturday morning along with one of the sacks of hay and a couple of old bowls for food and water. He settled the rabbit in the cage and then showed Bertie how to hold it and lift it in and out.

"Young rabbits have very sharp claws Mrs. Bannister and it would be better if you could make young Bertie an apron to wear to protect him and of course his clothes," said the old man.

"I have a piece of calico Mr. Bromsgrove, would that be suitable?" asked Alice.

"Yes that would be perfect. Rabbits actually need to have their claws clipped from time to time as they keep growing, just like our finger nails, but I like to wait until they are at least six months old before I do that, so I will come down in a few months time to see to that for you. Well Bertie, if you need any help or advice you know where I live and you are always welcome to come and see me and have you decided on a name for him yet?"

"I am going to call him Dandy, because you said that he really likes dandelions and I know exactly where to collect them for him, there are lots of them, just down past where my friend Dave lives."

And so Bertie's lifetime association with animals, started with a rabbit, from a neighbour, who taught him how to care for his pet and who in later years when the old man was not able, helped him with his rabbits in return. It was indeed the rabbit, or so Bertie said, that led him into his first anti-social escapade.

It was late October that year and he and his friend Dave were collecting dandelions on their way home from school, on the piece of ground down past Dave's house, when they happened to spot some apples hanging from the tree that was the other side of the fence they were standing by.

"Look at those apples Dave, I could really eat an apple just now, pity that fence is so high," said Bertie.

"I saw some other boys scrumping apples in there yesterday," said Dave, " I think there is a loose plank here somewhere - yes here it is, you watch out while I go in and get some."

Dave squeezed through the gap in the fence and emerged a couple of minutes later with a few apples. He gave one to Bertie, had one himself and put the rest in his pockets.

"Boy, that was great," said Bertie, "you keep watch this time and I'll go and get some more."

"There's no more low ones left, you'll have to climb up the tree a bit to get some now," replied Dave.

Bertie squeezed through the fence and climbed the tree and had filled his pockets with apples when a lady came flying down the garden shouting at him,

"You young thief, you come down from there at once or I will call a constable."

Bertie was so shocked that he forgot where he was, lost his hold on the branch and fell out of the tree at the lady's feet and landing badly, twisted his ankle and started to cry.

When she saw how young he was and realised what had happened to him, she felt a bit embarrassed, but left him on the ground and went over to the fence and called out to Dave.

"I know you are there, your friend is very badly hurt, go at once and get his mother and tell her to come and see me, do you hear, you young scallywag!"

While Dave ran off to Bertie's house, the lady helped Bertie to his feet and took him into her house and sat him down in her kitchen, taking the apples out of his pocket as evidence of his misdemeanour.

Meanwhile Dave had knocked loudly on Bertie's front door, which was opened by Aggie as Alice was out of the house shopping. He explained what had happened, without actually mentioning his own part in the proceedings and was told to wait while Bertie's Gran got her shawl from the hallstand and a packet of tea, as a peace offering, from the larder. They then walked down the road together and Aggie knocked on Miss Snellfield's front door.

"Oh, Mrs. Bannister, I didn't recognise the young lad as being your grandson," said the good lady of the house, "please come in, he is in the kitchen."

Aggie turned round and spoke to Dave, "Dave, home. I will be in to see your mother later. Off with you now."

Dave did not need to be told twice and ran off down the road, wondering what his mother's reaction would be to the impending visit by Bertie's Gran.

Miss Snellfield led the way into the kitchen, where they saw this very sheepish little boy, sitting on a big wooden chair, staring at the floor, wishing he was somewhere else.

If truth be told, both ladies had to try very hard not to smile at the spectacle, but Aggie put on her fiercest face as she scolded her grandson for breaking into someone's garden and stealing the fruit that they had worked hard to produce.

Miss Snellfield seemed satisfied with the reprimand and accepted Bertie's apology and both agreed that he should be sent home while they had a drink and a chat.

When Aggie produced the tea and presented it as a gift to Miss Snellfield and her sister, who had now joined them; explaining that her husband and son had been given it by the master of a steamship that they had helped unload earlier in the week and had been assured it was the very finest Darjeeling; it was smiles and goodwill all round.

Bertie and Dave kept waiting for their mothers to speak with them about the apple tree accident, as they called it, but in the end they realised that Gran had forgotten to mention it and so neither did they.

It was about a month later in November, when there was a knock at the door and Bertie, who was in the dining room playing with his toy soldiers, looked out of the window and saw a policeman standing there. His worst fear had been realised, as he guessed that Miss Snellfield had reported him and Dave for stealing her apples and the policeman had come to arrest him.

His mother opened the door, spoke with the policeman and then invited him into the dining room and said to Bertie, "Stop playing for a moment dear as Constable Hughes would like a word with you."

He sat there shaking, not knowing what to say, which was probably a good thing, as Constable Hughes had come round to see him about the watch he had found and not the apples he had stolen.

"Hello Bertie," he said, "you will remember me from the station when you brought the watch in that you found in the mud. Since you have not come back to see me, I thought that I had better come round and see you."

"Oh yes sir, I remember," he said with obvious relief, "did you find out who it belonged to?"

"Well, I sent it away to the jewelers as I said I would, but the watch repairer was away ill, so it sat there for several months doing nothing. Eventually he returned to work and cleaned it all up, to discover there was an inscription on the back which had the name of the owner in it. To cut a long story short, he has managed to get the watch working again and has contacted the owner and returned the watch to him."

"Thanks for telling me," said Bertie in a disappointed tone, "I can't tell the time yet anyway, so a watch would not have been any use to me," with which he turned and picked up his soldiers again.

"Not so fast my lad, the man's name is the Right Honourable Walter Dovehouse, a very important businessman in this town and the watch was very special to him and he wants to meet you at his house, to thank you himself, for being so honest. I have given your mother the details, as he has invited you both to have tea with him on Saturday afternoon and he is sending his horse and carriage to collect you. So what do you think of that my lad?"

Chapter 3
Mikesh Palk

As we look back on our lives, certain dates stand out as being turning points for us, although often we do not realise it at the time. Saturday the 14th of November 1885 was one such date for Bertie Bannister.

By two pm he had been washed, dressed in his Sunday best and threatened with terrible consequences should he get dirty again. His mother was also dressed in her best frock and had bought a new hat for the occasion. The excitement was tangible and when Bertie saw the carriage coming down the street, he almost fell off his chair. "Look Gran, it's a 'Growler' with two big black horses, c'mon mum lets go."

"No Bertie, we wait for the driver to knock and then we go, so just sit down again please," said his mother.

A moment later the knock came on the door and wild horses would not have stopped him from being the first one to the door, first onto the street and first into the cab. The driver laughed as he helped Alice up into the cab and said,

"If only we could bottle all that energy and keep it for when we get older, eh Mrs. Bannister?"

"If only," she replied smiling.

The Right Honourable Walter Dovehouse lived in a mansion on the outskirts of Gravesend and as no-one was in any great hurry to get there, it took almost thirty minutes to reach the house and this time Bertie waited for his mother to descend from the carriage before he got down after her.

"Is it all right to stroke the horses Mr. Driver?" he asked.

"Best not to son, if you were to get a kick or even if one of them just trod on your foot, you would never be the same again," replied the driver.

They were shown into a big front room by a maid who told them to sit down on the settee and that the master would be with them shortly.

"This room is massive mum, we could almost get the whole of our house in here and look at those pictures of old people, why are they all looking so miserable?"

"Shush Bertie, be quiet now and don't speak unless you are spoken to, you hear me now!" she scolded him.

"That's a very good question young man and I used to ask my mother exactly the same question when I was your age and do you know what she replied?" asked the Right Honourable Walter Dovehouse.

"No sir, what did she say?" asked Bertie.

"She said that since they had to sit for hours on end to have their portraits painted, they had nothing to think about but all their problems, so that is what made them all so miserable. Please sit down Mrs. Bannister and thank you so much for bringing this young man to see me, as I personally wanted to hear the story of how he found the watch and to thank him myself."

Just then the maid brought in the afternoon tea with scones and cakes and a jug of ginger beer, just in case Bertie did not drink tea. The maid poured the tea and offered the scones and cakes to everyone and then left them to continue their conversation.

"Well Bertie, please tell me the whole story and I want to hear every single detail and do you mind if I ask you questions as you are telling the story?"

Bertie had a good memory and was able to recount in detail exactly what happened to him that day and answered all the questions he was asked with confidence and clarity.

"You say it was about halfway down the old Morrison jetty that you slipped and fell, can you remember which side of the jetty you found the watch?"

"I was walking up towards the shore and it was my right leg and arm that went into the mud so the watch was on the right side of the jetty; but why does it matter?"

"Bertie, don't be so rude, just answer the question," said Alice.

"That's quite alright Mrs. Bannister, he is a very bright little boy. The reason I asked Bertie, is that when we were burgled and the watch was stolen, some more items were taken from the house as well. In thinking about it afterwards, it crossed my mind that if the watch was dropped in the mud, then maybe some of the other things were dropped at the same time, so I will get a few of my men to search the area and find out for me."

"What is the name of your husband's barge Mrs. Bannister, as one of the companies I own, the Dovehouse Import Company, is a shipping company and we often use the watermen to unload our vessels and I will tell my manger to use your husband when he can."

"That's very kind of you sir, our barge is the Florin and we actually did some work for you last month, unloading tea from your steam ship The Calcutta Star and I have met your manager, he is a good and fair man to do business with."

"I am delighted to hear you say that, did your husband happen to mention the problem we found on board, after the cargo had been landed?"

"No, I don't recall him mentioning anything, was it serious?"

Before he could answer, Bertie stood up and pointed out of the window, "There's a brown boy in the garden playing with a ball, can I go and play with him mum?"

"No Bertie, sit down at once, you are embarrassing me," she replied.

The Rt. Hon. Walter Dovehouse got up and stood beside Bertie looking out into the garden, "Well actually Mrs. Bannister, that is the problem I just mentioned. He was a stowaway on the ship. No-one knows how he got there, he obviously cannot speak any English and he refused to speak to any of the Indian crew on the steamer, which has now left for the return voyage to Calcutta. He is a mystery to us all. He was very weak when we found him and he is still not strong and seems to be pining away, so I would be very interested to see if he is willing to play with Bertie, if that is alright with you."

Alice gave her permission and Bertie went out into the garden while the adults watched with interest. Within a few minutes they seemed to be communicating with each other and then they were playing with the ball and then they seemed to be playing hide and seek among the bushes.

"They seem to be getting on well together, sir," said Alice, "do you not have any children living here that are his age, that he could play with?"

"No, my children are all grown up and only the butler lives in the house with us. That truly is remarkable you know, it must be the first time I have seen him laugh since he came here last month. I have instructed my agent to make inquiries in India concerning the child, but it will be at least another six months before I hear back from him, so the conundrum I am facing is what is the best thing to do with him in the meantime?"

"Would you like him to come home with us?" suggested Alice, "we have a guest room in the house, but it is only used one night a month on average, when my husband's uncle comes to visit. I am sure it would be alright with my in-laws and Bertie has always said he would like to have a brother and they seem to be about the same age."

"That would be wonderful Mrs. Bannister, if you are sure you do not mind. I will of course pay for his lodging and keep in touch with the boy from time to time. May I suggest that you return home with Bertie and check with your family that the arrangement is acceptable to them all and I will send the boy next week, once I have heard from you. Perhaps I could ask my driver to call by on Monday morning and obtain your answer, if that is acceptable?"

The two boys were both laughing loudly when they came in from the garden and sat down next to each other on the settee and both consumed a large glass of ginger beer.

Alice explained to Bertie what had been discussed and he somehow managed to get the gist of the arrangement over to the boy, who seemed to be very excited at the news. The Rt. Hon. Walter Dovehouse thanked Bertie once again for finding the watch for him and gave him half a guinea as a reward, which he gave to his mother for safe keeping.

Having said goodbye to the boy and their host, they boarded the carriage once more and were driven home. Gran had cooked a meat pie for tea and everyone was eager to hear what the house was like and what had transpired that afternoon.

"I did hear some sort of commotion going on," said Bob, "as we finished unloading the tea. I saw one of the officers carrying a bundle into the office, but I had no idea it contained a little boy."

"Poor little soul," said Aggie, "he must have been frightened out of his life and to think no-one even knows his name."

"Mikesh," said Bertie, "his name is Mikesh and he is eight and I think his dad is a fisherman."

Everyone looked dumbstruck at Bertie, "How do you know that, son?" asked his dad.

"He told me. I said my name and he said his name, he is great fun dad, it would be great to have him stop here with us and he doesn't have to stop in the guest room, my bedroom is plenty big enough for two."

When they discussed the matter in later years, no-one could remember actually making the decision to have Mikesh stay with them, Bertie seemed to have settled the matter on his own. He arrived the following Tuesday and actually ended up staying with the family for almost two years. True to his word, the Rt. Hon. Walter Dovehouse sent two guineas every month to pay for his keep and regularly invited Mikesh and Bertie to the 'Big House' to have afternoon tea with him.

It was Bertie who taught him to speak English and Bertie in turn learnt some words in Tamil, which was the native tongue of Mikesh. He discovered his name was Mikesh Palk and that he came from a town called Pamban and that his father was indeed a fisherman. As to how he got left on the boat, it remained a mystery which no-one could fathom and which Mikesh did not explain.

The initial inquiries by the agent had found out nothing, but armed with the information that Bertie had discovered, they were able to track down his parents and give them the good news about their son.

The time just flew by and Bertie, Dave and Mikesh were inseparable and became the very best of friends, but on Friday the 30th September 1887, the S.S. Calcutta Star was once more leaving for Calcutta and Mikesh Palk was on board and frantically waving goodbye to his friends and their families who were standing on the wharf.

The two boys promised to stay in touch, but they were only young and could hardly write, so after two or three letters, contact was lost and they each got on with their individual lives in their own countries.

Once Mikesh had returned home the direct contact they had enjoyed with the Rt. Hon. Walter Dovehouse ceased, but his manger did continue to use the services of Bob, Robert and the Florin on a regular basis, with Bertie being allowed to help them on the barge from time to time. It came as a surprise therefore, when in April 1891, Robert and Alice received an invitation to have afternoon tea at the Dovehouse mansion.

The carriage arrived on time and Bertie was upset that he had not been invited as well, "Are you sure I wasn't invited, I always have been before?" he asked.

"Bertie, I have told you twice already that the invitation is specifically for your mother and me only, this time, it is probably a business matter and you are not required, now let that be an end to the matter. Goodbye son and don't forget you promised to help Mr. Bromsgrove with his rabbits today," his dad reminded him.

"He's right you know Robert, it is strange that he was not invited, I wonder if they have had some bad news about Mikesh and don't want him to hear about it just yet," commented Alice.

"Let's wait and see dear, the Rt. Hon. Walter Dovehouse has been very good to us over the years, so let's not go jumping to conclusions," Robert replied.

The maid showed them into a different room to usual, which they assumed was a study, judging by the books in the shelves and the charts lying on a large table by the window. The Rt. Hon. Walter Dovehouse was looking at the charts and talking to a man in naval uniform. He looked up as they entered the room and then walked across to where the maid had left them, smiled and shook hands with them.

"So nice to see you both again Mr. and Mrs. Bannister, let me introduce you to my good friend Lieutenant Frost." The other man came over to them and shook hands and said hello and then they all sat down round a low table at the other side of the room, which had been laid with afternoon tea.

"I know you are both busy people, so I will come straight to the point as to why I have invited you to come here today. Unless I am mistaken, young Bertie will be twelve sometime around now, am I correct?"

"That's right," said Robert, "his birthday was last week and he was indeed twelve. Quite the young man now."

"That is good to hear Mr. Bannister. My good friend Lieutenant Frost is an instructor at the Training Ship Mercury which is located at Binstead on the Isle of Wight, have either of you heard about it?"

Alice shook her head in a slightly nervous manner as Robert replied,

"Only by reputation, it seems to be well thought of, but why do you mention it?"

"It is an institution which I support and regularly sponsor young lads to go there for a three year training course and I wondered if you would consider letting Bertie attend. He is a very bright boy with a real love and understanding of the sea and could have a very good career as a merchant seaman, if he chose to."

"Would he be away from home all the time?" asked Alice, "he has never been away from home before."

"Pretty much so Mrs. Bannister, but it would give him the sort of grounding in all things nautical that would otherwise take him ten years to acquire, from experience alone. Many of the lads go on to take their 2nd Mate's Certificate of Competency, followed by their 1st Mate's Certificate of Competency and some of them have actually taken their Master's Certificate of Competency and become a captain on their own ship. One of our lads has actually achieved all that in a little over ten years, but I will let Lieutenant Frost tell you about the training they provide there."

The Lieutenant described to them the regime at Mercury and the various subjects which would be covered and gave them a good idea of what would be expected of Bertie should he go there.

"I must stress that he does need to be physically strong and be able to take care of himself, but I am sure Mr. Bannister would agree, that the same principal applies whether you are sailing a Thames Barge on the river or a steam ship on the great oceans of the world," Lieutenant Frost informed them.

"Very true Lieutenant and I am confident that my son would be able to hold his own no matter where he is or who he is with. The decision will of course have to be his, but it is a very generous offer and we are extremely grateful to you sir. How long does he have to think about it?"

"The Lieutenant is going to London for three days and will be back here before he returns to the Isle of Wight. I will need to know by Wednesday and Bertie will need to be here on Thursday morning to travel down with the Lieutenant."

"Oh so soon," murmured Alice, "I'm not really sure about this Robert."

"Look Mrs. Bannister, I understand this has come as a bit of a surprise but just go home and discuss the matter among yourselves and let me know your decision please."

Dinner that evening was a strange affair with everyone thinking aloud, rather than having a serious discussion of the pros and cons of the offer to go to a naval training school.

"He's far too young to go off on his own," said Aggie, "but then again, how old were you Bob when you started on the barges?"

"I was working unofficially when I was ten, but I was just thirteen when I started full time with Patch. But I did of course go home at night, if you can call it home."

And so it went, round and round in circles until at last someone thought to ask Bertie if he would like to go to TS Mercury.

"Look dad, Granddad, I love the Florin, it's the best barge on the river, but every time I see one of those big steamers going off to India or Australia or America, I just wish I could jump aboard and go off with it. I would love to see the world, but I know that the ordinary seamen do not have a good life, but the officers seem to have a great time and I would love to learn to do all the things that they do. I was talking to the Third Mate on the Calcutta Star last time it was in port and he just loves his job and all the places he visits and he told me that he is only twenty one!"

Bertie was there for eight o'clock prompt at the mansion and he travelled down to Portsmouth with Lieutenant Frost who barely said two words to the boy the whole trip. There was another lad named Derek waiting at the ferry and they all crossed to the Isle of Wight together. A wagon was waiting the other side of the Solent which took them across the island to TS Mercury that was located at Binstead.

Bertie and Derek remained firm friends during their time at Mercury and often stood back to back in fist fights, between themselves and other boys.

Whilst Bertie enjoyed the lessons and the comradeship he did miss his family quite badly at first, but because of his good nature and natural friendliness, he made many good friends among the boys and staff, that is, with the exception of Petty Officer Fisk, the Bandmaster. Bertie claimed he was always picking on him and reprimanded him if even one rope on the bass drum, which was Bertie's instrument, was marked or not tightened properly.

"But sir," he would say, "my drum is four times the size of the side drums and takes me over two hours to clean. Couldn't I play the cymbals instead sir?"

"No Bannister, you are the bass drummer and the bass drummer you will continue to be while I am in charge of this band," would come back the answer. "And remember Bannister, this is a training school where you will learn values which will accompany you throughout your whole career and as my old petty officer used to say to me," at which point the whole band would join with him and say, **"You don't spoil the ship for a ha'porth of tar!!"**

"One day you will thank me for this Bannister," he always added, "two laps round the field, now boy!" Which meant that Bertie got out of band practice for as much as half an hour, while he slowly jogged round the field.

The only other thing which he found perplexing was why they had to practice moving a heavy old canon around the field, when so many of the boys wanted to go into the Merchant Navy rather than the Royal Navy. Nevertheless, over the three years he was there, he became very fit and exceptionally strong and quite capable of looking after himself when the need arose.

In July 1894 Bertie and his friend Derek left Mercury and both of them went back to Gravesend for the rest of the summer. Derek was hoping to get a job on one of the old Clipper Ships that still sailed to Australia for the wool trade, so Bertie had suggested that since Derek's family were all in the Birmingham area, that he stopped with him until something suitable turned up.

The two boys worked well together on the Florin with Bob and Robert, but had to be reminded on several occasion, that whilst the two older men might not have actually gone to a nautical school, they did have over seventy years experience of working on the river between them and were fully competent and able, to manage the boat without any advice from the youngsters.

Bertie called round to see the Rt. Hon. Walter Dovehouse one day in September in order to thank him for his sponsorship and to let him know that he was now home from college.

"Well actually Bertie, I did know you were home and were hoping you would come and see me. Petty Officer Fisk, who I believe was your bandmaster among other things, has been sending me a copy of your Annual Report each year, along with his own assessment of how you have been doing."

Bertie was somewhat taken aback by this information and was conscious that he was sitting there with his mouth wide open.

"Did you want to say something Bertie? I gather the band was not your strongest pursuit, but I have been very pleased to see how well you have done at Mercury and how often you were placed in the top three of your class for the different subjects you were taught. Petty Officer Fisk has always spoken well of you and has asked me to wish you well in the future. Tell me, what are you doing with yourself at the moment, working with your father and grandfather I presume?"

"That's right sir. I brought my friend Derek back with me from college and he is staying with us for a while and we are both working on the Florin. We actually helped with one of your wool clippers back from Australia the other day and Derek got very excited because that is what he hopes to do for his first passage."

"Does he indeed, well we are actually a couple of crewmen short for the return trip to Melbourne and I would be delighted to offer him and yourself, if you were interested, a job on the clipper. You would both have to be deck hands on your first trip, but I would have a word with the captain for you and ask him to get you both started with the training for your 2nd Mates Certificate."

"Oh wow, thank you sir, that would be fantastic. I will let Derek know, when does it sail?"

"It sails the first week in October, just let my manager know and he will sort out all the details for you."

Two weeks later, the whole Bannister family and Derek's uncle, were all standing on the dock waving good bye to the boys, as they set off on their great adventure to Australia.

The trip out was uneventful and the boys normally worked together on the same watch and impressed everyone with their knowledge, discipline and ability. True to his word the Rt. Hon. Walter Dovehouse had spoken with the captain and he had asked the First Mate to start the boys training. They arrived in Melbourne ten days before Christmas and were invited to spend the entire festive period, including the New

Year, with the Third Mate and his family, who lived just outside of town.

Whilst Bertie took the opportunity to learn how to ride a horse, Australian style, Derek made the acquaintance of the young lady from next door and declared to Bertie one evening that he was desperately in love with her and had been thinking about jumping ship in order to stay in Australia, with his new girlfriend.

This news was taken as a joke to start with, but when Bertie realised that Derek was serious, he was very worried for his friend and had a word with the Third Mate about it, as to what he should do. The Third Mate promptly arranged for a handsome cab to come to the house the next day and had the two boys taken back to the ship and had Derek placed under guard until the ship sailed a week later.

Derek never spoke to Bertie again and asked to be put on a different watch to his 'treacherous friend' as he called him and became surly and offensive to everyone on board, which of course, meant he got all the rotten jobs to do.

The seas were a lot rougher on the return leg and everyone had to work twice as hard to keep the ship more or less on time with the schedule. Bertie now had his lessons with the Mate on his own, as Derek had expressed no interest in completing the training and had said that he would get a one way berth back to Melbourne and then give up the sea for good. This did mean that Bertie had the undivided attention of the mate and his training fairly flew along.

The boys kept their distance from each other, which really upset Bertie for he had never fallen out this badly with a friend before. One day their paths crossed at the end of Bertie's watch and he approached his friend and said,

"Derek, I want you to know how sorry I am for what has happened. I had no idea he would have you taken on board and locked up. I made a terrible mistake and I am truly sorry."

Derek took a pace towards him, looked him straight in the eye and hit him as hard as he could in the face. Bertie went down like a sack of potatoes and fortunately for him, Derek only managed to kick him once, before some of the other men intervened and pulled him off. They were going to report the incident to the Captain, but Bertie begged them not to and as everyone on board new of the history between them, the men agreed that they wouldn't, but warned the boys to stay away from each other in future.

As they neared South Africa the weather continued to get worse and as they rounded the Cape of Good Hope the seas were treacherous and the Mate happened to notice that one of the headsails was beginning to work lose from the bowsprit, where it had been fastened. He summoned the officer of the watch and pointed out the danger to him and told him to order the man originally responsible for tying the headsail down, to go out and fix the problem, before the ship was put in any worse danger.

That man was Derek and despite his bad humour and recent behaviour, he was a good enough sailor to understand the danger to the ship and admit that the fault was his and it was down to him to fix the problem. Before anyone had time to fix a safety rope to him, he was out on the bowsprit, making the headsail fast. He had managed to carry out the tricky operation and was on his way back down the bowsprit, when a giant wave came and lifted him up and carried him overboard, never to be seen again.

Fortunately Bertie was below deck when it happened, so he did not actually see the tragedy himself, but he was devastated by his friend's death and was still in a state of mild shock when the ship docked in London.

No-one could get him to talk about the incident and although he helped out on the Florin from time to time, his heart was not in it and he mostly just sat around the house reading. He was walking down his road one day after coming back from town, when he heard a weak voice calling to him, "Bertie, is that you?"

He stopped and turned and saw Old Mr. Bromsgrove sitting on a kitchen chair by the front door indicating for him to come and sit with him.

"Mr. Bromsgrove, how are you keeping and how are the rabbits?" he inquired.

"Not so good Bertie and I am down to just a couple of rabbits now, but I do have something new which will interest you, come with me and have a look."

The last thing on Bertie's mind was to look at rabbits with Mr. Bromsgrove, but the old man had been so good to him in the past, that he did not have the heart to refuse, so he followed him dutifully as he shuffled through the house and out into the yard and into his shed. He opened the hutch and took something out and turning to Bertie said, "And what do you think of this beauty then?"

"Gosh," said Bertie, "what a beautiful animal. I have never seen a rabbit like it before, what is it?" He held out his hands and took the animal from its proud owner.

"It is called an Old English, isn't he lovely, feel how soft the fur is and I have even broken my own rules and given him a name, he is called Spot."

"What you, give a rabbit a name? The man who told me, if I may quote you, 'In truth son, there are only two types of rabbits, 'Winners' and 'Dinners'.' Well I'll be!"

And so Bertie's recovery from remorse, depression, call it what you will, had started. Eventually he was able to tell his dad the whole story about Derek and how he had felt responsible for his death, by betraying his friend's intentions to jump ship in order to stay with his new girl friend in Melbourne.

"It just never occurred to me dad that the Third Mate would forcibly take Derek and me back to the ship and put him under guard. I was not even allowed off the ship to get any presents for all of you or let his girl friend know what had happened to him."

"You made a mistake son, make sure you learn from it. But in the end, Derek could have re-acted differently and still be alive today. And you did apologize and offer him the hand of friendship, which he refused. It was his decision Bertie, this was a tragedy that did not need to happen."

Chapter 4
Calcutta Return

Bertie spent the summer and autumn helping his dad and Granddad on the Florin. It was mostly unloading the big ships anchored in the Thames, but there was also another run to Harwich with Spanish wine and once again a small cask for Mr. Wulters who received it most gratefully and apologized for the problems with the excise officers that they had again experienced on the previous trip. To compensate them for the trouble they had been put to, along with the large box of cigars for his good friend at Tilbury, he also presented them with a smaller box for themselves and this time Bertie received the one crown tip. The return cargo was made up of hay and vegetables for the London markets and Bertie invested the five shillings in some sacks of potatoes, carrots and cabbages which were mainly for the corner shop in Gravesend and which enabled them to go into credit once again.

In late October they were unloading tea from the S.S. Calcutta Star when the first mate called Bertie aside and asked if he would be interested in acting as third mate on their next trip to India. Bertie said that he would very much like to do that job and was told to let the agent know right away, that he would be pleased to accept the offer and to be on board the ship, with all of his gear, by 10:00am on the following Thursday.

"What was that all about son?" asked his dad.

"He was asking me if I fancied a trip to Calcutta on the next voyage dad."

"Well judging by the guilty expression on your face, I am assuming that you said yes to him, am I right?"

"Dad, I really enjoy working with you and Granddad and I have learnt a lot from you both, but the Florin is not really where my heart is. I just loved being on the open sea and I want the chance to travel and see different places, you know that."

"It's all right son, your Granddad and I understand, of course we will miss you, but its your life and you have to live it. Just be a bit tactful how you tell your mum and Gran though, as they have enjoyed having you around again."

Bertie saw the agent later that day and signed the requisite papers and received a month's pay in advance, along with a list of suggested items he would need for the trip. He had most of the things he required already, but his mother and Gran were sent off to the shops the next day with the list he had been given and his advance pay, to procure the remainder of the items for him.

The following Thursday he arrived at the ship in good time, along with a very handsome sea-chest that his Great Uncle Harry had purchased as a gift for him, from the lost property office of the London General Omnibus Company.

The first mate introduced him to the captain of the ship, who had originally been a captain with the Royal Navy and was a keen disciplinarian and who despised untidiness and malingerers. A man of few words, he shook hands, grunted something, which turned out to be, "Don't ever let me catch you being idle on my ship," and returned to what he was doing before being interrupted.

He shared a small cabin with two other young officers named Prop and March, who were two and four years respectively, older than Bertie. They had both gone to a private school and Prop, who received the nickname from the position he played in the school rugby team, was short and wide and appeared to have little or no neck and had made one previous voyage on this ship. March, no-one seemed to know what his first name was, had been on another of the company's ships for several trips to North and South America and was senior to both the other two lads and was happy to remind them of this fact whenever the occasion merited it.

Bertie soon discovered that life aboard a steamship was very different to life aboard a sailing ship and thoroughly enjoyed his first voyage to Calcutta. He spent every opportunity he could in talking to the older men aboard and listening to their stories and learning about the sea from them.

After they had arrived in Calcutta and unloaded the cargo of machinery and railway engines, they were eventually allowed to go ashore and discover the town for themselves. Bertie and Prop were walking down the gangway together, discussing their options for the day, when they heard someone shout at them from behind, it was Stoker Jones.

"I'll come with you lads, if you don't mind the company of a dirty stoker, that is."

"Jonesie, of course you can come," said Bertie, "have you been here before?"

"Many times boy-o," Jonesie replied in his deep south Wales accent. "What is it to be today, the sites, girls or some Indian food? By the way, what happened to March, get his nose stuck in the ceiling or something?"

They all laughed and decided that it would be good to see some sites, then eat some food and then, well, who knows what then!

Between them they managed to book a carriage and driver for the day, see everything that was worth seeing and a lot of sites that were not and finished the day back down near the docks at a restaurant that Jonesie claimed served excellent food at a very reasonable cost.

The restaurant was about three quarters full, mainly with sailors of every nationality under the sun, many of whom were entertaining young women who appeared to be of Indian extraction. The three men found a table near the back wall and sat down and waited. A waiter came over who spoke reasonable English and asked them what they wanted to eat and drink. With the help of the waiter and Jonesie's knowledge of Indian food, they each ordered something different and a large glass of the local brew to wash it down. The food tasted great, particularly after eating ships rations for several weeks and the waiter seemed to keep bringing fresh courses for well over an hour. They totally lost track of who was eating what, when Bertie bit into something, the like of which, he had never tasted before. He thought his mouth was on fire and it had such an impact on his metabolism that he actually seemed to stop breathing for several seconds. Prop was the first to notice and assumed he had got something stuck in his throat, so whacked him across the back. Whilst this had the desired effect and got Bertie breathing again, unfortunately he had a full glass of beer in his hand which went flying across the table and soaked the back of the young woman on the next table.

The Italian sailor, who was her escort and his three friends, took exception to this slur on his companion and immediately started a fist fight with Bertie and his two friends. Needless to say, the other gentlemen present in the restaurant, felt it a matter of honour to take sides in the proceedings and by the time the police arrived, a full scale riot was underway in the once peaceful restaurant.

The owner of the restaurant pointed out the three friends as the ringleaders of the trouble and these were duly arrested and taken to the local police station and locked up for the night. Fortunately another member of the ship's crew had been present in the restaurant and had been able to leave the affray before the police had arrived and was able to return to the ship and inform the mate that he thought the three may have been arrested. The mate duly informed the captain, who gave his permission for the mate to go to the police station to secure their release.

Whilst the English magistrate was very understanding as to what had actually happened, he fined them two guineas each for a breach of the peace and ordered them to pay the restaurant five guineas each to cover the damage caused by the fight. The mate had come prepared for this eventuality and paid the respective fines and damages on their behalf and ordered them back to the ship.

The captain interviewed each miscreant individually, with the mate taking notes of the proceedings. The fact that each man gave exactly the same story, bothered him slightly, but he decided that they had been punished enough for their misdemeanour and simply made a note on their record and ordered them to repay the relevant costs from their pay and to remain on board for the remainder of their time there.

Whilst Bertie and Prop initially felt ashamed that they had been arrested and had spent the night in jail, Stoker Jones, with the able assistance of the crew member who got away, circulated such a story of courage, fortitude and fighting ability that the reputation of the three became highly esteemed on the ship and throughout the whole company and they were henceforth known as Jones the Fist, Prop the Powerful and Basher Bertie.

It was later that day that Bertie felt a slight rumble in his tummy and only just made it to the toilet before the whole of his inside exploded and left him a virtual prisoner in the loo for the next twenty four hours. The ship's doctor eventually heard about the problem and invited him to drink the most foul tasting solution imaginable, which did eventually do the trick. Although he was back on his feet by the time the ship left port, he was still feeling very weak and it took him another six days to get his strength back and properly carry out all of his duties again. Mysteriously, Prop and Jonesie had no such problems to deal with, which seemed most unfair to Bertie.

During the return trip to England, Bertie spent a lot of his off duty time down in the engine room with his new friend Jonesie and the chief engineer; learning about steam engines and how they work and what can go wrong with them and how to fix them when they do go wrong. He was allowed to stoke the fires and assist with minor routine maintenance and only managed to get scalding steam on his arm once!

When they arrived back in London, Prop was not feeling well, so he stayed with the Bannister's for a few days until he was better and then Bertie travelled back with him to his home in Aylesbury, Buckinghamshire. Bertie was well received at first but when the story of the fight in Calcutta was mentioned over dinner one night, his father, who was a local magistrate, was horrified that the story would get out and ordered Bertie to leave the house the next day and never to return. Prop was truly embarrassed that his friend should be treated this way, but Bertie made no fuss about the matter and quietly left the house the next day.

On his return home he found a note from The Rt. Hon. W. Dovehouse requesting him to call round and see him 'As Soon As Possible'.

"His driver was most insistent that I give you the note and that you go round to see him as soon as you arrive home," his mother informed him. "He must have heard about the fight and the trouble you were in Bertie. Oh dear, I hope he is not angry with you."

Bertie dropped his bag and washed his hands and face and set off for the Dovehouse mansion. He arrived sweaty and out of breath, just as afternoon tea was being served and the maid showed him into the study. Bertie stood up as The Rt. Hon. W. Dovehouse entered and offered his hand to the man.

"I am not sure it is safe to shake the hand of Basher Bertie, will I be safe or will I be murdered in my own study?"

Bertie withdrew the hand and started to turn red, when he saw the other man start to smile and hold his hand out towards him.

"I am only teasing you Bertie, I have read the captains report and I have personally spoken with the mate and am convinced that the whole thing was an unfortunate accident and have instructed that the unfortunate incident be removed from all of your records."

"Thank you sir, I was really concerned at what you might think of me. I would hate for you to think that I had let you down."

"Well I think no such thing, but I am afraid that your young friend, Prop I think you call him, will not be sailing with you again. I have had a very unpleasant letter from his father, informing me that his son will not be working on one of my ships ever again. A real shame because the lad showed a lot of promise."

"He will be devastated, sir. He loved the Calcutta Star and working for the company and he was a good friend to me. I will miss him."

"Never mind, these things happen. While I was talking with the mate, he said that you had shown a real interest in the engine room and that the Chief Engineer had told him that he thought you a quick learner and had acquired a very good idea of how things work down below. Is that true?"

"I certainly found it interesting and loved to work on the engines, so yes, I suppose it is."

"Good. We have a smaller steamer going to Valencia in Spain in two days time and the engineer needs an assistant as the previous incumbent has been sacked for insubordination. Would you be interested, the round trip should not take more than three weeks and the experience would look good on your record?"

"Thank you sir," Bertie replied, "I would love to."

The first trip was indeed to Valencia and the second trip was to Naples and then to Algiers and then back to Valencia and by the time that December came, there was little that Bertie had not learnt about the workings of a ship's engines.

During the last trip to Valencia the ship was damaged as it entered the harbour and had to undergo some minor repairs. Bertie decided to take the opportunity for a bit of sightseeing and travelled to the small fishing village of Benicarlo. He stopped at the local inn, ate the local food, drank the local wine and tried chatting to the local senoritas. He met an old Englishman who had made the village his home and he acted as a guide and introduced him to the locals and started to teach him basic Spanish.

By the time he returned to the ship he had made several friends, been out with a couple of the fishermen and had helped to repair the engine on a local boat. The skipper was very grateful and told Bertie that he was welcome to stay with him the next time he visited the area.

Back home, things had not been so good. The Florin had been helping to unload tea chests from a ship when the sling that they were in split and a couple of the chests fell onto the barge, hitting Bertie's Granddad on the head and legs. He was knocked unconscious and had his left leg broken in two places. They got him to shore and a doctor was called, who set the leg as best he could and applied a cold compress to the large lump on the side of his head.

"You were very lucky Mr. Bannister that it did not kill you," said the doctor.

"I don't feel particularly lucky at the moment doc," he replied, "how will my boy run the boat on his own, eh?"

Bertie arrived home a few days after the accident, full of the joys of Spain, to find his Granddad in bed and out of action for several months. He did no more but went down to see the agent and explain the problem his father now faced and asked that he be allowed to help on the Florin until a suitable replacement be found.

Father and son worked well together and to be honest, neither tried too hard to find a replacement crew-member. One night in May 1897 the three Bannister men were enjoying a drink in the local pub when who should walk in but Bertie's old friend Dave, who came over and joined them.

"What'll you have Dave, a beer?" asked Bertie, Dave nodded.

Bertie bought the drink and set it down in front of his friend. "Cheer up mate, it might never happen!" said Bertie.

"It already has. After three years with that lot, they have sacked me. Said there was not enough work for four of us. Well if they hadn't taken the bosses nephew on last month there would only be three of us and I would still have a job. Mind you, with all this cheap furniture coming in from abroad, few people are prepared to pay the fancy prices that they charge any more."

"Do you have your own tools Dave?" asked Bertie's Granddad.

"Pretty much so Mr. Bannister, why do you ask?"

"We have a few things that need fixing on the Florin, as do most of the boats out there on the river, if your price was right, you could be kept pretty busy for most of the year, in my opinion."

"I would be happy to give it a go, you know me, I wouldn't overcharge you, when can I come over and see what needs doing?" Dave asked.

So a casual conversation over a drink in a pub, started a whole new career for Dave, repairing Thames barges and other boats. It also happened to be Dave, a week or so later, who suggested that his cousin, who was a porter at Smithfield and was looking for a new job as he had moved to Gravesend, could give them a hand on the Florin.

Within a month Robert and Dave's cousin were working so well together that Bertie felt comfortable at leaving them to it and going back to sea.

His next birth was once again on the S.S. Calcutta Star and he was soon on his way, back out to India. This time he decided to go into town on his own and explore Calcutta on foot. He was constantly being jostled by beggars and was happy to go into a large market area where all sorts of goods were on display. He had only brought a little money with him as he had been warned of pick-pockets and was haggling with a stallholder over a leather bag, when a wealthy looking lady a few yards away let out a scream as she was pushed to the ground and her necklace grabbed off her throat by a young thief. As the youth ran past Bertie he struck him in the chest with his elbow, knocking the lad to the ground and making him drop the necklace.

The woman was being helped to her feet and kept shouting something in Bertie's direction, so he walked over towards her holding the precious necklace. She had just taken it from him when a policeman turned up and began to ask what had happened. Everyone was shouting and pointing at Bertie who began to wonder if he had done the right thing in stopping the thief, who had incidentally, disappeared into the crowd. The policeman and the lady, with the stall holder and Bertie were all driven to the local police station where their statements were taken. The sergeant explained to Bertie that the lady was from a very wealthy and influential family and that the necklace had been worth a great deal of money and that the lady wanted to reward him in some way. He naturally refused the offer, but gave his permission for the lady to know which ship he had come from, so that a small note of appreciation might be sent to him.

He was about to leave the police station when he saw a picture of two men on the wall, with something written in Indian beneath the picture.

"Excuse me sergeant, can I ask what this poster is all about please?"

"I think your ship is too big for those pirates to trouble sir, but they are a real nuisance in the Bay of Bengal and around Ceylon. They say the two men are father and son and that they command at least half a dozen small ships, filled with cut-throats like themselves. These two are a very nasty duo, by all accounts."

Bertie left the police station in a daze and slowly walked back to the ship, he had just seen his old friend Mikesh Palk and a man who was probably his father, on a wanted poster in a police station.

The following day a messenger arrived at the ship carrying a small parcel addressed to Mr. Bannister. Inside was a leather bag, similar to the one he had been negotiating for in the market the previous day, but of much better quality, along with a note of thanks from the husband of the lady, whose necklace he had rescued. It so happened that the captain had also received a note from the same gentleman, expressing his appreciation of the young officer's gallantry and he was smiling benignly, when Bertie entered his cabin a little later in the day.

"Well Banister, last time in Calcutta you were a villain and this time you are a hero. The lady you assisted is from a very influential family, which we have done a little business with in the past and would like to do a lot more with in the future, so well done young man; this act of chivalry of yours, may well prove to be most beneficial to the company."

Bertie made several more trips to India that year with nothing exceptional happening to him apart from bumping into Prop in a bar one night and both of them making an occasion of it and being the worse for wear the next day.

At the end of the year he accepted a third mate's position on the S.S. Melbourne Glory and arrived in the city of the same name, in April and decided to spend his nineteenth birthday ashore. He booked into a nice hotel in town for a couple of days and just enjoyed relaxing and eating and drinking and generally doing nothing. After two days of this decadent lifestyle, he decided that he should look up Derek's old girl friend and let her know what had become of her true love.

He was able to give the driver of the carriage rough directions and with a little bit of perseverance and good fortune, finally found the house where the girl lived. He was walking up the path to the front door when he spotted the girl sitting on a couch at the side of the house reading a book.

"Excuse me Miss, I don't know if you remember me, but my name is Bertie Bannister and I was stopping with my friend Derek at your neighbours house over there, during the Christmas of 94."

The girl was about to reply when a man walked round the corner of the house carrying some glasses and stopped dead when he saw Bertie.

"What are you doing here Bannister and why are you bothering my fiancée?" asked the third mate and instigator of the whole unhappy incident.

Bertie was dumbstruck, suddenly everything dropped into place as to why the man had done what he had and he stood there for a few seconds, quietly deciding what to say.

"Does she know the truth?" asked Bertie. "Have you told her what happened to him?"

With which he turned round and walked back down the path to the carriage, just hearing the girl's gentle voice say, "I remember that man and his friend, what did he mean about the truth, what was he talking about, I want to know!"

Bertie sailed to Sydney, Perth, Buenos Ayres and Cape Town over the next two years and then in December 1900, at the ripe old age of twenty one and after two weeks of cramming at a nautical college in London, he sat and passed his Board of Trade Second Mates Certificate. He found the oral Seamanship examination quite easy but struggled with the written Navigation paper and was told that he needed to improve these skills if he was to pass all the examinations in the future.

Christmas and New Year were very happy times at the Bannister house in Gravesend that year, as everyone celebrated Bertie's success and looked forward to the future with confidence.

Chapter 5
The Boer War

While Bertie waited for his first post as a second mate, he helped out on the Florin for a few weeks. He and Dave's cousin Fred, did most of the heavy work while his dad acted as skipper and as for Granddad, he really came along just for the ride. They were all helping to manoeuvre a large piece of machinery into the centre of the barge, when Granddad stepped back onto a large piece of wood, fell awkwardly and badly damaged his knee.

"Stay where you are dad," said Robert, "we have the weight between us. Just move it to the left a bit boys, bit more, down with it. Good."

"Can you put your weight on it Granddad?" asked Bertie, as the older man tried to stand and then promptly sat down again with a gasp and shook his head.

The two younger men lifted him up and carried him to the stern of the barge and sat him down on a crate. Bertie found a couple of pieces of battening and some string and gently straightened the leg, decided that everything was in its correct place, as best as he could tell and then put the leg in a splint until they could get him to the doctor's.

"I have seen the surgeons do this on the ships I have served on Granddad," Bertie explained, "but if you want my opinion, your leg is still not right after breaking it last year and you will have to think about not working on the Florin anymore."

"If you had tidied up the boat properly, like I taught you to Bertie, I would not have tripped over that piece of wood and I'll thank you to keep your opinions to yourself," snapped the old man, "it's my boat and I'll work on it for as long as I like. Understand?"

Bertie was stunned by this re-buff and just nodded, it was the first time his Granddad had ever spoken this roughly to him.

Fred could see Bertie was upset and about to respond, so he grabbed his arm and pulled him to the other end saying, "Give us a hand with these other two crates mate, then we are all done and can go." While they were lifting the crates and making them safe, Fred quietly said to him, "This isn't the first time Bertie that the old boy has tripped or stumbled, even when lifting light stuff. Your dad and I have tried to work without him, but he insists on helping and to be honest he has become more of a liability than a help. What you said about his leg was quite right and I am fearful that if he carries on working, there really will be a nasty accident."

Later that day, the doctor confirmed that the knee had been badly wrenched and would need to be rested for several weeks and might never be strong enough to undertake heavy lifting again.

"I know your dad likes Fred and he would never say this to you himself Bertie, but he is really disappointed that you do not want to work on the Florin with him," said his mother, as they were enjoying an evening drink together after supper, that night.

"Mum, I am not stupid and I know exactly what dad is thinking, but he and Granddad have made their own decisions for their lives and I will do the same, thank you. It's my life, so don't try and tell me how to live it. It really is time Granddad retired, as he cannot handle the heavy work anymore and you and dad should think more about your own futures rather than mine; the Florin is only a barge after all."

"What on earth are you implying by that Bertie?" she said.

"Look mum, I am never going to work with dad on the Florin on a regular basis again, so maybe it's time that both he and you sat down and talked about your own lives for a change and consider your options and what is best for the two of you. You might even consider doing something different, neither of you are getting any younger you know!" With which he got up from the table, kissed his mother on the cheek and went to bed.

His mother was speechless at what her son had said to her and the moment Robert came upstairs repeated the whole conversation to him, half expecting him to go immediately into Bertie's room and give him a piece of his mind.

Instead of getting angry, Robert sighed and sat down next to his wife and calmly said to her, "He must know me a lot better than I thought, love."

"What do you mean by that? Oh no, you are not serious, we could never sell the Florin, it's been such a big part of our lives for so long now," Alice blurted out.

"You do the books Alice, you tell me. Are we still making the same profits we did a few years ago and what would happen if we stopped getting work from the Dovehouse Import Company?"

"Oh no, don't say that Robert, has the agent said something to you?"

"Not exactly, but things are changing out there and he did say we would have to adjust our prices if we wanted to keep his business. I tell you, life is a lot tougher for the watermen these days and if dad does decide to stop, well it might be time for a change all round."

Nothing more was said on the subject for a week or so by any of the men, but Aggie and Alice had managed several discussions when Bob was not around, one in particular left the two women very worried.

"So you say mum, that the landlord came round while I was out at the shops yesterday, what did he want?" asked Alice.

"He informed me that they had somehow omitted to put our rent up for the last three years and was giving us formal notice, that come March the first, it was to go up by almost half again. He also said that he had a list of people who wanted our big house and who were fully prepared to pay that sort of rent to get it."

"Didn't you remind him of the all the years we have been in his house and never once failed to pay the rent; when other people were not paying their rents and then doing a moonlight flit?"

"I most certainly did, but this was the new son-in-law who came to see me and he was not interested, his final words to me were, 'Pay the increase or find somewhere else that you can afford to live in', cheek of the fellow. Of course we can afford to pay the increase Alice, can't we?"

"Well mum, things were already getting a lot tighter with the profit we make on the various jobs we do, but what with dad not being fit to work anymore and having Fred's wages to pay, I am not sure that we can afford the increase!"

It was the last week of January and The Florin had tied up at Harwich and had just unloaded another cargo of wine, when the Feed Merchant, Mr. Alderton climbed aboard the barge.

"Good day to you Mr. Alderton, nice to see you again, everything OK with the cargo of hay for the LGOC tomorrow?" asked Robert.

"Good day to you Robert, the hay is fine, hello Fred, and is that Bertie hiding away at the back there? I thought they would have had a man of your experience and qualifications, taking supplies to the troops in South Africa by now. I am assuming you actually passed your Second Mates Certificate."

Bertie smiled and then came over and shook the man's outstretched hand.

"Good to see you again sir and thank you for asking. I did manage to pass the Second Mates examinations, but have to admit that I struggled a bit with the Navigation paper. That book you gave dad for me was really most useful and probably saved my bacon, so thanks very much, but I am sorry, I forgot to bring it with me this time."

"Not to worry, you keep it as a present from me. Where is the elder statesman of the Bannister trio today, not injured again I trust?"

"Well actually he is. Dad twisted his knee a week ago and will be laid up for a few more weeks yet. To be honest, I am not sure he will be able to come back and work on the barge again, not that he has admitted it yet!" Robert explained.

"That's interesting Robert, I actually came down to speak with you and your father on a separate issue, why not let the lads finish up here and you and I can discuss the matter over a drink."

It actually took several drinks at the inn for Mr. Alderton to explain what the 'separate issue' was all about. "So you see my problem Robert," he said, "having got the new contract for the warehousing of supplies for South Africa, I just don't have anyone with the experience and ability to manage the new operation for me and also I need someone who I can trust implicitly and who will not to rip me off, someone like you, in fact."

"I don't know what to say Mr. Alderton, it is a very generous offer and I know my dad has always liked Harwich, so I don't foresee any problems there. However, my wife and mother are a different kettle of fish. To be honest with you, I don't think either of them has ever been here, so I would have to bring them for a visit to see the town and let them decide for themselves. As for me, yes, I would be very interested in managing the warehouse for you and I am sure my wife would be up to keeping the books and dad would make a great foreman for the loading and un-loading job you mentioned. When do I need to give you an answer?"

The three men spent the whole return journey discussing the pros and cons of Mr. Alderton's offer and by the time they reached Gravesend, they had convinced themselves it was the right thing to do.

It is truly amazing how some life-changing decisions are just right and everything seems to work itself out, right down to the smallest detail. The ladies came to Harwich the following week and were shown round the town by Mrs. Alderton and they just loved it. Mr. Alderton then showed them all round a cottage he owned about half a mile from the Low Lighthouse overlooking the estuary and said that they could either rent or buy it from him if they liked it or they could choose somewhere else to live, just as they pleased. Whilst it needed some decorating, it was a lot larger than it appeared from the outside and everyone thought it would be an ideal location for them all. It had good sized rooms upstairs and down, as well as a large loft that the previous tenants had used for drying their nets, which Bertie was informed, would be his room.

When Fred told his cousin Dave what was happening, they called a family conference to discuss the matter and in the end made an offer between them for the Florin, which amounted to two hundred guineas cash and five guineas a quarter for the next three years. A solicitor in Gravesend drew up the contract and all the parties shook hands on the deal. It also meant that

Fred and his crew had somewhere to stay whenever they visited Harwich, which became quite a regular affair, as Robert used them whenever possible, to bring goods scheduled for South Africa, round to Harwich from London.

The last job the Florin carried out under the old ownership was to transport all of their furniture and belongings from Gravesend to Harwich and all of this was completed just a day before the deadline set by their landlord. Bertie moved all of his things into the attic and paid a local joiner to put a larger window in the roof, to afford him the most magnificent of views over the estuary. Within six months they had all settled into their new home and new jobs and had decided to use the proceeds from the sale of the Florin to purchase the cottage from Mr. Alderton and to treat themselves to one or two new pieces of furniture.

After all the weeks of waiting, Bertie finally was appointed Second Mate on the S.S. Melbourne Glory in April 1901 and his first voyage in that role, was to Cape Town with a boatload of supplies for the troops. They actually loaded a large part of the goods in Harwich from his father's warehouse and set sail from there, with a full cargo, of food and machinery as well as a large amount of ammunition and artillery pieces.

As they approached Cape Town they were met by a Royal Navy gunboat, which instructed them to wait some distance off shore as the Boers had managed to site a field gun in the hills above the town. This meant that they could fire with impunity at the harbour and dock area and had already managed to set fire to the oil depot and had only just missed hitting a battleship that had been anchored in the bay.

The captain did exactly as he had been instructed and kept the ship well off-shore, safely out of reach of the field gun. It took the troops just over a week before they could over-run the position and remove the gun, hence making it safe to steer the ship into Cape Town harbour and unload its precious cargo.

The owners' intention had been for the ship to sail to Ceylon from Cape Town in order to load a cargo of tea and then return to London with it, but a big problem was brewing in Cape Town with all the Boer 'Prisoners of War' (P.O.W's) that had been captured in the recent battles. A very large internment camp on the outskirts of Cape Town held thousands of prisoners and there was a concern that if this camp was raided and these prisoners escaped, all the good work of recent months would be wasted.

A decision had been made to transport some of the prisoners to other parts of the British Empire and already over five hundred had been shipped off to St. Helena in the middle of the South Atlantic and it was decided to set up some more camps in Ceylon and India as well. The owners of the Melbourne Glory had very little say in the matter and when an army of joiners and fitters arrived on the boat to make the necessary arrangements for carrying prisoners, the officers and crew just had to stand by and watch. The work was finally finished at the beginning of August and the first of the prisoners' boarded the ship a few days later. The last to arrive were about two dozen injured men who were carried aboard with great care and concern for their welfare, which in view of some of the stories which had come out of South Africa of late, about the conditions in some of the camps, was of great relief to Bertie and the other crew members. A couple of nurses from the local hospital accompanied the injured men on the voyage to Ceylon and Bertie willingly gave up his cabin for the young ladies to use.

By the time the ship docked at Colombo, Bertie had become a regular visitor to the injured men and had played dozens of games of dominoes and cards with them and had somehow managed to lose a large proportion of his cigarettes and sweets to them. He became good friends with one man in particular who was named Jan Van Royt. He had been badly wounded in the chest and head as well as losing part of his foot when a shell landed close by, to where he was kneeling. Since Jan was not able to walk unaided, Bertie submitted a formal request that he might be permitted to leave the ship and accompany the prisoners in order to assist his friend on the journey to the camp. They were going to a facility at Mount Lavinia, which was a few miles south of Colombo and had been specifically earmarked for the wounded P.O.W's.

The officer in charge of the prisoners instructed Bertie to come and see him, in order that he might vet him and also check out his reasons for accompanying the prisoners.

"You do understand that these men are prisoners Bannister and that your sympathies should lie with our own men who are held as prisoners by the Boers and of our own dead and wounded who have fought and suffered so bravely for their country."

"May I remind you Captain that I volunteered for this whole voyage; not just the bringing of supplies to Cape Town, that our troops so badly needed; but also taking the prisoners to Ceylon. I could have just as easily got a birth on a ship to Australia or India or America, but I chose to come on this particular ship, on this voyage, in order to support our troops. As regards Jan, err prisoner Van Royt, we only met once he was on board and despite the fact that the shell that wounded him finished off the rest of his family, including his young brother aged six, he does not hold any bitter feelings towards us. Most of the other prisoners shun him, for reasons I do not understand and I would like to give him what support I can, while I can."

"Very well, permission granted. Speak to the Sergeant Major about receiving a weapon and some shooting practice."

This last instruction left Bertie shocked and bewildered, but he immediately went and found the Sergeant Major who seemed to be expecting him.

"What on earth do I need a gun for Sergeant Major, these men are all too ill or crippled to try and make an escape?"

"You might well be right Mr. Bannister, but these men are skilled warriors and should not be under-estimated, even the wounded ones. Have you ever fired a hand gun before?"

"No, I haven't, what do I do?"

Bertie and the Sergeant Major spent several hours together over the next couple of days as he learnt to fire and maintain the Browning M1900 pistol. He was given a holster and a cleaning kit and a box of ammunition, all of which he had to sign for in duplicate.

The able bodied men were first off the ship when it docked and they were taken to a camp northeast of Colombo and then the wounded disembarked, but their numbers had dropped by two, as a couple of the men had died from their wounds during the voyage.

They were carefully loaded into the train carriages with the nurses going in with the most injured men and guards with rifles in the front and rear carriages. Bertie and Jan sat at the back of the train with several other prisoners and they all just chatted and enjoyed the view and the fresh air. There were no escape bids or rescue attempts and when they reached Mount Lavinia, the train stopped at the station and the men were helped off the train and into large covered bullock carts, which took them right into the camp.

The two men said their goodbyes and Bertie promised that if he ever came back to Ceylon, he would do his best to come and visit his new friend. Most of the soldiers who had escorted the prisoners remained at the camp as guards, so it was a much reduced party made up of a couple of the soldiers and Bertie, who made the trip back to Colombo.

As the ship had already been converted to take prisoners, it made several more trips between Cape Town and Colombo, before it finally returned to London with a cargo of Ceylon tea in early March 1902. Although Bertie did manage to visit the camp at Mount Lavinia on one of these trips, he discovered that Jan had recovered from his wounds and had recently been transferred to another camp, which unfortunately, he did not have the time to visit.

He never ran into the Sergeant Major or the Captain again and no-one else asked him to return the pistol and ammunition, so he just held onto them.

When he returned to Harwich for some shore leave, Mr. Alderton asked to see him in order to hear about all that had happened to him while he was away.

"Well Bertie, you seem to have acquired a taste for a bit of adventure, life is going to seem very boring to you from now on."

"Looking back on it, I suppose it was all a bit of an adventure, but at the time, I just felt I was doing my job. I don't think I was ever at risk, not really, if I am honest."

"Are you still planning to take your Mates Certificate this year, or has all that been forgotten?"

"I guess it all depends on where I am sent and if I can be home at the right time. I would certainly like to and feel I have learnt a lot over the last year or so."

"The reason I ask Bertie, is that a ship is leaving for Brazil in a couple of weeks and I know they need a Second Mate and the captain is an old acquaintance of mine and I did happen to mention your name to him. You have been with the same company for a few years now and a change might be good for your career. What do you think?"

"I have been to Buenos Ayres but never to Rio, so thank you for mentioning my name, yes, I would be most interested, how do I get to meet this captain?"

A meeting was arranged for the next day and the two men hit it off straight away, despite their differences in rank and age. Bertie was delighted when he was told that they would be picking up a cargo of coffee in Rio and then taking it to New York, before the last leg of the voyage back to London. If everything was on time, he expected to be back in England in time to take his Mates Certificate at the end of the year.

He found Rio to be both exciting and dangerous, but unfortunately Yellow Fever and Cholera were in town, so the ship ended up in quarantine for a month. Bertie used the time to good effect and improved his knowledge of Seamanship and Navigation and spent many hours under instruction, from the captain and mate. They were finally cleared to load their cargo of coffee and set sail for New York but once again had to wait longer than expected due to a labour dispute at the docks.

The ship finally arrived back in London in January 1903 and Bertie spent ten days swatting for the examination before finally taking the Mate's Certificate in February of that year and this time he passed all the examinations with flying colours.

Chapter 6
'El Burro Volando'

"You're up early today dear, not going sailing again, surely?" Alice asked her son on a cold February morning.

"I can't let Mr. Alderton down mum, this new dinghy of his needs at least two of us to sail it and just one more day out on the estuary and he will have cracked the finer points of his new Bawley."

"I would have thought that you would be sick of the sea after your last trip, but here you are off out again and hardly a moment to spend with your old mum! Oh, did you see the letter that came for you yesterday? From Ceylon and looks like a woman's handwriting. I left it on the dresser for you. You never mentioned any lady friend in Ceylon."

"Are you working as a book-keeper at the docks or are you now a detective with the police force?" he asked quietly and then quickly strode into the dining room, dodging the wet dishcloth that had been thrown in his direction and retrieved the letter from the dresser and opened it with the pencil he found in the coloured pot that the letter was resting against.

"Well I'll be!" he said. "It's from that young nurse, Charlotte, one of the girls I gave up my cabin for, you know, she was with the injured POW's we took on the first trip to Ceylon. I posted a parcel for her when we got back to Cape Town."

"You didn't say that you were writing to each other Bertie," commented his mother.

"Don't read anything into it mum, we are just friends. Anyway, she's writing to say thank you for posting the parcel and she hopes to come home later this year and says it would be nice to meet me again if I am home, but most importantly, to let me know that Jan Van Royt and some of the other prisoners had escaped from the camp and were roaming loose on the island."

"What does she mean 'it would be nice to meet you again if you are home'," queried his mother, who had retrieved her dishcloth and was now standing behind her son, studying the document in question.

Bertie was away again by the beginning of March with another round trip to Rio de Janeiro, New York and back to London. This time there were no problems with sickness at Rio but while out in town with another young officer they were robbed at knife point by a gang of youths who escaped with their watches and wallets. Unfortunately George, the other young man, also received a serious knife wound to the chest. Bertie helped him back to the ship where his wound was cleaned and stitched up by the doctor, who kept the young man in sick bay for the next week while he recovered.

The captain called Bertie into his cabin, sat him down, gave him a tot of rum and asked him what had happened?

"We had just left a pavement café, when this gang of five or six scruffy youths approached us. They all pulled out knives and one demanded our money and watches. I gave them my watch and the few dollars I had with me, but George thought he could fight them and took a swing at the leader of the group, who promptly took one step back and then another forward and knifed him in the side. Luckily for us, someone then shouted out 'police, police' and they all ran off."

"Well, according to the doctor, he is lucky to be alive," the captain informed him. "Why he should think a watch and money are worth dying for, I do not know. In a town like Rio, you either go in a crowd, as there is safety in numbers, or you travel by carriage and eat in a nice restaurant. If I were you

Bertie, in future when in Rio and other such places, go armed and expect trouble, but never go looking for it though."

While the ship was in New York Bertie managed to do a bit of sight-seeing with George, which included the Statue of Liberty, Broadway and The Brooklyn Bridge, all without incident or injury. On the way back to London, during one of his many conversations with the captain, he asked about the possibility of him becoming a Mate in the near future. The captain told him that it was most unlikely at his age and that it would probably be several more years yet, before that particular position would be available to him, with the company they were both currently working for. He went on to say, however, that he had himself worked for a Spanish company in the past, that operated smaller steamships in the Mediterranean Sea and around North Africa and that it was far more likely that they would be willing to give a younger man a Mate's job. He went on to say that he would happily give him a reference and an introduction to one of the owners, if Bertie so wished.

He considered the matter for several days and then spoke to the captain again who agreed to write the necessary Letter of Introduction and also provided Bertie with an excellent reference when they docked in London. Within a week of being back home, Bertie had received a letter from the Spanish company's London office, inviting him to go for an interview the following week, when several of the company's directors and senior captains would be in town.

Luckily for Bertie, Mrs. Alderton was a staunch catholic and had mentioned to his mother that a Spanish priest was currently working in the local church she attended. When Bertie approached the man about giving him some Spanish lessons, he willingly agreed and the two men spent an hour a day for the next week, learning and practicing, everyday, conversational Spanish.

The fact that he had obviously made an effort to learn a little Spanish had impressed the interviewers and this along with his Mate's Certificate, reference and answers to their questions, earned him the opportunity to become Mate on the company's next ship to leave Valencia at the end of August. The only thing which worried him slightly were the number of questions he was asked about his time as an assistant engineer back in 1896 when he was seventeen and when he asked for more details about the ship, no-one seemed particularly keen to talk about it and said that some more information would be sent to him, at a later date.

About a week later, he received the formal offer of employment in the post, with instructions to catch a lift to Valencia on one of the company's ships leaving in a week's time from London. The priest willingly continued with the Spanish lessons, but they now lasted for two to three hours a day and were on the understanding that he would accept some remuneration for all the time and effort he was spending on Bertie's education.

The letter informed Bertie that he would be First Mate on the S.S. El Burro Volando, which the priest informed him meant 'The Flying Donkey', which once again left him feeling a bit anxious.

The captain from his previous voyage met him in Harwich the day before he was due to leave for London and they had lunch together at the local inn.

"So tell me captain," asked Bertie, "did you by any chance ever come across the El Burro Volando during your time with the company?"

Unfortunately for Bertie, the captain had just taken a mouthful of beer when he asked this question and although the man tried his hardest, he could not control his mirth or the mouthful of beer. "The Mad Donkeys," he said, trying to put the glass down without spilling the contents, "I really should have warned you about that, but it was so long ago that I assumed they had scrapped the old ship by now."

"You should have warned me about what exactly," he enquired, "and I was told that 'El Burro Volando' meant 'The Flying Donkey' not 'The Mad Donkeys'."

"Oh Bertie, what have I done to you? I just never thought!" With which he almost fell off his chair laughing and had to hold his sides because they were hurting so much.

"The captain of El Burro Volando is a wonderful but eccentric old man named Capitan Burra and the chief engineer is his younger brother Luca which means that 'The Flying Donkey is in the charge of 'Captain Donkey' and the engines are cared for by a younger Donkey; so everyone in the company refers to the ship and crew as 'The Mad Donkeys'. Although the ship was pretty old and the engines used to constantly break down in my time, they somehow, never failed to complete a voyage, although they did get lost from time to time and often turned up in the wrong port and several weeks late, but it had the reputation of being a good ship to be on."

"Why does the company still employ them if they are so unreliable?" asked Bertie.

"Because they are an institution and everyone in the Mediterranean knows of them and who else would ever be prepared to take on that rusty old ship? But don't get me wrong, Capitan Burra will teach you more about the sea than any other ten men you will ever run into. Treat this as part of your education process and just soak up everything you see and hear, but just a couple of points to remember and now I am being serious. Firstly, never question an order he gives you no matter how crazy it might seem; secondly, never repeat anything that goes on aboard his ship to anyone else in the company or outside of it and lastly, make sure you get on really well with the ship's cook, his name is Paco if I remember correctly, who is another distant relative."

The men finished their meal and shook hands and parted company. The next day Bertie got a ride back with Dave on the Florin to London and the day after that he got a birth to Valencia, where he was informed that El Burro Volando was going to be at least a week late and the suggestion was made that he take a short holiday until it arrived. He managed to arrange a lift down the coast to Benicarlo where he knocked on the door of the skipper whose engine he had repaired and who welcomed him into his home like a long lost son.

A week in Benicarlo gave him the chance to practice his Spanish and a couple of days in Valencia gave him a chance to talk to some of the other mates and skippers and learn the correct Spanish for all things nautical, or so he hoped. The departing Mate from The Mad Donkeys was not willing to talk to Bertie and seemed very glad to be leaving the ship and the company.

When he took his things aboard the old ship he was surprised to see that under the shabby, rusty exterior, lay a well organised, well fitted out vessel. He was further astounded to find that the ship's cook was already making himself comfortable in his cabin, which happened to have two bunks in it. Remembering the warning he had received, he smiled, shook hands and stowed his own gear in the space under the other bunk. The man seemed pleased with this reaction and as he was able to understand a little English, started to explain what life was like aboard ship and said that everyone called him Paco.

That evening Paco took Bertie to a local restaurant where they seemed to eat like kings for just a few pesetas and where the wine flowed freely. The next day Bertie met the chief engineer and had a tour of the engine room. To his surprise the engine was in pristine condition and could only have been about four or five years old. He explained that he had worked on engines before and said how impressed he was with the way the chief engineer had looked after it.

Back in the privacy of their cabin he tried to tell the little cook what he had been told about the ship beforehand and the man just nodded and smiled, he then put his finger to his lips, in a gesture of keep it to yourself, as he said, "Ask me no questions, I tell you no lies! I like you Bertie, we will have good time – yes!"

They started loading the cargo of large wooden crates the next day and Bertie was impressed with the way that they were so carefully handled and then secured in the hold of the ship, but when they had finished loading the boxes, the hold still seemed to be about a third empty and then he noticed the line of about thirty metal seats that had been welded to the side of the rear hold, away from where the crates had been secured.

The captain finally came aboard about mid-night on the second day of loading the cargo and no sooner was he on board than the engines were started and the ship was underway almost immediately.

Bertie went to the wheel-house to find the captain and Paco in the middle of a deep and heated conversation and to his annoyance, was waved away very brusquely as he tried to enter, so he returned to his cabin. The cook came into the cabin about five minutes later and started to speak, "It OK now Bertie, Capitan, he not know you here, I tell him you good hombre, come he want see you."

They both returned to the wheel-house and now the captain warmly greeted him and to Bertie's surprise spoke very good English. Paco left the two men together to get to know each other and the captain seemed very impressed when Bertie told him of all that he had done and the places he had been to.

"Did anyone in London explain to you what I do on my ship?" the captain asked him.

"No sir, they just said that you normally work in the Mediterranean but occasionally have to go to North Africa, but that was all they would tell me."

"Everyone calls me Capitan, I do not like sir, it sounds a bit too much like your English word cur, for me. Very well, we need to chat my young friend and you need to have a very good understanding of the way I like to work, if we are to work well together."

And so the Capitan explained the way he liked to operate the ship and what he expected from his Mate. He also explained that whilst he worked for the Spanish shipping company the ship was actually owned by his family and he carried whatever additional cargo he wished to and went to whichever ports suited him. He was well aware that everyone called them 'The Mad Donkeys' and explained how it suited him very well to have this reputation, because no-one was ever too surprised when they turned up late or arrived in a port that they were not expected in.

"Some of the things we do are dangerous Bertie, so it is important that you can look after yourself in a fight and of course be able to handle a gun. Do you have a gun Bertie?" he asked.

"Yes, I have a Browning M1900 which I picked up during the Boer War, but I have to confess that I am not a very good shot with it though."

"While we are at sea I expect you to wear it at all times, but only to draw and fire it at my command, is that clear?"

"Yes sir. Err Capitan. But why should that be necessary?"

"I am going to be honest with you my friend; we carry a lot of very valuable and desirable cargo on this ship. For instance, most of the crates you saw being loaded contain weapons and ammunition for the Foreign Legion in Algiers, plus we often trade in ivory, gold, diamonds, rare animals, spirits and other such things. I have plenty of ammunition for the Browning so I expect you to take every opportunity to practice with your weapon. Your ability to shoot straight may not only save your life, but the lives of the rest of the crew as well."

"I see," said Bertie, not really seeing at all.

"Another thing I should mention is that we will often be within a mile or so of the coast and usually get approached by several small boats during that part of the journey. You must always be vigilant and let me know the moment you see another boat approaching us. Most will be friendly, but not all, hence the need to be alert and armed."

"A small boat has been heading in our direction while we have been talking, is that the sort of thing you need me to be alert over?"

The Capitan raised his binoculars to his eyes and studied the small boat coming towards them.

"Well done, this boat is friendly and will come along side very shortly, but go and put your pistol on, just in case of trouble."

Sure enough the small boat came along side and a rope was thrown aboard and made fast just as Bertie was returning from his cabin with his holstered Browning on his hip. A couple of kegs of something were transferred from the small boat to the larger one and something was said in Spanish by the Capitan to one of the men in the small boat, who waved at Bertie and said something which he did not understand. Bertie waved back and then picked up one of the kegs and followed one of the crew who had picked up the other one, to the captain's cabin. They were both put into a large cupboard and Bertie noticed another similar keg that had already been opened and caught the distinct smell of fine old brandy.

As he returned to the wheel-house, he noticed that someone had removed part of the cover from the rear hold and to his amazement watched three men climb from the small boat onto his boat and then descend into the hold.

As he was watching, the cook came up beside him, put his finger to his lips and slowly shook his head, the meaning being very obvious.

The small boat was untied and was quickly on its way and out off sight and when Bertie next went into the wheel-house, the Capitan explained what had just transpired.

"Not only do we take supplies to the Foreign Legion, but we also take new recruits and sometimes legionnaires who are returning from leave. Many of these men are criminals, escaped convicts or just men who want to get away from something or someone and start a new life. We offer them a confidential service, in helping them escape from Europe and getting them across to Algeria."

Bertie realised that he was standing there with his mouth and eyes wide open, so he closed them both, nodded to the Capitan, who continued with his narrative.

"Sometimes they are chased by the police or military and we have to move very quickly to escape their pursuers, which is why we have such a powerful engine on this ship and why my brother keeps it in such excellent condition. We never ask questions about the men we transport but if anyone ever proves too difficult to handle, he just goes over the side and has to take his chances, but that is a very rare occurrence."

Three other small boats approached them as they made their way up the coast towards Barcelona and another ten men climbed aboard and went below to join those already down there. Just after the last one had left Bertie noticed a much larger ship approaching them and informed the Capitan who took one quick glance through his binoculars and gave the order for full steam ahead as he steered the boat towards Toulon and was soon outside of Spain's territorial waters and well away from the Spanish coastguard vessel.

"Well done Bertie, I can see you are going to be a most valuable addition to my crew."

"What would have happened if they had caught up with us?" he asked.

"To be honest with you, I am not sure, as it has never happened. They think I am a smuggler and have been after me for years, but they know nothing of my transporting men to Algiers and they (pointing to the hold containing the men) certainly would not want to give up without a fight, of that I am most sure," with which he turned away and went to his cabin, leaving Bertie wondering what he had got himself mixed up in.

They arrived at Cagliari in Sardinia about mid-night and tied up to an empty dock where some men were waiting or them. One of the wooden crates was unloaded and several large barrels of Italian wine were loaded and secured in its place and three more men came aboard and went below. Four hours later the ship quietly sailed out of the port slowly heading for Algiers and Bertie was left in charge of the wheel-house while the Capitan had a quick nap in his cabin.

They had been steaming along for a couple of hours when Paco arrived at the wheel-house with a mug of coffee and some food for Bertie.

"Here amigo, Paco thought you would like coffee!"

"Gracias Paco, te estoy muy agradecido," Bertie replied in his best Spanish.

Paco smiled and was about to sit down next to Bertie when a crew member rushed in and said something to him which made him jump up and leave immediately and Bertie saw them rush past the window heading for the rear hold where all the men were located.

While he was still wondering what was going on, the Capitan came in followed by a crew member and he immediately instructed the engine room to stop the engine and told the crew member to take charge of the wheel and then told Bertie to follow him outside.

"We have a problem with one of the men in the hold, he is English and you had better find out what the problem is pronto, or he may be swimming to Algiers, understand?"

The Englishman had been brought on deck and was spilling the contents of his stomach over the side of the ship. When he had finally finished being sick, he sat back on deck and Bertie could see that he had received several vicious blows to the face and had been kicked several times in the chest. A large man Bertie had not seen before was speaking to Paco in what sounded like German and when he had finished speaking, Paco nodded and the man returned to join the others down below.

"Not good Bertie," Paco said, "this man sick on another man's boots and when fight start, he not able to defend himself. Sergeant say he not last two weeks in Legion, best get rid of him now."

"For goodness sake Paco, let me talk to him, we can't just throw him overboard like this, he will drown."

"And we can't take criminal back with us or we all be in big trouble, including you. Five minutes talk, then we decide what to do, O.K."

In the next five minutes Bertie learned that the man's name was Michael, he was twenty years old and he came from Winchester in Hampshire. He was the youngest son of a well-to-do middleclass family and that he had grown up in the shadow of an exceptionally clever and athletic elder brother and a beautiful and talented elder sister. He had just about managed to pass the entrance examination of a minor university but had been thrown out after the first year for misconduct and as a result had virtually been disowned and disinherited by his parents. His father had lectured him about his responsibilities and of being a man, so he had decided to run away and join the Foreign Legion.

When Bertie explained all this to the Capitan and Paco, they burst out loud with laughter and told Bertie that the man could stay aboard with the rest of the crew, but that he would have to earn his keep, or be put off at the next convenient port.

Michael did not take too much convincing that he was not right for the Foreign Legion and gladly accepted the offer of working his passage back to Valencia.

The ship duly landed at Algiers and the cargo unloaded and the new recruits disembarked, Michael having been instructed to stay below out of sight. The story was put about that he had been dumped overboard and no more questions were asked about him. They loaded a cargo of carpets and leather goods and left port two days later. By the time they returned to Valencia both Bertie and Michael had established themselves on board the ship and both were invited to stay by the Capitan for as long as they wished to serve with him.

Michael was taken to the Company Office where he signed all the relevant papers and was given a few pesetas to cover his expenses while in town. He later told Bertie that those few pesetas represented the first wage he had ever actually earned and that he felt really good about it. Bertie was surprised to find that not only did the company pay his wages, but the Capitan gave him a much larger wad of pesetas, as his share of the extra profit made on the voyage. He made a point of telling him to be discreet with what he did with it, so after some careful thought on the matter, he opened a bank account in Valencia and deposited half the wage the company had paid him into the account, but kept the remainder of the money on him.

Since El Burro Volando was to be in port for several weeks as there was some sort of family event that the Burra's had to attend, Bertie decided to take Michael down to Benicarlo with him and they both stayed with the old skipper and spent several days fishing with him. On the last trip the ancient engine finally gave up the ghost and they had to be towed into port by another boat that was fishing nearby.

The old man was truly distraught that he would not be able to fish any more as he could not afford a new engine and when Bertie pulled out his wad of pesetas and gave them to his friend and told him to buy a new engine, he was speechless and close to tears. In the end he would only accept the money if Bertie took a share in his boat, which he reluctantly agreed to do and so started Bertie's business interests in Benicarlo.

The holiday was soon over and the two young men returned to Valencia to see what further adventures were waiting for them on 'The Mad Donkeys'.

Chapter 7
Trouble in Lagos

Bertie and his new friend Michael spent the next eighteen months sailing the Mediterranean Sea with Capitan Burra and his crew aboard El Burro Volando. There was hardly a port or bay they had not visited or a cargo they had not handled. Only twice did Bertie get the order to open fire on an approaching boat, both times concerned pirates off the coast of Morocco and in both instances fire was returned and the wheel house had the bullet holes to prove it. After the first incident, Bertie took his shooting practice a lot more seriously and became a relatively good shot with his Browning M1900, but Michael managed to acquire a Lee Enfield bolt action 303 which he was able to use with deadly effect.

Both men had managed to save a large proportion of their company pay and whilst Michael had enjoyed spending his extra cash in the bars of Valencia, Bertie had continued to invest his in the town of Benicarlo, where he now owned shares in another fishing boat and had purchased a small block of land next door to where the old skipper lived and where he still stayed whenever he was on leave. It was his dream to earn enough 'bonuses' to be able to build his very own hacienda one day, right next door to his old friend. He did manage to get back to Harwich for a quick visit in late October and was distressed to find his Granddad was now having to use a stick to get around and had given up his new job on the docks. He was very guarded about what he said he did in the Mediterranean but everyone was delighted with the beautiful leather bags and jewellery he had brought them back from Africa.

He returned to Valencia in early November 1904 and after several 'Algiers runs' as they were called, the Capitan announced that they had been asked to take some very special machinery to Lagos in Nigeria, with the opportunity to trade at the various seaports on the way. He said that everyone would be on double pay with the company, plus the usual bonuses for any boat profits, but that they would be away for at least five months and that there would be the risk of a lot more danger than was normal. Only one crew member refused to go and his place was filled by an experienced seaman from one of the other company boats.

They sailed first to Cagliari but once again were spotted and actually stopped by the Spanish coastguard vessel that had chased them on that first trip. This time, of course, they had nothing on board of an incriminating nature, so the coastguard had to let them go, but assured them that he knew what they were up to and that he would get them next time.

Once at Cagliari, various barrels and casks of wines and spirits were loaded along with several dozen wooden crates, which were handled with great care and made secure in the hold.

As they travelled south towards Nigeria, they stopped at various ports on the way where some cargo was unloaded and new supplies of coal along with fresh food and water were taken on board. Paco seemed to know his way around every port they visited and whilst the Capitan invariably stayed on the ship, Bertie accompanied Paco on his trips ashore, both armed to the teeth with their sidearms, a large knife and often a rifle over their shoulders.

While the ship was docked at Freetown, Sierra Leone, Paco announced that he was going ashore to try and buy a monkey, something he had always wanted and asked Bertie to go with him. The market they were going to was not far from the dock so Bertie did not bother to arm himself and Paco just had his 'fisherman's knife' which he was never without.

There were several monkeys for sale in the market and Paco was particularly taken with a young male Vervet monkey that seemed to be in a very healthy condition and was full of life. It was about sixteen inches tall and had a tail that was even longer and with its light coloured fur set against its black and hairless hands, feet and face, was a truly striking animal.

He sat down and started to negotiate with the stall holder and had just agreed a price and paid the money, when a large, rough looking, white man pushed his way in to the front of the stall, snatched the monkey whilst thrusting some money at the stall holder and started to walk away with the now frightened animal, much to the annoyance of the stall holder and the anger of Paco.

The stall holder pulled the lead that was attached to the collar around the monkey's neck, which jerked the poor animal's head forward and caused him to sink his teeth into the man's arm. He immediately let the animal go, which jumped into Paco's arms and as he turned round to face the stall holder and Paco, he pulled a long curved knife out of his belt. What followed next happened so fast that all Bertie saw was a flash of steel, as Paco pulled his own knife from his belt and slashed the man across the wrist of the hand which held his knife. The knife fell to the ground and Bertie quickly picked it up and stood there menacingly in front of the man, as Paco held his own knife to the man's throat as he pushed past him, still carrying the monkey.

Bertie, Paco and monkey made it safely back to the ship, whereas the man with the cut wrist and monkey bite, spent several weeks in hospital and upon his release was charged with assault and attempted theft, by which time all on El Burro Volando were safely out at sea on their way to Lagos. Whilst

Bertie did not mind sharing his cabin with Paco, he made it abundantly clear that he was not prepared to share it with the monkey, so a makeshift cage was made and the monkey spent the nights in one of the holds and his days wherever Paco happened to be.

Apart from a couple of storms off the Ivory Coast which gave them some trouble for a few days, the ship arrived safe and sound in Lagos in the middle of June. Much to everyone's surprise the Capitan was the first to leave the ship and gave strict instructions that everyone else stay on board and be fully armed and ready to protect the cargo during his absence.

Bertie and Michael were reviewing their situation as they stood on the gangway with rifles over their shoulders and were discussing why the dock that the ship was tied up to should be so desolate, despite it appearing to be quite a modern structure. After about four hours of guard duty, a narrow gauge railway engine pushing five open wagons slowly steamed down the dock and stopped level with the ship, the driver getting out to chat with the two men and the co-driver climbing the ladder of the nearby crane.

The Capitan returned to the ship shortly after the steam engine had stopped alongside and promptly came on board. He was accompanied by a British army officer and a detachment of twenty four, fully armed soldiers. The dockside crane immediately came to life and the soldiers stood guard over the ship while most of the cargo was unloaded onto the waiting wagons. At a signal from the officer the soldiers climbed aboard the wagons and the train steamed off down the track.

When the train was completely out of sight, Bertie decided it was time to speak to the Capitan about the cargo and the way that everything was done in such secrecy aboard the ship.

"Excuse me Capitan, but may I have a word with you please," he asked in his most formal voice.

"Of course Bertie, let us go to the wheelhouse, we can chat while I fill out the Log."

Bertie realised that he had to be careful in what he was about to say, but knew that if he did not express his true feelings now, then he never would.

"Capitan, I have served you loyally for about two years now and have never once questioned your orders or asked about the other 'non company' cargo that you carry aboard this ship. I have, of course, been very happy to receive the very generous bonuses that you have given me, but I do feel as mate on this ship that I deserve to be taken into your confidence and should be aware of what cargo we are carrying and the risks that we are taking. Fighting off pirates is one thing, but the police, coastguard and military is quite another."

"I see Bertie, is there anything else you wish to say, before I reply?"

"Well actually there is! As much as I like Paco and enjoy his friendship, I have never been on a ship where the 'cook' has shared the mate's cabin and is taken into the captain's confidence, the way Paco is with you."

"Firstly, let me confirm to you, that you have served me well and have been an excellent first mate, but how I choose to run my ship is my business and who I choose to take into my confidence, is nothing whatsoever to do with you. I will continue to tell you only those things which I consider you need to know in order to do your job and if that is a problem to you Bertie, then we will have to part company when we get back to Spain, because I am not about to change the way I do things aboard my ship. As regards Paco, he actually owns a thirty percent share in the boat and is the one who organises the extra cargos that you have so benefited from since joining the ship. Tell me, do you really mind sharing a cabin with one of the owners?"

"No, of course not; that isn't the point. Why didn't you tell me about him before?"

"Because you were young and inexperienced in the ways of the world and I was not prepared to take the risk of telling you things which if discussed outside the boundaries of this ship could endanger all of us. The company cargo we unloaded today, for instance, consisted of weapons and ammunition for the British army stationed here and the cargo which is left and will be unloaded tomorrow is made up of some high explosives and specialist equipment for the tin mining industry that is based on the Jos plateau. If the cargo we had been carrying aboard this ship had become widely known, we would have had every pirate working off the coast of Africa after us. Now do you understand? You did not need to know this to do your job properly, did you Bertie?"

"I guess not, but what about the crates and barrels and casks we loaded in Sardinia, what do they contain?"

"I could say none of your business, but I won't. The crates contain rolls of very expensive Italian silk and the barrels and casks contain some of the very best wines that Italy produces, along with some fine old Scottish whisky and French brandy, which are all much sought after commodities in these parts of the world. Paco will trade them for gold, precious stones and ivory and whatever else he can find. His knowledge of these types of goods is very extensive and he always goes for high value non bulky items that we can dispose of at a dozen different ports around the Mediterranean Sea. We are high value smugglers Bertie, but I am sure you have already worked that out for yourself."

At this point Paco came into the wheelhouse and intimated that he wanted to speak with the Capitan.

"It's O.K. Paco, I have been telling our young friend here what cargo we have been carrying and your role in running the other enterprises that we are involved with. It is safe to speak in front of him, I trust him now, just as you said I should."

"That's good Capitan; Bertie good man. I have buyer for some of the silk and he pay in gold coins or diamonds, so Bertie can come now and be my escort."

The two men fetched one of the crates of silk from the hold and carried it onto the dock where a bullock cart took the crate and the two of them to a small shop in one of the back streets of Lagos. The merchant opened the crate and examined the rolls of silk and satisfied himself that it was the same quality as the sample he had received and left them enjoying a cool drink while he went into the back of the shop. After a few minutes Paco became restless and took his knife from his belt and stood up and positioned himself to the side of the door. He intimated that Bertie should withdraw his pistol from the holster and sit with it on his lap and be ready to use it if needed. The man returned to the shop shortly after Bertie had done as instructed but was accompanied by two large African men, both of whom were carrying machetes. As the man was about to say something, Bertie raised the pistol and pointed it at the man's chest while Paco stepped forward from where he was standing and held the man tight with one arm round his chest and placed the blade of the knife against his throat and pressed just hard enough to cause a trickle of blood to start to flow down his neck. Paco said something to the man who immediately took a leather bag from his pocket and threw it to Bertie.

"Count the coins Bertie," Paco instructed, "there should be twenty five gold coins inside there, which is the price we have agreed for the silk."

Bertie stood up and moved to the side of the shop and tipped the coins onto the wooden counter keeping the pistol trained on the now terrified shop keeper.

"There are only twenty coins Paco, do you want me to shoot him?" enquired Bertie.

Paco said something else to the man who immediately took off the rings he was wearing on both hands and threw them to Bertie.

"Pick up the coins and rings and open door, we are going now," instructed Paco.

Bertie scooped up the coins and the rings and put them in his pocket and moved towards the door. He quickly checked outside and saw that the street was empty and opened the door and went out backwards followed by Paco who threw the man forward as he left the shop, slicing down into his leg as he did so, hence giving the man something to think about, rather that worry about the two men who were leaving his premises.

They kept to the main streets as they walked back to the ship and were on constant alert in case they were attacked, but no-one followed them and on reaching the ship they immediately informed the Capitan of what had happened and suggested that a constant guard be maintained while they were docked in Lagos.

The Capitan took the coins and the rings and put them in his safe, but before he did this, Paco took a small gold ring with a single diamond and gave it to Bertie.

"When you said to me, 'do you want me to shoot him' I could barely stop myself laughing, you were very good Bertie, you keep this as reward from Paco, but not to wear here in Lagos, O.K.?

They were still tied up a week later as they were waiting for a cargo of tin and of rubber to be delivered but there had been no sign of the merchant or his henchmen, so the constant guard had been removed, but everyone was still being vigilant.

Finally word came that the cargo should arrive the next day so Bertie and Michael were sent into town to purchase fresh supplies for the homeward trip.

"I was wondering Bertie if you would mind making a slight detour with me before we go to the fruit market, it shouldn't take more than an hour or so," suggested Michael.

"This wouldn't by any chance have anything to do with a certain young lady working for the Church Mission Society, would it?" replied Bertie.

"Well sort of. My family have supported the CMS for years and I have used my time here to make contact with one of the old missionaries that I used to write to as a child. She has asked me to drop bye before we leave, so that she can give me some letters and parcels to take back to England for her; but yes, I have also become acquainted with a certain young lady and I do expect her to be present as well. You don't really mind do you?"

The one hour delay turned out to be more like a two hour delay and by the time they left it was mid afternoon and they needed to take a short cut through some of the less respectable areas of the town, to get to the fruit market before it closed. Unfortunately one of the areas they went through was very close to where the silk transaction had taken place and one of the merchant's henchmen happened to spot the two young white men as they made their way through the alleyways and immediately went and told his master, who summoned two more of his henchmen, with which they all set off in pursuit of the two Englishmen.

Their contact in the fruit market was expecting them and once the cash had been handed over, he instructed his porters to take the requisite fruit and vegetables to the ship.

"I don't much like the look of those two fellows over there Bertie, they have been watching us the whole time we have been here!" exclaimed Michael.

Bertie looked across to where Michael had indicated and immediately recognised the merchant and one of his henchmen, who had his machete hanging from his belt.

"Those men tried to rob us last week, while I was out with Paco, this could get nasty, are you armed at all?"

"Only a knife I'm afraid, is your pistol loaded?"

"Yes, but we can't risk anything here in case some innocent bystander gets hurt. When I give the word, we both make a dash down the road across there and then take the second left after about thirty yards; its downhill all the way to the docks. Are you ready?" asked Bertie.

His friend nodded, Bertie said, "Go," and they both accelerated across the square, along the main road and down the side road towards the docks. They looked back over their shoulder and although the two men were behind them, the gap had grown from twenty yards to over a hundred yards and the two friends slowed up and began walking while they got their breath back. Just as they were beginning to feel safe three men with machetes stepped out from the shadow of a building just a few yards in front of them and Bertie immediately recognised the large African he had seen in the shop with the merchant. Bertie went for his gun, which was still in the holster as the large man swung his machete at the two young men. Michael had the presence of mind to step backwards, but Bertie's pistol had got snagged on a loose thread in the holster and as he battled to extract it, did not realise the proximity of his adversary and received a deep cut to his left leg. The power of the blow knocked him backwards and as he fell back the gun came free and he somehow managed to fire it, at short range, at his attacker. The shot went through the man's side just above his waist and stopped him momentarily, but when he realised it was only a flesh wound, he roared in anger and was about to pounce on Bertie when the second shot hit him full square in the right side of his chest and knocked him off his feet. The other two men had stepped back from their accomplice and when the third shot was fired in their direction, they quickly disappeared from whence they had come.

"Give me the gun Bertie, the other two are only a few yards behind us now and we need to scare them off too," said Michael.

Bertie passed the pistol to his friend who aimed for the ground between the two approaching men and fired a single shot at their feet. He then slowly raised the pistol to their head height and waited. They in turn came to a sudden halt and like the other accomplices disappeared into the shadows.

Michael had fortunately been wearing a tie for his meeting with the young lady at the CMS and this proved to be most effective in conjunction with Bertie's handkerchief, as a tourniquet and pad, which he applied to the wounded leg.

The large African was badly wounded but not dead and managed to shout at the two men as they approached him. Bertie picked up the large machete and threatened him with it and then used it as a walking stick, which coupled with the assistance of his friend, enabled him to get back to the ship without further mishap.

A doctor from the local hospital came to see him and cleaned the wound and stitched it up and although it was a long deep cut, it had fortunately missed the main artery so the blood loss was not deemed to be significant. He also left some quinine just in case he developed a fever, once they had left port.

Bertie stayed in bed for the next two days, while the cargo of tin and rubber was loaded and Michael was interviewed by the local police about the whole incident. Since Bertie had developed a bit of a fever and could not talk coherently, the police sergeant left him alone. It appeared that the African had been found dead the next day, with a neck wound that had almost severed his head from his body, so the assumption had been made that some old score had been settled. The merchant had already left town without a forwarding address and his shop had been cleared of all goods, so he could not be interviewed about his involvement in the attack.

Two days out of port the fever had got much worse and the leg had swollen like a balloon, so the Capitan decided that the wound needed to be opened up again and thoroughly cleaned, to prevent Bertie from losing the leg or possibly dying from the infection.

The Capitan performed the operation with Michael's assistance and a large piece of diseased flesh was removed along with some muck that must have been on the blade of the machete, which the doctor had missed, first time round. The wound was stitched up again and the remainder of the quinine used to try and break the hold of the fever and Paco and Michael took it in turns to nurse him for the next two weeks. They fed him and washed and cleaned him and changed his dressings as the ship slowly steamed back into home waters again. No man had more considerate nursing or selfless friends than Bertie Bannister had on that return trip to Valencia. By the time they finally reached port he was up and about although still very weak and it was Michael who organised the carriage that took them both down to Benicarlo and who stayed with him for the next two weeks while he recovered his strength.

The trip had proved to be very successful for the owners and crew of the El Burro Volando and with his share of the profits, Bertie was able to pay a local builder to erect a two bedroom dwelling on his plot of ground in Benicarlo, just like the one that belonged to his friend, the old skipper, next door.

While the building was going on, he was still too weak to return to sea so he returned to England accompanied by Michael in time for both of them to spend Christmas with the Banister family in Harwich. Michael was encouraged by Alice to write to his family and to tell them of what he had been doing and where he had been. He received a reply back about a week later, telling him how pleased they were to hear from him and inviting him and Bertie to travel to Winchester to see them all. In the end Bertie did not feel he was up to any more travelling just yet and Michael went to Winchester on his own. His family were truly impressed with all that he had done and the transformation he had gone through and were delighted that he had taken the trouble to visit the old CMS missionary in Lagos. He mentioned the certain young lady that he had met, but refused to give any more details, much to the consternation of his mother and sister. His parents managed to persuade him to apply for a commission in the Royal Navy, having recognised his new found love of the sea and obvious interest and ability in nautical matters.

He, therefore, wrote to the Spanish Steam Ship Company in early 1906 resigning his post on the El Burro Volando and joined the Royal Naval College, Dartmouth later in 1906 to start his training. He and Bertie kept in touch for a few months but eventually the correspondence dried up and they went their separate ways.

While back in England Bertie decided to study for his Master's Certificate, so he wrote to the Spanish company's agent in London saying that he would have to resign his post on the El Burro Volando and expressing his gratitude to Capitan Burra, Paco and the rest of the crew for all that they had done for him and taught him. He studied hard for several weeks and then attended the nautical school in London that he had used before, for a further two weeks of intense study and then he sat and passed the Master's Certificate in early March.

Much to his surprise he received a letter from the Rt. Hon Walter Dovehouse a few days later, congratulating him on passing his Master's Certificate and saying that he had heard excellent reports from a friend of his at The Spanish Steam Ship Company, and that they had been most impressed by all that he had done for them. The letter went on to say that the First Mate's position on the S.S. Melbourne Glory had now become vacant and that Bertie was invited to attend the offices in London for an interview, if he was interested in the post.

There were two other candidates who were interviewed for the position, both a lot older than Bertie, but neither had his breadth of experience; so it was a very jubilant Bertie who set sail in mid April on the S.S. Melbourne Glory, bound for Australia, as the youngest First Mate in the company's history. The only downside to the occasion was that he was not going to be present when his new house in Spain was completed later the same month.

Chapter 8
The Iquique Massacre

The S.S. Melbourne Glory stopped at Cape Town for a couple of days to take on fresh supplies and to give the few passengers on board a chance to stretch their legs and see the sights. When Bertie happened to mention that he had spent some time there a few years ago to one of the young ladies on board, he was immediately coerced into organizing some transport for the group and acting as a tour guide for a day. Luckily the captain came to his rescue the next day and ordered him to carry out a thorough check of the cargo, as one or two crates had come loose during the storm they had passed through as they had sailed down the coast of Africa. .

They arrived in Sydney in late May and proceeded with great caution to their dock in Darling Harbour, in the knowledge that there had been a serious collision earlier in the month between a 2,000 ton steamer and a clipper that was being towed into the harbour, the pilot pointing out the stranded vessel as they went by. The passengers disembarked and bid the captain and crew goodbye and as one young lady shook hands with Bertie, she secretly slipped a note into his hand, being careful to stand between him and her mother who was watching her most carefully. He put the note into his jacket pocket with the intention of reading it later but unfortunately he forgot all about it and the note was not read until several weeks had passed. She said that she was stopping with friends of the family and gave him the address and that if he would like to call on her, she would be most pleased to receive him.

"I wonder what that means in plain English," he said out loud as he read the note in his cabin, "she might be 'most pleased to receive me' but I am pretty sure her mother would not be."

They unloaded some of the cargo in Sydney and collected a few passengers who like the remainder of the cargo were on their way to Christchurch, New Zealand to take part in the 1906 International Exhibition being staged in Hagley Park later in the year. They reached Christchurch in early June and unloaded the exhibits which included a model Battleship and other such items for the British Court and many crates of British machinery which needed to be assembled and then to be exhibited in the Machinery Hall.

A cargo of wool was taken on board and the ship set sail for England in late June and arrived back in London at the end of August. When Bertie was asked by his father how the trip had gone he replied, "Yes, it was good. No trouble, nothing I couldn't handle and to be honest a bit boring." And that was about all he had to say about it. He sailed once more with the Melbourne Glory, this time missing out New Zealand but calling at Melbourne, Adelaide and Fremantle instead and arrived back in London just in time to spend Christmas with the family.

For many parts of the country it was a white Christmas and despite the freezing temperatures Bob Bannister insisted on taking his usual walk before lunch on Boxing Day. When he did not arrive back home by two o'clock, everyone began to get worried and Bertie and his father went out in search of the old man. They found him about two hundred yards from the house waist deep in mud at the side of the path. He was shaking with the cold and was only just able to say that a large dog had come running towards him and in trying to get out of the animal's way, he had stepped on some ice and gone skidding off the path into the muddy river bank. He had twisted his bad leg again and was unable to put any pressure on it, so he had just been waiting for someone to come along and help him.

The old man was no 'light weight' and it took all the strength of Robert and Bertie to pull him free of the mud and then they had to carry him back to the house. Aggie and Alice were horrified to see the state he was in and once he was safely in bed; Bertie was sent off to get the doctor.

The doctor was in the middle of lunch when Bertie called and his wife insisted that he finish lunch before he went off to see yet another patient. He duly turned up around a quarter to four, checked the leg for serious damage and confirmed that it was just twisted and not broken. He gave him some medicine to perk him up and said he would call round again the next day.

That night Bob Bannister passed away peacefully in his sleep, he was seventy two.

The funeral took place a week later and despite none of the watermen being able to make the trip from London to Harwich, there were well over thirty people present at the service, showing what a well known and well liked individual he had so quickly become in his new home town.

Aggie spent the next month sorting out all of her late husband's affairs and got Alice to go with her to the solicitor, where she dictated her new will, which in essence left everything to her only son Robert. Having done all this, the grief of losing her beloved husband suddenly caught up with her and she became quite depressed and inconsolable. The doctor came to see her as she was growing steadily weaker, but said that her problems could not be treated with his medicines. She died at the beginning of March aged seventy and was buried in the same plot as her husband. This time many of their old friends from Gravesend were able to attend the funeral service and many people took the opportunity to speak with fondness, of their memories of Aggie and Bob Bannister.

For Bertie's parents, Robert and Alice, this was the first time in their married life that they had not shared a house with Bob and Aggie and they seemed lost as to what they should do next. Bertie decided that they needed a holiday and having spoken with Mr. Alderton about the need for them to get away for a while, found a ship that was calling at Valencia and booked a passage for the three of them to travel there at the end of March. He also took the opportunity to write to the Rt. Hon Walter Dovehouse, resigning his position as mate on the S.S. Melbourne Glory and to thank him for his sponsorship and encouragement over the last twenty years.

"Are you sure about this son?" his father asked him. "Your mother and I don't want you to give up your big chance, just to take us to Spain for a holiday and we are also concerned about how much this is all going to cost you."

"Dad, I have never been surer about anything; believe me. While I was serving on El Burro Volando, it was fun, it was exciting and each day was so very different to the next. Whilst I know I cannot go back to that job and really want to be Master of my own ship, if I did one more run with the Melbourne Glory, I think I would die of boredom. As regards the cost, this is my treat, you two just enjoy yourselves."

They all stayed in a hotel in Valencia for a few days while Bertie withdrew funds from his bank and bought some things for the new house and arranged transport down to Benicarlo. His parents could not believe how well he spoke Spanish and how he seemed to know everyone they came across when out walking in the town. The house had been painted white and the old skipper had planted some flowers in the garden for his young friend and had arranged for some basic furniture to be installed.

"Oh Bertie, this is beautiful," said Alice, "I understand now why you spend so much of your time here. We thought that perhaps you had a young lady that you didn't want to tell us about!"

"Mum, could I ever keep a secret from you? If I ever find a girl and fall in love, you will be the first to know, I promise."

During the next couple of weeks the two men went out fishing in both the boats that Bertie had shares in, while Alice got the new house into a proper order. They had long walks together along the beach, but mainly just relaxed and enjoyed themselves in the warm Mediterranean sunshine. As with all good holidays, it was over too soon and it was with many tears and hugs that they left Benicarlo, promising to come back as often as possible.

When they got back to Harwich, the warehouse was in a terrible muddle and it took Robert and Alice, assisted by Bertie, several weeks to get things the way they liked them to be again. It was while Bertie was helping his father to re-position some crates that Mr. Alderton approached them in an obvious hurry.

"Bertie, I have been looking for you everywhere, can I speak with you for a minute please?"

"Of course Mr. Alderton," he replied, "what can I do for you?"

"A German freighter has been loading cargo today and the Second Mate has managed to get crushed by a crate and has been taken to hospital. The captain has already lost several crew who have jumped ship and desperately wants to be on his way today and needs to fill the slot immediately. He asked me if I knew anyone and I said that you were the only person I could recommend at short notice. So what do you think?"

"Where is it heading for, this freighter and how long will it take?"

"It's on its way to Hamburg which should only take a couple of days and I have no idea after that, but if you just signed on till then, it would be a big help, but I need to know right away."

"I know it's a Second Mate's position, but they would have to agree to pay me as a First Mate and pay for my time and expenses in getting back here. If they agree to that, then it's fine by me."

"Well, they are an excellent company to work for Bertie and I am sure they would consider your terms most reasonable, so go and get your things and I will inform the captain."

The freighter left a few hours later with Bertie communicating with the captain in a mixture of Pigeon English, Spanish and hand signals. The mate did speak a little more English than the captain and between them they safely sailed the ship to Hamburg and unloaded the cargo. The agent in Hamburg spoke with Bertie after the cargo was unloaded and settled up with him, as had been agreed with Mr. Alderton. He was very grateful to him for stepping in at such short notice and was very interested in his qualifications and experience.

"So you have been to South America on quite a few occasions Mr. Bannister and speak excellent Spanish, I wonder if you might be interested in an opportunity that has just come up. I have a Swedish ship leaving for South America in two weeks time. It will be calling at Rio de Janeiro, Buenos Aires, Valparaiso and Iquique, but the problem I have is that the captain wishes to leave the ship at Valparaiso, so I need someone to take it on to Iquique and then return here to Hamburg. You would be First Mate up to

Valparaiso and then Captain for the rest of the trip. I would have to check references of course, but assuming everything is in order, would you be interested?"

"I most certainly would, I really enjoyed my trips to South America; but I have to be honest with you, I do not speak any Swedish whatsoever."

"That is not a problem, for they all speak English. I will send the necessary telegrams to your past employers and of course, to anyone you need to inform back home in England. I would prefer you to buy whatever clothes or equipment you are short of here in Hamburg rather than have you return to England for them and risk being delayed. I am prepared to fund you up to a month's pay in advance to cover your costs. The ship will dock here in two days time and I can get my secretary to book you a room in a local hotel in the meantime, which the company will, of course, pay for."

And so another chapter of Bertie's life started quite unexpectedly on a wet Tuesday in Hamburg at the start of June. He did not need to buy too much in the way of clothes and equipment, knowing that he could get whatever he needed in Rio at half the cost. He spent the two days exploring Hamburg and when the S.S. Avesta Prinsessa arrived in port, Bertie went aboard straight away to meet the captain and crew and to find his way around his new ship.

During the voyage to Rio de Janeiro the captain allowed Bertie to do everything that he would have to do when he took over as captain, but still kept command and made all the final decisions, but took time to explain why he had made a different decision to the one Bertie had suggested, on the few occasions that their opinions differed. Bertie then sailed the ship to Buenos Aires on his own and only when the ship had docked and unloaded its cargo did the Captain make a few suggestions of things that could have been done differently.

From Buenos Aires they headed south, round a very rough and unfriendly Cape Horn and arrived in Valparaiso in November, where the captain left the ship and Bertie took over his first command.

The first thing he did was to meet with all the officers and to tell them how much he had enjoyed working with them so far and how highly he valued the experience and professionalism that they each brought to their various jobs. Everyone was given the opportunity to express any opinions they might have about the way the ship should be run, but the general consensus was that the previous captain had done an excellent job and that there was not much that could or should be changed.

They then went on to discuss the voyage to Iquique and Bertie informed them that it would be the first time he had gone there and asked if any of the officers had been to the port before. Only one man, the very large and elderly Chief Engineer, had been to Iquique before and he said that it had not been a pleasant experience.

"It took several weeks to load the cargo of Saltpetre and the town was dangerous for Westerners and the local water was not fit to drink and had to be brought in by boat and was therefore very expensive," he said.

"I see," said Bertie, "that sounds to me like an opportunity for us all to make a small profit out of this enterprise. Where did they get the fresh water from, do you happen to know?"

"I was told that they got it from Antofagasta, why, what did you have in mind?"

"Well apart from a few dozen crates in the forward hold which are bound for Iquique itself, we have unloaded all of our cargo; so instead of just adding ballast, why don't we go into town here and purchase as many large tanks as we can both find and afford and then sail to Antofagasta and fill up with fresh water. We can then sell the water and hopefully the tanks as well in Iquique and all share in the profits. What do you think?"

"I think it is a good idea, but I am not sure that the owners would approve," said the newly promoted First Mate.

"Well we won't tell them until we get back and if they do not approve, the worst thing that can happen is that they will not employ me again. Besides, if we are stuck there for several weeks waiting to load the Saltpetre, we will need the water ourselves and hence will have saved them a lot of extra expense."

"Oh another thing," said the Chief Engineer, "I believe that there is also a real shortage of firewood there, the locals scavenge any piece of driftwood that washes up on the beach and I know where we could get some old timber in Valparaiso at a very low price, if you think it worthwhile."

Everyone thought it was an excellent idea and then the First Mate asked the question that everyone else was wondering about.

"How do we split the profits from these ventures?"

Bertie looked to the Chief Engineer who coughed twice and then said,

"In my experience for this kind of venture, it normally goes something like this. The Captain who is taking the biggest risk and I assume putting up the necessary funds, gets ten shares. The first Mate and myself get five shares each, the remaining officers assembled here, get three shares each and each member of the crew gets one share each. Is everyone happy with that arrangement?"

No-one intimated that they were not happy with the arrangement, so the necessary plans were put in place to make it all happen.

Fortunately Bertie had remembered to pack some of the gold coins he had acquired during his time on the El Burro Volando and these proved to be sufficient funds to purchase the wood along with ten very large tanks and enough water to fill them when they called at Antofagasta, on their way north. They arrived at Iquique at the beginning of December and anchored in the bay along with more than a dozen other ships, all waiting for their cargo of Saltpetre.

Bertie and the Chief Engineer went ashore the next day, leaving the First Mate in charge of the ship and eventually managed to find the office of the agent who was handling the crates they still had on board and was organizing the cargo of Saltpetre that they intended loading.

The front office was deserted but they could hear the voices of a man and a woman in the back room. They were speaking mostly in Spanish but it was a South American version that Bertie had not come across before, so there were some words he did not fully comprehend.

They stood there for a few minutes and nothing happened, so then they both tried coughing loudly and still nothing happened, so Bertie tried calling out to them but for some reason spoke in English rather than Spanish.

"Hello, is anyone there, hello, can we speak to Capitan Chavez please."

The woman came flying through the door and stood with her hands on the counter glaring at Bertie, "Of course someone is here, idiot, you must have heard us talking, just wait a moment will you!"

As she turned to go back into the rear room she said loudly in Spanish, having assumed that Bertie did not speak the language, "Ignorant English ass!"

To which he replied in his best Spanish, "Bad tempered Spanish fish-wife!"

She turned round slowly to face him again, hands on hips, eyes and mouth opened wide, not knowing whether to laugh or cry, but by now Bertie was just creased up laughing and the Chief Engineer and the man from the back had also joined in the hilarity.

"Good morning gentlemen, my name is Manuel, who have I the honour of addressing?" said the man from the back room.

"Good morning Manuel, I am Captain Bannister form the S.S. Avesta Prinsessa and this gentleman is my Chief Engineer, can I assume that you are Capitan Chavez?"

"I am afraid that Capitan Chavez is no longer with us, he died of a fever several months ago. This young lady, however, who was so very rude to you just now, is his daughter, Makaa, who is the new owner and knows far more about the whole business than me, who has only worked here as the manager for the last twenty years, which means that I was here before she was born in fact!"

"Manuel," interjected the now red-faced young lady, "I am sorry for getting cross with you, but you do know I was right! The miners are very un-happy at the moment and they have every right to be, the way they are treated. If we had something to encourage them with, maybe they would change their minds and help us with the cargos."

Holding her hand out to Bertie, she said, "Capitan Bannister, it is nice to meet you and you speak excellent Spanish, but I was expecting a much older man."

"Senorita Chavez, the pleasure is all mine and I am sorry to hear about your father. We have about two dozen crates on board for you, can you organize a berth for us or will you send a smaller boat that we can unload them into and what is this you were saying about trouble with the miners, do you have our cargo ready?"

"Capitan, so many questions, why don't both of you come through to the office and we can discuss all these things over a drink."

The discussions in the end took several hours and the four ended up having lunch together at a local café. They discovered that the local miners were on strike over their pay and living conditions and that was the reason why so many boats were in the harbour, waiting for their cargo to arrive.

"Capitan Bannister, I will come tomorrow with a boat and unload the crates you have for me," said Manuel, "but you may be here for many more weeks yet, I am afraid."

True to his word Manuel arrived with a boat early next day and to everyone's surprise Makaa came with him. While the First Mate and Manuel saw to the cargo, Bertie gave Makaa a tour of the ship.

"So Capitan Bannister, I can see that I was wrong in what I originally said about you, you are not an ass, but a very capable sailor. My father would have liked you."

"I too must concede Senorita Chavez, that you are not an old fish-wife, but a very beautiful and intelligent young lady and I am also sure that my mother would like you too."

"I thought you said that there was no more cargo on board, but I can see some large metal boxes through the slit in the cover there," she commented as they walked past the rear hold.

"Oh we stopped at Antofagasta to fill those tanks you can see with water. We heard that it was a precious commodity up here," he replied.

She leaned over the side and called out, "Manuel, come up here quickly and see what they have brought with them."

Manuel came up and Bertie got some of the crew to uncover the rear hold, exposing the large tanks of water and the store of old wood.

"If you will give me some of the wood and two tanks of water senor," said Manuel, "I am sure that I can organize your cargo for you and get it loaded ahead of the other ships. The rest of the wood I will sell for you at a good price and I know of at least ten ships in the harbour that would buy the other tanks of water off you."

"I will need to speak with my officers, but assuming we can cover the costs we have incurred and make a small profit, I think we can do business," replied Bertie.

The officers readily agreed to the scheme and Bertie said he was sure the owners of the ship would be happy to pay for the water and wood they were giving to Manuel to secure an early delivery of the cargo.

Manuel arrived two days later under cover of darkness and unloaded one of the tanks and some of the wood into his boat. The following night he came again and took the second tank and some more wood and the remainder of the wood was unloaded over the next two nights and taken to his compound.

Bertie accompanied him back to shore on the excuse that he wanted to see the compound and be sure that everything was in order, but deep down it was really to see Makaa again.

"She is not here, senor," answered Manuel, when Bertie enquired after her. "Her uncle, her mother's brother, is a miner, so she has decided to go with him on the protest march. I told her it was dangerous, but she never listens to me."

"Why is it dangerous?" asked Bertie in a concerned tone.

"The military is said to be coming here and they might do anything, even arrest the leaders and Makaa's uncle is a leader and I fear that she will be at the front of the procession with him."

"I see what you mean. Will this protest march affect our plans to load the cargo of Saltpetre?"

"I do not think so. I have arranged for it to be loaded on the 14th and 15th of December and the miners march should arrive here on the 16th of December, so you will be able to leave here soon after that. I have also spoken with eight of the captains of the ships in the harbour, who would like to buy the water, but I have not told them who the supplier is, we do not want to start a fight over it, not yet anyway. If we load the front hold first of all on the 14th December, we can unload the water when it gets dark and then load the rear hold the next day."

Makaa did not appear again but stayed with her uncle on the march with the miners. Hundreds of them arrived in town on the 16th December 1907 as expected and they all stayed at the school of Santa María de Iquique.

Bertie tied up at the dock on the evening of the 13th December and spent the next two days loading the cargo of Saltpetre. The water tanks were duly unloaded and put in safe storage by Manuel. An auction was held for them from among the skippers Manuel had spoken with, on the morning of the 16th December, when Bertie and the S.S. Avesta Prinsessa were safely anchored out in the middle of the harbour again.

He was busy preparing the ship for sailing over the next couple of days and did not go ashore again until the afternoon of the 19th December when he got several of his crew members to row him ashore. He found Manuel in the office, but he was on his own and obviously very agitated.

"It is good to see you Capitan Bannister; I have all your money for you, Manuel has done well for you, no?"

"Wow, I'll say you have Manuel, I guess some of the other ships which have been anchored in the bay for many weeks, were getting desperate for fresh water, how much do I owe you for handling all this for us?

"I have already taken my fee; this is for you and your crew. It has been good to do business with you Capitan; I hope you will come here again."

"Is Makaa still with the miners?"

"She is senor and I am very worried for her. The soldiers have arrived and they know who she is, she will not be safe here again. It is not safe here tonight for you either senor, you should go back to your ship. Some of the other captains are very upset that you have loaded your cargo and they are still waiting. You should leave Iquique now before they cause any trouble."

Bertie returned to the ship and spent the next day doing a final check of everything aboard ship with the intention of leaving the day after, but he was disappointed that he had not had the chance to say goodbye to Makaa before leaving port.

He was still considering a final trip ashore to see Makaa when the sound of gunfire was heard coming from the town and it seemed to go on for ages. Everyone on board who owned binoculars was standing at the side of the ship, scanning the shore to try and see what had happened.

"It's no good," said Bertie, "I will have to go ashore and see what has happened and to make sure that Makaa and Manuel are all right. Are there any volunteers willing to go with me?"

Virtually everyone on board wanted to go, but Bertie took just three of the larger crew members with him, all armed to the teeth and with the instruction for the Mate to get the ship ready to leave the harbour as soon as he returned. He checked his pistol and made sure he had plenty of ammunition and had a few practice shots on the way to the shore. He left two men by the boat and got the other one to accompany him to the agent's office. Manuel was there by himself in the front office in a terrible state of shock. He was covered in dirt and could barely speak for crying.

"It was awful senor. I was helpless to do anything. I just watched as the soldiers opened fire on the miners and their families at the school. Hundreds have been killed, women and children shot down as well as the men, they were all unarmed and it was just plain murder."

"What has happened to Makaa, is she dead?"

"Not yet. She was here with some of the other women, getting some water for the miners and their families when the shooting started. I begged her to stay here but she went back to see if anyone was still alive there. She is so young and high spirited that I am sure she will do something silly and put herself in danger."

"Which way is the school Manuel? I will go and find her; you stay here and wait for her. If she should come back here without me, do not let her go again. Tie her down if you have to."

Manuel went to the door and pointed the way to go to the school and Bertie and the crewman went off at a run, Bertie explaining to the man, what had happened as they went. The crewman, who was an ex soldier suddenly stopped at the corner of a building and pulled Bertie back to where he was standing. He had heard male voices and guessed that they might be soldiers. He slowly peered round the corner of the building and sure enough there were a couple of soldiers standing just round the corner, a yard away from the wall, enjoying a cigarette together. They had their Mauser rifles slung over their right shoulders and their spiked helmets firmly on their heads.

As he watched them, he saw an officer approach and shout an order to the men who immediately put out their cigarettes and walked over towards the compound that stood in front of the school. One man stayed there while the other accompanied the officer down the road and out of sight. Bertie stood by the crewman's side and was almost sick as he saw the dead bodies lying all around the schoolyard. Men, women and children had all been shot down in cold blood and just left there.

The other man noticed someone crouching down behind a cart that had been abandoned about fifty feet in front of where they were standing and pointed it out to Bertie. As he turned to look at the person, she turned towards him and Bertie realised it was Makaa. He waved to her and she was about to wave back when a side door opened in the school and a little boy, no more than a toddler, dazed and bleeding, stumbled out. The soldier un-slung his rifle and raised it to his shoulder and took aim at the little boy. Makaa leapt from where she was hiding and ran screaming towards the soldier, who turned towards her. At that moment a priest came running out of the side door, picked up the little boy in his arms and shouted out at the soldier who turned back towards him, now pointing his rifle at the priest. Fortunately, the man hesitated and appeared to be unwilling to fire at the priest, who went back inside the school, carrying the little boy in his arms.

By this time the hysterical Makaa had almost reached the soldier, who just about had time to turn towards her, swivel his rifle round in his hands and strike her a forceful blow on the side of her head, with the butt of it. She dropped to the ground like a sack of potatoes and the man did no more, but put the rifle to his shoulder and took aim at the helpless young woman at his feet.

This time it was Bertie who was shouting and charging forward and as the soldier turned towards him, away from Makaa, two shots rang out. The shot from the crewman's rifle hit him in the heart and the shot from Bertie's pistol, hit him in the stomach. The man was dead when he hit the ground. Bertie picked up the Mauser and put it over his shoulder and then gently picked up Makaa while the crewman covered their retreat. No-one else appeared on the scene, as rifle shots had become quite a familiar sound on that bloodthirsty day and they were able to escape round the corner of the building, to where the crewman was standing.

With Bertie continuing to carry Makaa, the two men made their way to the shore, where the other two crewmen were ready and waiting with the boat. The journey across the harbour seemed to take forever and the crewman kept his rifle trained on the shore in case any soldiers had followed them, but they reached the ship without further incident. The Mate was ready and waiting for them and he immediately raised the remaining anchor and the ship was on its way out of the harbour within forty minutes of Bertie's arrival. Although a group of soldiers did eventually appear on the shore, they were not certain which ship Makaa was on, so no more shots were fired and no-one gave chase.

Makaa was laid out in Bertie's cabin and given smelling salts and kept cool. She was delirious for several days and despite the risks involved, it was agreed to call in at a small port that the Chief Engineer had once visited, which lay halfway between Antofagasta and Valparaiso, to seek the advice and ministrations of a doctor. The Chief Engineer went ashore and made contact with a doctor who was willing to come to the ship and attend Makaa. He came aboard in the late evening and was most concerned at the state of her head wound and the symptoms of concussion which she still displayed. He dressed the wound and told them to keep her cool and that he would return in the morning to see how she was, but warned them that she might need to go to hospital.

When he returned in the morning, he brought a nurse with him and between them they washed all the sand and dirt off her and put her into fresh night clothes that the nurse had brought with her and confirmed that she had improved over night and that it would be safe to continue with their journey in another day or so.

The nurse returned the next day having purchased some new clothes for Makaa with some money that Bertie had given to her and was pleased to see her sitting up in bed and feeling a lot better. She mentioned that the massacre and the killing of a soldier, had been reported in the local newspaper and that the authorities were now seeking a young local woman and an English sea captain, that had apparently assisted in her escape. She smiled politely and left the ship, which in turn left port two hours later.

Bertie and Makaa discussed what options she had open to her regarding her future, but both agreed it would be too dangerous for her to stay in Chile, while the authorities were actively looking for her. As she was still feeling very unwell, it was agreed to put off any decision about her future until the ship stopped in Rio de Janeiro for fresh supplies, which gave her plenty of time to consider her options.

Chapter 9
A New Life

By the time the ship reached Rio de Janeiro, Makaa had become a firm favourite with the whole crew and they insisted on having a whip-round for her, so that she could go ashore and buy herself some new clothes and other items. The ship was only in port for three days while it took on fresh supplies and enough coal to safely get them back to Hamburg, but in that time she must have visited over a hundred shops and been escorted by every officer on the ship, including the Chief Engineer.

Bertie had spent most of his off duty hours nursing her and talking with her and there was not a lot they did not now know about each other by the time they docked in Rio. When he described Benicarlo and his little house by the sea, that he seldom had time to live in, she quickly made her mind up that Spain, the native country of her father, was by far the best option for her and when Bertie suggested that she could manage his growing business interest for him there, the matter was completely settled in her mind.

When the S.S. Avesta Prinsessa finally docked in Hamburg there was a very mixed reception committee waiting for Bertie, once the cargo had been unloaded. The owners of the cargo were delighted that Bertie had managed to load the cargo in December, when all of their competitors ships had been delayed and had only recently left Chile, which meant they were able to get a better than expected price for the Saltpetre. When Bertie explained how he had achieved this for them, they were more than willing to recompense the crew for the water and wood that they had been obliged to give away to Manuel, to encourage the miners to help them.

The owners of the ship, on the other hand, were furious with him. As soon as the ship had docked, the agent informed the owners who immediately dispatched two of their directors to Hamburg. They were very angry that he had upset the Chilean authorities and been involved in the shooting of a soldier and told him that he could never go back to the country again, which meant he was no longer of any use to them, so they fired him.

While he was waiting for the Swedish directors to arrive, he was able to find a Spanish ship which was leaving for Barcelona in a couple of days and booked a cabin for himself and Makaa. With the help of the Chief Engineer and the crewman who had saved her life at Iquique, they managed to smuggle Makaa off the Avesta Princess and get her aboard the Spanish ship, without anyone noticing.

The agent was nowhere near as hostile as the owners and he was in fact very impressed with his ingenuity and the way he had handled matters in a very difficult and dangerous situation.

"I am certain I will be able to find you another ship Captain Bannister, when your affairs are settled and you are ready to go to sea again," he confirmed.

He also sent a telegram to Mr. Alderton on Bertie's behalf, telling him that he had arrived back in Hamburg but had decided to go to Spain to check on his house there, before coming back to England to visit his parents.

Having drawn the rest of his pay and settled the profits from the water and wood venture with the officers and crew, he was delighted to find that it had turned out to be a very profitable voyage for him. "Capitan Burra would be proud of me," he thought.

The ship stopped at various other ports before arriving at Barcelona, including Cadiz, where Makaa's father originally came from. They went ashore and started to ask around after him or any of his family, but no-one seemed to know him or remember him. As the ship was about to leave they gave up the search for the time being, which Bertie felt quite pleased about, although he was not sure why he should feel that way. They discussed what they should tell the neighbours in Benicarlo and decided it would be easier to say that she was a distant cousin who had returned from South America after becoming unwell, to look after the house for Bertie. Since she was also concerned that the Chilean authorities might try and track her down, as she had been responsible for the death of a soldier, it was decided to change her name to something more English and after Bertie made several suggestions she chose Deborah as her new name. They further agreed that Makaa no longer existed and should never be used by either of them again.

The old skipper was enchanted by Bertie's cousin Deborah and regularly took her out fishing with him as did every other fisherman, whose wife did not object to her going along. Her business skills started to come into play after a couple of weeks and she was soon finding better markets for the fish that Bertie's business partners caught, plus several other local fisherman joined the group, when they saw how well this newcomer was doing for them.

The weeks seemed to fly bye and Bertie decided that it was about time he went back to see his parents in England. He had received several letters from his mother saying how well things were going for them now and how settled they both were in Harwich and how nice it would be to see him and his new lady friend. Towards the middle of May Bertie finally made it back home, but he was on his own, much to his mother's disappointment.

"What do you mean, 'she didn't want to come'? Aren't we good enough for her?" enquired his mother, shortly after he had arrived at their cottage.

"Mum, she is nineteen. In the last twelve months she had to nurse her father and then watch him die of the fever. She saw her uncle, his family and friends, shot down by the soldiers. She was knocked unconscious by the butt of a soldier's rifle and has had to flee the country of her birth, probably never to return again. She just did not want any more changes in her life just yet and is actually feeling settled in Benicarlo. Is that too hard to understand?"

"I'm sorry dear, but your letters have been so full of this Deborah, that she is obviously someone very special to you and we were just keen to meet her. You have obviously never felt this way about a woman before."

"Mum, there you go again, reading too much into a situation. I saved her life, I nursed her and helped her to escape; of course I am concerned about her, but nothing more, you hear!" With which he went up to his room to unpack his things.

"Well, you got that one wrong Alice," said Robert.

"Oh did I? You just wait and see Robert Bannister, you just wait and see."

After a few days with his parents he travelled up to London and called at the London offices of the Spanish Steam Ship Company. They were delighted to see him and said that they had heard of his adventures on the S.S. Avesta Prinsessa and would be very happy to have him back as a captain on one of their ships when a vacancy came along and said that his friends on the El Burro Volando sent him their best wishes. He left them his address in Benicarlo and suggested that if anything did come along, then they should send a letter to each address, to be on the safe side.

He worked with his dad in the warehouse for a couple of weeks and Mr. Alderton did try and tempt him with a couple of offers, one to sail to Australia and the other to sail to North America, but he knew where he wanted to be and who he wanted to be near, so he made arrangements to go back to Spain the second week of June. He left on the Wednesday and arrived on the Friday and before he had got through the door and sat down, Deborah threw her arms round him and gave him a big hug and a first kiss.

"I have missed you so much Bertie, please do not leave me again, you are all I have in the world and I love you so much."

He held her in his arms and stroked her hair and kissed her. "I have missed you too, I could not bear to be away from you, my heart was aching so much it hurt. I love you so much Deborah." No more words were necessary; they just held each other close and enjoyed the moment.

"Oh, this arrived for you yesterday; I did not know what to do with it," she said, holding up a telegram from the Spanish Steam Ship Company. She gave it to him and he read it and smiled.

"Is it good news?" she asked.

"Yes, it's from the company I used to work for in Spain. I saw their London agent while I was in England and told him I would like to work for them again. I am to go and see their agent in Valencia about becoming a skipper on one of their freighters that operates in the Mediterranean Sea. This would mean no more long trips away, Deborah. If I can get a job with them it would solve our problems, it would be wonderful."

He travelled to Valencia on Sunday and saw the agent first thing Monday morning.

"Senor Bannister, it is so good to see you again," he said, "please sit down and join me in a drink."

It turned out that they had just lost the previous skipper of El Puente Volante, The Flying Bridge, to a competitor and if Bertie was willing, he could start right away as the new captain of the ship. Bertie explained the situation he was in with regard to Deborah and said that he would be very interested in the job, but certainly in the short term, would not want to be away for more than a week at a time.

"That will not always be possible senor, you know the way we work here, but we would not object to the wife of a captain travelling with him from time to time."

Bertie asked for a few days to discuss the matter with Deborah, which the agent agreed to.

He travelled back to Benicarlo and decided to discuss the matter over dinner at the local café.

"So you see Deborah," he said, "the sea is my life and until I met you, it was my first love, but now of course you fill that slot."

She smiled and said, "Thank you Bertie, however, I can feel a 'but' coming, am I right?"

"Well yes, the problem is that I will have to be away for some trips that will last more than a week from time to time, it cannot be avoided, it comes with the job I am afraid."

"Bertie, my father was a sea captain, I understand that, but before I was born, my mother did sometimes go with him, would it not be possible for me to go with you occasionally; would you mind if I came along with you?"

"No, of course I wouldn't mind if you came. The company does allow that, but it also has very strict rules on the matter. Deborah, the company will only allow a captain to take his wife on a trip with him."

"I see, so what are you saying to me Bertie?" she said softly.

He reached across and held her hands, he gulped and he looked into her eyes and said, "Deborah, you know how much I love you, would you be willing to marry me please?"

Whether the "Yes," came first or the kiss across the table came first, is open to debate, but everyone in the café clapped and cheered as they realised what had just taken place between the popular young couple sitting at the table in the alcove.

They finished their meal and the café owner insisted that he pay for them and also gave them a bottle of wine to take home with them.

They chatted as they went home and then Bertie had an awful thought. "Oh dear, what will people think when they hear that I am going to marry my cousin?"

"I don't think that will be a problem," she replied, "I was talking with the lady who cleans the house for our neighbour while you were away and it all sort of came out; so I am sure everyone knows the truth about us by now."

The letter informing his parents that he was to get married, arrived at the end of June and caused much consternation in the Banister household.

"See Robert, I told you he was in love with that girl, I know my own son!"

"How could I ever doubt you Alice?" he replied.

"They want to get married in Benicarlo on Saturday the 19th September and suggest that we get out there about a week beforehand. It would have been nice to have met the girl first though!"

"What does it really matter, as long as Bertie has found someone he truly cares for; anyway, it gives you an excuse to buy a new outfit as 'mother of the groom'," Robert replied.

Robert arranged with Mr. Alderton for them both to take about two weeks off in September and the necessary arrangements were made for them to travel to Spain. In the meantime Bertie had started his new job as captain of El Puente Volante and quickly decided that it was in fact, more like a donkey, than the ship which actually bore that name.

Once their engagement had been announced, propriety demanded that Bertie stay with the old skipper when he was at home, so when his parents arrived in Benicarlo, they had Deborah and the house all to themselves, for the best part of a week, which gave everyone the chance to get acquainted and become good friends.

The ceremony took place in the local church, which was packed full for the occasion. The old skipper gave Deborah away and he was so proud to be asked to do it, that you might have believed that she was actually his own daughter. Robert acted as best man for his son, but was relieved when he was told that he did not need to make a speech, as no-one present would be able to understand it. The service was in a mixture of Latin and Spanish so Robert and Alice were not always too sure what was going on, but the priest was very considerate and kept the whole service quite short and they were standing outside, posing for the photographs, in less than an hour.

The reception was at the café where Bertie had proposed to Deborah and was full of their local friends, as well as Capitan Burra and Paco who had managed to arrange the ship's itinerary so that they could attend the celebration. The party went on late into the evening with the newlyweds eventually going to their own home to spend their first night together and Robert and Alice going off with the old skipper to spend the night in his house.

The next morning Alice made breakfast for Robert and their host, which they sat down to eat at around 9:30am on the veranda at the rear of the house.

"Do you think I should go and wake them Robert, it is getting on for ten and they have to be on their way by mid-day."

The two men looked at each other and raised their eyebrows.

"Are you out of your mind woman? Would you want someone to disturb you if you were them? Give them another hour at least," Robert suggested.

By 10:30am she was getting really agitated and remembered she had left something important in Bertie's house, which she had to go and fetch and before Robert could stop her, she was out of the gate and into next door.

"Hello mum, did you want something?" said Bertie, who was eating breakfast at the kitchen table.

"Oh, there you both are, I think I left my hairbrush here somewhere, have you seen it?" asked Alice.

"It is over there, on the cupboard," said Deborah, who was sitting close up to Bertie drinking a cup of coffee.

"We will have to leave soon mum, would you mind tidying things here for us, once we have gone. I guess you and dad will have a few more days holiday here, before you both head off back home."

"Of course I will, you two just have a great honeymoon, where is it you are going again?"

"Formigal, in the Pyrenees. We may even get to do a bit of skiing if we are lucky. Deborah says she would like to come and spend Christmas with you this year, work permitting of course. Would that be O.K?"

"Oh that would be wonderful. We would love to have you come and visit us, wait till I tell your dad, he will be thrilled."

They arrived at the small hotel in Formigal on Monday afternoon and spent the first couple of days just relaxing and enjoying each other. They started to go for short walks on the

Wednesday but did not venture very far from the hotel. By Friday the weather had turned a bit warmer and they decided to try a much longer walk. The receptionist gave them a local map and showed them a series of paths that smugglers used to travel, which stretched all the way across the border to the little French village of Soques, a distance of just over four miles as the crow flies.

They put a drink and something to eat in a bag and set off on their walk just after ten. It was uphill all the way and the going was a lot harder than they had expected and they had only managed two or three miles by mid-day. They sat down on a grassy bank and opened their bag with their lunch in it and were about to pour themselves a drink, when a little boy came running out of the woods from the opposite direction to which they had come, stopped suddenly when he saw them and sat down on the grass next to them. Bertie said hello in Spanish and then in English, while Deborah tried offering the boy a cheese roll.

"Merci Madame," the little boy said in French, "Je m'appelle David."

Fortunately Deborah had learnt enough French to talk to the occasional French captain that had come to Iquique, so she started to chat to the boy as he ate his way through their lunch and drank their lemon cordial.

"He said he is staying with his parents and big sister at their cabin in Soques, but his dog started to chase a rabbit and as he is a silly dog and often gets lost in the forests, he ran after him to bring him back, but has not managed to find him yet," related Deborah.

"Ask him if he knows how to get back to the cabin from here," said Bertie.

Deborah asked the boy the question and then explained, "He thinks so, but has never come this far before. I think we will have to go back with him Bertie."

They finished their lunch, or what was left of it and all three headed off down the path that David had come from. He held Deborah's hand and happily chatted away to her. They had walked for about forty minutes when they could hear a man and a woman, some distance away, shouting out for David. As soon as he heard his parents' voices, he let go of Deborah's hand and sped off down the path. They quickened their pace and followed him down the path and after a few minutes came across his mother, father, sister with a big dog on a lead, all remonstrating with the boy.

As Bertie and Deborah approached the group, David turned towards them and pointed and said something to his parents, which caused his father to walk over and speak with them. He spoke in French, with Deborah acting as interpreter for Bertie.

"It appears that David has been missing for several hours and his parents got very worried when their dog returned without him. He knows these woods quite well as they always come here for holidays and he often goes off on his own, but this is the longest he has been missing and they were getting very concerned in case he had got lost or hurt himself."

The mother then joined the conversation and the two ladies chatted for a bit and then Deborah explained what had been said.

"They are most grateful to us, for walking back with the boy and hope he has not been a trouble to us. They are returning to Tarbes tomorrow, where they have a jewellery business, Josephs and Son and have said that if we are ever in the area, then we would be most welcome to call in and see them."

"I don't think that is going to be very likely, but who knows. You had better say goodbye as we have a long walk back to the hotel and I am starving," said Bertie.

They said their goodbyes and David very formally shook hands with Bertie and they all went their separate ways.

They returned to Benicarlo the following Wednesday, by which time Robert and Alice had already arrived back in England and Alice immediately started to plan for Christmas and her visitors. It gave her the impetus she needed to sort through her deceased in-laws things, a job she had kept putting off and to get their bedroom re-decorated for her son and his lovely new wife.

Deborah did not accompany Bertie on any of his voyages that year as she was really getting into the fish business and he was only once away for more than a week. They went across to Harwich in late December and spent Christmas and New Year there, but Deborah found it very cold and caught a bit of a chill and was very glad to get back home to their little house by the sea and the warmer Spanish climate.

Chapter 10
The Great War

The first five years of their marriage were very happy ones and seemed to just fly by. The only sad point was that their good neighbour and friend, the old skipper, passed away quietly in June 1910 and whilst the house was sold to a wealthy merchant in Barcelona, as a holiday home, he left his half share of the fishing boat to Bertie and Deborah. They found a couple of local men whom they rented it to for a modest sum, on the understanding that they were responsible for all maintenance costs and that Deborah continued to handle the sale of all the fish that they caught.

Bertie sailed El Puente Volante mostly around the Mediterranean with the occasional trip to England, Holland and Germany and a regular voyage every six months to Accra in the Gold Coast and then on to Cape Town but he flatly refused to call in at Lagos again. Whilst he always carried his Browning pistol with him and had the Mauser cleaned and ready for action, they only had to be fired in anger once, when off the coast of Senegal and being approached by a lightly armed pirate boat. The ship's engine was replaced in August 1912 when they had to be towed into Valencia by The Flying Donkey, having broken down five miles out of port.

They were sitting at home in early September 1913 discussing how they should celebrate their fifth wedding anniversary when Deborah remembered that a letter had come for Bertie.

"It looks like your mother's writing and she normally sends us a card for our wedding anniversary, but it is only addressed to you, so I didn't open it, here it is," she said, passing him the envelope.

Bertie read it, pulled a face and then read it again.

"Well you are right, it is from my mum, but she is telling me to come home immediately as something has cropped up that needs my urgent attention. She says that she cannot be more specific but it involves Michael, who used to work on El Burro Volando with me."

"Wasn't Michael the one who nursed you when you were ill," asked Deborah.

"Yes. He's the one; I probably owe him and Paco my life. I wonder if he is in some kind of trouble, he was always game for a bit of fun! One of the other ships is due to go to London this week, I wonder if I can switch cargoes with them and go there myself instead. Probably not a good idea for you to come with me this time love, as it sounds like I could be busy."

After talking to the company mangers and to the other captain involved, Bertie was able to switch cargoes with the other ship and he also arranged a few days holiday so that he could go to Harwich and see his parents. He sent a telegram to that effect, saying he would be with them on Friday the 19th September and stop for three days. He arrived in London on the Wednesday and unloaded the cargo on the Thursday and got to his parents place late Friday evening.

His dad opened the door and greeted his son and then called out to Alice, "Put the kettle on mother, the prodigal has arrived!"

As he walked through into the lounge his mother came rushing down the stairs and greeted her son with a big hug and a kiss.

"Oh Bertie, it's so good to see you after all this time, we have really missed you both."

"I know mum and I am sorry for not having been to see you lately, but I have been away so much this year, that when

I do get any time off, I just want to stay in my own home with Deborah."

They chatted for about an hour, catching up on all that had happened to them since last they were together and enjoying a nice cup of tea and some fresh fish that she had bought for supper.

"Anyway, what was all this in your letter about 'something has cropped up that needs my urgent attention' and Michael being involved? I have never known you to be so mysterious. Is he really involved or was it just a trick to get me over here."

"It was certainly no trick," said his dad, "Michael came here himself and virtually dictated the letter to your mum. He was most insistent; 'a matter of National Importance' he said. We have already sent him a telegram and told him you are coming, so I expect he will turn up some time over the weekend."

"How strange dad, did he not give you any more information about what he wanted me for?"

"None whatsoever, it was a most peculiar meeting Bertie, had your mum quite flustered!"

Robert and Bertie went for a stroll after breakfast and called in at the local pub for a pint before heading back home, where they found Alice having a cup of tea with Michael. He immediately got up from the table and the two old friends shook hands and then Robert and Alice went out to do some shopping in town, leaving the two men to talk on their own.

"Well Michael, this is all very mysterious and I have to tell you that you have spoilt my fifth wedding anniversary, so I hope there is some point to all of this. By the way, Capitan Burra and the crew send their regards and I should ask, if you have managed to find a girl to marry you yet?"

"Yes I have and actually you have already met her." He replied with a smile.

"Not that little nurse you met in Lagos?" asked Bertie. His friend nodded and smiled.

"Congratulations, I am so pleased that all my troubles and woes were not in vain, how long has it been?"

"Two years in August; Anne and I live in Folkestone and she works at the hospital."

"So you are no longer with the Navy then?"

"Well yes I am, sort of!"

"What exactly does 'sort of' mean?"

"I work for Naval Intelligence, but am currently seconded to a British Intelligence Unit who are based down at Folkestone."

"Goodness, heavy stuff, what exactly do you do, or shouldn't I be asking questions like that?" queried Bertie.

"Actually no, you shouldn't old chap; but that is of course, why I asked you to come here to see me. This form," he said, producing an official looking document with a Government insignia, "is a copy of 'The Official Secrets Act' and I have to get you to read and then sign it, before I can continue. I hope you don't mind?"

Bertie took the form, quickly scanned it and pushed it back across the table.

"Michael, I actually consider myself as much a Spaniard as I do an Englishman, these days. I live there, I work there, my wife is of Spanish decent, I speak the language like a local, why on earth does the British Government want me to sign a document like that. What do you need to tell me, that is so secret and of such importance to me and to Great Britain, that I have to sign The Official Secrets Act?"

"We know a lot about you already, Bertie," he said and produced a manila folder from his briefcase with at least an inch of papers and photographs in it. "At my suggestion we have been observing you for well over six months and it was me who originally put your name forward and suggested that you would be the perfect person for what we had in mind. Please trust me and sign the document; I am sure that I know you well enough to say that you will want to be involved in what we are doing," with which he passed the document back across the table along with a fountain pen.

"You know Michael, if it was anyone else but you, this conversation would end right now and I would just ask you to leave; but we both know that I probably owe you my life and therefore I can't do that, but I guess that you have already worked that out for yourself," with which he signed the document and returned it and the pen to Michael.

"Everything I am now going to tell you falls under 'The Official Secrets Act' and must not be repeated or discussed with anyone, including your parents. You will need to tell Deborah something, but for her own safety, the least she knows the better. Is that understood?"

Bertie nodded.

"The Government firmly believe that by this time next year, we will be at War with Germany. The likelihood is that the Ottoman Empire, Bulgaria and the Austrians will side with Germany and we believe that Belgium, France, Albania, Russia and a few more will side with us. Most importantly as far as you are concerned, we believe Spain will remain neutral. Gibraltar will of course play a key role in the logistics of what takes place and the Mediterranean Sea will be extremely important to both sides."

"So what are you saying Michael, you want me and my wife to come back to England right now and sign up with the Royal Navy, just in case you are right and we have a war with Germany, all because I know my way round the Med?"

"No, not at all, that's the last thing we want. We believe that you can better serve your country by taking on the role of a natural born Spaniard and staying in Spain and pretending to be the captain of a Spanish ship that can freely go wherever it wishes to. You would then be able to keep us informed of all enemy shipping movements you came across or heard about, particularly anything you can find out about their fleet of submarines. A lot of the experts think that the naval war could be won and lost under the sea, as much as on top of it."

When Robert and Alice returned from shopping, the conversation immediately changed to more mundane matters of home and family, while they all had lunch together. After lunch Bertie and Michael went up to his room and they picked up their conversation at where they had left off previously.

"The only problem I can see to your suggestion Michael is that I have to travel all over the Mediterranean as well as down the coast of Africa with the company; I don't see how I could consistently find things out and then safely pass information to you."

"That is true, but you do have an interest in the local fishing industry. You now own one boat and have a share in another and an interest in several more; why not give up your job with the company and just do the fishing full time. I am sure Deborah would be very pleased if you did not have to go away for long periods of time any more."

"No doubt about that, but I just have a small boat, its good for a day's fishing, but to get the sort of detailed information you need, I would require something a lot bigger, in order to be able to stay out at sea for a few days at a time."

"What size of ship are we talking about exactly and how much would it cost?" asked Michael.

"A lot more than I could afford, something like that Buckie Steam Drifter that is moored up by the lighthouse at the moment. Now a ship like that would be ideal for what you had in mind."

"Suppose we gave you the money to buy the boat and all the necessary gear and get it shipped to Benicarlo, would you be interested in working for us?"

"Yes of course I would, I would be proud to serve my country, but as I said earlier, I am not a Spanish citizen and technically, neither is Deborah. If I got stopped by the enemy and they found out that I was spying for Britain, I assume they would shoot me and anyone who was with me on the ship."

"Good point, I will look into that when I get back to work. What was Deborah's maiden name?" asked Michael.

"Makaa Chavez, but she most definitely does not want to be called Makaa again. But why did you want to know?"

"Oh, just a thought, Spanish surnames, passports, that sort of thing."

"Right, so you can get the necessary papers for us both, sounds like you know what you are doing. O.K. so where do we go from here?" asked Bertie.

"You go back to Spain and I will go back to Folkestone and talk with my superiors. I will write to you in Spain and if I say I am going to Scotland; then you will know that everything has been agreed and you are to give up your job and come here for a holiday with Deborah, when all the details will be sorted out and we will give you some extra training. If I say that my trip to Scotland has been cancelled, then you know the whole thing is off and just forget we have ever had this conversation."

"Sounds good to me, but I really hope you are wrong about another war. It seems only yesterday that I was taking Boer Prisoners of War, from South Africa to Ceylon; doesn't the world ever learn?"

Bertie had only been back from England for ten days when a letter came from his old friend Michael, saying that he was now married and that he and his wife were going on a late holiday to Scotland and wondered if Bertie and his wife might be able to join them.

The managers of the Spanish Steam Ship Company were very disappointed when Bertie handed in his letter of resignation and immediately tried to get him to change his mind. When he explained that he had inherited some money and planned to buy his own 'Steam Drifter' in order to become a fisherman in the Mediterranean Sea, everyone assumed it had something to do with Deborah and them wanting to be at home together a lot more. They were relieved, however, when he told them that it would be well into the New Year before his new ship would be ready and he would have to actually leave the company to start his new venture; which gave them time to recruit a new captain to take his place.

A couple of days later a courier delivered a registered package addressed to Deborah Chavez, which she signed for and then of course opened. Inside were two Spanish passports, one made out to Senora Deborah Chavez and the other to Senor Bertram Chavez. Fortunately Bertie had decided to tell her everything and to make sure she was completely happy with his new role as a British spy, working undercover in Spain.

They first travelled to London and were a little anxious as they went through customs for the first time with their new passports, but there were no problems. They then took a cab to Kings Cross railway station and caught the overnight sleeper train to Edinburgh. Reservations had been made at a small hotel in Princes Street, where Mr. and Mrs. Michael Callard were already in residence and an adjacent room to theirs had been reserved for Mr. and Mrs. Chavez.

The two ladies got on really well together and although Anne did not speak any Spanish, Deborah had learnt enough conversational English over the years for them to be able to chat freely. After two days in Edinburgh they all travelled up to Aberdeen and stopped there for another four days, during which time, the two men left the ladies sightseeing and travelled to Buckie to speak with the boat builders that Bertie had chosen. A friend of Michael's who was a very keen salmon fisherman had given him the address of a small Bed and Breakfast place, just outside of town, that he regularly used, to enable them to keep a low profile while up on the Moray Firth.

The ship was to be built mainly of wood but with some iron having to be used for the wheelhouse. It would have an overall length of just under eighty feet and a breadth of nineteen feet and a total weight of forty tons. The boat builder explained that the engine would be supplied and fitted in Aberdeen and that it would be sufficiently powerful to enable the ship to sail at speeds in excess of ten knots and that the ship could carry enough coal to keep it at sea for over a week. He expected everything to be completed and the ship to be available for sea trials at the start of April.

A deposit of six hundred pounds was paid to the builder, which Michael supplied; along with a few minor modifications which Bertie explained to the designer. The pair travelled back to Aberdeen and after spending a day with their wives, paid a brief visit to the company supplying the engine. Michael produced an official looking document which he gave to the chief engineer, which detailed a few modifications to the engine. He produced a copy of The Official Secrets Act which the man then signed on behalf of the company. A six hundred and fifty pounds deposit was paid to the engine company and they all shook hands on the deal and then left for their hotel.

"He seemed very impressed with the design changes you suggested Michael, do you have someone who is an engineer on your team," asked Bertie.

"Not exactly," Michael replied, "I just know someone who knows someone, if you get my drift. While I think of it, we will send the rest of the money we discussed to your bank in Spain. It will come from a solicitor we use and will verify the story you have put about, regarding an inheritance."

After collecting their two wives from the hotel, they all caught the overnight express and travelled back to London where they said goodbye to each other.

Bertie and Deborah then spent a few days at Harwich with Robert and Alice, before going back to Spain.

Bertie finally left his job as captain of El Puente Volante in the middle of February and travelled to Folkestone for specialist training, while Deborah stayed behind in Spain to run the business. They first of all brushed up his Morse Code skills and then went on to firearms training and some basic lessons in German. They taught him about the use of codes and how to answer difficult questions and even how to deal with being tortured. Before he left, they gave him an old leather-bound copy of 'He would be a Gentleman', by Samuel Lover, which they would all use when communicating with each other in code.

He went back up to Buckie and Aberdeen on several occasions and paid the balance due on the boat and engine by bank transfer from his Spanish bank account. The sea trials were mainly carried out by a local skipper named Joe, a short, bearded, powerhouse of a man, who skippered a fishing boat out of Macduff. Whilst Bertie judged Joe to be an extremely competent and experienced skipper, with a great understanding of the local conditions, he did have problems understanding his broad local accent some of the time. Joe made some suggestions regarding the design and steering of the ship which Bertie had implemented and agreed that it handled a lot better after that. The two of them then sailed the boat to Harwich, where they took his mother and father for a short trip around the harbour. Joe then returned home to Scotland, as Bertie had arranged for a couple of men from Benicarlo, who had agreed to become his crew on the new fishing boat, to come to Harwich and sail it back to Spain with him.

They all spent a few days together trialing the ship in the waters around Harwich and Robert helped Bertie to install one or two pieces of equipment that Michael had supplied for the ship, including a small radio set, with a second radio which was to be set up at their house in Spain. When everyone was satisfied with the way the ship handled, they set off on its first long voyage back to Spain, arriving in Benicarlo at the end of April 1914, to a tumultuous welcome from all the locals who had gathered for the occasion.

Bertie spent a lot of time teaching Deborah how to use the radio set and to both receive and send Morse code. He explained that it would allow them to stay in touch while he was away and to give her some idea of the amount and variety of fish he was bringing back with him. They decided to call the ship El Burro Suerte, 'The Lucky Donkey' as the other 'Donkey' ship had been so lucky for Bertie and of course the new 'Donkey' was registered in Benicarlo and flew the Spanish flag. They purchased the requisite fishing nets and other equipment from local shops and set out on their new venture.

Bertie told everyone that they had decided to be known as Senor and Senora Chavez, which news was normally just greeted by a nod or a shrug. When he met anyone away from home, he introduced himself as Capitan Chavez and opened a new bank account in that name, which received all monies from the fish business and all the creditors bills were also paid from this new account. Over the next couple of months, Bertie Bannister just disappeared and Capitan Bertram Chavez, (Bertie to his friends) took his place.

The first time he was away on a trip for a couple of weeks with the ship, there was a big surprise waiting when he returned home. Deborah had bought herself a two month old puppy she had called Veto, to keep her company while she was on her own. Veto was a Spanish Water Dog and as his name meant 'Intelligent', and so he proved to be.

By the time that war broke out in the summer of 1914 El Burro Suerte was already getting to be quite well known around the Mediterranean and with its new gear and modern equipment, was starting to bring home some excellent catches of fish. The fact that Deborah knew in advance the details of the fish they had caught, meant she was able to get top prices for the catch. Because the ship was able to stay at sea for several weeks at a time, it was able to visit any port it chose to and to sell its fish wherever there was a market for it.

Bertie was prepared to trade in most currencies and would barter for goods, jewellery and other produce, when the occasion required it. The modifications he had asked the Buckie boat builder to make, allowed him to safely carry, wines, spirits, cigarettes and other goods that people needed in war time, but which he did not want the various customs authorities to discover. He traded with anyone and everyone and within six months, Capitan Chavez was welcomed by all sides of the conflict, as well as all the neutral states.

He got into the habit of communicating with Deborah at ten pm each night and used a simple code to inform her of his current position, the fish they had caught and where they had caught them. He would always enquire after her health and what sort of day she was having and sometimes would enquire after the dog Veto. His nightly broadcasts were monitored by both the British and German navies, who often stopped the friendly Spaniard and bought fish and other supplies from him and got a liking for Spanish wine, port and sherry. He once made the mistake of mentioning a certain fish which they had not in fact caught that day, so when a German ship stopped him and asked to buy the particular fish in question, he had to make up a story of passing it to another Spanish ship who were heading back to port that night and to then selling them an expensive fish at a low price to compensate.

The British navy always took down his messages in detail, but only ever de-coded them, if they contained a reference to Veto the dog. If they needed to pass information to him they would send his call sign out at hourly intervals until he was in a safe position to answer. The first time this happened was at the end of December when a British merchant ship had hit a mine and gone down off the Balearic Islands. By the time Bertie arrived most of the crew had drowned, but he did manage to pick up half a dozen men and take them to Barcelona and hand them over to the authorities. The whole time the survivors were with him, he kept up the pretence of being Spanish and not understanding what they were saying, as the instructors had warned him never to relax the pretence of being Spanish and never to admit he was British. Once he was at sea again, he was able to inform the British navy of the details of what he had seen and where he had left the survivors.

On another occasion he picked up a German sailor who had fallen overboard and took him to Barcelona, just like the British sailors; but this time he was able to pass on the name of the sailor's ship and its position in the Mediterranean, to the Royal Navy.

Christmas 1914 was a very strange affair for Bertie, knowing that his parent were still in England, coping with all the shortages and doing their bit for the war effort and here was he, with his wife in Spain, safe and sound with plenty to eat and drink. It just did not feel right to him; but he knew it was the way it had to be.

Deborah decided that they should go to Valencia for a few days at the end of the year, as they had enjoyed a most successful six months fishing and trading with the new boat and although Bertie was not very enthusiastic, he eventually agreed to the suggestion.

"Besides," she said, "people will expect us to go away and enjoy ourselves, they all know how successful we have been Bertie, it will do us both good to celebrate the New Year properly!"

So off they went on New Year's Eve and had a great time in Valencia and stayed at a very smart hotel and had a large bedroom with its own bathroom. They had a good meal and danced till midnight and saw in the New Year at The Plaza de la Vergen with hundreds of other people. They walked back slowly to their hotel and as they reached the foyer, Deborah noticed that the little café was still open, so she suggested that they had a coffee before going to bed. They sat down and ordered a drink and Bertie could not help noticing that she was fiddling with her hair and bag and did not seem comfortable with herself.

"Are you alright Deborah," he asked, "you do not look very comfortable, is something bothering you?"

"Nothing is bothering me exactly Bertie, but I do have something to tell you, which the doctor confirmed when I went to see him this week. I am pregnant; we are going to have a baby, probably at the end of August. I do hope you are pleased about it!"

"Ahhh, that's fantastic Deborah, that's the best possible news I could ever wish to hear," with which he got up from his chair and went over and kissed and hugged his wife.

Veto on the beach at Benicarlo   Artist – Peter Rugendyke

Chapter 11
The Big Fish

As the war continued throughout 1915 so Bertie became more adept at obtaining information and passing it on to the British Navy. He provided little luxuries to both sides and in some weeks made a lot more money from his trading than he did from his fishing. Gold and silver coins, perfume, jewellery, watches, leather goods, silks and other materials all passed through his hands, but he was always careful never to trade in arms or ammunition or anything else that could lead to future complications or questions that he would rather not have to answer.

He was chased several times by the Spanish coastguard, but the modified engines on his wooden ship always gave him that slight advantage and he was able to evade them. When he was eventually stopped by the coastguard in early June, he vehemently protested his innocence to the two officers who boarded his boat, but they ignored his pleas and went about their business of searching the entire boat, looking for contraband. The initial search yielded nothing apart from a couple of packets of British cigarettes, which one of the crewman claimed were his and had been bought from a French fisherman the previous week, but they confiscated them anyway. They then spent another two hours conducting a much more thorough search of the entire ship and even came close to finding one of Bertie's hiding places among the store of coal. At last they decided they had wasted enough of their time and left the boat with all sorts of dire threats of what they would do to him when they finally caught him out, but despite the unpleasant comments, they still left the ship with enough fresh fish for all of their suppers.

Whilst Deborah enjoyed the benefits of his extra trading activities, she did worry what would happen to them all if he got caught and of course, how to keep the growing pile of money and valuables safe.

"But what are we to do with all the profits you have made?" asked Deborah, after a particularly successful trading week. "If we just take the money to the bank it will create a lot of questions and the last time I sold a piece of jewellery in town, I got a very funny look from the shop manager and he only gave me a fraction of what it was worth, so we cannot go there again. So tell me, do you have any ideas of what we should do, have you even given the matter any thought at all Bertie?"

"Well, last time I had this problem, I used the money I made on the Mad Donkey to buy the land here and then pay to have this place built. No-one seemed bothered by what I was doing then and not a lot has changed in the intervening years! I guess the first thing we can do is to make some enquiries and find out who owns the piece of land behind us and buy that from them and then get an extension built. When the baby comes, we will definitely need a bit more room anyway."

"Good idea, I will ask around in town and find out who owns the land. But you should think about getting a safe or digging a big hole or doing something to keep our things secure and out of the way. My father used to have a loose brick in the wall and hide his money behind it, but he never had as much as you have managed to collect. Is all of this ours or do you still have to pay the men their share out of it?"

"I make a point of settling with the men each week, so they can treat it as part of their wages, so everything you see here is all ours! The other idea that I did have was to do with that boy we found on our honeymoon. Didn't his parents say they owned a jewellery shop?"

"That's right, Tarbes, over the border in France. What were you thinking?"

"Not really sure, but just thought there might be an opportunity there, they seemed the sort of people who might be interested in dealing with us. Alternatively, we could go over to England after the war and use our profits to buy land or a property of some sort near where my parents live. But the opportunity to do that is probably going to be years away yet."

"Talking of England," said Deborah, "are they going to want the boat back after the war or will they expect you to buy it from them, it all seemed a bit vague to me, as to who really owned it?"

"Good point, but providing we continue to make a profit on the legitimate fish sales, we should have enough money in the bank to be able to buy it in a couple of year's time," her husband replied.

Deborah kept in quite good health throughout her pregnancy and with Veto to keep her company and a baby to knit and sew for, the months soon passed and right on time her waters broke on Monday August 30th 1915 and a baby girl was delivered by the local mid-wife just after three o'clock in the afternoon. Bertie had realised she was getting close and had not gone out in the boat that day, so he was able to be present at the birth of his little daughter and hold her in his arms and experience the thrill of gazing at his first child.

The local women gave her great support for the first few weeks, especially when Bertie was at sea and most days someone popped in to see the baby and help her out in the house.

They had already had long discussions over what names to give their child and had decided that if it was a boy, it would be named Roberto after his father and if it was a girl she would be called Deborah after her mother. Bertie did point out that Deborah was not her real name, but she was adamant:

"The name Deborah has been good for me and has kept me safe and possibly, even kept me alive. Remember what we agreed, Makaa died on the boat back from Chile, my past is forgotten, we said we would not even discuss it again. I want my baby to be called Deborah, after me, if it is a girl."

The Spanish priest who had originally taught Bertie to speak Spanish, while he was still living at Gravesend, had returned home to Spain, but a younger man had gone out to the same church just before the war started, so Bertie had arranged to use this ecclesiastical avenue to get messages to his parents. He wrote to them straight away, giving all the details that he could possibly think of, and a few which Deborah suggested, about the birth and the new baby. His letter eventually reached Harwich about a month later and the new grandparents were thrilled to read about their new grand-daughter, especially when they read that the baby had been named Deborah Alice Chavez and was a bouncing seven and a half pounds and had emerged safely into the world, crying loudly.

"Are you sure there is no possible way I could go over there and be with them?" asked Alice. "Fancy, after all these years, a little girl named after me. I am dying to see her and Bertie and Deborah, of course."

"No love. It is just not possible. It would be very dangerous for you and could completely blow Bertie's cover of being a Spanish fisherman. I am sure they will try and send a photograph as soon as they have one. We will ask the priest to ask for this in his reply."

In November, mother and baby made the trip to Valencia and had several photographs taken, one of which found its way to a certain cottage in Harwich in time for Christmas.

Baby Deborah slept well and fed heartily, right from the start. She was crawling at six months and walking at ten months and once she was up on her feet, there was no stopping her. She proved to be a very tough, strong willed little girl and her and Veto played together for hours each day and their shouts and barks could be heard by all the neighbours.

Finding out who owned the land behind them, took a lot longer than expected, due to the complexities of the Spanish legal system, when it comes to property ownership. Eventually someone was found who knew the auntie of the owner of the land and contact was made with them; so just before the time that baby Deborah started to walk, the legal documents were signed, the requisite cash was paid over and the builder, who had built the original house for Bertie, was instructed to start the work. Basically the floor area was doubled, but only one extra bedroom was added, but all of the other rooms were increased in size. They were able to stay in the house for most of the time, except for a couple of weeks in June 1916, when interior walls were being knocked down and repositioned. During this time they stayed in the house next door, having become very friendly with the new owners, who were not using it at that time.

The building work was finally finished around Deborah's first birthday, which gave them an excuse for a big birthday party. Unfortunately, as it turned out, this was not a very happy event for the birthday girl, as she had teething problems for the whole of the party and cried solidly throughout.

Life continued in much the same vein for the next year, the Great War taking a terrible toll, as hundreds of thousands of lives were lost on both sides of the conflict. Around the middle of July 1917, when Bertie was fishing off the coast of Spain, just east of Barcelona, he received a message from the British Navy, instructing him to go to the Ionian Sea and to start fishing there, as some 'big fish' had been sighted. This was only the third time he had been given a specific instruction to go somewhere and on all of the previous occasions, there had been a certain amount of danger involved for both him and his crew. He had two regular crew members with him on the trip, Jacobo an older man in his fifties and Santo who was just a bit younger than Bertie. The third man was Santo's young brother, who had stepped in at the last moment when the other regular man had gone sick.

Bertie called Jacobo and Santo into the wheelhouse and informed them that he had decided to go and fish in the Ionian Sea, just west of Corfu and that if they did not wish to go with him for any personal reason, then he would not think ill of them, but would endeavour to transfer them to another boat or drop them off at Cagliari on the way there.

Jacobo and Santo smiled at each other and Jacobo acted as spokesman for them both.

"So Capitan, the British Navy wants us to go to Corfu, do we know why?"

Bertie was surprised and for a moment he was speechless.

"How long have you known?" he asked.

"More or less, right from the start, we guessed you were up to something when you suddenly became a Spaniard," replied Santo.

"I see, does everyone in town know of this?" asked Bertie.

"Of course not; we are not stupid," said Jacobo. "Anyway, we don't like the German's any more than you do. It may not be our fight, but we are happy to assist you wherever we can and after all, it has proved to be very profitable for all of us, what with the fish sales and the trading with both sides, we have never earned as much money as this before."

"So neither of you mind coming with me to Corfu then?"

"Of course we will come with you, but I do not want my young brother to come. He just thinks we are fisherman and if anything happened to him, I would never forgive myself," said Santo.

"Right, so we transfer him to another boat or drop him off at Cagliari, but what reason will you give him, won't he be suspicious?" asked Bertie.

"No, he has an interview for a job next week and I will simply say that we have decided to be away for a couple of weeks. Just pay him his wages for a few days and he will be happy."

As it happened, they did not need to call in at Sardinia, as they passed a fishing boat from Valencia that they often fished with, who was heading back to port and transferred Santo's brother, with a full week's wages to the other boat. As captains do not tend to tell each other where they find their fish, no-one on the other boat bothered to ask Bertie where he was heading, so after transferring the young man, they both went their separate ways.

They arrived off the North West coast of Corfu around dusk a couple of days later, having called in at Palermo for some fresh supplies. They decided to anchor in the bay overnight and to make the decision of where they should start to fish, once they had made an assessment of the area in daylight. They sent the usual message to Deborah, giving their position and details of the fish they had caught. Bertie asked after his daughter and Veto and mentioned that they had not caught anything big as yet.

About midnight Bertie was asleep in the wheelhouse when he felt a hefty bump against the side of the boat. He was up and out of the wheelhouse in an instant and there to his immense surprise was a submarine, on the surface of the sea, anchored alongside him.

As he studied the submarine he was able to make out the U-boat markings and then he realised that some of the crew were standing along the railing of the submarine pointing rifles at him and also the sub's mounted machine gun, was pointing directly at him.

He checked to see if his Spanish Flag was still flying on the mast and it was, so he pointed to it and shouted out, "We are Spanish, what do you want?"

An officer with a loud hailer appeared and replied in his best Austrian-Spanish,

"I can see the flag, where do you come from?"

"We are from Benicarlo, which is near Valencia," Bertie shouted back, cupping his hands round his mouth.

"Why are you so far from home Spaniard?"

"We have been out fishing for four days and caught very little and then we heard from a friend who was returning to port, that he had caught a lot of fish near Corfu, so we have come here to see if our luck will improve."

"I am coming over to speak with you, do not be frightened, we intend you no harm."

By now Jacobo and Santo had joined Bertie and they discussed what this new turn in events might mean for them.

"I don't think it's German, it must be one of those Austrian submarines," said Bertie, "I think it's called a U-27 class or something like that, I have never seen one before."

"I wonder if that is the type of submarine that they say is always breaking down with engine trouble," asked Santo.

"We will soon find out, act friendly towards them, here they come," warned Bertie.

The officer and two armed crewmen came aboard the boat and while the officer went with Bertie to the wheelhouse, the two crewmen proceeded to carry out a thorough search of the boat.

Bertie produced a bottle of cognac and offered the officer a drink which he accepted and they drank together and introduced themselves and made small talk. The crewmen then appeared and said something to the officer, obviously indicating that there was nothing unusual on the boat and that there were only a few fish on board. The officer carefully watched Bertie to try and see if he understood any German and came to the conclusion that he was most likely, what he claimed to be, a Spanish fishing boat captain.

"Well Capitan Chavez, I will come to the point. My ship has engine problems and I need you to tow me into Saranda, where I should be able to get some assistance. If we leave now, we can get there under cover of darkness and there will be no risk to you and your boat."

"Lieutenant, Spain is neutral, we cannot take sides, I cannot help you, I am sorry," said Bertie emphatically.

"And I cannot leave you here, knowing of my predicament. I will be forced to shoot you and your crew and sink your boat, if you do not help me."

Bertie now realised why he had been sent here in the first place and assumed that he was being watched by the British Navy, so he raged and blustered and protested a lot more, before he finally agreed to tow them to Saranda, which was about thirty miles away, North East of Corfu and part of the Ottoman Empire.

The officer and one crewman remained with Bertie and the other crewman returned to the sub and then came back with a cable for towing, before returning to the sub. The engine on El Burro Suerte was started up and the slack in the cable slowly taken up as Bertie eased his boat forward. It was slow going and they had to take a wider path than expected due to the rocky coastline and a few man made dangers that the lieutenant told him to avoid. Dawn was just breaking as they steamed into Saranda and Bertie was told to wait off shore until he was told what to do next. Within an hour a large tug had appeared and taken charge of the submarine and Bertie was ordered to follow the tug into port and was amazed to find two more submarines tied up together, along with several other large ships and a full marine workshop, all hidden from view.

Several armed soldiers were on the dock and helped to tie up the boat, after which, they were all ordered off the ship and taken to a room at the end of the dock where the lieutenant spoke to Bertie while the crew listened and the sub-mariner stood guard outside the door.

"I was not quite honest with you last night Capitan," said the lieutenant, "as you can see, we have all the help we could possibly need here to fix our engines, but I am afraid that you and your crew will have to remain as our guests until the end of the war, now that you are aware of our little secret."

Bertie complained loudly and became quite belligerent, so the officer drew his pistol and pointed it at him as he said, "I do understand how you feel Capitan, but you do not have any options, apart from one, that is. Would you like me to shoot you and your men now, or will you agree to stay here and be my guests until we decide what to do with you. The choice is yours."

Bertie looked at his two crewmen and then replied, "Forgive me lieutenant, but we all have families back home that will be worrying about us; in your shoes I would probably have done the same as you. You had to protect your ship and your crew and we understand that. We will be your guests, as you suggested."

"Very sensible Capitan. Here comes the sergeant of the guard, he will take you to a room where you can stay, but I regret to tell you that it will be locked and guarded."

As the sergeant came into the room the lieutenant left, but said something quietly to him as they passed each other in the doorway. While this was going on, Bertie pulled his cap down over his eyes and whispered to Santo that he should be the one to speak with the sergeant. Santo looked surprised but nodded and stepped forward in front of Bertie, "Sergeant the men and I are hungry and we need something to eat and drink and we want to know where you are taking us?" he asked the sergeant.

The sergeant did not reply but pointed his pistol at Santo and indicated that they should follow him. He stepped out of the room and walked along the dock and then into a large stone building which was obviously an old warehouse. The sub-mariner followed behind the party, keeping his rifle trained on them the whole time. They climbed a flight of stairs, walked the length of a first floor corridor and went into a room at the end. It had a small window halfway up the wall, with bars across it, three wooden chairs and an old table stood in the middle of the room and a candle holder hung down by a chain from a beam in the high ceiling. The sergeant indicated that they should stand against the far wall and he then called them one at a time to empty the contents of their pocket into a cardboard box that was on the table. Jacobo made a bit of a show when he put his knife into the box, but apart from that, the whole process went smoothly and the sergeant picked up the box and left. They heard a key turn in the lock and two sets of boots, marching back down the corridor and the three men sat down around the table.

"Why did you ask me to speak to the sergeant instead of doing it yourself?" asked Santo.

"Because I recognised him," said Bertie. "The very first time I was involved in taking recruits to the Foreign Legion, he was there, returning from leave. I am not sure if he saw me that night, but he may have done, in which case, should he recognise me, he will know that I am English and not Spanish and you know what that means!"

"Si, si," they both replied, in a very concerned way.

"Do you have any idea what the British Navy are going to do, or even if they know we are here?" asked Jacobo.

"To be honest with you, I don't," replied Bertie, "but they must have asked us to come here for a good reason, so I assume they have been watching us somehow and will do something when they are ready. The longer we are here, however, the greater the chance that someone will recognise me, so we need to be thinking about how to get ourselves out of this place, before we are either shot, or sent to somewhere which is a lot more secure."

From the window they could look out to the harbour and see all the boats coming and going, but all the naval boats were well out of sight and no-one viewing the harbour from the sea, would ever have guessed the secret that Saranda held.

Jacobo was looking out of the window when he called out to Santo, "Hey, come and see what is coming into the harbour Santo; see over there, just taking the sail down, do you see it?"

"Ah, Jacobo, do you remember when my uncle first took me fishing in his boat?"

"How could I forget, you were sick for six hours," Bertie joined them at the window and Jacobo continued, "do you see it Bertie? They are unloading fish by the wall, it is just like the boat that belongs to Santo's uncle; we used to sail with him a lot, when Santo was just a boy."

"Could we sail across to Italy in it, if we had the chance to escape?" Bertie asked.

"With Jacobo and me, we could sail back home to Benicarlo in it, if we had to," replied Santo.

Just then the door opened and a civilian worker carried in a tray with some bread and a jug of water and three beakers on it, while the guard stood at the door with his rifle pointing towards them. He then went out and came back into the room with a bucket and some newspapers, which he put in the corner by the door, which was then closed and locked again.

They ate the bread and drank the water and used the bucket and chatted and schemed the day away. The guard and civilian came back in the early evening, with more bread and water and some sort of sausage for them to eat. Santo indicated that they needed to empty the bucket, so he was told to follow them with the bucket. As he picked it up, some spilt on his shoe, which gave the civilian and guard something to laugh about.

Instead of going down the corridor, they turned the other way and went down a narrow winding staircase with a dark passageway at the bottom. The civilian opened a door to a windowless toilet and Santo went in and emptied the bucket. He indicated that he wanted to wash it out, so he was taken to the washroom next door, where he half filled the bucket with water and then went back and tipped it down the toilet. The three then went back the way they had come and Santo and the bucket were locked up with the other two men.

They had their food and drink and asked Santo what had happened and where they had taken him. He carefully told them exactly what had happened, trying to remember every detail and then answered their questions.

"I have told you already, I could not see out of the window in the washroom, it was whitewashed over," he said.

"You normally whitewash a window to stop people looking in, not looking out, which means it could be at the front of the building and look out onto the harbour, rather than at the back or side" said Bertie.

"Did you see the sun in the room Santo, it would have been quite low in the sky?" asked Jacobo.

"Yes, well no. I didn't see it as such, but there was a glow at the top of the window, it must have been the sun," Santo replied excitedly.

At this point the door burst opened and the sergeant, with his Luger pistol in his hand came into the room and stood by the table, while another soldier stood in the doorway with his rifle trained on them. The soldier shouted out in Spanish, "Everyone against the wall and you," pointing at Bertie, "take your hat off now and put it on the table."

Bertie stepped forward to the table and took his hat off and put it on the table, keeping his head low to his chest. The sergeant walked over and putting the barrel of his pistol under his chin, lifted it up, smiled at Bertie and said in broken English, "Well Englishman, we meet again."

"Me Capitan Chavez, Spanish, you have papers, I only speak little Inglsh," Bertie replied.

"Good try, but we have been watching you and your boat for many months Englishman, besides, the lieutenant has told me that he thought you understood some German and I am sure that I have seen you myself, before somewhere. It has already been decided, you are all spies and we will shoot you all tomorrow."

Bertie realised the game was up, so he spoke in English, "You are right about me sergeant, but these men are Spaniards and did not know anything about what I have been doing, you must not shoot them, Spain is a neutral country."

"I really don't care about them, but it is a lot easier for us, if we just shoot you all and as far as I am concerned," **Boom**!!

Which is as far as he got with the sentence, as there were several more loud explosions outside, accompanied by bright flashes of light and part of the outer wall of the building came crashing inwards. The guard standing in the doorway took the full impact of the flying masonry, which virtually severed his head from his body. Everyone else, including the sergeant, was blown against the end wall and although Jacobo was dazed, he had the presence of mind to remove the small leather covered cosh that was hidden at the back of the sheath that his knife had been in and promptly whacked the sergeant over the head several times with it.

"Is he dead?" asked Bertie, as he picked up the Luger that had fallen to the floor.

"Why should we care, he was going to shoot us tomorrow," said Santo, as he picked up the rifle that the dead soldier had been holding and they all climbed over the rubble and went out through the massive hole in the wall where the door had once been.

The corridor they had originally come down earlier that day had mostly been blown away, so they followed Santo down the back staircase, past the toilet and into the washroom. The civilian who had brought the food to them was lying on the floor, bleeding profusely, from where he had been cut by the flying glass. Bertie found some towels and tied them tightly over the wounds on his arm and chest and managed to put a tourniquet on his right leg, to stop the blood flowing.

Meanwhile, Jacobo had searched the room next door and returned with three heavy coats and a bag with some food and a bottle of wine in it and Santo had gone outside to see what was happening.

"Quick, we must leave now, some soldiers are coming this way, hurry!" he warned.

The other two climbed through the window and they all put on the coats that Jacobo had found.

"They cannot tell us from anyone else now," Santo said, "besides, I do not think that they are too bothered about us telling the British what we know about this place any more, are they?"

As they looked out into the harbour and dock area, they could see many ships burning and sinking and where the submarines and other naval boats had been anchored, there was now just a mass of fiery scrap metal. Some shells were still coming down on that area so the three men decided it would be safest, to head off in the opposite direction.

"Head for the boat like my uncle's one," shouted Santo, "I think it is just over there." They all ran in the direction he pointed to and no-one stopped them, or shot at them or even shouted at them, the confusion and general panic in the harbour area completely covered their escape.

When they reached the boat, they were relieved to find that no-one was there, so they quickly untied it and while Jacobo and Santo manned the oars, Bertie steered them out into the main channel.

"What if the British see us and start to shoot at us?" asked Santo.

"They are far too busy destroying the boats in the harbour to worry about us, but if we can head north and keep close to land, we will not be in any danger," Bertie replied.

The two men rowed steadily for about fifteen minutes and when he thought they were out of danger, Bertie said, "We are far enough away from the docks now, to risk putting the sail up, so let's see what this boat like your uncle's can do, shall we Santo!"

They sailed along the coast for a couple of hours and then decided to head off in a north westerly direction in the hope of being able to make the Italian coast by the following morning. They could hear gunfire long into the night and were aware of several large vessels steaming close by, but they were not stopped and the wind and the tides were kind to them and when dawn finally came, the Italian coast was clearly visible in the distance.

"I think we should make for Brindisi," said Bertie, "I have been there several times and know the harbour and have a business contact there that I am sure will be willing to help us. Is everyone in agreement?"

They kept sailing in a northerly direction for the rest of the morning and made their way into Brindisi in the late afternoon. As they tied up at the dock an old fisherman came towards them, shouting and gesticulating at them. No-one understood what he was saying and eventually he caused so much confusion that a policeman arrived on the scene and indicated that they should all go with him to the police station. Eventually a young lady teacher from the local school arrived who spoke Spanish and acted as interpreter, Santo, once again taking the lead.

"It appears that the old fisherman claims the boat belonged to one of his sons and was stolen several months ago from a beach south of here and insists that you are the thieves and should be put in prison," the young woman explained.

"We are all Spanish fishermen, from Benicarlo and we were fishing off Corfu two days ago, in our steam driven fishing boat," said Santo, "when we were stopped and arrested by an Austrian submarine and accused of being spies. They made us go to Saranda and locked us up. They told us that we were going to be shot today!"

Everyone gasped as the woman explained what he had said to her.

"Well how do they have my son's boat if they were in prison in Saranda?" asked the old man.

Santo went on to explain about the British bombardment of the harbour and how they had all managed to escape from their captors. He then told them that his uncle used to have a boat just like the one they had taken and that he knew how well it sailed and that it would be able to cross the sea and get them to safety in Italy. Finally an Italian naval officer was brought in, who confirmed that Saranda had been bombarded the previous night, so the three were congratulated on their escape and set free; but the old fisherman demanded that he be allowed to keep the boat, so that he could return it to his son.

Bertie was able to remember the address of his business contact who willingly lent them enough money to buy some new clothes and other essentials and gave them a bed for the night. The next day they bought a map and got their friend to send a telegram to Benicarlo, letting their families know that they were safe and were heading home.

They decided it was safer to cross Italy by land and then try to get a boat from the western side to Sardinia and thence home from there. They first went to Taranto and then down the coast to Trebisacce and then made their way across to the village of Fuscaldo, where Jacobo remembered that an old friend of his now lived. The journey took them four days and they slept rough to save money and in order not to have to answer lots of questions, wherever they went.

Jacobo was able to find where his friend lived, but his wife said he was away fishing and would not be home for another day. Whilst she was a bit wary of these rough looking men, Jacobo could recount enough stories to give her the confidence to allow them to sleep in her shed, wash in her kitchen and to supply them with food and drink.

It was actually two days before the friend arrived home and another two days before he was ready and willing to take them to Palermo where they were able to get another ship to take them to Cagliari in Sardinia.

As luck would have it, one of the El Burro Volando's sister ships was in the harbour and Bertie was able to arrange a lift back to Valencia for them all, arriving back in Benicarlo the next day, where they were all greeted like returning heroes.

Chapter 12
A Modern Form of Transport

"But what are you going to do now that you don't have your big fishing boat anymore?" asked Deborah. "You could still go fishing in the old boat, but the two brothers already use that most days of the week and I do not have the heart to tell them that we want it back."

"No, of course we couldn't do that," replied Bertie, "and anyway, the sergeant of the guard told me that they had been watching me for a quite a while, so it would not be safe for me to return to the sea at the moment, whatever boat I was in, so I could not even risk going back to the old firm that I worked for, in case I put anyone else in danger there. We have more than enough cash and valuables tucked away to live on for a year or so and anyway, you still have the fish selling business to run, so I will just have to be a kept man for the time being, until we decide what we should do."

Jacobo and Santo used some of their ill-gotten gains to put down a large deposit on a small fishing boat, between them and occasionally Bertie went out with them, if they were not going very far out to sea. Deborah handled the fish sales for them, so the family continued happily in this vein until the end of March 1918.

"We had a letter today from that priest in London, Bertie," Deborah informed him one day, after he returned from a fishing trip with his two friends.

"Really, another letter from mum already," he replied, "we only got one a week ago, is there something wrong over there?"

"No, it's not from your mother, it's actually from the priest and it is really strange, here, you take a look at it," she said, passing him the letter.

Bertie took the letter and read it aloud in his best Spanish:

'My Dear Senora Chavez,

Let me say how kind it was of you, to ask after my health and I am pleased to be able to tell you that I am feeling a lot better now. One of our parishioners owns a small cottage next to the church at Howam and allowed me to use it from last August until just the other week, so I was able to avoid the dangers of the English winter and enjoy the fresh clean warm air.'

"You see what I mean Bertie? I never wrote to him asking after his health, he must have confused me with someone else. What do you think?" asked Deborah.

"I think that my good friend Michael is using the priest to get a message to me. He says in the letter, 'next to the church at Howam', but I am not sure that there is such a place in England, but while I was being trained at Folkestone, Michael took me out to a favourite pub of his, which was at 'Church Hougham', do you see? And when he says 'from last August until just the other week, so I was able to avoid the dangers', he is in fact referring to the period since I returned from captivity in Saranda, until the time he wrote the letter."

"I see," said Deborah, "so what about the rest of it?"

Bertie continued to read the letter:

"I was very sad to hear of the death of your donkey, I know how fond of it you were, but I am sure that it served you well and all good things come to an end.

Perhaps now is the time for you to turn to a more modern form of transport; why you might even buy yourself a motorbike. I say this, as a good friend of mine in Barcelona, purchased one a few months ago and it really seems to have given him a new lease of life and proves to be a very useful form of transport on the dusty Spanish roads.

If it were not for this terrible conflict, I would be planning to return to Spain myself, as there are several family matters that urgently need my attention.

Anyway, let me say again how pleased I was to hear from you and that you are all safe and well. Please give my regards to David and to all my good friends at the church.

Bless you all,

Father Benedict.'

"Well, I think from this, that we can assume that Michael is planning to come and see us in the near future and is acknowledging that the boat has gone and that I cannot go back to sea," said Bertie.

"But what was all that about a motorbike, was he being serious or is that a code for something else?" asked Deborah.

"Very interesting," replied Bertie, "I think that he is actually telling me to go and buy myself a motorbike, as he mentions dusty roads, a new lease of life and David. The only David he would know about was that young lad we met on honeymoon, because I was telling him and Anne about it one night. But as to what it all means, I have absolutely no idea. Still, it gives me an excuse to go to Barcelona and buy myself a motorcycle; that will cause a stir with all the neighbours!"

It turned out that there were four places in Barcelona that sold motorcycles and Bertie visited each one of them in turn, starting with the one that had the biggest selection of bikes. He made a point of asking for the manager, giving his name and occupation and where he had come from and during the conversation, mentioning the need for a new form of transport since the old family donkey had died a few months ago.

Whilst the manager was pleasant and tried very hard to sell him a motorbike, there was no sign that he was expected or recognised, so he moved on to the second and then the third establishment, with similar results.

The last place he visited was a bit of a dingy workshop, down a side-street in a less reputable part of town and the owner did not seem very interested in talking to him and only had one motorbike on show, a 250cc 1910 Arbinet Freres.

"The motorbike has already been reserved senor, I do not have any more at the moment, you will have to look somewhere else," the owner told him.

"That's a real pity," said Bertie, "I have travelled all the way from Benicarlo to come here to buy a motorbike and this one would be ideal."

"Benicarlo, you say," queried the owner, "do you happen to know a friend of mine there, Capitan Chavez?"

"I am Capitan Chavez and you are not a friend of mine, so who are you?" asked Bertie, taking the Luger out of his pocket and pointing it at the owner.

"Easy, easy Capitan, we are all on the same side. I was told to expect a Capitan Chavez and to give him this motorbike; it has all been paid for and is ready to go. I just need to see a scar that you received in Africa; to prove that you are who you say you are. And please put the gun away Capitan, my mechanic has you covered anyway," he said, pointing to the far corner of the workshop, where Bertie saw a man in overalls standing with a rifle aimed at him.

"You were quite safe," said Bertie, "as I am out of ammunition, it was just for show."

The pistol was put back in his pocket and the scar on his left leg shown to the owner and the motorbike examined and discussed. The luggage rack and its supports had all been strengthened and a spare seat was supplied that could be fixed to the rack, to take an extra passenger. Bertie stayed a couple of days in Barcelona, during which time he learnt how to ride the motorbike and how to strip the engine and maintain all of the working parts.

When he finally headed off back home, he was loaded down with a tool kit, spare parts, spare tyres and plenty of fuel, with the promise that a delivery would come sometime in the next couple of weeks, with more parts and fuel.

Bertie and Deborah both loved riding on the motorbike, but unfortunately on one such trip, they ran out of fuel three miles from town and had to push the bike back home, only to be greeted by the cheers and jeers of their friends and neighbours. Bertie then stripped the engine and cleaned all the parts and had everything back together well before their delivery arrived from Barcelona, with the promised extra fuel and parts, along with a note telling them not to waste any more fuel on unnecessary trips. He did, however, do one more trip, just round the town, with baby Deborah strapped on her mother's back, who was sitting on the spare seat holding on tight to Bertie. She laughed and shouted with glee and waved to everyone that they passed.

Towards the middle of May, a 1300 ton British mine-layer left Gibraltar in the middle of the night and headed for Majorca. Just before dawn a small boat left the ship and ran ashore in a small bay on the South East coast of the island. One man got out and went ashore and the boat returned to the ship, which immediately steamed off towards Malta.

A day or two later, a Spanish fishing boat picked up a lone sailor in Palma and dropped him off in Benicarlo, before going on to Barcelona. The sailor slowly made his way to Bertie's house by the seashore and knocked at the door. Young Deborah got to the door first, accompanied by Veto,

"Mama, mama, hombre," she shouted out, while Veto barked loudly.

The man stood there smiling at the little girl as Deborah came to the door,

"Yes, can I help you," she asked.

"Deborah, it is me Michael, and this must be little Deborah and you must be Veto," he said to the dog.

"Michael, is it really you, I would never have recognised you, come in and sit down and make yourself comfortable. I will call Bertie, I think he is cleaning that new toy you gave him once again," with which she went out the back and fetched her husband.

The two men shook hands and chatted over a glass of wine and ate some bread and cheese, while young Deborah attempted to climb all over their visitor and Veto was put outside to calm down.

"So tell me the truth Michael, was I sent as the bait into a trap at Saranda? Did you know what would happen to me?" Bertie asked his friend.

"Yes, I am afraid that is exactly what happened. We had lost so much shipping to those submarines that we had to find a way to discover where there base was and then destroy it, with as many ships in harbour as possible. So yes, to be quite honest with you; you were the bait."

"But how did they find out about me spying for you, we had both been so careful; but the sergeant said they had known about us for months?"

"He exaggerated, weeks maybe, but not months. We had two people in our department that we thought could be enemy spies, but did not know for sure which one of them it was. We allowed the one we thought was loyal to find out about another boat we use from time to time and the one we really suspected of being the spy, we allowed to find out about you.

The first boat went to Corfu just a week before you, fished for a few days and then came away again, so we guessed we were right about the first person, who was just careless and has now been replaced. We were sure, therefore, that they would be forced to arrest you, once you arrived in the area and all we had to do was to keep track of where they took you, wait for a few more ships to come up in support and then blow Saranda harbour to kingdom come."

"But Michael, he was your friend," said Deborah, "how could you do such a terrible thing to your friend. Just because you once saved his life, did not give you the right to take it from him, just when it suited you!"

"It was not my decision Deborah, thank goodness; someone much higher up the chain of command than me, had the job of choosing the bait for the operation. What we achieved by destroying the submarines and their base at Saranda, probably saved hundreds of British sailors lives and it was the right decision to make; besides, I knew that if anyone could get himself out of there alive and save his crew as well, it would be Bertie; he just has the knack of surviving in dangerous situations."

"It's O.K. Michael; I agree with you, it was the right decision to make, so let us never talk about it again. I just hope the British Government is not going to charge me for a ship which it destroyed! But to change the subject, why have you come to Spain, I assume it was not just to see me and why the insistence that I get a motorbike and learn how to ride, am I going somewhere?"

"Not so much you, but we are going somewhere," Michael replied, "let me tell you all about it. Sorry Deborah, but this is for Bertie's ears only."

The two men left Benicarlo on the motorbike early the next day, to enjoy as much daylight as possible for the journey. They travelled light, apart from a small rucksack which Michael carried, a container with spare fuel and they each had a pistol and ammunition. They arrived in Zaragoza in the late afternoon and found a couple of rooms at a small hotel. They said that they were Spanish businessmen, on their way to Formigal for some late skiing or mountain walking. They had a good meal at the hotel and afterwards walked round town and found somewhere where they could get some fuel for the motorbike, the next day.

After a good night's sleep and an excellent breakfast, they were away again just after nine, having had to wait around town until that time, for the fuel to become available.

They arrived at Formigal in the afternoon and found rooms at another small hotel that hardly had any other guests. They topped up the fuel tank with the spare fuel they had brought and hid the container at the back of the hotel and then drove to the Spanish French border, where they were stopped by two border guards who were happy to chat with them and enjoy an American cigarette that Michael had brought with him.

"We have not seen anyone over there for days," they informed them, indicating the French side of the border, "we think all the German's have moved out and are fighting much further north and the French have other more important things on their minds at the moment."

They said goodbye to the guards and went back down the road, stopping at the top of a hill, where Michael got off the bike and pulled a flare gun out of his pocket. At precisely five o'clock, he fired the first flare into the air and then he fired the second flare, leaving a three minute gap between them. They then went back to the hotel and enjoyed a good meal and a bottle of wine.

The next day they set off after breakfast down the track that Deborah and Bertie had taken on their honeymoon.

"Can you remember the way to that cabin in the woods that David's parents owned, where you met them and his sister," asked Michael.

"I think so, but how on earth do you know about the cabin, I never mentioned it when I told you about the incident?" asked Bertie.

"I could tell you, but then I would have to shoot you," joked Michael, "you will understand for yourself soon enough."

They crossed the Spanish border and kept walking into France and Bertie was able to remember the route they had taken and lead his friend to the cabin. They heard voices inside as they approached it, so they both took out their pistols, Michael going to the back door and Bertie to the front door and they more or less entered the cabin together.

"Come in gentleman, we have been expecting you," said Mr. Josephs in excellent English, who was wearing the uniform of a French army officer.

"Hello, remember me," said his son David, jumping up and greeting Bertie, "I'm too young to join the army, but dad lets me run errands and accompany him on trips sometimes."

"I certainly do remember you David," said Bertie, "why Deborah and I were only speaking about you all a few weeks ago, it's so nice to see you again."

They chatted for a while and Bertie came to realise that the two men were used to talking with each other on a regular basis and had done so for some time now. In the end, Michael explained that he would be staying in France, to act as liaison officer with the French military for the remainder of the war, so the two friends said goodbye and Bertie walked back to the hotel on his own. He went to the front desk and settled the bill and collected the few things that he had left in the room and then drove a different route back home, arriving in Benicarlo in time for Sunday tea, with the engine just beginning to splutter from lack of fuel as he stopped in front of the house.

Nothing much happened for a few more weeks and Bertie continued his life of fishing with his friends and playing with his little daughter and having the occasional ride on his motorbike. Around the beginning of June, the man from Barcelona, who gave Bertie the motorbike, turned up with some more fuel and a couple of tyres and saying that Bertie was owed a free service for his bike, which he had come to carry out.

He duly performed the service and replaced one or two key components and then told Bertie that he should be prepared to return to Formigal on Tuesday of the following week, as he was required to pick up a package.

"What sort of package are we talking about?" asked Bertie.

"I do not know any more than that. It may be an envelope, it may be a parcel, it may even be a person for all I know. Just make sure you are ready for any of these options. Is that clear Capitan Chavez? Oh, and do not forget your gun, you may have to use it this time!"

With which he gave him two boxes of ammunition for his Luger and a proper holster to put it in and a cleaning kit.

"Find somewhere in the hills and get in some practise with the gun as it handles differently to your old Browning. By the way, I have made a few adjustments to make the bike go faster, so you may just need to practice with that as well."

The man left and Bertie immediately made an excuse to Deborah and went off into the hills with the Luger, a box of ammunition and a few tin cans. He found the Luger a totally different weapon to use than his old gun, but within an hour, he was hitting a can at twelve paces, two times out of three; something he was seldom able to do with the Browning.

He left quite early on the Monday and as there was only one of them on the bike this time, he was able to arrive at Zaragoza before three o'clock and get his motorbike tank filled with fuel, before booking into the same room in the small hotel that he and Michael had used before.

He left after breakfast the next day and arrived in Formigal around lunch time and went to the same hotel that he had used before.

"Mr. Chavez, how nice to see you again," said the manager, when he went to the reception desk to enquire about a room. "A French gentleman was here a week ago and said he was a friend of yours and that you would be arriving here today. He asked me to reserve the room right at the top of the hotel for you; he said that you liked exercise and would also enjoy the excellent view of the hills."

"Did he indeed, he loves a good joke. I hope you made him use the same room himself," commented Bertie.

"Well I didn't make him use that room, of course, but he did occupy the same room and said he loved to look out at the night sky and watch for shooting stars. He claimed he spotted a couple of them one night around mid-night, but I think he was seeing things, between you and me. Do you need a hand with your bag?"

"No, I left it on my bike, but I am travelling light as usual, I'll go and get it and then go up to my room."

The manager gave him the key and he then went outside and got the bag from his motorbike and went into the hotel and started to climb the stairs.

"One moment senor," called out the maid who cleaned the room that he was going to use, "Senor Josephs asked me to give you this and to say he was sorry he missed your birthday," with which she passed him an envelope with a birthday card in it.

Once in his room he took his binoculars from the bag and went to the window. "Why did he want me to have this particular room and what was all that about shooting stars at midnight," he said to himself.

"Oh, I see, that is the hill over there, where Michael fired the flare gun, so that hill to the right, must be in France. So what does he expect me to do when I see a flare at midnight?" he mused.

He realised that there must be some sort of instruction in the birthday card, so he opened the envelope and after giving it a good shake, in case something dropped out, read the greeting and the message.

'Happy Birthday my friend,
Sorry for being a bit late with your card.

David sends his regards and hopes to meet up with you soon, very close to where he met you the first time, but about eight hours later this time.

He will bring your present with him, as a gift from all of us here.

Keep safe and stay vigilant in these difficult days.
Kind Regards
From all at Tarbes'

Bertie kept watch that night from eleven pm to one am, but there were no 'shooting stars' and again nothing the following night. On the third night he saw two flares go up just after mid-night from the French side of the border, so he knew that things were about to come to a head.

He went for a short ride on his motorbike in the morning, to make sure everything was in order, had lunch at the hotel, after which he had a short nap. He managed to obtain some food and drink from the kitchen, which he put in his rucksack and set off for a bit of star watching, as he told the manager, shortly after five pm. He made his way along the path that he and Deborah had taken on their honeymoon and reached the spot where they met David around seven fifteen. Remembering the warning on the card about 'staying vigilant' he found a spot in some nearby woods to sit down and rest, but from where he could observe the small hill, without being seen himself.

David arrived about forty minutes later and after carrying out a brief reconnaissance of the area, waved to someone who was obviously hidden somewhere down the track behind him. An unfit, middle-aged man came up the path and sat down on the grass. He and David chatted in what sounded like a mixture of French and German and after about five minutes, Bertie emerged from his hiding place and greeted the young man.

"This is Hans," said David, "he is a senior German army officer and I have been told to tell you, that you must leave with him tonight and get well away from this area, as there are search parties out tonight. You must not let him be seen by anyone here, but must take him back to Benicarlo with you. As soon as possible, once you are back home, you are to take him out on a fishing boat and go to Palma in Majorca, where a British Navy warship will be waiting to take him from you."

Bertie was surprised, to say the least, with his instructions and tried asking David a few questions, but he knew nothing more and after sharing his food and drink with them, David returned to France and Bertie led Hans, if that was indeed his name, back down the track to the hotel.

They arrived on the outskirts of Zaragoza while it was still dark and found a deserted barn where they could hide. The German spoke a little English, but neither men were in the mood for conversation and Bertie kept watch, while Hans got a few hours sleep. Around eight o'clock Bertie went into town on his own to get some food and drink and to fill the motorbike with fuel, telling Hans that he should not be gone for more than two hours and to stay out of sight while he was gone.

Bertie decided that now they were away from the border, there was little chance of anyone stopping them, so they just took their time in riding back to Benicarlo, with the occasional stop to stretch their legs and obtain food and drink; just giving the appearance of two old friends enjoying a ride in the country.

Deborah was not too happy at having a German house guest, but understood that Bertie had not really had any choice in the matter and Hans was obviously a family man, as young Deborah and Veto, took to him immediately, so her concerns were soon forgotten.

Bertie was not too disappointed when he discovered that Jacobo and Santo were away fishing and had to wait until the following evening before he could ask them to take him and a friend on a fishing trip.

"This fishing trip to Palma," queried Jacobo, "I don't suppose it has anything to do with the British warship that we saw there yesterday, does it?"

Bertie smiled but did not answer the question, but said that his friend would pay them well for the trip, so of course they agreed.

They set off after breakfast and reached Palma in the afternoon and found the warship anchored in the bay, with a large launch tied up next to it. Bertie hailed the launch and said that they wanted to come alongside and they were told to approach. Bertie went onto the launch first and spoke with the officer in charge and told him that he had been told to bring a certain person to them. The officer knew exactly what he was talking about and assisted Hans in crossing from the fishing boat to the launch and then gave Bertie a small bag containing some gold sovereigns.

"I have been told to give you these to cover your expenses and to reward the other men on the boat. I have also been told to inform you, that you have served your country well Mr. Bannister and have undoubtedly speeded the peace process in bringing this officer to us. Please leave now and instruct your men to say nothing about the German to anyone or to mention where they have been today."

Bertie and friends left the bay at Palma immediately and the British warship left within the hour and made its way back to Gibraltar. Santo suggested that they should do some fishing while they were out at sea and managed to catch a few nice fish to take home with them. The little bag contained fifty gold sovereigns and the two men were delighted when Bertie gave them five sovereigns each for their trouble and warned them to say nothing about Hans or what had happened to him.

The Great War finally came to an end on the 11th November 1918, having resulted in the deaths of sixteen million people, of whom almost seven million were civilians. A further twenty one million people were wounded physically and countless millions more carried the psychological wounds with them for the rest of their lives.

Some people called it *'The War to end all Wars'*, how wrong they were!

Chapter 13
Stormy Weather

"For the last time Deborah, I do not want to go back to sea, I will find some work in Valencia or somewhere," Bertie shouted as he stormed out of the house, "you just tidy up this mess you call a home and leave me to worry about the finances."

She was still upset an hour later when Santo's wife Daria came by the house.

"Is mummy in Deborah?" she asked the little girl who was playing with Veto in front of the house.

"Yes, but she has been sick and is crying again. What's wrong with her?" she asked.

"Oh, I am sure she is just not feeling well, but I will go and find out, you stay here and play."

Daria went into the house and found Deborah at the table with a glass of water and red swollen eyes. She got up when her friend came in and hugged her and started to weep all over again. Eventually she calmed down and the two ladies sat down together and started to chat.

"Why is he being so stubborn about going back to sea Daria, I just don't know what has got into him? It's not like he or the others were blown up with the boat and it's not like it was our boat either. Santo and Jacobo are fishing again, so why can't he? As you well know, the price of fish has dropped lately, so I am only making very little now and we have used up nearly all of our savings and there is no other work round here that he would be willing or able to do."

"Have you told him yet Deborah?" asked Daria.

"Told him what?" Deborah replied.

"That you are expecting a baby; what else!"

"Oh, you know then."

"Of course I know, do you think I am stupid or something. How many months is it now?"

"About two I think, maybe a bit more. How can I tell him when he is being so unreasonable to me? I don't know what he would say or do. And before you ask, no I haven't seen the doctor yet."

"I guessed as much; but I had to see him yesterday and mentioned to him that you were pregnant and suggested he come and see you today. He said he would come this morning and that sounds like it could be him right now. I will go and let him in." With which she opened the front door and let the doctor into the house, telling the little girl to play with Veto for a bit longer.

"Well Senora Chavez, congratulations and everything seems to be in order. I would agree with your own estimation of two and a half months and would expect the baby to be born at the end of June next year," the doctor confirmed. "Come and see me at the surgery in a couple of weeks time and I will be able to give you a better idea of the exact date. Goodbye and remember what I said about taking things a bit easier," with which, he picked up his bag and left.

"Thank you Daria, you are a good friend," Deborah said, at which moment Bertie came breathless into the room.

"What's up? Someone told me that they saw the doctor coming into the house and Deborah and Veto are playing outside, are you ill or something?"

Before Deborah could answer Daria replied for her, "No Bertie, she is not 'ill or something' but she does have something to tell you, so I will leave the two of you alone," with which she got up and left.

"What's going on exactly Deborah?"

"Bertie, I am pregnant. We are going to have another baby at the end of June. That's what is 'going on' as you so nicely put it."

"So I suppose everyone else around here knows all about this except me then! Thanks a lot," he exclaimed.

"Bertie, ever since the war ended, no before that; ever since you lost the boat, you have not been the same person that you used to be. We seem to have drifted apart, I can't speak to you any more without it ending in a row and when I realised that I was pregnant, I wanted to tell you, but I was frightened of your reaction."

"Oh of course, it's my fault, I should have known and you're frightened of me; it must be something to do with the way I beat you up. Is that what you have told all of our friends? Is that why people are starting to ignore me and give me funny looks? Perhaps if you had been the one to see a man decapitated by a lump of concrete, in front of your very eyes, it may have upset you too!"

"I had to watch my friends and family being gunned down in cold blood, remember;" Deborah screamed at him, "but I never moped around, refusing to work, looking for sympathy. I got on with my life and you need to do the same, before you destroy all that we have. Go and get a job and don't come back here until you have one, I am tired of being the only breadwinner of this family!"

This last tirade just stunned him. Who was this mean, spiteful woman sitting in front of him, screaming at him? He shook his head in disbelief, not knowing what to say to her. He went into their bedroom and got his coat and hat and money, walked out of the house, said goodbye to young Deborah and Veto, got his motorbike out of the shed and left.

He slept that night under a boat that had been pulled up onto the shore on the outskirts of Valencia and enjoyed a meal at a café he used to use when in town and where he met a few of the old sailors from the company he used to work for. They talked about old times over a meal and a few bottles of wine and one of them mentioned that Capitan Burra had recently passed away and the company was deciding what it should do about El Burro Volando.

"As you know Bertie, the Burra family own the boat and not the company; but without a skipper that they know and can trust and that the company approves of, they will probably be forced to sell it. You should think about it Bertie, they were good to you when you needed a job; even if you only skippered the boat for a short time, to give them a chance to decide what to do with it," the old sailor said, "besides, you were not meant to be a land-lubber, the sea is in your blood, man."

He thought about it for most of the night and was woken early the next day by the fishermen, coming to launch their boats for a day's fishing. He went back to the café for breakfast and then had a wash and smartened himself up in their washroom and arrived at the company's office around ten a.m. The manager was pleased to see him, particularly when he explained what he had been told the previous night about Capitan Burra and his beloved boat.

"I am expecting Paco to call bye around mid-day and the boat is tied up in the harbour, why don't you go down and have a look at the old 'Donkey', she needs a coat of paint, but is still in good condition, apart from a few new bullet holes," he informed Bertie, smiling.

Word had already circulated around the tight-knit seafaring community that Bertie was in town and by the time he got down to the harbour, Paco and Luca were on board the ship with a bottle of cognac opened and drinks already poured.

"Bertie my friend, it is so good to see you again, come aboard," shouted Paco, "we were only talking about you yesterday and all the good times we had together before the war, you are a veritable answer to our prayers."

He climbed aboard the familiar old boat, greeted the two men and sat down with them and shared a drink as they remembered old Capitan Burra.

"We all heard about your narrow escape at Saranda and the loss of your boat, we are truly sorry my friend," said Luca, "we all grieve for your loss, just as we all grieve for my brother."

And that was all that it needed. One sailor to another, expressing heartfelt sympathy about a lost boat, which only another sailor could truly understand. They discussed the family's wishes as far as the boat was concerned and then possible future trips and certain repairs and modifications to the ship that Bertie suggested would make life a lot easier for them all. It was just being assumed, somehow, that he had applied for the position and been accepted as the new skipper on El Burro Volando.

The company, were of course delighted with the new arrangement and extended the contract with the family for another year, with the understanding that Bertie would be taking some time off in June or July, when the new baby came.

When her husband had not returned home that evening, Deborah assumed he had gone fishing with some of the men from town, but when he did not return the following day, she began to get worried, in case there had been an accident with the motorbike, or that he had left her for good.

When her friend came round the following morning to say that Santo had checked with the other fishermen and no-one had seen him, panic really began to set in.

"He has never done this before Daria," Deborah told her, "he always lets me know where he is going, but he was so angry when he left, he could have done anything, gone anywhere!"

"This is Bertie, we are talking about here, Deborah," replied Daria, "not some stranger who does not love you, your husband of more than ten years, remember! The father of your beautiful little girl and the baby you are carrying. You told him to get a job and not come back until he had one and he told you that there was nothing round here, am I correct?"

Deborah nodded and Daria continued, "So, may I suggest that he has probably gone to Barcelona or Valencia, or one of the other big towns to look for work. Santo and I often argue and he goes storming off, but he always comes back and so will Bertie, you just wait and see."

She was of course quite right and when Bertie turned up later that day, with an armful of flowers and news of working on The Mad Donkey again, she was relieved and overjoyed and the next day she posted a letter to Bertie's parents telling them the good news.

The Mad Donkey started to be away on trips for several weeks at a time and although her friends and neighbours were very supportive, Deborah started to struggle on her own and wondered if Bertie was doing it deliberately, but did not want to risk another argument so she said nothing. When Alice wrote to say that she wanted to come over and spend some time with her daughter-in-law, especially since she was unable to help her when Deborah was born, she jumped at the opportunity for some company and assistance.

"Do you want to write to your mother or shall I do the honours?" Deborah asked him over dinner one night.

"No, if you are happy to have mum come over, then I am sure she would be delighted to hear it from you. Just give me a shout if you need help with any of the English spelling," he replied.

The next few months rushed bye and although some of Deborah's baby clothes were still in the house, Bertie insisted that she go and buy some new things for his new baby son, as he had become convinced it was going to be a boy.

Alice was due to arrive at the beginning of June and had curtly told Mr. Alderton when he queried her request for six weeks off work, that she would take as much time off as was required as her family came first and since she had been thinking of retiring, then perhaps he should find someone else to replace her, so there!

By the end of May, Deborah was enormous and everyone told her to relax and slow down, but the thought of her mother-in-law arriving to a dirty untidy house, was just too much for her, so as Bertie was away on a trip again, she started on the 'Spring Cleaning' all on her own. The first day, she swept and dusted and took lots of rests, so did not feel she was overdoing it. The second day she changed all the beds and washed the linen, knowing that Bertie was due home the following day and would not mind helping with the ironing. She was in the garden, hanging out the first load of washing and noticed that Deborah was playing 'Hide and Seek' with Veto. She had hidden in the bushes behind her and then called the dog, who soon discovered her hiding place and came bounding across the garden towards his young friend. Just at that moment a sea breeze came up and blew the sheet that she was trying to peg up, onto the line, in front of the dog, who swerved to avoid it and ran straight into Deborah's legs, knocking her off her feet.

She hit the ground with a loud thud, as she was trying to save the washing from getting dirty and let out a terrible scream as the pain from her womb swept through her whole body. Little Deborah came running over and started to cry, Veto barked loudly and several neighbours came running into the garden to see what the matter was. The doctor was fetched from his surgery and several of the men carried her into the house and laid her on the bed.

The baby boy was born four hours later after a very painful delivery and he was stillborn. One of the neighbours whose young daughter often played with little Deborah, took her and Veto home with her and Daria volunteered to stay the night with her friend, who had been sedated by the doctor and who also took the little body of the dead baby, back to the surgery with him.

Jacobo had the difficult job of meeting Bertie when he arrived home and of breaking the sad news to him, before he got into the house.

"Right, thanks Jacobo," he said, "I had better go in now, you did say that Deborah was in bed?"

His friend just nodded as the tears streamed down his cheeks, "I am so sorry my friend, my wife lost our second child, I understand the pain you must be feeling right now."

Veto came running up to him as he walked towards the house and he lashed out at the dog with his foot, giving it a hefty blow in the ribs, causing it to whelp loudly, before it slumped off to hide somewhere.

He quietly opened the front door and taking off his coat, went through into the bedroom. One of the other neighbours was sitting, talking with Deborah and she got up and left the room as he came in.

"Jacobo just told me," he said slowly, as he sat down on the chair by the bed.

"A little boy. I was right then. I don't know what to say Deborah, I just feel numb, he's dead. That little life; just gone. Why?"

He got up and walked around the room, trying to take it all in. She started to sob, but he barely noticed, the thing in his stomach was getting bigger and bigger and the lump in his throat was almost choking him. The neighbour came back into the room and went over to Deborah and hugged her, he had to get out of the house, go somewhere else and be on his own. He started the motorbike and drove to a deserted beach he knew and just stood there, all alone, shouting at the top of his voice, "My son, my son, no, no, no."

He returned home a few hours later and Deborah was in bed sleeping. Jacobo and Santo were both there, waiting for him, outside on the veranda with a couple of bottles of wine and some glasses.

"She is asleep my friend," said Santo, "Daria is sitting with her. Sit down and drink with us. Here, we will toast the little one who is now in heaven."

He sat down and took the glass and Santo continued, "To the little one who is in the arms of Jesus, heaven's gain is our loss, may the Lord comfort Deborah and Bertie and their family, in their loss. Amen."

From somewhere deep within him, the anguish of his soul was unlocked and Bertie started to grieve for his dead child. The tears flowed for an hour or more and his friends sat in silence and supported him. When he finally stopped weeping, he just nodded to his friends, thanking them for their support.

"Now you must go to Deborah," said Jacobo, "she too has lost her child and needs you."

He went indoors, thanked Daria for her support and said that he would take over now, which he did. He held his wife in his arms and kissed her cheeks and told her that he loved her and cried with her. He then went and fetched little Deborah from the neighbour's house, who had mercifully undertaken the task of telling the little girl what had happened to her baby brother, something which Bertie had been dreading.

The funeral was arranged for the next day and someone found a wheelchair, so that Deborah could be safely taken to the local church, as she was in no state to walk, but had insisted on going.

The church was packed and prayers were said for the little boy they had called Roberto Bannister Chavez, who was buried in a corner of the cemetery that was kept for children.

Alice arrived ten days later and stayed for almost two months in the end. She laughed with her little grand-daughter, whose English improved tremendously during her Granny's visit and cried at her grandson's graveside and prevented Bertie from shooting Veto with his Luger.

"You cannot blame the dog for what happened, son," she said to him, "it was a terrible accident. Deborah herself does not blame him and neither should you. You need to go back to sea and I will stay here and take care of things until Deborah has recovered and she is able to look after the home again."

Bertie did go back to sea and his mother did return home to Harwich in August, but there was always a sadness in the house that had not been there before. To all intents and purposes, Deborah got over the death of her baby son, but Bertie knew that she was never the same again and that their relationship was never quite the same again either.

Before she went back home, Alice got a letter from Robert, saying that his uncle Harry, who had returned from the Great War a sick and broken man, had become ill while he was visiting Harwich and that Robert thought he might have to stay with them for a while. A year later, Harry was still with them and his condition had got worse. She wrote to Bertie saying that Harry had been asking for him and that he would love to see his Great, Great Niece before he died and asked him to come over and see them as soon as possible.

"You and Deborah should go and see your uncle Harry, Bertie; I know how much he means to you. Veto and I will stay here, I want to try and get started with the fish business again. Why not go over for Deborah's fifth birthday, your parents would be thrilled, I am sure."

She was right, his parents were thrilled at the thought of having their little grand-daughter for her fifth birthday, what plans they made. A passage was booked and the ship left Barcelona with Bertie and his daughter with Deborah waving from the quayside. It was a pleasant voyage and Bertie was thrilled to see how much the little girl took to the sea and enjoyed their trip together. When they arrived at the dock in London, Robert was there to meet them on his own, saying that Harry had not been too good that week, so Alice had stayed behind in Harwich.

Bertie could not believe the difference from the last time he had seen his great uncle, who was delighted to see Bertie again and loved his little niece to bits. Like a lot of soldiers returning from the war, Harry would never speak about the horrors he had seen during his time in France and he would sit up late into the night talking with Robert and Bertie on every other subject imaginable, rather than face the nightmares that haunted his sleeping hours.

Monday the 30th August 1920 was little Deborah's fifth birthday and Alice had managed to find a few young girls from her church to invite to the party. Harry had paid for a great big china doll for her and Alice had spent several weeks making doll's clothes for it. She got her first jigsaw puzzle and some books and some new clothes for herself and a new pair of black shoes. Deborah had given Bertie a small parcel for her, on the strict instructions that it must not be opened until her birthday and when just Bertie and his daughter were on their own.

"Can I have Mummies parcel now Daddy, please?" she said, when he had taken her up to bed at the end of a truly wonderful day.

"Of course you can, I hid it under your pillow earlier, see, there it is."

She pulled the parcel out from the pillow and started to pull off the paper.

"Two cards daddy, are they both for me?" she asked.

"Let me see. This one is yours and this one is for me," he said passing her the birthday card.

The card and parcel were opened and to Bertie's surprise, the parcel contained the crucifix which his wife normally wore around her neck and the card was a normal greeting card that a mother would get for her little girl.

"Put it back in the box tonight Deborah and I will ask Granny to help you with it tomorrow, goodnight love."

"Aren't you going to open your card daddy?"

"I'll do that downstairs, this is already way past your bedtime. Goodnight."

With which he turned the gas light out and went back downstairs to where the others were sitting with a cup of tea. His mum poured him a fresh cup as he sat down in the corner chair and looked at the envelope.

"What's that Bertie, a note from Deborah? I recognise her writing," Alice said.

He nodded and opened the letter and read silently for a few minutes and then said aloud, "Oh Deborah, you fool, what have you gone and done?"

Everyone looked at him and waited for him to explain, but he was speechless. He stood up and gave the letter to his father and went outside for a walk in the fresh air, to clear his head and to think.

"Well go on Robert, read it out to us, what does she say for goodness sake," said Harry. Robert sat down and read the letter out loud.

'Bertie,

If you are now reading this letter, then Deborah would have had a lovely birthday party and I am on my way to Chile and you cannot stop me this time. You got so cross with me the last time I mentioned going back there, that I have just had to make my own plans and tell you about it once I was safely on my way.

I have written several times to Manuel, who you will remember was my father's manager at Iquique, asking how things are there now and how my relatives all are. He has told me that things are a lot better there now and it would be quite safe for me to visit again, but that my cousin, who I was particularly close to, has been very ill and has been asking after me, just like your uncle Harry asked after you.

Manuel also said that he had found some articles of value that belonged to my father, that he wanted to give me, including a document stating that dad owned a twenty percent share in a mine, that I did not know anything about. Manuel says that if I do not come over and claim it, then it will be lost to me and to my family for ever and as you know, they could all do with the revenue from it, as they are all so poor.

I will send you and Deborah a letter whenever I can, but please do not try and follow me, as Manuel says that there is still a warrant out for you, over the soldier you killed.

Look after my beautiful little Deborah for me and I trust you to do whatever you feel is in her best interests.

Love,

Deborah.

P.S. I have taken care of Veto.'

"Did you know anything about our Bertie killing a soldier, Robert?" asked Alice.

"He was not necessarily the one that killed the soldier, as the other man fired at the same time. But yes, to answer your question, I did know; if they had not shot the soldier at Iquique, then the soldier would have shot Deborah as she lay unconscious on the ground. They saved her life Alice, he is not a killer."

"Oh I see, thank you," she replied.

"Did Deborah say anything to you, while you were staying with them in Spain about going back to Chile?" Robert asked his wife in return.

"No, no she didn't. But I was handed a letter one day while I was in the garden putting out the washing and when I went into the house with it she snatched it right out of my hand, like she didn't want me to see it. She told me that it was not for them but for another family called Chavez who lived further down the road and that they often got mail for each other. I mentioned it to Bertie, but he did not know anything about it, nor was he bothered, so I said no more."

"Poor old Bertie, what will he do now, I wonder," said Harry, "it's not as if he can go after her, even if he wanted to."

"Well one thing is for certain, he cannot take little Deborah back to Spain with him, doing the job that he does and being away from home for so much of the time. She will have to stay here with us until her mother returns, if she ever does," said a determined and delighted Granny.

Two days later on Wednesday the 1st of September 1920 Harry died of a massive heart attack and was buried in the local church yard at Harwich, close to all the people he loved.

Chapter 14
So who are you now?

Bertie left his daughter with her grand-parents and went back to Spain, as he had a contract to fulfill with the shipping company and The Mad Donkey. He was not surprised to discover that the remains of their 'nest egg' had all gone, along with all of his wife's clothes and personal possessions. After a thorough search of the house, he found a letter from Manuel that had fallen down the back of a drawer in the desk which Deborah had kept all of her personal papers and fish business documents in.

It was in answer to what he guessed was her first letter to him, saying it was good to hear from her and that he was pleased that she was still alive. As he read the letter over and over again, he had the feeling that something was not right about it, but could not work out what it was and then it struck him, that the paper was spotless, like it had come from a box of stationery in a very clean office, rather than from a thick pad of paper, in a dusty shack in a mining town, where Manuel had done all of his work.

He pulled the old trunk out from under his bed, which had accompanied him on all of his travels around the world, unfastened the lock and opened the lid. Now whilst he was not the most meticulous of men, he did keep personal records for all of his trips and he also kept any paperwork or mementos that did not need to be handed in to the company that employed him.

"I know it's here somewhere, ah, what's that in the envelope? Got you, now let's take a look," he said to himself. Holding the receipt that Manuel had given him in 1907 for the wood and water he had sold for them; he sat down at the desk and compared it with the letter that he had supposedly written to Deborah in 1919. The handwriting on the two documents was completely different. The writing on the receipt was large and scratchy and sloped heavily to the right, whilst the writing on the letter was neat and bold and sloped slightly to the left.

"Well Manuel, I really did not believe that you would have encouraged her to go back to Iquique and this proves it was not you who wrote the letters and enticed her back to Chile. So who did write to Deborah and what is going to happen to her when she gets there?"

Towards the end of October a postcard arrived from Deborah with a picture of the Panama Canal on it. She said she had been sea-sick and hoped that they were both well. In early December another postcard came, this time with a picture of Lima in Peru and with the information that she had heard that there had been trouble recently in Santiago and a lot of people had been put in prison.

He took both of the postcards to Harwich with him, when he went there for Christmas, as well as lots of presents for his daughter and parents.

Meanwhile in Harwich, Deborah had been enrolled in the local Church of England Infant School and had started there a week after Harry's funeral. She loved being with her grand-parents, but missed her old friends in Spain and her mummy and daddy a lot and looked forward to receiving his letter each week. Although she struggled with her English a bit at first, since she really only used to speak it with her daddy, she was a bright little girl and was soon as fluent in English as she had been in Spanish.

The other friend she missed a lot, was of course her dog Veto, so her grand-parents bought her a ten week old puppy, of very mixed parentage, that she named Velvet, because his coat was so soft and smooth. Alice, who had now given up her job, used to take Deborah and Velvet on long walks each day after school and Robert used to take over at weekends, but always felt a bit self conscious in calling out the dog's name, if anyone else was around.

When she asked her Granddad why her mummy had left her and gone back to Chile, he just smiled and said, "She has a very sick relative that she wants to see and had to leave very suddenly. I am sure she will be back very soon, certainly by next summer."

Next summer came and went, with no more postcards, letters or other news. Bertie visited Barcelona on several occasions and spoke with various Government officials, who said they would pass on his enquiries to the Spanish Embassy in Chile. He waited patiently for several months but they did not reply to his requests for information, so he asked again a little more forcefully and eventually they confirmed that they had not heard from her or received any request to assist her in any way.

He carried on living and working in Spain, just in case she should return home or a letter should arrive, but he grew steadily more restless at his predicament.

While spending Christmas in Harwich in 1921, with his parents and daughter, his father made a suggestion to him.

"I don't suppose your friend Michael is still involved with that Secret Service outfit that he worked for in the War, is he son?"

"No idea dad, I haven't heard from him in ages, why do you ask?"

"Well, I was just thinking that South America is always a very volatile place and I would have thought that they would have had people working there; maybe they might have heard something; it's got to be worth a try!"

Bertie agreed with his father and wrote to Michael at the old address, telling him all that had happened, not knowing that they had moved to London and the letter would have to be re-directed to their new home. He had been back in Spain for well over two months before the reply from Michael reached him.

'Dear Bertie,

I was truly sorry to hear about Deborah going back to Chile and suspect you are right about her being tricked into returning there. The only photograph that we had of her was the one that I took of the two of you in Aberdeen, so I have sent copies of this to our 'friends' in South America, to make enquiries on your behalf.

I will keep you informed of everything I discover and if you let me know when you are coming to England next, Anne and I would love to come across to Harwich and meet up with you and your family.

Regards,
Michael'

Bertie went back to England in April and remembered to let Michael know the dates he would be there, so he travelled out to Harwich and met up with Bertie for lunch on a wet Saturday afternoon. After lunch and a game of 'Snap' with Deborah, the two friends went for a walk along the river.

"Anne wanted to come with me to see you all, but I am travelling on to Belgium from here, so it was not possible this time, anyway, she sends her love," Michael said.

"Thanks Michael, I really appreciate you helping me in this way, have you heard anything from your friends in South America yet, or is it still too soon?" Bertie asked.

"Well we started with Iquique and Manuel and quickly drew a blank there. It appears he was chased out of town soon after Deborah and you left in December 1907 and her father's business was given to the dead soldier's family, by way of compensation. That explains why it was not Manuel she was writing to, but probably someone in the soldier's family who was now running the business, or they may have just passed the letter on to the Military for them to handle."

"I never really thought that Manuel would have done that to her, he always seemed to genuinely care for her. So where did they go from there, Michael?"

"My friend in Santiago started to ask questions about her and to show her picture around the cafes and bars and very soon found himself in a back alley with a couple of knives at his throat and stomach. He tried to convince them that he was not a member of the Secret Police, but a private detective acting for the husband in England, who was trying to find his wife, who had returned to Chile from Spain and had now gone missing."

"Do you mind if we sit down Michael," said Bertie, "I am truly sorry that I have put another man's life in danger on my behalf." The two men sat down on a riverside bench and Michael continued with his story.

"They all thought my friend was lying, because they believed Makaa, as they called her, had married a Spanish sea captain and they might well have ended his days there and then, but an older man at the back of the crowd, told them to stop what they were doing and to leave my friend alone, which they all did. It turns out that the man was Manuel himself and he already knew that someone had been making enquiries about him in Iquique."

"Did Manuel know where she was or what had happened to her?"

"Yes, he did know of her whereabouts Bertie; he told my friend that she was in prison. It appears she soon found out that Manuel was no longer in Iquique and went out to visit her relatives in the mining towns. The cousin, who was supposed to be dying, was actually fit and well and although the family did their best to keep her presence a secret, it soon became common knowledge and it was only a matter of time before the police arrived and arrested her."

"But what was the charge against her; surely even in Chile they have to have a charge against someone to arrest them?"

"The soldier's family wanted her charged with murder, but the police knew that she would never be convicted on that charge, so they charged her with Civil Unrest and being an 'Accessory to Murder'. She was taken down to Santiago, tried and found guilty and sentenced to ten years in jail; the sentence starting in September of last year."

Bertie sat there quietly, with his head in his hands, taking in the bad news.

"Did your friend say if anyone had visited her in prison and how she was doing?"

"It appears Manuel has arranged for another cousin who lives in Santiago, to visit her once a week and to take in food and do her washing and to bribe the guards from time to time, so that they will leave her alone. He said that if you could send him money, he would pay for a decent lawyer to lodge an appeal against her conviction. He has located the priest who came out of the school and saved the little boy and he is prepared to testify that she was not part of the protest and was not in the building; so coupled with the fact that she was forcibly made to leave the country by you, he genuinely believes he could get the sentence significantly reduced, or even set aside."

"I never thought of myself as a 'kidnapper', but she was unconscious and I did not ask her if she wanted to leave, so I guess it is true. Did he give your friend any idea of how much money he would need to hire a lawyer?"

"Lawyers are not cheap, even in Chile, he said that you would need to send him at least two hundred pounds to cover all the costs. Do you have that sort of money available?"

"No, not in cash, anyway. If I liquidate everything we have, including the house, then I might be able to raise it, but it would take me a few months. But then how would I get the money to Manuel and can he be trusted?"

"I could use my channels to get the money to Chile and then to Manuel, we would consider him to be a very useful contact for us over there, so I am certain I could get approval to do that for you; as regards being trustworthy, without his support, who knows what would have happened to Deborah by now?"

"What about me, could I go to Chile or would I be arrested as soon as I landed, it is almost fifteen years now, surely they have forgotten about me by now?" Bertie pleaded.

"They may have done, but if the lawyer wins his case, there will be a new charge of kidnapping, to add to the one of murder, but I will make certain for you. Somehow I can't help thinking that if they arrested Deborah for being an 'Accessory', I would have thought it most likely that they are still after you Bertie. Putting her in prison might just be a trap to lure you into going back there," Michael replied. "But look, you go back to Spain, try and raise the money, but don't sell the house unless you have to and I will ask my friend to speak with Manuel again and to make discreet enquiries about your own status."

Michael continued on his journey to Belgium and Bertie returned to Spain, to continue working on The Mad Donkey and to raise funds for a lawyer for his wife. When he discussed his problems with Paco and Luca they said that they would speak with the rest of the family about his need for cash, to see if they would be prepared to help him in some way. They came back to him a week later; with the offer to buy his house for the equivalent of 250 pounds cash, on the understanding that they would hold it for at least eight years and sell it back to him, if he wanted it, at any time in the period, for the current market value.

"We know how much you and Deborah love that house and the family wanted to help you Bertie, so think about it and let us know," said Luca. "They also said that you could continue to live there, rent free, while you were Capitan of our boat."

"Thank you my friends, I don't know what to say, please thank your family for me, it is a most kind offer. As soon as I hear from my contact in Chile, I will talk with you both again."

It was late August, when Bertie returned from a lengthy trip to Africa, that he found a letter from Michael waiting for him at home.

'Dear Bertie,
We trust you are well and that the fishing trip was successful. My friend abroad also had a successful trip and has secured the services of a big fish who believes he can assist you with your problem.

I have also been authorised to help you with the transfer, so if you can let me have the sum we discussed I will pass it on for you.

I have been advised that the climate would be bad for your health, but we can discuss that when we meet.

Much love,

Michael and Anne'

"I wonder why he is talking in code to me," Bertie said to himself, "perhaps he thinks someone is reading my mail, now that they know where I live in Spain."

It took a few weeks to agree all the details of the house sale with the Burra family, which was handled by one of the younger members, who was a solicitor and was obviously trying to impress his elders. In the end, Paco took him to one side and had a word in his ear and things went through quickly after that.

Bertie had also told them that he would stop working for them as Capitan just before Christmas, as he had determined to go to Chile, some way or another.

"In your place, I would do the same as you, my friend," said Paco. "But they will be watching out for you in Chile now, especially once the re-trial starts. Any British or Spanish Capitan who arrives there, will be checked out most carefully, but a common sailor, from Australia or New Zealand, who would think to check him out."

"I am sure that is true, but how does that help me Paco?"

"Take this," he said, passing him a slip of paper. "It is the name of a man in Sydney that I helped once. Memorise the details, then burn the paper. He will be able to help you with a new passport and identity, but be careful, he is a dangerous man. Just as you once lost Bertie Bannister in Spain, so you must now lose Bertram Chavez in Australia."

The week before Christmas, Bertie packed his old trunk and left his home in Spain, not knowing if he would ever return again. When he arrived in London, he visited Michael in his smart new office and handed over the two hundred pounds, to pay for Deborah's lawyer.

"Why all the cloak and dagger stuff in your letter Michael, it seemed a bit unnecessary?" Bertie asked.

"We had information that you were being watched in Benicarlo, so I was just playing safe, just as you need to from now on. I will send the money this week and we hope to start legal proceedings in January, but we have no idea how long everything will take. One thing we are sure of, however, is that they know you are alive and that they are out to get you. So on no account must you go there yourself. Even though you are a British citizen, we could do very little to help, if you were arrested. I have been instructed to make that very clear to you Bertie."

"I understand Michael, Bertie Bannister, or even Capitan Chavez, will not be going anywhere near South America, I can assure you."

After Harry's death, Robert and Alice had re-decorated the other downstairs bedroom, so that it was suitable for a little girl, leaving 'Bertie's room' as it was, upstairs. Deborah settled well into her new home, she liked her school and made lots of friends. Although her Granddad seemed to take every opportunity he could to spoil his little grand-daughter, her Granny was a lot more level headed and treated her with a firmness that Deborah did not always appreciate.

Every time that Bertie came to visit, she would ask after her mummy and demand to know when he would come and live with them in Harwich; there being no real desire on her behalf, to return to Spain and leave her grand-parents behind in England. Once Christmas was over, he sat down with his parents one evening and explained what he had in mind.

"Michael thinks the trial will start around March or April next year and what with calling witnesses from Iquique and other places, could take as long as six months, which probably takes us to September 1923. This means that she would have been in prison for two years, which I have been told, is the part of her prison term that applied to the 'Civil Unrest' bit of the charge against her."

"Does that mean if they are successful with the appeal, that she would be set free?" asked Alice.

"Possibly," Bertie replied, "but Michael's people think it is more likely that her sentence will be commuted to some form of probation or freedom on license, a sort of 'house arrest', which could last for several years more."

"So I suppose you plan to go over there and rescue her again," his mother said, "that woman will be the death of you Bertie. Your responsibilities are here with your daughter, she needs you; Deborah chose her own path and she must reap the consequences of her choice."

"She wasn't well mum; she was still depressed over losing the baby. Michael told me that Deborah is not physically well either, it sounds like she has contracted Tuberculosis while in prison, I'm her husband for goodness sake, I can't just leave her there to die, can I?"

"You are the only one who can decide what you have to do son," Robert interjected, before Alice could speak again, "you know you can rely on your mother and me to look after little Deborah, but you have sold your house and given up your job, so you obviously plan to do something, why not talk it through with us."

"Thanks dad, mum, I really do appreciate all that you have done for us and we would be stumped without you two. The general idea is that I will get to Australia somehow and then take on a new identity. There are a lot of ships which sail between Australia, New Zealand and South America, so I will become an ordinary seaman on one of these and get into Chile that way. Officially, Michael has told me to stay away from Chile, but unofficially, he has said that he would help me if I should decide to go there. He has told me how to make contact with his man, once I am there, so I guess I will then just play it by ear, as always. Any information that I want to get to Michael, or he wants to get to me, we will either do directly through his office or we may decide to do it through you, if that is alright?"

"But how will you keep in touch with us if you are changing identities," asked his mother, "how will we know you?"

Bertie gave his mum a hug and laughed as he replied, "Don't worry mum, I'll think of something."

The next day father and son went to see Mr. Alderton, who Robert had suggested should be taken into their confidence.

"He has contacts all over the world now and could be very useful for finding the right ship or helping you out, if you get into a tight spot," Robert advised.

Robert was right about Mr. Alderton, who supplied Bertie with a list of contact names in virtually all of the major ports around the world and had actually identified a possible first leg, for his journey.

"There is a ship leaving for South Africa in a few days time Bertie, who could do with a second mate. Not quite what you are used to, but I could get you aboard without having to show any papers and without anyone but the captain knowing, if you were interested. From South Africa, you could make your way in a series of different voyages, down to Australia, using ships that I have contacts with. I am sure that once you are there, you could jump ship without anyone knowing and lose yourself 'down-under'."

"I don't know what to say Mr. Alderton," Bertie replied, "I will get a few things together in a bag and be here for whenever you think necessary."

They went back to the house, having decided that they should tell Deborah a slightly different story; that he was leaving for Liverpool in two days time, in order to catch a ship for New York. They also called at a second hand shop on the way home and bought an old leather bag that he could take with him, rather than cope with his heavy old trunk. He also went to a saddler's and bought a thick leather belt for his trousers, which had an inner compartment in the lining, for hiding coins.

"I have left my passport and papers in my trunk dad, along with a letter for Deborah, for when she is older; if for any reason I don't come back."

"Right'o son, I'll see she's alright, don't you worry about her, just try and send a postcard when you can, or get one of Mr. Alderton's contacts to send a cable, he told me that he was happy for you to do that."

Father and daughter had a great time together for those few days and since she was used to him going back to Spain, she was not unduly upset about him going off to New York.

"Send me a picture of the Statue of Liberty daddy and bring back one of those big hats that the cowboys wear, please," were her final remarks, as he left the house on a dark January evening.

He slipped quietly onto the quay where the ship was tied up and was in the process of loading the last few crates of her cargo. There was suddenly a problem with the crane and the last load of crates was set down on the dock a few yards from where Bertie was hidden. This was his cue and he immediately ran forward and jumped onto the crates, holding on tight to the netting as the crane started up again and raised the crates high into the air and down into the hold of the ship. As the crates were guided to their resting place, a man flashed a light at him, indicating that he should follow.

He was taken to a small cabin at the rear of the ship and the door was closed. His bag was already there, as Mr. Alderton had carried it aboard himself the previous day. A note was on the table which simply read, 'Wait here until I come for you.' Bertie looked at his watch and it was ten forty five pm and he knew the ship was not due to sail until five o'clock the next morning, so he stretched out on the bunk and went to sleep.

He was woken at six thirty by an old man who came into the cabin with a mug of tea and some breakfast. He appeared to be Chinese, but Bertie was not certain and he only had a limited vocabulary in English.

"He say wait," the old man said, pointing towards the ceiling, and closing the door behind him.

By nine o'clock, he was desperately needing to go somewhere, so he opened the door and gingerly looked out down the passageway. He walked a few paces down towards the stairs, passing the open kitchen, where he saw the old man at work. Bertie coughed loudly and the old man looked up surprised and then worried and rushed over, taking hold of his sleeve. He pulled him back to the cabin, but Bertie managed to convey his need to go the toilet, before the door was closed. The man returned in another ten minutes and said, "You come now."

Bertie followed the man along a maze of corridors, stopping at a toilet on the way, before going out on deck and then onto the bridge, where the Captain and Mate were waiting for him.

"Hi there Bob," the Captain said, "I am Captain Brown and this is Mr. Davis, my First Mate. Mr. Alderton told us that you were an experienced sailor and we needed a Second Mate for this voyage, but once we reach South Africa, you are on your own, is that understood? I don't care what you have done here, or why you have had to leave in such a hurry, just do your job well and we will get on fine."

"Yes sir," Bertie replied. "What are your orders for me?"

The Captain was a man of few words, but knew his ship and was a good sailor. The Mate was lazy and brutal and most of the crew seemed to live in fear of him, so for most of the trip Bertie acted as First Mate and was the interface between the Captain and his crew.

When they reached Cape Town the Captain paid Bertie his wages, which amounted to about half the rate for the job he had done, saying he had been forced to pay the Mate a bit extra to keep his mouth shut, which Bertie did not doubt. He managed to leave the ship un-noticed in the dead of night, with his bag and belongings and made his way to one of the hostels that seamen use, where they don't ask too many questions.

The next day he called on Mr. Alderton's contact, who was already expecting him and had arranged his next passage on an Indian ship that was returning to Madras in a couple of days. Bertie asked the man if he could send a cable to Mr. Alderton, telling him that Bob Harwich had arrived in Cape Town and would be heading for Madras shortly. He purchased a postcard of Cape Town which he sent to Deborah and another which he sent to his parents.

He was Second Mate once again on the trip to Madras, but this time he received the full pay for the job and was invited to spend a few days with the Mate, who he had become good friends with, at his home in Madras. The official 'Alderton' contact in Madras was not interested in helping Bertie, but his new friend the Mate, put out some feelers among his contacts and eventually another passage was arranged on a ship bound for Hong Kong.

The contact of Mr. Alderton's in Hong Kong was extremely resourceful and arranged for Bertie to act as Mate on an Australian ship returning to Sydney. The captain was very understanding of the fact that Bob Harwich (Bertie's assumed travelling name) did not have any official papers with him, but a two hour conversation with charts, compass and sextant, convinced him he was up to the job of Mate and as he said at the end of the interview, "If you aren't any good cobber, I'll just put a bullet in your brain and throw you overboard, because you really don't exist, do you?"

The two men got on really well together and eventually one day, Bertie told him the whole story of what he was doing and why he needed to change his identity in order to get to Chile. Skip, (as everyone called him) was very understanding and offered to help him in any way that he could. He suggested that Bertie stayed on the ship while they were in harbour, to save his precious finances and it was also Skip who helped to smuggle Bertie ashore and then went with him to meet the man that Paco had told him about in Sydney.

"Of course I know a man called Paco, I know several in fact. So what!" his new acquaintance responded when Bertie introduced himself.

"He told me to say three words to you 'Abidjan' and 'Yellow fever', you would know what it meant and that he had truly sent me to see you."

The man stared across the table at Bertie and bit his lip as he thought what to say.

"Did he tell you what significance those words might have for me?"

Bertie looked blank and shook his head.

"What did Paco tell you that I would do for you?"

"He said you would be able to get me an Australian passport and a new identity."

"And that is all you want from me, he did not tell you to ask for anything else?"

Bertie shook his head again.

"There is a photographer's shop two roads down, on the corner. Go there now and tell him to take a photograph for a passport and to bring it to me, Eduardo, when it is ready. He will know what to do. You will go back to the shop in exactly three days time and your passport and papers will be ready. Never come here again, never acknowledge me if you see me out in the street and tell Paco the matter between us is settled. Now get out."

Bertie and Skip left immediately and headed off in the direction the man had indicated.

"Nice friends your friend in Spain has Bob, you really don't want to meet up with him again," Skip said as they walked along the street.

"Do you know him then?"

"Only by reputation if it's who I think it is. The least you know about that one the better."

They went into the Photographer's and repeated what Eduardo had said and he immediately stopped what he was doing and took several photographs of Bertie. They went back to the shop three days later and picked up a package containing a passport, a birth certificate and a school report and were surprised when told by the young shop assistant that there was no charge for the service. They had a few beers at a pub and then headed back to the ship.

"So who are you now Bob?" asked Skip, as they sat down in his cabin.

"It would seem that I am David Raymond and I was born in 1884, that's good, I have just lost five years off my age. I was born in a town called Broken Hill and my dad was a miner and my mum a housewife and I was pretty awful at school, by the look of this report."

"That's interesting," said Skip, "my wife's sister married a bloke from there and his surname is Raymond. A nice bloke, I should let you meet him and you can ask him about the place and get some background information, you never know, it might come in handy one day."

A week later, Bertie was staying at Skip's place on the outskirts of Sydney, now that he had his papers and a new identity and it was safe for him to leave the ship. Skip had invited his sister, her husband Tom Raymond and their son, Tom junior, to come to tea, so that Bertie could meet them and get some information about Broken Hill and mining. It was agreed that Bertie would continue to be the English friend Bob, so that there would be no slip-ups with names or stories.

Tom was a huge man, well over six foot three and broad to go with it and his son, Tom junior was already taller than Bertie and he was still only fifteen. Bertie got on well with father and son and found he gained a tremendous amount of information from the gentle giant, whose family had worked the mines for many years, as he had done himself, until he met his wife on a trip to Sydney eighteen years earlier.

"Well Bob," said Skip, after they had all left, "was that a worthwhile exercise?"

"It certainly was, I really liked the two Tom's and your sister was a real lady, such a nice change from that brute of a brother of hers!"

Bertie stayed in and around Sydney for several weeks and eventually got a job as an ordinary seaman on a ship that was sailing to Auckland in New Zealand and then on to Santiago in Chile. Most of the crew were Aussies, so he had a chance to improve his accent and pick up the slang words and mannerisms of the other crew members. He only had to prove himself once on the voyage, when a cocky Kiwi tried to push him around one night and despite getting a black eye in the melee, he managed to floor the other man with his third punch, which impressed the rest of the crew and meant that the man gave him no more trouble for the remainder of the trip.

The ship arrived early in the morning in Santiago on Friday 12th October 1923, Columbus Day. There was a big carnival in town and everyone wanted to go ashore and see it and Bertie was particularly anxious to use the carnival celebrations as a cover for meeting with Michael's official contact and perhaps Manuel himself. He had managed to send Michael a letter from Sydney, giving him all the details of the ship and its expected date of arrival at Santiago, as well as letting him know his new name and details.

It had previously been agreed that he would go to the bar where contact with Manuel had first been made and that he would sit in a seat in the far corner of the bar between three and four in the afternoon, reading a newspaper and wait to be contacted.

He got through several drinks and had read most of the English newspaper, before a middle aged woman came into the bar and sat down at his table.

"Mr. Raymond, my name is Mrs. Michael, I believe you have been expecting me," she said in Spanish.

He looked surprised, he was not sure what he was expecting, but it certainly was not a middle aged lady, speaking Spanish.

"Wait for a minute after I have gone and then leave by the back door and keep walking down the road opposite. When you see a beggar in a blue doorway, push past him and go in. I will meet you again in there," with which she got up and left by the front door.

He waited for the minute, as instructed and then folded the paper, paid for his drinks and left by the back door. The road opposite was narrow and dirty and did not look like the sort of road that a visitor to Santiago should go down, but he went down it anyway. After fifty yards there was a beggar by a door, but it was not blue, so he kept on walking. After another twenty or so yards, there was another beggar and this time the door was blue, so he pushed past him into the front room of a house. It was pitch black and as he stood still and tried to focus his eyes in the gloom, he received a hefty thump to the back of his head, which knocked him out cold and he went down like a lead balloon.

When he came to, he was securely tied to a chair and appeared to be in a different room to where he had been knocked out. His head and shirt were soaked and he thought first of all it was blood, but soon realised that they had thrown a jug of water over him to bring him round.

A young man with a knife stood in front of him and the woman he had met in the bar sat at a table a short distance away.

"I will ask you some questions senor and if you get them all correct, you will live, if you don't you will die. Is that clear?" she said.

"Who are you people, why are you treating me like this?"

"We are friends of Makaa Chavez and now no more questions."

They asked him about himself, Deborah, their daughter, their home in Spain, the motorbike, even Michael, which he refused to answer. If they were the Secret Police, he knew that he was incriminating himself, but if they were Michael's contacts, then he knew he would be safe. Eventually the questions stopped and he was untied.

"Well David Raymond, we believe you. You are a brave man to come back to Chile to save Makaa. She was released from prison two weeks ago, but the military want time to put a new case together for treason. We know it is just a trumped up charge, just to keep her here, so that they can lure you to Chile to entrap you. She is not allowed to leave the house unaccompanied and has to report every day at four pm, to the police station, which is a short walk from the place where they are keeping her."

"Is she well?" asked Bertie.

"No, she is not and the quicker we can get her out of the country, the better for her and for us."

"My ship leaves here in ten days time and returns to New Zealand and then Australia. Once she is on board and we are in international waters, she will be safe," Bertie informed them.

At that moment an older man came towards him and held out his hand, "It is good to see you again Capitan, do you remember me?"

Was it a greeting or one last trap, Bertie looked intently at the man, "Manuel, it's good to see you again, after all these years. How can I ever thank you for all you have done for Deborah, err, Makaa. We owe you so much."

The next day Bertie and the young man who had wielded the knife, were having a drink in a bar, that was on the route that Deborah took, when reporting to the police station.

"You must not acknowledge her in any way," the young man warned, "she does not know you are here and must not know of your presence until the last minute, in case we have to change our plans."

Bertie sat there, pretending to read a newspaper, as Deborah walked past. She was thin and looked like an old woman and had to keep stopping to get her breath. He felt tears come into his eyes and wanted to dash out into the street and hold her, but he just sat there and watched her walk bye.

"She does not have to go to the police station on a Sunday and your ship leaves early on Monday the 22nd of October, I think you said."

"That's right, we leave at dawn," Bertie replied.

"Can you arrange for the ship's boat to be at a small dock around ten o'clock on the Sunday evening beforehand?"

"Yes, I can do that, no worries," he replied with a confidence he did not feel.

He spent the next few days doing the things that sailors in a strange port are expected to do and got to know one or two members of the crew really well, particularly the Kiwi he had fought with, who was game for any sort of activity, legal or otherwise.

Between them they bought up all the spare bottles of drink and cigarettes that were on the ship and sold them for a hefty profit to one of the bars by the docks. They also robbed the ships sick room of a lot of its supplies and sold them to a man they met in the same bar. As the Kiwi did not speak any Spanish, Bertie did all of the negotiating.

"Can you get me any guns David, I would give you a good price for guns?" the contact said.

Bertie was about to say no, but asked his friend about it, before replying to the man. He thought about it for a few moments and then said, "Tell him yes, I know where there are some rifles on board, but we would have to be very careful. They are inspected each day, except Sunday of course; yes, we could bring them Sunday night, but not here, somewhere a bit quieter and tell him that we want gold coins this time, not his local money."

Bertie informed the man that they believed they could get some rifles and ammunition if he was interested, but that it would have to be on Sunday night and at a quieter dock than the one they were now at. He would meet the man here on Saturday evening and agree the final details.

Bertie informed Makaa's friends what he had arranged with the man from the bar and they told him which dock they wanted to use on Sunday night. He met with the man from the bar on Saturday and agreed a price for six Lee Enfield rifles which his Kiwi friend said he could obtain for him.

The mate was spoken to regarding the use of one of the ship's boats on Sunday evening and for a small fee agreed to help. The Kiwi friend used the pretext of seeing a senorita, he had fallen for, for a last time before he left port.

Six Lee Enfield rifles and a box of ammunition were taken from the armoury right after they had been inspected on the Saturday and were hidden down in the scuppers somewhere. Bertie did not inform his friend about Deborah coming aboard the ship, but he was concerned as to where he would hide her initially, knowing that he would have to tell the Captain about her and get her to the sick bay, once they were safely out of reach of the Chilean authorities.

Deborah's guard changed over at three in the afternoon on a Sunday and as there was no trip to the police station, the new man would just sit in an armchair and fall asleep, after drinking a couple of glasses of Deborah's wine, while she stayed in the bedroom upstairs. Over the previous few days, her friends had managed to acquire a key for the back door and during the 'changing of the guard', two of them had slipped into the house and added something to the wine, to help the man sleep.

By five o'clock he was fast asleep and to make it look good for the man, they thumped him over the head and tied him up securely and put him in the large laundry cupboard.

They went upstairs and woke Deborah and told her what was happening, apart from making any reference to Bertie. At nine o'clock they left the house by the backdoor and using side streets and alleyways, made their way to the dock.

Bertie arrived promptly at ten and exchanged the rifles with his contact for the gold they had agreed on and he then made some excuse to go ashore for a couple of minutes, much to the annoyance of his friend. As soon as it was all clear, Makaa's friends made contact with Bertie and they all took her to the waiting boat. Bertie explained to his friend that this was his wife and she was coming with them and he just laughed and said, "If you say so chief, on your head be it, but it is going to cost you."

The Mate helped them winch the boat aboard, Deborah being told to stay still and keep quiet as she lay under a tarpaulin. For his silence and assistance, the Kiwi was offered all the gold that they had got for the rifles, which he accepted. It was agreed that Bertie would keep the Mate occupied, while his friend took Deborah down below, to a hidey-hole he knew about. Bertie went to see her when all was safe and they held each other tight and wept together.

The boat left on time the next morning and once it was in International Waters, Bertie went to see the captain and told him about Deborah. Although he was furious, that his ship should be put in danger this way, he agreed that no-one need ever know that she had been aboard and told Bertie to take her to the sick bay and to stay with her himself. He announced that Bertie had come down with a recurrence of Yellow Fever and that no-one was to go into the sick bay apart from the on-board medic.

When Deborah did not turn up at the police station the next day, a search was made of the house and the unfortunate guard was found tied up in the cupboard. He claimed that at least three people had jumped him and he had a large lump on his head to prove it. They searched for her in Santiago and Iquique without success and assumed in the end that she had disappeared over the border, or had died of her illness and her body buried somewhere.

By the time that the ship reached Auckland, Deborah was a lot stronger but still had a nasty cough and the Captain had visited her regularly to see how she was. It was announced to the crew that David Raymond did not have Yellow Fever but was still not well and would be leaving the ship in Auckland. He left at night, in the same ship's boat that had been used in Chile, with Deborah under a tarpaulin and the Mate and the Kiwi acting as crew.

Chapter 15
You Owe Me One

The Mate had discovered the missing rifles on his Monday inspection of the armoury and immediately went to speak with Bertie and Zac, his Kiwi accomplice, about it. They flannelled him about the need to set up a profile with the people they were dealing with in Santiago, in order to ensure the release of Deborah.

The three of them then went to see the Captain and explain what had happened to the rifles and the medical supplies and naturally he was furious about the whole matter and castigated the three of them, having guessed the Mate's complicity in the affair. After further discussions, he was assured that replacement rifles and supplies would be purchased in Auckland and would be in place before the ship sailed for Sydney, so he agreed to let the matter lie; which meant that when the small boat returned to the ship, the Mate was on his own and the other three had landed on a quiet beach at Home Bay, to the west of Auckland.

"Any ideas of where we are or what we do next Zac?" Bertie enquired.

"I used to come here fishing with my dad and uncle when I was young, there is an old hut about half a mile that way," he said, pointing along the beach, "that we used for overnight stays, it's a bit rough, but it will do as a base while we sort ourselves out. Can Deborah walk that far?"

"I'll be fine," Deborah replied, "it's so good to enjoy clean air again and to be free, I owe you two so much, for all you have done for me." She made this last statement, as Bertie had told her that Zac had helped in her escape, rather than say that his 'friend' was just a common thief.

Anyway, Bertie smiled and Zac actually blushed, as he had never been in the role of 'hero' before and thought it would go down really well with his family, who did not have such a kind opinion of him.

"I heard the Mate say that he would come back in the boat in three days time to collect Zac and the rifles and the medical supplies, will you be able to get them by then?" Deborah enquired.

The two men looked at each other in a funny sort of way, as they had not really discussed this part of the operation and said nothing in reply to the question.

"Surely the Captain and Mate will get into trouble if you don't at least replace the guns. After all, you did make a good profit on them, of that I am certain," she said.

"Of course we will replace them," Zac answered, "we will find somewhere safe to leave you and then Bertie and I will go into Auckland tomorrow and get what we need. I know a man who can get the rifles and there are plenty of shops Bertie can get the medical supplies from. You just leave it to us Deborah."

They found the hut and the key, which was under the same old stone where it was always left and made Deborah comfortable on some old tarpaulins that were stacked on a shelf inside.

They all slept badly and woke early in the morning and discussed what they should do next.

"Let's find somewhere to eat and then we can ask for information about getting a decent room to stay in," suggested Deborah, "do you know of any cafes in this area Zac?"

"It's been more than twenty years Deborah since I fished off this beach and there was nothing here then, I think we will have to get a bit closer to town before we find somewhere, so shall we get started?" Zac suggested.

The first person they met while walking into town was a policeman, who was just on his way home after finishing a night shift.

"Where are you three off to so early in the morning?" he asked.

"We were stranded on the beach overnight officer," Bertie explained, "our friends were getting us back for a trick we played on them a few months ago, but my wife is not feeling too good today and we need to find a hotel or guest house to stay in, while I make arrangements to get us home."

"And where exactly is home?" the policeman asked, in a suspicious tone.

"Gisborne," Zac replied, "but my friend's wife really is not well and we need to get her somewhere she can rest, do you know of anywhere round here?"

At this point Deborah started coughing and Bertie had to support her, to keep her from falling over.

"Your wife needs to see a doctor chum, you should take her to the City Hospital right away, she does not sound at all well. Do you know where it is?"

"Good idea," said Zac, "I went there several times with my mum. Can we get a bus there as it's a bit far to walk?"

"If you walk down that side street, it will bring you out on Jervois Road and there is a bus stop just round the corner. You may have to wait half an hour, but it is better than making the lady walk. Good luck," he said and left them to it.

In the end they had to wait only twenty minutes for a bus and then change buses once more, before they reached the hospital. The doctor took one look at Deborah, heard her cough and immediately said, "We will have to keep you in, it sounds to me like you have TB. Do you have any history of this?" he asked.

"Can I assume that the normal doctor patient privileged relationship is working here?" asked Bertie.

"Of course," the doctor replied, so Bertie informed him of where Deborah had come from and the fact that she had been in prison for two years and had only recently been released.

"If you go with the nurse Mr., what did you say your name was?"

"Bannister and this is my wife, Deborah Bannister."

"We have a specialist ward here for TB sufferers and your wife will be well looked after," the doctor informed him.

Deborah was taken up to the ward and put to bed and the necessary paperwork completed. Bertie and Zac found a guest house not far from the hospital and booked a couple of rooms for two nights. Bertie found a large chemist shop in town and gave them the list of supplies that they had taken from the ship and returned an hour later to collect them. Since Zac was paying for the rifles, Bertie had agreed to pay for the medical supplies, which cost him a lot more than his half of the proceeds, from the sale of the ships supplies in Chile.

He met up with Zac again in the evening at the guest house and discussed how they had got on.

"I managed to get all the supplies from the chemist shop, but obviously not manufactured by the same company, they are in those two boxes behind the door," said Bertie.

"I have arranged to pick the rifles up in two days time, but they were not sure about the ammo, still the rifles are the main thing," said Zac, "you know Deborah could be in that hospital for weeks, it could be quite costly for you, have you thought about what you are going to do?"

"Not really, one thing at a time and I want you to know how grateful I am for the way you have helped Deborah and me. I know we did not hit it off to start with, but without your help I could never have got her out of Chile alive. I will always be in your debt Zac."

Zac nodded and smiled and then suggested that they go out for a meal at a café he had found near the waterfront. They had a big helping of fish and chips with pie and custard to follow, all washed down with several mugs of tea. Around seven thirty a big man came in and sat down at the table with them.

He looked straight at Zac and spoke quietly, "Eight o'clock Thursday, under the pier. Bring the money and don't mess me around Zac. I have only managed to get half the ammo, but had to pay more for it than I thought, so the price remains the same. Understand? And come alone!"

He got up and left and Zac breathed a sigh of relief.

"Sorry Bert, but they insisted on seeing who my partner was, that's why we had to come here tonight," Zac explained.

"Zac, can they be trusted. Will you be safe to go there on your own," asked Bertie.

"To be honest, I can't be sure. I haven't dealt with that big chap before, but my usual contact has been replaced, so I had no alternative. We will take a walk down to the meeting point tomorrow and do a recce of the area."

Both Bertie and Zac went to see Deborah the next morning, but the doctor would not let either of them in to the ward.

"Sorry Mr. Bannister, but your wife is still undergoing tests and until we are certain what is wrong with her, we are keeping her in isolation. I can tell you that she had a good night's sleep and ate a full breakfast this morning, so come back tomorrow afternoon please and I should have a better idea of her condition by then," the doctor informed him.

"C'mon lets go down and check the pier out," suggested Zac, "we can't do any good here Burt."

They walked down to the pier which was away from the main dock area and was not well lit or easily seen from the road.

"If you were to stay up there by the road," said Zac, "and stand among those trees, they would not be able to see that you are with me, but you would be able to come and help me carry the guns and ammo, once the deal has been settled. I don't think they will be hanging around for long, so I will whistle when I need you. We can take the medical supplies to the beach hut we used the other night, during the daytime tomorrow. If anyone sees us they will just think we are preparing for a nights fishing."

Bertie went on his own to the hospital, after they had both carried the medical supplies to the hut on the beach and Zac went and bought a large canvas bag to carry the guns in.

The doctor told him that they had confirmed that Deborah had developed TB but that it was not in an advanced stage yet and that her general health was very poor.

"We gather from your wife that you have a home in Spain and that you want to return there as soon as possible, is that right?"

"No, doctor, it isn't right. I have had to sell our Spanish home, but she does not know that yet. We will in fact be returning to my parents house in England. Does that make a difference?"

"Not really, I know for certain that there are some very fine centres for treating TB in England. She will have to spend at least another six months in New Zealand, before we have got her to a stage where she will be strong enough to travel back there. I am afraid that you will have to plan on staying in Auckland until at least May of next year Mr. Bannister, maybe even longer."

"Thanks doctor. My wife's health comes first, of course; I will make arrangements to that effect," Bertie replied.

He walked slowly back to the Guest house and told the owner that he would like to extend his stay for a couple more days, but that his friend would be leaving that evening. He settled what they owed to date and paid for two more nights and then went up to his room. Zac came and joined him an hour later, carrying a large canvas bag, which he had already put his few possessions into. They discussed what had to be done that evening, counted out the money into a pouch that Zac had bought and went out for a meal together.

Bertie did not mention that he had loaded his Luger pistol and had it in his belt, just in case there was trouble. They had their meal and walked down to the pier, arriving there forty minutes early, so that Bertie could find a good spot among the trees.

Zac walked around for a while to get his courage up and arrived at the pier at a couple of minutes to eight and sat underneath it, out of sight of the road, with the empty canvas bag beside him. He was suddenly aware that a small boat was coming in from the sea and was making for the spot he was sitting by. Two men got out of the boat and searched the area quietly calling for Zac, he could see they were carrying guns and he became very nervous, but slowly made his way down towards them, having left the pouch with the money, buried in the sand by the post he was sitting next to.

One of them searched him for weapons, but he was carrying none, so they put their guns away and went and fetched the rifles from the boat.

He checked the six rifles as best he could and they seemed to be exactly what he had asked for and seemed to be in good condition. They walked with him up the beach and he retrieved the money bag and handed it over to the big man he had been dealing with, who presented him with the rifles and the ammo.

Just before they left him there, the big man hit him hard in the face with a huge fist that sent him flying into the sand.

"I told you to come on your own Zac, do you think I am stupid, I know your friend is up there in the trees. I should kill you for this."

"We have to get these rifles and some more supplies to Home Bay by midnight; he has just come to help carry everything, that's all. His wife is sick in the hospital; we have done all this to pay for her treatment," Zac blurted out.

"I know about his wife, I have had him followed, just tell him to keep his mouth shut and not to come looking for me again. Got it?" with which he gave him a hefty kick in the chest.

The two men walked back down the shore to the boat and when they had rowed a safe distance away Zac whistled the agreed signal. Bertie was horrified when he saw the state Zac was in and moped up the blood as best he could. They managed to carry the rifles and ammunition to the beach at Home Bay where they had landed three days before and Zac stayed with them while Bertie went and fetched the medical supplies from the hut. Around mid-night the Mate arrived in the ship's boat, accompanied by the medic who had looked after Deborah. The canvas bag with the guns was put aboard and then the ammunition and the other boxes and Zac then followed them into the boat.

"You owe me one Zac," the Mate informed him, "the Old Man wanted me to leave you here tonight, as a punishment; but I talked him out of it. I said it was all Bertie's fault and you were only helping a friend, just like I was. So there, you owe me big time."

Bertie walked back to the guest house and let himself in and went up to his room, he lay down on the bed and slept for just over fifteen hours. When he woke, he checked his finances and realised he still had all the gold coins bar one, in his belt, plus a mix of foreign currencies, that he had acquired on all of his travels. He then went to see the owner of the guest house, to try and arrange a long term rate for the room and perhaps a slightly bigger room to boot.

"Let me get this straight Mr. Bannister," the landlady said, "you are a Merchant Navy captain, but you do not currently have a ship. Your wife is in the City Hospital with TB which she caught in Chile, but you refuse to give me any more details than that. The doctors have told you that she could be in hospital for several months and your friend, who has been assisting you, but you won't say with what, has re-joined his ship and left for Sydney. Have I got your story about right?"

Bertie sighed and nodded that she had.

"I really don't think I can help you and would like you to get your things right now and leave my Guest House today. I will of course, repay you what I owe you. Henry, Henry! Help Captain Bannister with his things, he is leaving right now."

Henry was the landlady's husband, who was on a day's holiday from his other job and came running when summoned. He followed Bertie up the stairs and when they were outside the room he finally spoke up, "I am so sorry Captain Bannister for all this inconvenience, I know my wife can be very difficult sometimes, but her father died of TB and she is petrified just by the thought of it."

"I am sorry to hear that," said Bertie, "but I still need to find somewhere to live for six months."

"I appreciate that captain, but we really don't have anything suitable for a lengthy stay at a price you would consider reasonable. However, may I make a suggestion that you might find acceptable?"

"Go ahead, I'm all ears," Bertie replied.

"If you go down the street opposite and take the second left, my sister has a house there, number twenty six and I know she is looking for a lodger, as she has recently been widowed and is struggling to make ends meet. Tell her Henry sent you and that I will try and pop round and see her as soon as I have some spare time."

Armed with this new information, Bertie felt a little bit more hopeful than he had done twenty minutes earlier and set off to find Henry's sister at number twenty six, round the corner. It was a lot further than he had guessed and it took him well over half an hour to reach the house. He knocked on the door and heard a dog barking and waited, but as no-one came to the door, he knocked a second time. Again the dog barked and again no-one came to the door. Suddenly a window went up in the house next door and a woman put her head out and shouted, "You want Mrs. Glass?"

Bertie assumed that this was the woman's name, so said that he did.

"She's in the garden love, taking in the washing, I'll let her know you are there."

Bertie thanked her, the woman disappeared and he waited.

Eventually the door was opened by a short, middle-aged woman in an apron, who was followed by a middle-aged terrier, who was barking at a safe distance behind her.

"Yes, can I help you, sorry to have kept you but it's my washing day and I was in the garden taking it in and Mrs. Cross said there was someone at my door and I have only just got in from work, have you been here long?"

Bertie guessed this one-way conversation could have lasted a lot longer, so he butted in at this point, "Mrs. Glass,

Henry told me to come and see you, he said that you might have a room that I could rent for a couple of months."

"Henry, my brother Henry, that's nice, is he a friend of yours dear?"

"Not exactly Mrs. Glass. I have been staying at his wife's Guest House for a couple of nights, but she is not able to put me up for the period of time that I need and he suggested that I should come round and see you. Oh, and he said that he will try and pop round and see you soon."

The last piece of information took a second or two to sink in and then the lady on the doorstep erupted at him.

"Pop round and see me soon, I'll give him 'pop round and see me soon'. My own brother has not bothered to 'pop round and see me soon' since my husband's funeral and that was in January this year, eleven months ago. The spineless halfwit is frightened to do anything on his own and she certainly won't give him permission to 'pop round and see me soon'."

"I'm sorry Mrs. Glass; I have obviously come at a bad time," Bertie offered, "perhaps I can come back tomorrow, when it is more convenient."

Just then a young woman arrived at the house and pushed past Bertie and went up to Mrs. Glass who had started to cry.

"What have you said to my mother, who are you?" she demanded.

"Look, I am sorry if I have upset your mother. Your uncle Henry told me to come here because I need a room for a couple of months while my wife is in hospital and he said that your mother might be able to help me."

"Oh yes really, which hospital is she in then and what is wrong with her?" she asked sarcastically.

"The City Hospital and she has TB and I need somewhere to stay that is reasonably near bye, is that good enough for you?"

"Oh, Mr. Bannister, it's you. I am sorry, but I didn't recognise you straight away. We met in the ward where your wife was yesterday. Come into the house and we can chat. Mum, its O.K. mum, I know this man and his wife is in the ward next to the one I am working in."

Mother, daughter and Bertie went into the house and sat down in the front room and chatted for well over an hour. Bertie was totally honest with the two women and told them exactly what had been happening in his life and that the doctor had said that Deborah would have to stay in hospital for about six months; before she would be fit enough to travel back to England.

He learned that Mr. Glass had been severely injured in the Great War and had come home a broken and dispirited man and had finally died of his wounds in January that year. He was offered the big room at the front of the house, which used to be Mr. and Mrs. Glass's bedroom, but which she could no longer bear to sleep in. It was agreed that he would take the room for an initial month, just to see how they all got on and his meals would be included in the weekly rate. He moved in straight away and paid for a month in advance and enjoyed his first home cooked meal of lamb chops, potatoes and peas that very evening.

"Can I ask what you intend to do about getting work Mr. Bannister," asked Mrs. Glass, "will you try and get a job at sea again or something on land?"

"Mrs. Glass, I would really prefer it, if you and your daughter called me Bertie, if you don't mind, that is."

"Of course we don't mind Mr. Bannister, err Bertie. My name is Rosie and my daughter is Flo."

"Thank you Rosie. To answer your question, I would like to go back to sea again. I have the name of a contact to see in Auckland, that a man I have worked for in Harwich gave me, so I hope to be offered some work by him. The only problem is that if I am away for days at a time, I will not be able to visit my wife and we don't know anyone in New Zealand, so she could get very lonely."

"Well I could visit your wife sometimes," Rosie replied. "I work at the library and could pop in after work. If you would like me to, that is!"

"That would be marvelous, but I think visiting times are between two till three in the afternoon and between six and seven in the evening, that might not be convenient for you," he replied.

She smiled as she answered, "Don't you worry about that, I know one of the nurses there, don't I Flo?"

The next day was Saturday and Rosie had offered to go with him to the hospital to meet his wife. Deborah had been warned by Flo that Bertie had taken a room with her and her mother, so she was not too surprised to see Bertie come into the ward, accompanied by a lady. The introductions were all made and the two ladies seemed to hit it off straight away. When Bertie left the ward for a few minutes, Rosie discreetly asked Deborah if there was any shopping she could get for her and a list of items was agreed between them and Bertie was told that he should give Rosie some money to pay for them, when he returned to the ward.

On Sunday morning, Rosie and Flo went to the Methodist Church, not far from where they lived and Bertie took a walk into town to find out where Mr. Alderton's Auckland contact was situated and wrote letters and postcards home in the afternoon, which he posted in the box outside of the post office.

On the morning of Monday the 10th December 1923, for the first time in months, Bertie felt that he was back in charge of his life once again. He walked into town to see Mr.

Alderton's shipping contact and had a long conversation with the man, who took copious notes of his experience and qualifications.

"I will have to cable Mr. Alderton and check all this information out Captain Bannister, but if you do not mind taking a First Mate's position to start with, I am sure I can find a suitable job for you. Why don't you come back on Wednesday afternoon and we can talk again."

Bertie then walked to the Telegraph Office and sent a Telegram to his parents:

'Deb and me safe in Auckland. Deb in hospital with TB. Letter in post. Send passport and marriage cert to following address…………………………………………Bertie'

He then went to the largest bank he could find and asked the clerk on the reception desk if they would change his foreign currency into pounds and the clerk directed him to the foreign currency desk. The clerk there was surprised to see so many different currencies and such a lot of it and asked Bertie if he would mind waiting in the lobby, while he spoke with the assistant manager.

The assistant manager took one look at the scruffily dressed man in the lobby and went and spoke with the manager as to whether he should get security to escort the man out of the bank or they should call the police. Just then, one of the bank messengers stopped by the man and spoke with him for a while and then continued walking towards his normal seat.

"Call that man over, I want to speak with him," the manager said to his secretary.

"You wanted to see me sir," the messenger said shyly.

"Yes, come in. I didn't say sit down," the manager barked at him.

"Who was that man I saw you speaking with out there in the lobby?"

"Captain Bannister, sir," Henry replied, for this was his other job when he was not assisting his dear wife in the Guest House.

"He was staying at my wife's Guest House for a few days, nice man, his wife is sick in the City Hospital. He has just arrived from South America, Chile I believe."

"What sort of a captain is he?" the manager enquired.

"Merchant Navy I believe, sir."

"Very well, you can go."

Much relieved Henry left the office and noticed that Bertie had seen him leave, so he gave him the thumbs up sign, although he was not really sure why!

"Well that explains all the different currencies and why he needs pounds right now. Tell the clerk to exchange the currency and suggest that Captain Bannister opens an account with the bank," the manager instructed his assistant, "and do remember that we cannot always 'judge a book by its cover'."

The assistant manager went over and instructed the clerk, passing on the same pearls of wisdom about books and covers, as he himself had received. The clerk duly looked up the various exchange rates and calculated the combined sum that Bertie was due in pounds and having asked Bertie to come back to his desk, offered to open a bank account there and then, after saying that he would need to see some form of identity, before he could withdraw any money or be issued with a cheque book. Bertie opened the account with five pounds, taking the rest in cash and saying that he did not have his passport with him, so he would give proof of identity another time.

He visited Deborah in the evening, to find that she and Rosie were engrossed in a deep conversation, which stopped the minute he arrived.

"Talking about me already," he quipped, "how are you today Deborah, hello Rosie?"

"I thought I asked you to give Rosie some money for my shopping, you owe her four pounds ten shilling and nine pence Bertie," Deborah said, ignoring his questions to her.

Rosie got up from her seat and said, "I have to go now Deborah; I'll see you again tomorrow and get those other things you asked me for. Goodnight."

"Bye Rosie and thanks for everything," Deborah replied.

"What was all that about between you and Rosie?" he asked, a bit taken back.

"Women's things, nothing for you to worry about, now, what have you been doing today?"

He told her what he had been doing and that he had seen Mr. Alderton's contact and that he was hoping to get a job soon, not wishing to worry her about his current shortage of money.

"I have been meaning to ask you Bertie, who has been looking after our house in Spain, all the time you have been away?" she asked.

"Deborah, we don't have a house in Spain any more, I had to sell it to raise the money for your lawyer. How else do you think I paid his fees. You took all of our savings to pay for your passage to Chile, remember! Mum and dad are paying for Deborah, not that they have said anything and the rest of the money I used to get to Chile and help you escape the country. We are broke. We have the clothes we stand up in and about thirty five pounds in cash. That's it love, the rest has all gone."

"What do you mean, you sold our lovely home by the sea, how could you Bertie, you had no right to sell it, there must have been some other way to pay for the lawyer."

"And you had no right to go behind my back and write to Manuel and get fooled into going back to Chile. It took me five minutes to work out that those letters were not from him. How could you be so selfish and so stupid Deborah? You have cost us our home, our savings, your health and goodness knows what else!"

At this point the ward sister appeared, told them that they were disturbing other patients and suggested that Bertie leave right away, which he did.

Flo had also been working in the hospital that evening and when she arrived home at nine o'clock, Bertie had still not arrived back at the house.

"I would forget about his tea mum, he was really upset with his wife, the ward sister had to separate them. He is probably in a bar somewhere, does he have his key on him?"

"Yes dear, it's not on the hook. I feel so sorry for him, after all that he has done for her, but she is not well and I am sure she will regret what she has said when she is feeling better."

"I am on the early shift tomorrow mum, so I am going to bed. I wouldn't wait up for him; he will probably not want to talk with anyone tonight."

She was quite right; Bertie arrived home just before midnight, the worse for wear but not completely drunk. He had problems getting his key in the lock and stumbled up the stairs, hitting his knee on the corner of the blanket chest on the landing. He swore once, but then remembered where he was and went to bed as quietly as he was able and slept through until ten o'clock the next day, by which time he was relieved to find that he was on his own in the house once more.

Chapter 16
An Interesting Place

If Bertie had felt great on the Monday, well he felt awful on the Tuesday. It was the worst row he had ever had with Deborah and he was feeling hurt, un-appreciated and un-loved. He made himself some toast and found a jar of homemade marmalade and sat down by the kitchen window with his breakfast and looked out into the garden. It was a warm sunny summer's day and he started to think of his daughter and parents back home in Harwich and really wished he was there with them.

"I can't sit here all day feeling sorry for myself," he said out loud, "so what shall I do? I cannot see Mr. Alderton's contact until tomorrow and I could do with another pair of trousers and a new shirt to wear and I probably need a haircut, if I might be attending interviews this week. Come on Bertie, there's a lot worse off than you, pull yourself together man!"

He put some of the money he had got from the bank in his wallet and the rest he left in his bag under the bed; picking up his key from the hook in the hall, he left the house and headed off into town.

He found a barber shop and sat down next to another man to wait his turn and picked up the newspaper on the seat next to him. The main story was about the battle between the Government soldiers and rebels at Vera Cruz, Mexico and the fact that American troops had left New Orleans with the intention of sailing down there in order to protect their country's interests.

"That's a very interesting place Vera Cruz," said the old man sitting next to him, "I was there first in the seventies while I was still a young man, boy did we have some fun. That was real sailing then, with the old schooners, not like today when everything is done for them, these modern sailors don't know what proper seamanship really is!"

Bertie folded the paper, put it back down on the seat and started a debate on seamanship, which continued while the old man and then he, had their respective hair cut; it lasted while they walked down to a café that the old man frequented and expanded to include the proprietor, who was also an old sailor and kept going till after they had eaten lunch together and only ceased when Bertie looked at his watch and realised it was gone two o'clock and that he still had his shopping to do.

"I'm sorry gentlemen," he said, "to leave your education at this critical point of the discussion, but I need to depart and buy myself some new clothes, if I am ever to get another job on one of these new fangled steam monsters, that you both dislike so much. Any suggestions of where I should go?"

The two old men came up with several suggestions of exactly where they thought he should go and Timbuktu was probably the politest, which gave Bertie his best laugh for many months.

Finally the proprietor suggested that there was a Gentleman's Outfitters on the High Street, which would probably supply all he needed and Bertie left the café to further comments and whistles, with the instruction that he should come back tomorrow to finish the argument.

He got a smart, but tough, pair of trousers, several shirts and some underwear and a very nice striped tie that the manager gave him for being a good customer. He passed a Greengrocer's shop and bought some grapes for Deborah and then went into town to the Passport Office to see what forms he would need to complete, in order to get Deborah put onto his passport, when it arrived from England.

When he got to the hospital Rosie and Flo were both talking to Deborah and had obviously just been laughing at something Flo had told them. As he sat down at the end of the bed, Flo left, but Rosie remained, seated on the other chair.

"Hi love, these are for you," he said, as he passed her the bag of grapes. "How are you feeling today?"

She took the grapes, smiled and put them on her locker and then said, "Much better thank you. The doctor said I was responding well to the treatment and that my general health was much improved already. Plus Rosie has managed to get all the shopping for me that I wanted; you will remember to reimburse her what I owe, won't you?"

"Oh sorry Rosie, I forgot, remind me later please. I decided to go shopping myself and get some new clothes, just in case I have an interview this week."

"And have a haircut, by the look of it, very smart," she commented, "but not before time, if I might say. Which reminds me, the sister said that a hairdresser comes into the hospital each week and I desperately need to get mine done, do you have some change you can give me please?"

Bertie gave her a ten shilling note and a handful of coins which she put into a new bag that Rosie had got for her.

"Isn't it nice," she said holding it up, "Rosie got it in the market for me."

Rosie chatted about an awkward lady she had dealt with at the library and Bertie told them about his lengthy encounter with the old sailor at the Barber's shop and no-one mentioned the house in Spain or the flight to and from Chile, but just kept to safe non-confrontational subjects.

As Bertie said goodbye and turned towards the door, he did not see Deborah give Rosie's hand a little squeeze as she mouthed the words "Thank you for staying" to her. Rosie smiled and mouthed back, "You are most welcome my dear."

They went home and had dinner together and Bertie gave Rosie the money she was due, plus a bit extra, in case his wife wanted anything else. He was dying to ask her if Deborah had requested that she stay the whole time he was there or whether she just did it on her own account, but in the end, he decided that he did not really want to know, so he said nothing.

On Wednesday he replaced a couple of light bulbs that had blown and which Rosie had said she could not reach and then went into the old shed in the garden to find a saw and a chopper, as she said she needed some more firewood for the copper in the scullery. Apart from a few cobwebs and some dirt that had blown in under the door, the shed was immaculate. Every tool had its place and every tin and jar was clearly labeled. The bench had a large woodworking vice attached to it and the wood was either up in the rafters of neatly stacked in the corner.

"My word, this is the way to lay out a shed, if I ever get one in the future, I must remember all of these ideas that he has used. This wood is far too good to use for firewood, ah, that looks more like it underneath the bench. Looks like some bits off the end of railway sleepers, they'll do fine."

He took the blocks outside, chopped them into kindling and put them in the box outside the back door. He then made himself a drink, washed and changed into his new clothes and walked into town to the shipping agent, by way of yesterday's café and the two old men, who made suitable comments about his changed appearance.

The agent was seated in his office when his secretary showed Bertie in and he had some papers in front of him on his desk as he rose to welcome his guest.

"Captain Bannister, good to see you again, please take a seat. I have heard from Mr. Alderton who has confirmed that you are who you say you are, and he speaks very highly of you. He asked me to tell you that your father has posted the documents you asked for and that I am to say 'Hello' from him."

"That's good to hear, thank you," Bertie replied. "I should explain that one of the documents I have asked my father to send over to me, is my British passport."

"How on earth did you manage to leave England without it, or shouldn't I ask?"

"During the war I obtained dual citizenship and was issued with a Spanish passport, as well as having my British one, but unfortunately I have managed to mislay that one somewhere."

"How odd, can I ask you why you were given a Spanish passport?"

"I am afraid I am not allowed to give you any more information, as everything I was involved in is covered by the Official Secrets Act. This means of course, that I really cannot apply for any 'out of country' jobs, until my British passport arrives from England," Bertie explained.

"Oh I see, what a pity. Because of your past experience, I have been in contact with a shipping company who would be very interested in employing you on their New Zealand to Great Britain runs, a job you could continue to do irrespective of whether you were based in England or New Zealand. Would you be interested in seeing them, I guess your passport will be here in a couple of months and they might be willing to give you some local work in the meantime?"

"Sounds ideal," Bertie enthusiastically replied, "I have seen quite enough of the Mediterranean and Africa, to last me a lifetime already. It would be good to return to the long distance routes again."

"What about your wife and family, how would they react to you being away for long periods of time?"

"My daughter knows no different and things are a bit difficult between me and my wife at the moment, so I am sure it would not be a problem for her either. Who is the company and when can I meet them?"

The Auckland based manager, for The Christchurch Wool and Shipping Company, met with Bertie on Thursday morning and was so impressed with him, that he cabled the head office and arranged for him to travel down immediately, on one of their ships, in order to see the Managing Director himself, the following Monday.

Deborah was sceptical at first but when he explained that it would be a very convenient way to get her safely back to England once she was well enough to travel, she agreed that he should go to Christchurch for the interview.

"At worst, I will resign once we have you safely back home," he concluded, "if the job does not work out."

They had a good time together that Thursday evening and a certain warmth, that had been lacking of late, seemed to have found its way back into their relationship.

"And don't you worry about me Bertie, I am doing fine. Rosie comes in to visit me every day now and Flo stops by for a chat whenever she can, they are such nice people. She was ever so grateful to you for chopping the wood for her yesterday, she said that she has tried doing it herself, but always ends up hitting her fingers."

He gave her some more money in case she needed anything while he was away and when the bell sounded to mark the end of the 'Visiting hour', he was pleased to hear a, "Good luck in Christchurch," from her, as he left the ward.

The ship left Auckland around six am on Friday and Bertie was invited to join the Captain on the bridge. The two men liked each other immediately and talked about their different experiences and their favourite places to visit.

"I don't suppose you would mind acting as my Mate once we get to Wellington, would you Bertie?" the captain asked, after a couple of hours into the voyage.

"No, of course not, is there a problem with the Mate then?" he replied.

"Not a problem as such, but his mother lives there and she has been very ill lately and his father has asked him to come and visit her as soon as he is able. If you are prepared to step in for him, I could let him leave the boat there and save him the return trip to Christchurch."

The Mate left the ship at Wellington and some cargo was unloaded before the ship steamed on to Christchurch, arriving around Sunday lunch-time. Bertie worked well with the Captain and was able to demonstrate his competence to everyone aboard. A room had been reserved for him at a small hotel in town, which was only a short distance from the headquarters building. He was there at nine o'clock prompt the next morning and the managing director's secretary showed him into the Board Room and poured him a cup of tea.

The walls of the room were full of pictures of ships, both large and small, ancient and modern and he was busy studying these when the Managing Director (M.D.), accompanied by Captain Bilby, from the ship he had travelled down in, came into the room.

"Captain Bannister, nice to meet you," said the M.D., offering his hand to Bertie, who shook it firmly. "Do you recognise any of the ships on the wall?"

"Only the clipper, it's the first ship I sailed on when I finished at nautical school. It brings back memories, that's for sure. Nice to see you again Captain Bilby," he said, shaking hands with his new acquaintance.

Captain Bilby has spoken well of you and I have made a few enquiries of my own, since you first saw my manager in

Auckland. Apart from a few years that appear to have gone missing during the war and since for that matter, you have had a very diverse and interesting career and everyone seems to hold you in high esteem. Now Captain Bilby is one of my most senior captains and a fellow director of the company and we need to know exactly what you have been doing since 1914 before we offer you a job with us.

It took Bertie almost five hours to explain what he had been doing in the last nine years, being careful not to give any secrets away. They stopped for drinks at eleven and had sandwiches brought in at twelve and finally there was a barrage of questions which he tried his best to answer, culminating in a formal job offer at three pm.

"We can certainly start you straight away Bertie on the local routes and on one or two of the island trips where we know the customs officials, but if we make sure that we always have crewman 'David Raymond' on your ship, then we can use you elsewhere if we get stuck. Are you O.K. with that?"

"Sounds good to me, I can't wait to start, but as I said before, I do have my wife's medical bills to pay, so a couple of weeks pay in advance would be most welcome. The other thing is that since I have to be in Auckland and have rented a room there, does the company have somewhere I can stay when I am here in Christchurch?"

"No problem there, I have a small annex in the garden that I keep for visiting friends and relatives, you can use it whenever you like," said Captain Bilby.

"And if that is not available, you are most welcome to come and stay with me," said the M.D., "there is acres of space at my place."

And so yet another chapter in the life of Bertie Bannister had started, one he always looked back on with a tremendous amount of pride and pleasure.

He spent the first month or so, as Mate on a variety of ships, visiting every major port in New Zealand and quite a few of the islands as well. He did manage to be in Auckland for Christmas Day and Boxing Day and had asked Rosie to buy a new outfit for Deborah, for when she was well enough to be up for more than a few minutes at a time.

His first command with his new employer was a small tramp steamer type of ship that just sailed wherever it was needed around New Zealand and across to Melbourne, Brisbane and Adelaide in Australia. David Raymond was able to leave the ship each time with no problems and collected one or two stamps in his passport to prove it.

The package from his father arrived in early February and armed with the requisite documents and forms, he visited the passport office to have his wife, Deborah Bannister added to his passport.

Deborah continued to get better in hospital and was finally discharged at the beginning of May and went to live with Rosie and Flo, staying in Bertie's room.

His first round trip to England was during the months of February, March and April and he was First Mate to Captain Bilby on that trip. During the time the ship was in Southampton, he was able to travel up to Harwich and visit his family.

His daughter was overjoyed to see him again after all the time he had been away and was disappointed he did not have a picture of her mummy. He could not get over how much she had grown in the last twelve months and was a little envious at the strong bond that now existed between his parents and his daughter.

"Will Mummy come home with you next time?" she asked him.

"I expect so Deborah," he said, "it really depends on how well she is by then, but I am hoping that she will be well enough to travel and we might possibly arrive here at the end of June or in early July."

Once his daughter was in bed, he sat down with his parents and talked with them well into the night, describing the escape from Chile and life in New Zealand.

"So how is Deborah really son?" his dad asked.

"I don't know dad, things are not the same between us these days. We had a tremendous row just after we arrived in Auckland. She was sounding off at me for selling the house at Benicarlo, as if I had a choice in the matter! I just lost my temper and told her exactly what I thought of her for going off the way she did and all the harm and expense she has brought on us. But if I am being honest, things were not right between us long before then."

"Ever since she lost the baby," his mother commented, "some women never get over a thing like that. I am sure that is why she wanted to go back to Chile, she had her family there who she thought could help her, she was just not thinking straight Bertie."

"I know mum and I have tried to understand what she must have gone through, but we do still have a daughter and she never even mentions her, it's like she doesn't exist. I read out bits from all of your letters and she listens, but never makes any comments and never asks me to say anything for her, when I write to you."

"She is still her mother and I am certain that once she comes home and sees her daughter, everything will be alright again. You just wait and see."

"I hope you are correct, I really do mum. On the practical side and I know you would never mention it to me; but how much do I owe you for looking after Deborah for all this time?"

"The answer would be nothing Bertie whatever the situation, but it really is nothing. Did we ever tell you about your Great Uncle Harry's Will?"

"No dad, I assume he left everything that he owned to you and mum."

"That is partly true and since he had hardly worked after coming home from the war, there was not an awful lot left, but there was one thing of value, do you know what that was?"

"No idea," said Bertie, "did he have stocks and shares or something?"

"No he didn't; but he did own the flat in London that he lived in. Your mother and I had always assumed that he rented it, but it turned out that he owned it and left it to little Deborah, to become hers when she reaches twenty one. In the meantime, we are allowed to rent it out and the rent we receive, more than pays for her keep and in fact we have opened a Post Office Account in her name and the extra money is paid into her account each month. Wasn't that good of Harry to make arrangements for her like that?"

"It certainly was, I had absolutely no idea, how wonderful, does she know about it?" Bertie enquired.

"Goodness no, she is just a child," his mother said, "we will tell her when she is eighteen and able to understand what it all means. That will be soon enough."

For reasons he could never explain, Bertie forgot to mention Uncle Harry's Will and that their daughter was a property owner to his wife when he got back to New Zealand and never got around to discussing the matter with her ever again.

Deborah was indeed very happy with her new life and friends in New Zealand and really had to be coerced into returning to England. She finally arrived in Harwich in late October 1924, a year after she escaped from Chile and was met by her exuberant daughter and her playful dog.

Alice had been quite right about Deborah's attitude changing when she met her daughter again and whatever fears had haunted her while she was away, seemed to disappear the moment they were in each other's arms.

At first the two women were a little hesitant with each other and each expressed concerns to their respective husbands about sharing the house long term; but when Mr. Alderton offered Deborah the same job in the warehouse that her mother-in-law had done before her, she found it gave her a new lease of life and the tensions between them evaporated and they started to become good friends and even went out together to church functions and the like.

Little Deborah proved to be a bright little girl and passed out top of her class two years running in 1925 and 1926 and won a place at the Grammar School when she was eleven.

Bertie continued to work for The Christchurch Wool and Shipping Company on the New Zealand to Europe run and when Captain Bilby retired in 1929, Bertie was appointed Senior Captain of the company and given a seat on the Board at the age of fifty.

The same year he arranged to take his parents on a return trip to Australia and New Zealand, giving them the holiday of a lifetime, that they had always dreamed about, as a thank you for all that they had done for him and his two 'Deborahs' over the years.

Chapter 17
Comings and Goings

Robert and Alice returned from their trip to Australia and New Zealand in early December 1929 and could not wait until they got their photographs back from the chemists, in order to show everyone where they had been and the wonderful sights they had seen. They had some snaps of Auckland which included Rosie and Flo outside in the garden of their home and Deborah was thrilled to see her old friends again.

Young Deborah had been telling her teacher about the photographs and was so excited about them, that the teacher sent an invitation to her grandparents, asking them if they would be willing to come to the school during the last week of term and to show the photos to Deborah's classmates and talk about their trip.

Alice made the excuse that the week before Christmas was the busiest week of the year for her, so she declined the invitation, but suggested that Robert should go on his own, to the school and tell Deborah's classmates about their holiday.

Wednesday the 18th of December turned out to be a nice bright day so Robert set off bright and early as he wanted to get a few things in town before he went on to visit Deborah's school. He had been asked to be there for two o'clock, so he had plenty of time to shop and get something to eat before walking to the school.

As he came out of the restaurant it started to drizzle and as he had not bothered to take his raincoat with him, he quickened his pace and stepped out briskly, hoping to avoid the downpour that was about to hit the town. He had managed to get to within a quarter of a mile of the school gates, when the heavens opened and the rain fell down like a torrent. In those few remaining yards, he got soaked through.

The School Secretary found him a towel and suggested that he should forget about showing the photographs and talking to the children at this time and just go home straight away.

"Thank you but no," he replied, "my granddaughter would be so upset if I did that; I will just give a quick talk today and show some of the photos and then leave. I could always come back again next term if they wanted me to."

The talk was quite brief, just forty minutes and he could have left then, but he made the mistake of asking the class if there were any questions and there were, a dozen or more. By the time he had finally finished answering them, it was ten to four and the school ended at four o'clock anyway, so Robert and his granddaughter walked home together that day, accompanied by some of her friends, who were still asking him questions.

It started with a cold and then a cough developed and by Boxing Day he was obviously a sick man, but he still insisted that they wait until the Friday before they disturbed the doctor during the holiday. When the doctor came he was very worried by Robert's condition and arranged for an ambulance to come and take him to hospital, where it was confirmed that he had Pneumonia.

His condition deteriorated throughout January and when he asked his son to get the family solicitor to come and see him in hospital, it was clear that he feared the worst.

He died quietly in hospital on Sunday the 2nd of February 1930 with his wife and son at his bedside.

He was buried in the plot of land next to his Uncle Harry, after a well attended funeral service at the local church. Alice, her daughter-in-law and her granddaughter, all wept for most of the service and burial, but Bertie remained dry-eyed throughout, much to everyone's surprise, it was as if he felt nothing. Alice was speaking to the vicar about it a week or two later and asked him if there was anything she could do?

"It is not un-common for the loss of someone we really love, to leave us quite numb and unable to grieve. Your husband and son were very close Mrs. Bannister and he just needs something to trigger his grief, because if it remains bottled up inside of him, it will definitely not be good for him. It will be like an open wound, deep inside, that won't heal."

"Do you have any suggestions as to what I might do Vicar?" she asked.

"It's very difficult to know what to suggest, but sometimes sorting through a deceased loved one's papers, or clothes, or tools if it's a man, can act as a trigger. May I suggest that you pray about it Mrs. Bannister and see if God gives you any suggestions."

It was a week later that Alice said to her son, "Bertie, I would like a picture painted of the Florin, your Granddad and father's old boat. I have found an artist in town who will paint it for me, but he said he needs some photographs of it. Do you think you could take your dad's camera and get some for me, before you leave on your next trip?"

"Great idea mum, I know Fred and Dave don't use it for work anymore, but I think they still sail her occasionally, I'll find out and get some photos for you, you just leave it to me."

A trip to Gravesend was arranged for a week later and Fred and Dave had been glad to assist Alice in her quest for some pictures and had cleaned the boat out and patched the sails and with Bertie's assistance had the old boat out on the Thames by early afternoon. Bertie got all the photos he wanted of the Florin and afterwards, the three friends took her for a sale up the river and back.

They had taken the sails down and were putting them away when Bertie stepped back and caught his foot on a lump of wood and would have toppled over and hurt himself, if Fred had not grabbed hold of his coat and yanked him hard towards himself, keeping him on his feet.

Without thinking, Dave immediately joked with him and said, "I don't know Bertie, all your years at sea and you are still as clumsy as you were when we used to go out with your Granddad and your old man when we were kids!"

Those few words were all it took to unlock the maelstrom of grief that was pent up inside him. He just sobbed out loud for a good five minutes and his friends had the good sense to just sit him down and leave him alone in his sorrow.

They finished tying the boat up in the dock and stowed all the gear away and managed to get down the pub for a drink, just before it closed. Bertie met a few more of his old acquaintances in the pub, who all asked to be remembered to Alice and all had different stories to tell about his dad and granddad. Having thanked his friends for their support and after promising to send them copies of his photographs, he made his way back to Harwich and took the reel of film in for processing.

While he was away on his next trip to Australia, Alice got the photos developed and gave them to the local artist she had spoken with, who painted the most magnificent picture of the Florin, which took pride of place on her living room wall.

Although Deborah had continued to do well at the Grammar School to start with, she slowly slipped down to the bottom of the class and after her Granddad died, she appeared to lose all interest in her lessons and friends for that matter and just sat in her room reading or going for long walks with

Velvet. Her friends called round to start with, but in the end grew tired of her rejections and left her to her own devices.

When Bertie was home in Harwich, the two of them would go sailing together and it was during one of these times on the water that she asked him a strange question.

"Dad, did I kill Granddad?"

Bertie thought he must have misheard her and replied, "Sorry love didn't quite catch that, did you do what?"

"One of my friends at school said that I killed Granddad, because he came to school to please me and got Pneumonia and died; because I was trying to impress everyone."

"What a terrible thing to say Deborah, of course you did not kill your Granddad. He was an old man and obviously not as fit as we thought he was. When he was out on the Florin, he would get soaked through once or twice a week, with no harmful effect whatsoever. Even now, on my long trips to New Zealand, I often get wet but cannot leave the bridge until my watch is over; a lot longer period of time than Granddad was wet for."

"So it wasn't my fault then?" she queried.

"No Deborah, his time on this earth was up and he has gone to a better place and he would be terribly upset if he knew someone had said this hateful thing to you. Now listen carefully to me; it was not your fault in any shape or form and I never want you to talk or even think about the matter again. Is that clear?"

"Yes dad and thanks, I loved him so much you know. Oh I love you and mum and Granny, of course I do, but Granddad was so special to me," she sobbed.

He steered the dinghy into the bank, so that it would not capsize and went over and hugged his daughter until she had stopped crying and was herself again.

"Are you O.K. now love? Is there anything else you have wanted to ask me?" Bertie asked his daughter.

"There is actually dad, but I am afraid you will laugh at me or get annoyed with me," she replied.

"Of course I won't. What is it Deborah?"

She took a deep breath and then said, "Would I be able to come with you to visit New Zealand and Australia dad. I would love to see all the different animals and visit the places that Granny and Granddad went to. Would it be possible, dad? I would not be any trouble; I could be your steward and look after you on the ship."

"I honestly don't know Deborah, let me think about it," he replied hesitantly, "I will need to talk to mum about it and to my boss, of course; so leave it with me."

"Well she leaves school next July when she will be almost sixteen and has absolutely no idea what she wants to do," Deborah said to her husband, when they were discussing their daughter's request. "I think it would do her the world of good to go with you. It's about time her horizons were broadened and she started to experience a bit of life. You are a director of the company after all and if you want your daughter to go with you, surely that should be your decision. Your position has to count for something Bertie."

"I agree, but I will still need to discuss it with the M.D., I can't just decide this on my own, it would be setting a wrong precedent."

When Bertie was discussing the matter with his mother a short while later, she was not so certain, but whether it was concern for Deborah, or she was worried about being left on her own, he could not tell.

"What does Deborah think about it, does she mind her daughter going to New Zealand with you; or perhaps she plans to go there with you as well and leave me on my own back here," Alice wondered.

"No mum, she plans no such thing. She said she would like to have come with us, but she does not want to lose her job at the warehouse, besides which, she is not the world's best sailor, so she will stay here; but she does think it would do Deborah a lot of good to go abroad and experience new things."

When Bertie got back to Christchurch, Shep the M.D., was very enthusiastic about Deborah coming to New Zealand as Bertie's steward.

"Just one proviso Bertie," he said, "my daughter Sally would love to go to England and to visit Europe, so assuming the two girls get on together, you might have to put up with two stewards on the return trip and possibly my wife and I as well."

"Oh, I am sure the two girls will hit it off together Shep, they both love animals with a passion, but I am not so certain about having two V.I.P.s to entertain on my ship!"

With a voyage to New Zealand to look forward to, Deborah worked hard at school for her last year and passed out in the top half of her class, for most of her subjects. The School Netball team, that Deborah captained, did particularly well, winning the local schools league and coming second in the County competition, for which she received a medal. Since Bertie was not due to leave for his next trip until the middle of August, she went to work with her mother in the warehouse for a few weeks, to help with the filing and to do a bit of stock taking, for which she earned a few pounds of pocket money.

The ship left from Southampton and Alice and Deborah travelled down there to wave her goodbye as she set out on her great adventure, dressed in her new ship's uniform that Bertie had got for her. He thought it would make her feel part of the crew and help her to be accepted by them as well.

She served all of the ships officers in their mess and helped the cook prepare the meals for everybody on board and even when it got very rough through the Bay of Biscay, she was not affected by sea-sickness and only dropped a tray of crockery the once, which was of course deducted from her pay!

They stopped at Gibraltar for a day and then set off through the Mediterranean Sea and Bertie took the ship along the coast to Alicante to give her some idea of what his old house in Benicarlo used to be like.

"It must have been beautiful there Daddy," she commented, "will you take me to see it sometime after we get back, so I can see where I was born, or would it be too painful for you to go there again?"

"No Deborah, it would not be painful and I would like to take you there and show you the town you were born in. That's a good idea, but I am not sure if your mother would want to come, as we have not discussed it in years."

They passed safely through the Suez Canal and down past Aden and made their next stop at Colombo where they unloaded some cargo and took on some Tea, destined for the Tea Shops of Sydney and Auckland.

By now several of the younger men had discovered the Captain's pretty daughter and Bertie realised he was becoming quite protective towards her and that his little girl had actually become an attractive young woman.

When they docked at Colombo he had some ship's business to attend to and left Deborah in the care of the cook, who was an older man and who had agreed to take her ashore and accompany her as she saw the sights of the town.

When she returned to the ship she had purchased a piece of Ceylon glass for her Granny and asked Bertie what he thought of it?

"It's beautiful Deborah, I am sure Granny will be thrilled with it," he said, "did you remember to get a receipt from the shop, like I told you to?"

"Yes dad, I am not a child you know. It was really strange though, because the man who served me was white and about your age, but he wasn't English, cook said that he might be Dutch but wasn't sure. Anyway, he asked me my name to put on the receipt and I said my name was Deborah Bannister and he replied, "I once had a friend named Bannister during the Boer War, I think his first name was Bert or something like that."

"Well I'll be blowed, did he sign the receipt that he gave you?"

"Hold on and I'll look. Yes, here it is," she said, taking it out and giving it to Bertie, "can you read what it says?"

"It looks like J Van Royt to me," Bertie replied, "where was the shop?"

She told him where the shop was located and he jotted it down in his diary before replying, "I may just know this man Deborah and it was during the Boer War that I met him."

Unfortunately Bertie did not have an opportunity to visit the shop to see if it really was Jan, but he made a mental note to look him up the next time he came to Colombo.

The ship's next port of call was Sydney and this time Bertie found time to take his daughter into the City to enjoy the sights. They both marveled at the new Harbour Bridge that was almost completed now and walked around Circular Quay and down through the area known as The Rocks, where a lot of the old buildings had been knocked down to make way for the new bridge.

She went shopping at The Rocks and found some opal earrings for herself and a nice opal brooch for her mother.

They finally arrived in Auckland in the middle of October 1931 and Rosie and Flo were delighted to meet Bertie and Deborah's daughter and insisted on her spending several weeks with them so that they could show her all the beautiful sights of North Island New Zealand.

They swam with dolphins in the warm blue waters of the Bay of Islands, they stood spellbound by the geysers at Rotorua and watched as the geyser that erupted at 10:15am each day, sent its plume of hot steam almost sixty feet into the air.

They visited lake Taupo, which is almost 240 sq miles in area and had been formed thousands of years ago by a super volcano, but Deborah's particular favourite activity was just to sit and soak in the hot mineral springs to the south of Lake Taupo.

The 'few weeks' soon became two months, as she enjoyed being with Rosie and Flo so much and in the end, it was agreed she could spend Christmas with them as Bertie had to start his next voyage back to England.

While Deborah spent her first Christmas in the sunshine of Auckland, Bertie his wife and Alice were in the cold damp climate of Harwich and all of them missing the youthful liveliness of Deborah; so while Christmas in Auckland was full of fun and excitement, Christmas in Harwich was the opposite.

"Did I mention that Deborah asked me if I would take her to visit Benicarlo next year when she comes back," Bertie announced over Christmas dinner.

"You mean if she comes back," snapped Alice, "I don't know why you allowed her to stay over there on her own

Bertie; goodness knows what might happen to her over there, a young woman by herself."

Bertie and Deborah looked at each other in Surprise and then Deborah answered, "I have told you already mum, that she is not on her own. You and dad met Rosie and Flo while you were there and you agreed after your own trip what a delightful pair they were. I know you are missing her, but she is sixteen and not a little girl and just remember Bertie was twelve when he went off to the Isle of Wight on his own and he was sailing to Australia and back on a Clipper when he was sixteen."

"I know, but it's different for a girl and since Robert died, I have relied on her company so much," Alice explained.

That evening, after they had gone upstairs to bed, Bertie and Deborah picked up the earlier conversation again.

"What did you say to our daughter after she asked you if you would take her to Benicarlo next year?" Deborah asked him.

"I said that I thought it was a good idea that she should visit Spain and see the town where she was born," he answered evasively.

"And what did you say about me?"

"What do you mean Deborah?"

"You know perfectly well what I mean. What did you say about me?" she repeated.

"I told her that I was not sure how you would react to the suggestion, but that you might not want to go there again."

"I see," Deborah said, "and why exactly did you think that I might not want to go there again Bertie?"

"Deborah, I am not looking for an argument with you. She asked me a question and I gave her that answer because I have absolutely no idea, whatsoever, how you might feel about going back to Benicarlo again. We have not talked about it for years and you never share any of your thoughts or feelings with me anymore, so how on earth could I tell her what you might decide to do!"

"Calm down Bertie. Let me point out that you are never here to have a conversation with. I spend more time talking to the dog than I do with you and when you are home, we can't have a conversation without your mother butting in."

"Leave my mother out of it Deborah, this is her house after all, remember? I had to sell ours to get you back from prison, or have you forgotten again?"

"How could I forget, you are so quick to remind me. I just find it incredible that the big shot sea captain, who is also a director of the shipping company he works for, can't afford to buy his own house to live in! I don't believe you Bertie, you just don't care about me anymore and I should have stayed in Chile or New Zealand where I had friends who cared about me and wanted me!"

"Well that says it all Deborah, now I know exactly where I stand, don't I?"

With which he rolled over onto his side, facing the other way and tried to go to sleep and she rolled over onto her other side and wept quietly. They both lay there for almost an hour when Bertie decided to get up and make himself a cup of tea downstairs.

He was sitting on a chair at the kitchen table when Deborah appeared in her dressing gown and sat down on the chair next to him. He got up and poured her a drink and then sat down again next to her.

"How could you possibly think I don't care about you Deborah? You are the only woman I have ever loved, I just don't know how to treat you or what to say to you any more, it feels like I have lost you to someone else."

"Maybe if we moved back to Spain and had our own house there again, things would be different," she said.

"But I thought you hated the idea of moving back to Spain, that's why I have never mentioned it to you," he replied.

"And I thought you were so cross at selling our lovely home, that you could not bear to go back there again, which is why I haven't mentioned it to you," she explained.

"So would you be happy to go to Spain next year, when Deborah comes home from New Zealand?" he asked.

"Yes, I would love to go there and visit Benicarlo and put flowers on Roberto's grave and see our friends. Maybe we could buy another piece of land and build a holiday home or something; could we afford to do that?"

"I don't see why not," he replied, "after all, you still speak to Deborah in Spanish and I still use mine occasionally, it would be good to have a place in the sun again. Don't say anything to mum about this yet though, I hadn't realised how much she had relied on her granddaughter since dad died and I am not sure it is a good thing, for our daughter's sake. She has her own life to live and her own mistakes to make!"

Meanwhile in Auckland, Rosie had started to take Deborah to work with her in the library and to teach her all about being a librarian.

"This is much more interesting than working in that draughty warehouse where my mum works," she said one day.

"Someone with your mother's condition should not be working in a draughty warehouse, in my opinion," Rosie replied. "Not at all suitable! You should think about taking a librarian's course when you get back to England Deborah, I will speak to your father about it when I see him next, if you would like me to?"

"Do you think so Rosie? Good idea, perhaps if you mention it first, I can tell him later. Isn't it what they call a 'Pincer Movement' in the army?" she said smiling.

"Which book did you get that from?" Rosie joked in return.

When Robert got back to New Zealand in February, he discovered that Shep and his family had already left on their tour of Europe and that the two girls had only met once, when Shep stopped for a few days in Auckland on the way out, but had not really hit it off together.

Rosie told him that in her opinion Deborah would make an excellent librarian and that he should enroll her on a course when she returned to England. Deborah confirmed that it was something she would like to do, so he agreed that she could make enquiries, but suggested that she might have to be eighteen or over to enroll.

They left Auckland on a sunny day at the beginning of March and arrived in Southampton on a wet day in April. Alice had not been feeling too well, so she and Deborah had decided not to travel down and meet the ship when it docked. Bertie spent a few days sorting out company business and then travelled to Harwich, where his presence almost went unnoticed due to the joyful celebrations at his daughter's return.

Before he left on his next trip, he made arrangements for them all to go to Spain in September for a holiday and had secured a junior position for his daughter in the local library, just to give her a year or two's experience on the job, to be sure that being a librarian was what she really wanted to do, before enrolling on a course.

"Your mother said she did not want to come with us at first," Deborah said, one evening after dinner, as they sat together on the settee, "but when I pressed her about it, she said that she didn't want to be in the way and that it would be good for us to be on our own."

"What did you say to that?" Bertie asked tentatively.

I told her that I would not listen to such nonsense and that I wanted her to come with us, so she changed her mind and said that she would love to go to Spain again."

"Well done Deborah, thank you, I appreciate that," he said cuddling up close.

The voyage back from New Zealand was held up in Sydney, so Bertie finally got back to England at the end of August with just two days to spare, before they had to catch a ship across to Valencia. They stopped there for a few days and then travelled, a little apprehensively, to Benicarlo, where Bertie had booked them all in, at a new hotel in town.

The next day they got up late, had breakfast and decided that they needed to go down to the beach and visit their old home. As they approached it, they saw two old men, sitting on the veranda, mending their nets.

It took Paco and Luca a little while to realise who was walking up their path in the morning sunlight and it seemed to dawn on the two of them at once, as they both jumped up out of their seats and rushed forward to greet their friend.

Having greeted the three ladies in a similar exuberant manner, they fetched a bottle of wine and some glasses and celebrated the arrival of their old friends. Word seemed to spread like wildfire that the Chavez family had come home and within an hour there was a party on the front veranda which must have included well over forty people.

When things had quietened down, Paco explained that he and Luca had only moved into the house that year, as the eight years they had promised to hold it for him were up and as they had heard nothing, decided to live in it themselves and just run a small fishing boat off the beach, for their own enjoyment.

That evening, back in the hotel, Deborah and Bertie discussed their options.

"I am sure if we pressed Paco and Luca, they would sell us the house, but it has become their home now and I would not want to ask this of them," Bertie said.

"I quite agree Bertie and if I am honest, I always had a slight feeling that it was your house and never 'our' house, as you already had a house there before we met. So I would really prefer to see if we can buy that piece of land a hundred yards down the beach from them and build something new, that would be 'our' home," she replied.

The next day they all went to the churchyard to lay some flowers on the grave of Roberto Bannister Chavez and were amazed to see the grave was neat and tidy and that flowers had obviously been placed there a few days before. They made enquiries about this and were told that each week Daria and Santo came and attended the little boy's grave.

Deborah went on her own to see her old friend and to thank her for the kindness which she and Santo had extended to her and her family over all the past eight long years. The two women hugged and cried and as Deborah explained later, "It was like a great dark cloud had lifted from me, that afternoon in Benicarlo."

They left Benicarlo at the end of their holiday but not before they had all agreed to build a holiday home there and had gone to the local solicitor, to instruct him to purchase the piece of land for them, that they had chosen.

Chapter 18
Three's a Committee

When Bertie got back to Christchurch, he discovered that both Shep and his wife had picked up a mild case of Malaria on their trip around the world, so he decided that he should remain there and run the business until Shep was fit enough to return to work. He became very worried one day, when the bank manager rang up and asked him to make an appointment to come and see him, as the bank were reviewing all of their customers overdrafts and were becoming concerned at the size of the overdraft that his company now had with them.

Shep finally came back to the office at the end of March and accompanied Bertie on his visit to see the bank manager, but it was another month before he was really fit and well again and Bertie was able to leave him to manage the company's affairs on his own and return to England to see his family.

He skippered the next available ship that was going to England and arrived in Harwich in the middle of May, to find that his daughter was still enjoying her job at the library, but was distressed that her dog Velvet had recently died, after being frightened by a horse. He was surprised to discover that his wife had given up her job at the warehouse, as the cold and damp atmosphere there had finally proved too much for her and given her a permanent cold, but she had failed to mention this in any of her letters to him.

"Bertie stop fussing," she snapped at him, after dinner one night, as they all sat around the table chatting. "I do not have T.B. again, it's just a cold; but I agree with you, that it would be good to go to Spain on holiday and enjoy the sunshine for a few weeks."

"OK Deborah, you win, now tell me about the house," he said.

"Well, I wrote and told you that we had finally purchased the land, just after Christmas and the builder you spoke to while we were over there, sent us some designs of both modern and traditional buildings. The three of us then discussed the good and bad points of each design and then picked the bits we liked from all the various buildings and got the local artist, who painted the picture of the Florin for mum, to paint a picture for us, which we sent to the builder, along with all of our notes."

"Goodness," said Bertie, "this reminds me of the definition of a camel!"

"We know dad," his daughter replied, "a camel is a horse designed by a committee."

"Shame on you Bertie," his mother scolded, "look at the picture first, before you make any more disparaging comments."

The copy of the picture was duly fetched and placed before him on the table and to be honest, it would have been a very brave man to find fault with something that his mother, wife and daughter had all agreed upon.

"Hey, I like it," he said, in genuine surprise, "I think that it will fit in well with the other buildings that are already there, but will still be very different from our old house. Well done ladies, good job."

They all beamed at him, confirming he had said the right thing.

"Do we know how far on the builder is with it yet?" he asked.

"He should have had the outside finished a week ago and be working on the inside of the house now, so everything should be completed by the end of August, if we are lucky," Deborah informed him, "when are you due back here again?"

"All being well, I should be back by the end of September," he said, "so why don't we plan on a family holiday to our new home in Spain for early October; the weather is still quite nice then. Will you be able to get time off from the library?" he asked his daughter.

"I will have to check with the chief librarian, but I am sure it will be all right for me to take my annual holiday at that time of year, as most people want to go between June and September and anyone with children, invariably wants to go in August, when it always seems to rain!"

Bertie returned to New Zealand and spent a couple of weeks working with Shep as they needed to recruit some new staff, as they had sold one of the older less efficient ships which had regularly travelled between Europe and Australia and purchased a smaller cargo/passenger ship to replace it. The new ship would handle some new lucrative contracts that Shep had negotiated around the home ports of New Zealand and Australia. Luckily Deborah had allowed an extra week on the date he had suggested for the holiday, so come Saturday 14th October 1933, the Bannister family set off for Valencia in Spain, with Bertie actually having three days to rest in England, before he had to leave again on holiday.

They stopped in the same hotel they had used previously, for a couple of nights, while they got some furniture and sorted the house out. Everyone had already chosen who was having which bedroom, so it was just a case of ordering their own bedroom furniture, Bertie having made it very plain to his mother and daughter, that his wife would choose all the other furniture in the house, without any assistance from them, unless specifically requested.

When the furniture van arrived, Bertie had strategically arranged to go fishing with Paco and Luca for the day, so he left Deborah in charge of the whole operation, while he had a pleasant day out with his friends. They fished and they talked about the good old days and how difficult life had become as a result of the Great Depression which had started in 1929.

"Does your New Zealand shipping company have plenty of regular work for its ships Bertie, or is it mostly occasional contracts that you pick up, like we did on El Burro?" Luca asked during their conversation.

"It used to be mostly regular business, but things have changed in the last few years and competition is so stiff, that we have to take what we can, when we can these days," he replied.

"And are you still managing to make a profit and pay your way then?" Paco enquired.

"Good question Paco," he replied thoughtfully, "like most companies these days, the profit margin is almost non-existent and we owe a small fortune to the bank, why do you ask?"

"The family still has the money it made from the sale of El Burro Volando to invest and they asked me to speak with you about an investment in the company you work for. What do you think?"

"Your family has been very good to me Paco and I would hate to take advantage of them, simply because we could do with a cash injection right now. I will talk to Shep, our Managing Director, when I get back to Christchurch and then write and let you know. But I really appreciate the trust your family has in me."

When he got back to the house the next day, everything was installed and in place and there seemed to be a reasonable peace among the three ladies. Bertie took them all out to a nice restaurant for a meal in the evening, where they discussed their plans for the rest of the holiday.

At the end of two weeks young Deborah had to go back to work at the library in Harwich and Alice had intended to go back with her; but her daughter-in-law's cough seemed to be getting worse and was giving them all cause for concern, so she opted to stay in Benicarlo with Deborah, in case she got any worse and was unable to travel home.

Bertie went with his daughter to Valencia to see her onto the ship that would take her back to England and her parting words to him were, "Now don't you worry about me dad, I am eighteen now and quite capable of looking after myself, so there is no need for you or gran to rush home to keep me company; stay here and look after mum for as long as you need to."

When the doctor called a few days later, he confirmed that Deborah had developed T.B. again and made arrangements for her to go to a specialist hospital in Valencia. Alice remained at Benicarlo and visited Deborah every third or fourth day with Luca, who had bought himself a Citroen C4 and had learnt how to drive. He was happy to assist his new neighbour by taking her to hospital to see Deborah and the two became good friends over the ensuing weeks.

Bertie was back in Christchurch in December and was devastated to discover that the company was in serious financial difficulties, due to the Depression and would have to fold. Unfortunately ship prices had crashed and the bank was cancelling their overdraft, which in effect, meant that it was going to take everything they possessed, leaving them with nothing.

Bertie wrote to Luca and Paco telling them the bad news about the company and they immediately cabled back to enquire if the new small cargo/passenger ship that he had told them about, had been sold yet, because the family would like him to bid for it on their behalf and continue running it for them in New Zealand and Australia in the short term, while they decided what they wanted to do with it, in the long term.

The ship came up for auction ten days later and Bertie duly bid on behalf of the Burra family and ended up buying it for them, for just under two thirds of what The Christchurch Wool and Shipping Company had paid for it only a year earlier.

Bertie spent a few weeks visiting the various shipping agents he knew in Australia and New Zealand and was able to re-sign most of the contracts that Shep had originally obtained for the ship and sign up a couple of new ones as well. This meant that there would be enough profitable work for the ship for the next twelve months, which would give him time to return to Spain to be with his sick wife and to discuss the Burra family's long term plans for their new acquisition. The captain and crew were happy to keep their jobs and work for another company, although they were surprised when the ship was renamed El Burro Volando II.

Although Shep was ruined financially, his spirit was not broken by the loss of the company and he happily agreed to run the back office for Bertie and manage things in New Zealand, while he was away in Europe.

He arrived in Spain in May to discover that Deborah's condition had worsened and the doctors had given up any real hope of her recovering. He and his mother discussed the situation and decided that Deborah should come home from hospital, to spend her last few months with them. With the help of his mother and the support of the local doctor and their many friends, they nursed her throughout her illness, right to the very end.

In November, young Deborah gave up her job at the library and shut up the house in Harwich to help nurse her mother and was there in Benicarlo with her Granny and dad when her mother died in late January 1935.

She was buried in the same cemetery as baby Roberto, just a few yards away, so that she could be with him in death, even though she had not been able to be with him in life.

Bertie and Deborah's house in Benicarlo Artist-Lynette Lilley

Bertie had many business discussions with the Burra family and agreed with Paco and Luca that he would return to New Zealand as soon as he had made proper arrangements for his mother and daughter; who had both expressed a preference of returning to England and keeping their house in Spain as a holiday home.

They all returned to Harwich in February, but the house now seemed very cold and empty and neither Deborah nor Alice wanted to live there anymore. As fortune would have it, there was a letter from the Rental Agent, informing them that the tenant of Harry's old flat in London had retired and gone to live in the country and that the flat was now vacant; but suggested that it should be re-decorated throughout, before it was advertised for renting out again.

Alice and Bertie sat down with Deborah and informed her that the flat had been left to her by Harry, but that it would not legally be hers until she was twenty one next year and that she had a post office account with several hundred pounds in it, as well.

"Can we go and see it Granny, I have always wanted to live in a big city, ever since the time I spent in Auckland with Rosie and Flo. There were so many things to see and do there in the City, I hated coming back here again," she announced, "there is nothing at all to do here in this little town!"

They all went to London a few days later and got the key from the agent and went to see the flat, which was not far from the Olympia Exhibition Hall. It had a large lounge with a small kitchen and bathroom and two fair-sized bedrooms and looked out onto a tree lined side street.

"It's so shabby," Alice remarked, "it does not look like it has been decorated since Harry moved in here, all those years ago. What do you think of it Deborah?"

"Granny, it's fantastic, is it really mine?" she answered. "It would be wonderful to live here, right in the middle of everything. Will you come and live here with me gran?"

"Me, live here! You don't want an old lady like me in your way, Deborah, surely!"

"Please gran, say you will. Dad has to go back to New Zealand soon and will be away for months again and I couldn't stay here in London on my own, now could I?"

They arranged for a decorator to come in and re-paper the walls and to paint the ceilings and woodwork and then for a carpet shop to come in and lay new carpets throughout the flat. Deborah brought her bedroom furniture from the house in Harwich and one or two choice pieces from the lounge and dining room that her Granny said she could have. Alice purchased a new single bed for herself and a new bedroom suite, leaving all her other furniture in the house at Harwich, just in case things did not work out for her, living in London with her granddaughter.

When the two ladies moved into the flat in late March, Bertie was already on his way back to Auckland, having obtained the position of first mate with a company he had previously dealt with in New Zealand.

"Well young lady, I guess now is the right time to discuss our finances," Alice decided over lunch one day. "I am sure that you are not expecting your father to be able to support us both in his current position. I have a small income from my savings and if we decide to sell the house in Harwich, once we know this arrangement is going to work, I will be quite comfortably off; but it will not be enough to support you as well."

"I don't expect you to support me gran, I know I have to work and I will look for a job tomorrow, I promise."

Despite several weeks of scouring newspapers and writing applications, nothing materialized for Deborah and in the end it was the Rental Agent who rang up and asked Deborah is she would be interested in working for him for a few weeks, while his receptionist was off getting married. Although it was not a job she had done before and Alice was not certain if it was her granddaughter's supposed business skills, or good looks, which had prompted the enquiry; she started on the Thursday before the woman left work to marry, in order to get two days handover, before she was working completely on her own.

Her experience in the warehouse and library had given Deborah the opportunity to see how different office systems should work and she soon came to the opinion that there was no actual system at work in that office, so she set about creating one herself. The Rental Agent noticed the difference quite quickly and was certain that the volume of business had increased in the short time Deborah had been working for him. When the two weeks were up he was sorely tempted to sack the original woman and keep Deborah instead, but she had realised by then, that a small office like that, was not where she wanted to spend her working life and happily left after a further couple of days during which she explained her new system to the returning newly-wed. The manager was so pleased with what she had achieved for him, that he wrote a glowing reference for her and told her that she might use him in the future as a referee.

Next, she wrote to the six top insurance companies in London, asking if they had any clerical positions vacant and was invited to attend for an interview with two of them. Each interview took well over an hour and included a written and oral examination, as well as a formal interview by the manager of the department she would be working for and the personnel manager. One company wrote to say that they had no suitable position to offer her at the moment, but would keep her name on their books, but the other company offered her a job as a trainee insurance clerk in their 'Household Insurance' department, based at their head office in Holborn.

She wrote back immediately accepting the offer and they confirmed that she should start work with them on Monday the 10th June 1935 at 9:00am.

"It will be so easy to get there gran, I can travel on the underground railway all the way, this is going to work out so well for us," she confirmed.

"I am so pleased for you my dear," Alice replied, "but I really think you should draw some of that money out of your saving account and go and buy yourself a nice suit to wear at the office, you want to impress everyone on your first day, don't you."

"Sorry to hit you with this as soon as you arrive mate," Shep said as Bertie sat down in the visitor's chair in the small office they now rented in Christchurch, "but I have had to sack the captain of El Burro Volando II and the ship is currently in Wellington waiting for a new skipper."

"It's nice to see you too Shep" Bertie replied, "what did he do, rob a bank?"

"Much worse than that," Shep replied, "he hit the dock at Wellington and the harbour police were called and found that he was drunk. I had no option but to sack him. I knew you were due back about now and would probably want to take over the ship yourself, so thought that if the crew knew it was my decision and not yours, that there would be no animosity against you."

"I appreciate that Shep and I will head up there tomorrow and take over as captain. I assume it is on its way to Auckland and then across to Australia. Please ring our agent in Wellington and let him know I am on my way. How many days have we been delayed so far and what did you do about the passengers that had booked with us?"

"We are about ten days late so far and I have informed the next three customers in Auckland, Brisbane and Sydney of the delay and they all said that it would be OK. The ship is not due to be in Melbourne till three weeks after that, so you have time to catch the schedule up by then. There were only a dozen passengers that were affected, of whom six are regulars, so I have returned all monies paid in advance and booked them on to other ships and told the regulars that we would give them 15% off their next two trips with us, to keep them loyal to us."

"Well done Shep, good thinking. Are we still making a profit on all of our contracts?"

"To be honest, the answer is no, but we are breaking even, which is more than most operators are doing these days. It's the growing passenger trade that is making the profit for us and if we can build that side of the business, whilst maintaining the freight contracts at just above cost, we should be able to do very nicely, thank you."

"I had long talks with the Burra family and you will be pleased to know that they hate bankers as much as we do and are willing to put up another five thousand pounds in cash, if we should need it."

"Marvelous, but at the moment, I am pleased to say that we don't need it. Everyone is paying on time and the passenger trade is all cash, but it's good to know that it is there if we do. Have they said what their long term plans are for the ship?"

"At the moment they are happy to leave the ship here, at least for the next year or so, but they know the Mediterranean so well, that I am certain they plan to take it back there to work, sometime in the future."

Bertie left the next morning and arrived in Wellington later that evening and went straight to the dock where El Burro

Volando II was tied up. The paint on the side that had hit the dock was scratched but there seemed to be no other damage to the ship. The Mate was there to meet him and to discuss the incident with Bertie.

"The captain had started drinking just after his eldest son was badly injured when he fell off his horse last year, but it did not seem to affect his judgement or his ability to run this ship. The boy died a month ago and the captain has not been the same since. I should have reported to Shep that his drinking had got worse, but the captain had enough on his plate already, poor chap, I just couldn't do that to him as well. I am sorry Skipper; I feel I have let you down."

Bertie carefully considered what he had just heard, before he replied, "Being First Mate, isn't just about your nautical ability and qualifications, it's about taking responsibility for yourself and those under your command; as well as the ship you are in charge of. We are lucky that the ship is not seriously damaged and no-one on the ship or on the dock was injured. Consider yourself lucky that Shep has spoken highly of you and that you have acted in the company's best interests since the police got involved. I am going to take no further action this time, but remember that the new owners are a very experienced group of seaman and will not tolerate this sort of behaviour on one of their ships."

Once the Mate had left the bridge and the door was closed, Bertie started chuckling to himself, as he remembered the antics that they had all got up to on the original El Burro Volando and felt a bit of a hypocrite over the lecture he had just given.

They sailed up to Auckland and Bertie left the Mate in charge of unloading and loading the cargo and went to visit Rosie and Flo to tell them about Deborah having died of T.B.

"I told your daughter that a warehouse was no place for her mother to be working," Rosie commented, "I am so sorry for your loss Bertie, I know how much you loved your wife."

With which she put her arms around him and held him while he wept on her shoulder.

"I'll make us a cup of tea, can you stop the night or do you need to get back to your ship? Flo and her husband are using your old room now, but I can easily make up a bed for you downstairs on the couch if you like. He's a nice man and likes to go and meet her from hospital when he can, they should be home soon. He's a good bit older than her, they actually met through me as he works with me in the library."

"Thanks but no, I won't stop. I want to get back and check how things are doing, new crew and all that, I want to keep them on their toes. So how is it working out with you and Flo and her husband in the same house together?"

"To be honest Bertie, it is not ideal. This house is far too big for me on my own, but nothing is selling right now, even though I would like to move to something smaller. Flo wants to carry on living here as it is so convenient for both of their jobs, but can't afford to buy it off me and as you well know, she is a very independent, strong willed woman and should really be in a place of her own now that she is married. Added to which, I am due to retire next year when I am sixty and I would love to go on a long holiday and visit Europe and especially Aylesbury in England, where my grandparents originally came from."

Flo and her husband returned home and after introductions and the swapping of good and bad news and several cups of tea, he left his friends and walked back to the ship, but not before Rosie had told him to make sure he had a few days spare next time he was in Auckland and to come and stay with her for a day or two.

The ship left Auckland and sailed to Brisbane and from there went on to Sydney, where Shep had arranged for the damaged paintwork to be sorted while it was in dock. As Bertie had a few days to spare, he took a ride out to the house of his old friend Skip on the off-chance that someone might be at home. Skip's wife Edna opened the door when he knocked.

"Look what the dog dragged in, Bob Harwich, what are you doing here?" she exclaimed.

Bertie gave Edna a big hug, which also gave him a moment to stop and think who Bob Harwich was and once the penny had dropped he replied, "Edna, you look more gorgeous than ever, what a beauty you are!"

"Come in Bob, Skip is in town getting supplies, he should be back in an hour, can I get you a beer?"

He sat down in a big old armchair and thought about his situation and decided it was easier to remain 'Bob Harwich' than to give Edna a lengthy complex explanation. A very large man in his late twenties walked into the room carrying two beers, one of which he gave to Bertie.

"Good to see you again Bob," he said, offering his hand.

Bertie shook the outstretched hand and looked at the man, "I'm sorry mate, but I am afraid I don't remember your name."

"You must remember him, he's Tom, Skip's sister's little boy," Edna reminded him as she bounced into the room.

"Of course, Tom, good to see you, what are you doing with yourself these days?"

"Bit of this, bit of that, you know the sort of thing Bob," he answered evasively.

Bertie nodded, indicating that he understood what Tom meant and as if to save them any more embarrassment, as to what Tom actually did, Skip arrived back from town and they all went outside to meet him.

"Bob, you old pirate, it's good to see you, we were only talking about you last week, what do you think of my new Ute?" Skip asked.

"Looks great mate, I haven't seen anything like this before, what did you call it?"

"A Ute. I think it stand for a Utility vehicle, Ford make them. It is posh enough to go to church in on a Sunday and keep Edna clean and dry and tough enough for me to use on the farm or for taking animals to market, want a ride? Get in, you can drive, I'll tell you what to do, it's easy and there is nothing to hit out here anyway."

While they drove round the farm, they chatted about what each of them had been doing over the last few years and Bertie learned that Skip had given up the sea to become a farmer, supplying food for the Sydney market.

"Edna was getting fed up with me being away all the time, so in the end it was a question of giving up the sea or giving up Edna. Easy choice, eh mate?"

"Too true," Bertie replied in a non-committed way, "so what's this about young Tom, sounds a bit dodgy to me?"

"That nephew of mine has got in with a really bad lot, like that bloke in Sydney that you and I met, remember Bob. I don't think he has done anything really bad yet, but it's only a matter of time. He is so big and strong and totally fearless, he can't go into a pub without having a fight with someone and has been in the local lock-up so many times that my sister has just given up on him. No-one knows he is here with me and I want it to stay that way, so please don't tell anyone about seeing him here. I don't suppose you are going to Fremantle in Western Australia on this trip are you."

"Afraid not, why do you ask?"

"It's a different country over there; he could lose himself there and start over again, if you get my drift."

"I have been trying to secure a contract with an importer in Fremantle, shipping machinery from Sydney to there and to Broome, if it comes off I will let you know and I would be happy to take Tom with me, has he been to sea before?"

"Yes, he came with me for a few years before I became a farmer, so he is pretty handy on a ship, he acted as my Second Mate before I retired, but he has no qualifications or anything. It was after he came back here that he started to get into trouble, so I feel sort of responsible for him."

Bertie stopped the night on the farm and had a few more 'driving lessons' in the Ute before going back to the ship. He oversaw the repair work, loaded the cargo and then headed out to sea again.

When they arrived in Melbourne, he went along to the Ford garage and test drove the latest model Ute and promptly purchased one for himself. The manager recommended someone in town who would give him some proper driving lessons, which he diligently undertook, for every day the ship was in port.

The Ute was covered with tarpaulins to protect it from the elements and was made secure on the foredeck. Shep had placed an advertisement in a Melbourne newspaper offering a special group rate for six or more people travelling between Melbourne and New Zealand, which proved to be very successful, as all berths were filled with a waiting list.

He arrived back in Christchurch in late May, having deposited most of his Melbourne passengers at Auckland and Wellington, with just a few going all the way to Christchurch in South Island. The Ute attracted a lot of interest when it was unloaded and driven round town by its new proud owner, who also instructed Shep on how to drive it. Various enquiries were made by interested parties about bringing more Utes back on the next trip to satisfy the expected demand from local farmers and Shep agreed to have discussions with the customs people on the matter.

Bertie made three more round trips that year, bringing a further eight Utes into New Zealand and always having a full compliment of passengers on the return leg from Melbourne.

He was pleased to write to Paco and Luca at the end of the year, telling them how profitable the venture was proving to be and sending them their first cheque for their share of those profits.

The icing on the cake for Bertie and Shep, was that they finally managed to agree favourable terms with the Fremantle agent, for shipping machinery from Sydney to Fremantle and Broome.

Chapter 19
Family Problems

Bertie spent the first anniversary of his wife's death in Christchurch, with Shep and his family. They kept him company, when he wanted company and left him alone when he needed to be on his own.

Deborah and Alice were at the flat in London, although they had managed to get across to Benicarlo during the previous September for a couple of weeks and stay in the house and visit the two graves and take flowers. Luca was delighted to see them again and took them out and about in his motor car most days, although Deborah preferred to stay home on her own sometimes.

Bertie was kept very busy with El Burro Volando II, but when Luca wrote to say that they wanted to see him on business, he made arrangements with Shep and a recently retired captain friend, to look after the ship for a couple of months and then wrote to Deborah and Alice, suggesting that they all met up in Spain at the end of August for Deborah's twenty-first birthday.

Alice had travelled out on her own to Spain at the beginning of August, as there were a few repair jobs that needed to be carried out on the house, according to Luca's letter to them, which needed someone to oversee. He met her at the dockside and drove her to Benicarlo and the two friends had a most enjoyable three weeks together before Bertie and Deborah arrived.

The party was held at the same restaurant where Bertie had proposed to Deborah all those years before and he could not help noticing that his daughter seemed to spend an awful lot of her time with Santo's son Marco, a good looking lad about the same age as her.

Bertie, Alice, Luca and Paco were having breakfast together the next day, when Deborah joined them looking rough and holding her head. It was the first time she had woken up with a 'hang-over' and was not enjoying the sensation.

"Morning," she said, "ah, the glare, I need my dark glasses," and went back into the house again.

Alice followed her in and found her an Aspirin for her headache and made her some toast and coffee and sat her down in a cool shady part of the house.

"Oh Gran, it feels like someone is using my head for a drum and I was violently sick in the night."

"I know, I heard you and don't look to me for any sympathy. Let this be a lesson to you young lady, everything in moderation. I don't ever want to see you in this state again. I am seventy eight and have only been drunk once in my lifetime and that was enough for me and I hope that when you are my age, you will be able to say the same thing too," with which she left her alone and went back outside.

"That was a bit harsh mum," said Bertie, "it was her birthday after all."

"In polite society Bertie, it is considered very rude to listen to other people's conversations," and that was the final word on the subject.

When Bertie sat down with Paco and Luca to discuss business, the first item on the agenda, was the Spanish Civil War, which had commenced in July of that year.

"It is not good Bertie," Paco said, "Spaniard will be fighting Spaniard and it could go on for several years yet. Who knows how it will end."

"Does this affect your decision to bring El Burro back to Spain then?" Bertie enquired.

"It most certainly does my friend. The family have discussed the matter and firmly believe that since the ship is our biggest asset, it is best kept where it is, until things have settled down here and it is safe to sail her to Benicarlo. We are delighted with what you and Shep have managed to achieve in New Zealand, despite the world's business problems and we are asking you to consider staying over there for another year or so, at least until early 1938, when things should be a lot more peaceful and settled here. Are you prepared to do that for us Bertie?"

"I love it over there and we have a great team working with us and I believe the business opportunities should continue to be good for us, but I am a bit worried about my mother and daughter, things seem to be getting a bit strained between them."

"Your daughter is a grown woman and needs to be on her own now Bertie," Luca commented.

"That's exactly what I mean Luca, but I can't let my mother live on her own in Harwich, the loneliness would be devastating for her and she has given up so much for me and Deborah."

"Let me stop you right there my friend," Luca interrupted, "I have already taken the liberty of discussing this with your mother and she would be quite happy to stay here in Benicarlo and leave Deborah on her own in London. She was just worried what your reaction would be to the idea."

"My reaction, why should she be worried about my reaction?"

At this point Paco blew a kiss towards Bertie's house and then one towards Luca and smiled.

"Oh I see, I see, I had no idea. I would be delighted for the two of you Luca, absolutely delighted," Bertie said smiling from ear to ear.

When Bertie discussed the 'idea' with Deborah, she was not at all impressed with the possible new arrangements.

"I admit that I do not need Gran watching over me any more Dad, but surely she can just go to Harwich and live there, she has plenty of friends there after all. I really don't see why she would want to come here on her own and for you to suggest that she might want to be here because of that old man next door, is just ridiculous!"

"Calm down Deborah and keep your voice down, let's try and have a civilized conversation here. This is my house, not yours and if your Gran wants to come here to live, then that is O.K. by me, I am not asking for your permission. You have your flat in London to live in and it would make a lot of sense to sell Gran's house in Harwich. The proceeds would give her enough funds to enjoy her twilight years to the full, in any way and with anyone that she chooses."

"You are right dad, I was being selfish, goodness knows, she has the same right to a little bit of happiness as everyone else."

At the end of the holiday, Deborah went back to London and her job at the insurance company, where she was now a clerk in the 'Life' department and Alice and Bertie went to Harwich. They packed up Alice's and Bertie's personal things and had them shipped to Spain, took a few more small pieces of furniture to Deborah, for her flat and then sold what was left and put the house up for sale with a local Estate Agent. They saw a solicitor and drew up all the paperwork, before heading back to Spain.

She continued living in Bertie's house down the road from Luca and although the two behaved like an old married couple, they never actually went through a formal ceremony, but their love, consideration and respect for each other was there for all to see and they were regularly seen together on their long drives out in the countryside.

Bertie eventually returned to Christchurch in December and took over being captain of El Burro once again. The ship had suffered a minor altercation with a tug boat and was in the dock at Wellington for repairs. To be on the safe side, Shep had laid her off for the whole of December and given the crew a month off, just in case things took a bit longer than expected.

"Let me get this straight Bertie," Shep queried, "they do not want us to send them a cheque this year for the profits, but to hang on to the money over here and to use it to knock four of the smaller cabins apart and make two deluxe cabins instead and to put some new equipment in the galley to provided some better cooking facilities for our passengers."

"Got it in one," Bertie replied. "They eventually want to take the ship back to the Mediterranean and offer two week cruises to people. They believe it will be the most profitable thing to do with the ship, once the Civil War is over and they want us to get some experience of the cruising business now. So while the ship is in dock, we should go up there and organize the re-fit, which would allow us to start again fresh in January."

"You're the boss, but it could have a detrimental effect on our freight business you know."

"I know and I told them that, but they are prepared to take the risk and what's more, they want us to buy another similar boat, while prices are still depressed, to add to the fleet."

They both went to Wellington and found a marine architect with the relevant 'refit' experience and through his contacts, the work was started during the second week of

December. The company commissioned to do the work said that while it was not a major job, with the Christmas holidays about due, they could not guarantee that everything would be completed until early January; so Shep went back to Christchurch and Bertie decided to go up to Auckland and visit Rosie for Christmas.

"She does not live here anymore Bertie," Flo informed him when he knocked on the door of the house she used to live in. "Mum retired from the library in October, I thought she wrote and told you."

"I probably passed her letter in mid Atlantic somewhere Flo, where has she gone to, on her grand holiday I suppose?"

"No, that's all on hold at the moment, she fell off a ladder at work in her last month and broke her arm and is only just out of plaster. I rent her house off her now and she has a small cottage that she rents, it's actually quite close to Home Bay, where you first came ashore with your wife. She would love to see you again; I'll give you the address."

Bertie got a taxi to Rosie's new home and after several attempts to rouse her, decided to walk round the back and see if she was in the garden, as Flo had warned him that it was a bit of a wreck when she moved in and she was spending several hours each day, getting it in order.

The side gate was a bit stiff and as he pushed it open, he realised it had been wedged shut by the dustbin, which was now making its way across the garden. Luckily, Rosie had just walked into the house to wash her hands, so when it fell over and tipped its contents onto the grass, no-one was injured.

"Whoops, sorry Rosie," he said, "I didn't realise the dustbin was there. I'll clear up the mess."

"You most certainly will not clear up the mess in your best suit, you can go and change into that old boiler suit you used to wear first Bertie, how wonderful to see you again, come in; we can deal with that mess later."

While Bertie was visiting the bathroom, Rosie cleared up the mess from the dustbin and pulled it back against the gate. She then gave him a quick tour of her little house before they sat down for a drink.

"This is nice Rosie, ideal for you now that you have retired. How long have you managed to lease it for?"

"It actually belongs to an old neighbour of mine, so there is nothing formal between us, but I can stay here for as long as I like. Which reminds me, how long are you in Auckland for, are you stopping for Christmas?"

"I have to be back in Wellington for early January and I have booked a hotel room for a couple of nights, while I just checked everything out," he said.

"I was going to run a Bed and Breakfast again here once I have decorated the other bedroom, so why not stay here with me, then you can help me decorate it and earn your keep."

"You sure I won't be in the way?" he queried.

"Don't be silly Bertie, you know how much I enjoy your company and you will be most welcome to stay here."

After a drink and a chat, Bertie went back to the hotel to get his case and cancel his accommodation and took the opportunity to telephone Shep at his home in Christchurch. They talked about the first cruise with the new deluxe cabins and Shep was delighted to report that one of the cabins was already booked from Auckland to Fremantle and back, but that the other one was still vacant. He said that they could do with a new cook on board, as the old one was not really up to anything more demanding than the basic food that the crew were served.

"You are not seriously suggesting that we should get rid of old Brock," Bertie said, "he has been working for you since before I joined the company; the crew would mutiny if you did that."

"No of course not, but we need to do something, do you have any bright ideas," Shep responded.

"Well I do actually. At least for this first trip, while we iron out all the wrinkles. Rosie, my friend in Auckland, has recently retired and she is an excellent cook and I am sure that if we offered her the other cabin, on the understanding that she would cook for and look after the other passengers, that she would jump at the opportunity."

"Sounds great to me," said Shep, "let me know if she is not interested and I will make enquiries elsewhere, but let's go forward on the assumption that you can sweet talk her into it."

"But I have never done anything like this before Bertie, I have been a librarian all of my working life, I would hate to let you down."

"You won't let me down Rosie and there will only be two deluxe passengers and maybe six or eight others to worry about it. You said you have always wanted to travel and this is your chance to try it. Brock will still be around to help you and to look after the crew and we could really do with someone with your skills, to write us a set of procedures for handling our growing number of passengers, rather than just play it by ear as we do at the moment."

"All right then, I'll give it a go. Fancy starting a new career at my age, Flo will be surprised."

She was right, Flo was astounded, "Are you sure you know what you are doing mum, you have never seen inside of a ship before, let alone sailed on one and suppose the new kitchen equipment isn't working properly, what will you do then?"

"Bertie has suggested that I go down to Wellington with him and meet this Brock that I will be working with and try out all the equipment for them on the way up to Auckland. Anyway Flo, don't be such a spoil sport, I have only just retired, there is plenty of life left in me yet."

Rosie arrived in Wellington with Bertie on Wednesday 6th January 1937 and spent the rest of the week finding her way round the ship and getting to know the crew and testing out the new equipment. Everything was made to work eventually, but she was not very happy with the layout of the galley and got the workmen back for a day, while things were changed round to suit her requirements.

Shep and Bertie were a bit worried as to how Brock would react to a lady cook in his galley and to be honest the first day or so was quite difficult, but Rosie was her normal pleasant self and when she happened to mention that her husband had served in the same regiment in the War that Brock had served in, a bond was formed and a new friendship was created.

Apart from being seasick a couple of times, Rosie managed well on the ship and soon proved that she and Brock were a formidable team. News soon spread of the deluxe cabins and four more of the smaller cabins were turned into deluxe cabins later in the year.

Shep purchased a second cargo/passenger ship for the Burra family in July and after a refit of the galley and passenger quarters, it was back in service by September under the care of the Mate from the El Burro, who had now passed his Masters Certificate. Rosie and Brock carried on working together until October, but when she fell and hurt her arm again they decided it was time for both of them to retire. He proposed to her, she accepted and they were married in Auckland on Saturday the 6th November 1937, with Flo acting as Maid of Honour and Bertie as Best Man. The happy couple had a two week honeymoon at Paihia in the Bay of Islands, before taking up residence together in the cottage at Home Bay, Auckland.

Bertie had completely forgotten about Skip and his problem nephew when he called at their farm in February 1938. He knocked at the door several times and was surprised when Skip opened it and stood there, pointing a loaded pistol at him.

"Bob, grief mate, I thought you were someone else. Come in and put your hands down, you look ridiculous."

"Hi Skip, Edna, good to see you both, what's going on here exactly?" Bertie enquired.

Skip got him a beer and they all sat down together around the large wooden table.

"Before we go any further, I have to tell you that my real name is not Bob Harwich, but Bertie Bannister. Bob was just a name I used to get out of England un-detected and the rest of the story about my wife being in prison in Chile, you already know. Sorry to have misled you mate, but it was safer that way."

"No worries. It's that nephew of mine again Bob, err Bertie, he has really gone and done it this time. He was part of a gang that held up the bank in the city two weeks ago. Most of them got away with a large amount of cash and gold coins, but one man was wounded and is in hospital, the gang are pretty sure he will talk to save himself."

"Do you know where your nephew is hiding, is he wounded?" asked Bertie.

"I have him tucked away on the outskirts of the farm and he is in good shape. Although I think that he is safe there for the moment, we have had the police round twice already and

Edna thinks they have been watching the farm. They must have guessed that he was involved in the robbery and want to interrogate him."

"Last time I was here Skip, you mentioned getting him to Western Australia where he could start over; I am going to Freo and Broome this trip with some machinery, by way of Melbourne and Adelaide, perhaps there is something I could do to help you."

"Thanks mate, but I wouldn't want to put you in any danger," Skip replied.

"What's wrong with you Skip," Edna screamed at him, "Bob is offering us a way out of this nightmare. Of course we would like you to take Tom with you, good riddance to bad rubbish, I say."

"Edna, shut it," he shouted back at her, "she's right though, but how can we make it happen, without dropping you right in it?"

In the end the solution was quite simple. Bertie spread the word in port that he was looking for a Second Mate to go with him on a one way trip to Broome, as from there he had already got someone else lined up. Skip had a word with an older friend of his and he wrote a letter to Bertie recommending a certain Bob Harwich for the Second Mate position. Bertie entered the appropriate information in his log and Tom Raymond slipped aboard El Burro one dark night just before the ship left Sydney, bound for Melbourne.

He was introduced to the crew as Bob Harwich and spent most of his time down below in the engine room and only came up on deck at night, when there was no-one around.

The crew were not too sure about this rough looking giant in their midst, but the Skipper said he was O.K. and that was good enough for them. When they called at Melbourne and Adelaide, Bob did not go ashore with the rest of the crew but he did get caught on deck one night while at Adelaide, by one of the passengers who had also decided to stay on the ship. The passenger disembarked at Fremantle and no-one thought any more about it.

The plan was for Tom to leave the ship at Broome and find work up there for a year or two, before heading down south to Geraldton or Perth and Fremantle. Bertie had talked with him about changing his identity and said that from his experience, it was safer if the old and new names were similar, as it as easy to forget who you are supposed to be.

"Instead of being Tom Raymond, why not tell everyone you are Ray Thomas; that will make life a lot easier for you," Bertie suggested, "but not yet, you need to remain Bob Harwich while you are with me."

From Fremantle they steamed up to Geraldton where they unloaded some more of the cargo and once all the passengers had left the ship, Bertie and Tom went ashore. They found a pub and had a drink and something to eat and Bertie picked up the newspaper that a previous customer had left and started to thumb through the pages.

He got to page six and then gasped and turned white. The story was about the bank robbery in Sydney that Tom had been involved in and there were pictures of four men that the police wanted to interview, one of which was of Tom Raymond, as a young man.

"Look at this Tom, but don't make any reaction or say anything, do you understand?"

Tom nodded and Bertie passed him the newspaper which he studied.

"I am going to get up and pay the barman what we owe him, you just walk casually to the door and wait for me. Right, lets go," Bertie told him, tucking the newspaper into his jacket pocket.

The two men rose from their seats and left the bar, after Bertie had settled their account. They slowly walked back to the dock and boarded the boat, going straight to Bertie's cabin, where they each had a glass of whisky to settle their nerves.

"We have to assume that someone will recognise your photograph and report the fact to the police," Bertie said, "we know the passenger at Adelaide had a good look at you and even some of the crew may feel they have to say something."

"The photo was taken when I was twenty one Skipper, that's nine years ago, I have changed a lot since then," Tom replied.

"You have changed Tom, but because of your size, you do tend to stand out in a crowd. I am sorry mate, but it is definitely about time that Tom Raymond died, that is the only safe answer for you and me, that I can think of."

"Sounds a bit dramatic Skipper, what exactly do you have in mind?"

That evening, just before the ship was about to sail, a very drunk Bob Harwich staggered onto the ship and started to argue with Bertie about nothing in particular. He made the mistake of taking a swing at 'Basher Bannister' and was immediately flattened by a straight left to the jaw. He went out like a light and the captain ordered that he be dumped at the stern of the ship, where he could do no more harm.

Two of the crew carried him to the stern and Bertie went back there a bit later and covered him with a tarpaulin, along with a couple of sacks that were also at the stern of the ship.

"Good luck Tom," he whispered, "and make sure you stay out of trouble this time. A lot of people have taken some big risks in helping you escape, so don't waste this opportunity."

Tom nodded his appreciation and said, "Thanks Skipper, I won't forget you; are you sure you don't want some of the gold coins for all your trouble?"

"I am absolutely certain Tom! If they search my boat when I get to Broome, I don't want them to find anything of yours at all, is that clear?"

As the boat pulled out of Geraldton, no-one noticed a shadowy figure climb over the side of the ship and silently drop into the water. Tom was a good swimmer and soon made shore and disappeared into the vastness of Western Australia.

Some hours later when they were steaming through Shark Bay, Bertie walked to where Tom had been lying and after making sure that no-one was watching, heaved the largest of the two sacks, which had previously been filled with stones, into the water and shouted out loudly, "Man Overboard. Man Overboard!"

Several crew members came running up and Bertie gave the command to 'Stop Engines'.

"That drunk Harwich has just fallen overboard," Bertie announced, "I should have tied him down, damned fool!"

"You'll never spot him here Skipper," the Mate said, "if he doesn't drown, the sharks are sure to get him."

Just at that moment there was a faint cry, probably from a distant sea bird.

"That was probably him, I say again it is a waste of time searching for him," the Mate repeated.

Nevertheless, they did search for Bob Harwich for a couple of hours, before Bertie reluctantly gave the order to proceed on their journey and left the Mate in charge of things, while he made a detailed record of the whole incident in the Ships Log.

When they arrived in Broome, there was a reception committee waiting for them, just as Bertie had feared. While he was taken to the police station to be interrogated, the police and customs officers made a thorough search of the ship and interviewed all the passengers and crew.

With a few minor variations, the same story was given by crew and passengers alike. The man calling himself Bob Harwich had come aboard drunk and had been knocked unconscious by the captain, who incidentally had bruised knuckles to prove it. In the early hours of the morning they had heard a splash followed by the 'Man Overboard' cry and had then spent the next two hours, fruitlessly searching Shark Bay.

The search of the ship revealed a small portion of the captain's supply of whisky and other essentials, which were confiscated; but nothing else.

Bertie produced the letter from the old skipper in Sydney, recommending Bob Harwich to him and by the time this was properly checked out, the old man had conveniently passed away and could not testify one way or the other.

The police inspector closed the door to the interview room and put his mouth close by Bertie's ear as he said, "I don't believe a word of this letter Captain Bannister, because we both know that Tom Raymond was not only a nasty piece of work, but he was also related to an old friend of yours, wasn't he. Don't try and deny it, because my colleagues in New South Wales were watching their house and saw you go in there to visit them while your ship was docked in the harbour."

Bertie remained silent and sat still.

"I really don't envy you the task of telling his family that he just fell over the side of your ship and got eaten by the sharks. Someone is going to tell them that you knocked him out cold and they are all going to think that you pushed him over the side when no-one was looking and took the gold. You are going to be a very un-popular man in Sydney Captain."

"Can I go now Inspector, as I have a cargo to unload?" Bertie asked firmly.

"You can go, but if I were you, I would not want to come back to Broome again, we know you have hidden that gold somewhere. You are not welcome here; do I make myself clear? Tom Raymond may have been a badun, but he did not deserve to go like that!"

Bertie did not return to Broome any more, but when he was in Sydney some months later, he did call on Skip and Edna again, out at their farm.

"It's so good to see you again mate," Skip said greeting him, "Edna, come and see who's here."

"Bertie, wonderful to see you, how are you? It was a real shame that you were not able to make young Tom's memorial service the other month; it was beautiful, really beautiful, even his mother was able to say something nice about him."

"Glad to hear it Edna, he was a good lad, just got into bad company, but I didn't really think it would be appropriate for me to come to the church though," Bertie answered.

"Yeah, you're probably right," Skip said, "my second cousin on my mother's side was there and she told me how delighted she was to get a postcard about a week before the service, from a friend of hers in Fremantle, a young fellow called Ray Thomas. It appears he is well and has a job on a farm."

"That's nice to hear," said Bertie smiling, "let's hope he has learned his lesson though!"

Chapter 20
Here we go again

"Morning Skipper, welcome aboard, how was your weekend?" the First Mate asked, as Bertie boarded the El Burro Volando II in Auckland, after spending the weekend with Rosie and Brock.

"Very enjoyable thanks, Brock seems to have settled down to domestic bliss, a lot better than we all expected," Bertie replied.

"Are all the passengers on board and did we manage to get a booking for the other deluxe cabin, or is it still empty?" Bertie enquired.

"We have a booking, but they are not here yet," the mate replied. "Shep said they were an English couple on holiday in New Zealand and Australia; who were only arriving from Christchurch on Saturday, so they might still be a bit weary from their drive up here."

"Send one of the crew out to look for them, in case they are walking around lost somewhere. I can give them another hour and then we will have to depart."

Bertie went to his cabin and then to the bridge, where he was checking that everything was in order, when the Mate came in and announced that the last two passengers had arrived and were now on board and were getting settled into their cabin. He gave the order for starting the engines and soon had the ship slowly steaming out of port on its way to Sydney.

"Did I mention Skipper, that the passenger from England said that he thought he might know you?" the Mate informed Bertie, after an hour or so at sea.

"No you didn't," Bertie answered; but it was not unusual for a passenger to have sailed with a captain on a ship before, especially one with all of Bertie's years of experience on the world's oceans and seas.

"Sorry, I forgot. He said it might have been in the Mediterranean; his name is Callard, Michael Callard; ring any bells with you?"

Bertie turned towards his Mate and said, "It certainly does, I don't suppose his wife's name is Anne, by any chance?"

"Yes it is, so you do know them then!"

"Indeed I do. Michael Callard saved my life once, when we were in Nigeria," he said out loud, "and almost got me killed on several more occasions," he added quietly to himself.

"Tell the cook that I will be dining with the Callards in my cabin tonight, will you please," he ordered the crewman, who was on the bridge with them.

"Right away Skipper," the man replied and left to deliver the message.

Once he had gone, the Mate looked at Bertie and said, "You have suddenly turned very white Skipper, is everything O.K? Do you want me to join you for dinner this evening, or would you rather be with your old friends on your own?"

"Let's just say, that I doubt very much if they are the bearers of good news, but thanks for the offer. Whatever it is that Mr. Callard wants me for, I will need to be on my own with him and his wife to hear it. Please keep this conversation to yourself and I will keep you informed of any developments."

"Well this is nice Bertie, Anne and I were only saying a few weeks ago that it would be nice to catch up with you again and we were so sorry to hear of the death of Deborah, such a brave lady."

"Thanks Michael and it's good to see both of you again too, but this is no accident is it, but let's eat first and we can discuss why you are here later."

The main course was Snapper, which Brock had caught the previous evening and the fruit pie which followed was one of Rosie's specialties.

"I have to warn you that the food will probably not be this quality for the whole trip, but we will do our best for our important English visitors," Bertie quipped at the end of the meal. "A glass of Port, for both of you? Cigar Michael?"

He poured three glasses of vintage port and passed the box of Havana cigars to Michael. They made small talk while the steward came and served coffee and cleared the dinner things away and then Anne excused herself and went to their cabin, leaving the two old friends to talk.

"I assume you are still with the same Secret Service mob, that you were with before?" Bertie asked Michael.

"I did return to the Navy for about twelve years and sailed the seven seas, but I was invited to join them again a couple of years ago, just about the time when the Spanish Civil War was getting off the mark."

"Nasty affair that," said Bertie, "is that why you are here, because you know I work for a Spanish family, who own this ship?"

"Well sort of my friend, but before I say anything more, I have to remind you that you did once sign the Official Secrets Act and are still bound by it. Is that clear?"

"Perfectly clear Michael, but don't you people ever let a chap off the hook and allow him to retire and get on with his life again. I am almost sixty now, you know and not as strong and active as I was twenty five years ago."

"Rubbish, you are as strong as an ox and fitter than most men half your age, there isn't a pound of fat on you and you have excellent health and your own teeth. You'll have to do better than that to escape the evil clutches of his Majesty's Secret Service," Michael replied, laughing at him.

"Go on, you've got me, want do you want with me this time?"

"We believe the Spanish Civil War has only got a few more months to run, but by this time next year, we expect that the whole of Europe will be embroiled in another Great War. Herr Hitler will not be appeased and will not be content until Germany has control of the whole of mainland Europe."

"Good grief, that's terrible news. So much for the Great War, being the last major conflict. What about America, will they get involved this time?"

"We think so, but no-one is certain; but we are pretty certain that General Franco will keep Spain neutral again, which is why we are having this conversation, Capitan Chavez."

"But I have told you before, that the German's suspected me of being a British spy, when I was a prisoner at Saranda during the last war, surely it would be far too risky to try that charade again?"

"We don't believe so. Our people destroyed most of the German intelligence records after the last war and anyway, when was the last time you met anyone in the Mediterranean area, who knew you from back then? Most of them are dead or retired. At worst, people may suspect that you have used your dual Nationality to escape war service, but we honestly don't foresee any greater risk than that, if you are willing to become Capitan Chavez for us once again."

"Assuming you are correct, what is it that the British Government wants me to do for them this time?"

"Firstly, take this ship back to Spain and change its registration from New Zealand to Spain. It already has a

Spanish name and is owned by a Spanish family, so no-one will be too surprised at your doing this. We would like you to leave the other ship here, as it would be ideal for us to requisition and to use as a hospital ship, once hostilities start and that should, in theory, keep it safe from attack as well."

"What about my daughter, Deborah, she lives in London, can I move her to Spain as well, to be with me and her Granny?"

"Good idea, especially since your mother has not been too well lately."

"I didn't know that, what's wrong with her?"

"Nothing serious, she is just getting old, after all she is eighty and has probably had too much sun of late. We would like to suggest that Deborah sells her flat in London and buys a house in the fishing village of Roses, it's just by-"

"I know where it is," Bertie snapped, "I don't want Deborah involved in any of this, do you understand Michael."

"Bertie I am doing her a favour. London will not be a good place to live in during the next war. I will see she gets top price for the flat and I am offering her the chance to buy another property, at rock bottom prices, in a neutral country; that's all I am saying, nothing more."

"Don't let me down on this Michael, Deborah is even more headstrong than her mother used to be and I do not want her taking any unnecessary risks. Is there anything else I should know at this stage?" Bertie demanded.

"You will need to have your own transport in Spain once again, would you like another motorcycle or would you prefer a car, now that you can drive?"

"How do you know that? Is there anything about me and my family that your lot does not know Michael?"

"To be honest, yes there is. What did you do with the gold that you took from that chap Tom Raymond, who went over the side of your ship near Geraldton a few months back?"

Bertie stared at Michael in disbelief, but also realised that his account of Tom's disappearance had been accepted, so deciding that discretion is the better part of valour, he smiled thoughtfully and replied carefully,

"I would prefer a motorcycle again please. An Indian Chief with a sidecar would be ideal and as I told the police in Broome, he fell over the side while drunk and I don't have his gold, it must have gone over the side with him!"

"If you say so my friend, but he was a nasty piece of work by all accounts and between you and me, everyone was relieved to see the back of him."

Michael and Anne left the ship at Sydney after spending a very pleasant few days on board with Bertie and returned to England, after visiting certain Government Offices in town and sending certain cables of confirmation.

When the El Burro got back to Christchurch, Bertie sat down with Shep for a long conversation about their respective futures.

"Neither of us are getting any younger, so it will make things a lot simpler if we just agree to go our different paths Shep," Bertie explained. "I have heard that my mother is not too well at the moment, so I want to go back to Spain straight away and see how she is and take care of her if necessary. Assuming that the Burra family agree to our plan, you hire a captain to take the ship to Spain and I will see about getting a replacement captain over there, while I am involved in my own family matters. You carry on running the business here and I will suggest that they buy another small freighter, to take up the slack we will create, with our freight customers in Australia and New Zealand."

"Agreed Bertie, but there is a personal matter I would like to discuss with you. I don't suppose you would consider selling me the Ute would you, if you are going back home," Shep asked. "I really enjoy driving it and it is so useful at home, I would really miss it, if you took it with you."

"Make me a fair offer and it's yours," Bertie replied.

Bertie arrived in London in March 1939 just about the time that Hitler had marched his troops into Czechoslovakia and just before the Spanish Civil War came to a close. Deborah had not known that her Granny was unwell and was quite prepared to give up her job and go to look after her, but was not at all happy about selling her lovely flat in London and buying a house in a small coastal village in Spain, that she had not heard of before.

"Deborah, you are not a little girl any more, you are a grown woman, so I cannot order you to sell the flat, but for just once in your life, trust me and do what I ask!"

"What is it dad, you're frightening me, shouting at me like that. Do you know something that I don't? That story you gave me about giving up your job and coming home to look after Granny is just nonsense. We both know that, so what is going on?"

Bertie explained to her, all that he and her mother had done during the Great War, for the British Secret Service and that he had been asked to make himself available to help them once again, should the need arise.

"You're telling me that you and mum were spies for the British, with false identities, well I never! I wondered why Roberto was given the surname Chavez and not Bannister, but just thought it was a Spanish custom or something of the like. Will I be expected to spy as well?" she asked him apprehensively.

"No, I have made that very clear to them, that you are not to be involved in any of this. You will be my daughter and keep house for me in Roses and swim and fish in the sea and maybe ski in the mountains. Nothing more dangerous than that, I promise."

"But you said mum looked after the radio on shore for you; I could be trained to do that at least," Deborah said thoughtfully, "I would be keeping up the family tradition, eh dad!"

"We will have to see about that; but I will let them know that you have agreed to go to Roses and sell the flat. We will advertise with a local estate agent for some ridiculous sum and see what sort of offer they come up with."

While the flat sale was going through, Deborah packed up all her things and sent them to Benicarlo, arriving there herself in mid May and the proceeds from the sale being transferred to her new Spanish bank account, ten days later. Michael had provided a new Spanish passport for Bertram Chavez and one for his daughter, Deborah Chavez. Michael had strongly suggested that they buy a house on the outskirts of Roses, preferably with a few acres of land, so that if there were people seen on their property, it would be assumed that they were itinerant workers.

A suitable smallholding was found about six miles out of town that had an olive grove and some orange trees growing on it, plus room for some vegetables and a few chickens if they wanted them. Although the house was soundly constructed it had that tumbledown look to it and consisted of three bedrooms and a bathroom and a massive open plan, dining, cooking and living area. There were several sheds and a large stable block, come barn, just twenty yards from the rear entrance. Deborah used some of her profit from the sale of the flat to renovate the interior of the house and the British Government paid to have a wine cellar put under the stable block and for the walls and roof to be strengthened. They also paid to have a large aerial mounted on its roof and they supplied a powerful radio for Bertie, or someone else, to use. Their personal things were moved up from Benicarlo, but it was decided to purchase fresh furniture and bedding for the new house, leaving the old furniture in the other house.

They introduced themselves as Capitan Bertram Chavez and his daughter Senorita Deborah Chavez and allowed the story to circulate that they had moved to the area after the recent death of Bertie's wife from T.B.

Michael arranged for a large fuel tank to be installed and for the 1928 Indian Chief motorcycle and sidecar, which Bertie had requested, to be made available in Barcelona. Deborah had a dozen lessons with an instructor and soon became as competent a motorcyclist as her father.

There was always a steady supply of visitors from Benicarlo, who went up to Roses to keep Deborah company, so that she was not often left on her own. Alice, Luca and Paco were regular visitors and Santo, Daria and Marco along with Jacobo were often there as well. Bertie bought a thirty foot long fishing boat, with a powerful inboard diesel engine in it, which he told all his friends to make use of; so it was regularly seen going in and out of the harbour on fishing trips, on many days of the week and at various times of the day.

Paco and Luca informed the family, that they believed that now was the right time to bring El Burro Volando II back from New Zealand and that an old friend, Capitan Bertram Chavez was to be its new skipper. The ship arrived in Barcelona on the 31st August, just before Great Britain declared war on Germany on the 3rd of September 1939. The family had already changed the ships registration from New Zealand to Spain, so it was proudly flying the Spanish flag as it steamed into port.

Bertie was surprised to find Rosie and Brock were on board the ship when it arrived in Spain, having been offered a free trip to Europe by Shep, on the understanding that they would cook for the crew and find their own way back to Auckland, once their European holiday was over.

They were stopping with Alice in the house in Benicarlo when war was declared, so it was decided that Rosie would stay with Alice and Brock would sail with Bertie, for as long as he was able, or until a safe passage back to New Zealand could be arranged for them both.

Michael had arranged with Bertie a method of communication, similar to, but a bit more sophisticated than, the one they had used before and as a final thank you to him and Deborah, he paid for a skiing holiday in a small town called Rialp, which was high up in the Spanish mountains. He really did believe it was a genuine thank you present, until Michael mentioned that the town was situated quite near to the French border and that it would be very useful if he and Deborah could ski.

When Alice and Luca heard about the trip, they decided that they too needed a holiday and since Luca's family actually had an old house in the same town, that was rarely used these days, all four of them decided to stay in the house rather than in the hotel. They arrived on Wednesday the 20th December 1939, quite late in the afternoon, but Luca had written to his younger cousin Annette, who lived in the nearby town of Sort and she had been washing and cleaning the house for over a week, to get everything ready for them.

The house was built of stone and was well over fifty years old and was just a few yards down from the old church. The top floor was the main living area, with some great views looking out over the town. The middle floor contained five bedrooms and a bathroom and the ground floor was where they had a large workshop and would have kept their horse and cart originally, but where Luca's Citroen C4 fitted with room to spare.

Annette was single and middle aged and had recently lost her father, whom she had nursed for thirteen years and was easily prevailed upon to remain with them at Rialp for Christmas. They had a great time together and since the skiing lessons did not start until after Christmas, there were no broken bones or twisted joints to worry about.

The lessons actually started on Wednesday the 27th and lasted for a week. By the time they had finished, Deborah had become quite an accomplished Intermediate level skier and Bertie had just about managed to get his Beginners Certificate on the Nursery slopes.

At the end of the holiday, Deborah and Annette had become firm friends and Luca had told both her and Bertie that they were welcome to use the house any time they wanted to and showed them where the key was hidden for the front door, whilst adding,

"But of course we never use it, as we never lock the doors here!"

"We now have a telephone at the shop in the town square where I work sometimes," Annette told Deborah, "here is the telephone number for it," she said, passing a folded piece of paper, "if you let me know when you are coming, I will come up and get things ready for you and keep you company, if you wish."

"Oh thank you Annette, that would be wonderful and you must come and visit us at our smallholding at Roses, it is so beautiful there. I have a motorcycle, so you could travel with me."

"I would like that Deborah, it is years since I was at the coast, thank you."

"Excuse me," said Bertie, "but who has a motorcycle?"

"Dad, we both know you got it for me, you say you can drive a car, so buy yourself one. I saw the new Renault Juvaquatre in a garage, it's really nice and a lot warmer and safer than the bike, you do need to be careful at your age."

"I quite agree with you Deborah," said Alice, "a car would be much better for you and it's not like you cannot afford one Bertie, after the huge profit you told us that you made on that Hoot thing, or whatever you called it."

Luca and Alice took Annette home, while Bertie and Deborah enjoyed another day on the ski slopes and they all travelled back to Roses on Saturday the 6th January after a truly enjoyable time away, with plenty to eat and drink and just two days before the Government introduced Rationing into Great Britain.

Deborah was determined to have exclusive use of the Indian motorcycle, so before Bertie was allowed to return to sea, she drove him down to the garage in Barcelona where he purchased a brand new Renault Juvaquatre which he arranged to pick up on his next trip to town. Deborah returned to Roses accompanied by Rosie, who had been driven to Barcelona by Luca and Alice, along with Brock, who went aboard the El Burro with Bertie, which had been moored there over the festive period.

The Mate greeted Bertie as he went aboard and told him that he needed a private word with him straight away.

"We only have six passengers Capitan but all the cabins have been booked and I think one of them is a senior member of General Franco's Government. Another man seems to be his assistant and the rest seem to be policemen, but they are not in uniform and have all brought weapons aboard."

"Thank you for telling me that, has all the cargo been loaded?" Bertie enquired.

"We are waiting for a few more crates of fresh fruit and then we will be ready to leave for Naples."

"Good, I will go and speak with our passengers."

As he approached the deluxe cabins a man was standing guard outside the door and was holding a very large gun which he pointed at Bertie. He told him to halt and to wait, while he knocked on the cabin door. A thin faced man with a beard and wearing glasses answered the knock and spoke to the guard and said something to the other person in the room. He then stepped into the gangway and closed the door behind him and walked up to Bertie.

"Capitan Chavez, it is good to meet you. My name is Senor Moreno and you are to speak with me and only to me throughout this trip. You must instruct your crew to stay away from these cabins at all times and to make no attempt to speak with any of the passengers is that understood?"

"May I remind you that I am Capitan of this ship Senor Moreno, so make sure you instruct your men to stay out of my way and in no way to interfere with the running of my ship. Is that understood?" With which he turned away and went to the bridge and instructed the mate to assemble the crew, where he informed them of Senor Moreno's instructions. He also instructed Brock to bring a drink and a sandwich to his cabin.

"You need to keep out of the way Brock, while these people are on board. Get your assistant to do all the serving for the passengers and if one of the policemen should speak to you, act dumb, but it's best to stay away from them if possible."

"What are they going to do in Naples Bertie, do you have any idea?" Brock asked. "None whatsoever, but we will keep our ears open and see what we can pick up."

It turned out that one of the policemen, was in fact the Government Official's personal chef and went down to the galley and took over control there. Brock told his assistant to do whatever he was told and to find out as much as he could, about who they were and what they were going to Naples to do.

The chef was a very likeable man and excellent at his job and made enough food for the crew as well as the passengers. He liked to sing and he liked to talk and it did not take very long before he had told the assistant cook, who the V.I.P. was and the purpose of his visit to Naples.

They reached Naples the next day and the mysterious passenger and his entourage left the ship and were met by the Spanish Ambassador to Italy and a very impressive diplomatic car.

They unloaded all the cargo, apart from four large heavy crates that were marked as agricultural products, which they were told to keep hold of until the following day, when they would be collected separately.

"There is something strange about those crates Capitan, I don't think they are what they pretend to be, or why wouldn't they have just unloaded them and put them in the warehouse over night," the Mate said, when they were alone in the bridge.

"Good point, let's go and investigate, I like to know what I am carrying in my ship," Bertie replied.

They went down into the hold with a jemmy and a hammer and managed to prize up the corner of one of the crates and shine a light inside.

The Mate reached into the crate and took out a handful of the contents which he studied, "I thought as much," he said, "my dad used to work in the mines, that's Wolfram or sometimes called Tungsten. It's used in the manufacture of armaments."

"As long as it won't explode or damage my ship, we need not worry about it," Bertie answered, "put some more nails into that corner and hammer it down please."

The crates were unloaded the next day, directly on the back of some Italian army trucks, which were immediately driven out of the area.

From Naples they sailed to Palermo and then on to Tripoli, Algiers, Casablanca, Lisbon and then back to Barcelona. During the trip they were approached by many small ships who wanted to trade with them or to carry loved ones to the safety of a neutral port, like Lisbon or Barcelona. Bertie was prepared to trade in most hard currencies as well as gold, silver and jewellery and soon got back into the swing of how things were done in that part of the world.

He used his old Luger pistol on one occasion, to fire a couple of warning shots at an African trader that was becoming a nuisance, but apart from that, the trip went smoothly and was most profitable for the Burra family owners and for the Officers and crew.

The next time he spoke with Paco, he mentioned the need for protective firearms and was later supplied with a couple of German MP38's and three Lee Enfield Number 4 rifles, with enough ammunition to last them for the rest of the war.

He picked up his new Renault from the garage and drove himself and Brock back to Roses, where Deborah and Rosie were waiting for them.

After the usual greetings and delivery of gifts from Africa, Bertie announced that it was most likely that a future trip would probably go down to Cape Town and possibly Ceylon and that Rosie and Brock might like to consider this as a first leg in their journey home to New Zealand.

That evening he and Deborah made contact with their supposed relatives in Algeciras giving them the current news about their Olive Grove, health, lives ashore and afloat and other activities.

Next day in London, Michael chaired a meeting which discussed the recent information he had acquired about a forthcoming Trade Agreement between Spain and Italy and the movement of Wolfram from Spain to Naples and then on to an armament factory somewhere nearby.

"All we have to do is follow the crates and they will lead us directly to their underground factories," Michael said, "we need to get an agent into the dock yard at Naples as soon as we can and our contact will let us know the next time he is going there."

It was May before the El Burro went to Naples again and once more their passengers were the Government officials and police guard, that were present the first time. Just like last time the large heavy crates were unloaded the following day onto army trucks which left the port for the underground factories. No-one took any notice of the old man on his motorbike who was heading in the same direction as the convoy, nor did they link him to the Allied raid that completely annihilated the factory two weeks later.

When Bertie called in at Lisbon on that trip to pick up passengers and a supply of Port for his own use and for trading with, he found himself chatting in a bar to a middle-aged man who spoke very poor Spanish and who said he wanted to get to Barcelona.

"I am sorry my friend, I would like to help you, but without the right papers I cannot let you onto my ship," he told the man.

The man suddenly gave up trying to speak in Spanish and said in his best Oxford English, "Bertie old chap, Michael has told me to tell you that 'The cockles in Cockermouth are truly excellent this year'."

This was the coded introduction they had agreed between them, to be used when Michael was sending someone undercover to Bertie, or vice versa.

Bertie was taken by surprise and racked his memory for the correct reply, knowing that if he got it wrong, the man was likely to shoot him.

"I am delighted to hear that, but I prefer 'Kendal Mint-cake'," he said with obvious relief.

"If my friend has sent you to me, why don't you have the right papers with you," he then enquired.

"Last minute change of plans. I have to get into southern France as soon as possible, but we have a traitor there and my contact has been arrested and shot, so I was diverted here and to you."

"I see, do you have any other clothes with you?"

"No, they got lost en route, I have just what I am wearing, is that a problem?"

"You are about the same size and build as my Mate, I will come back here at dusk with some clothes and his passport, here is some money, buy yourself an old cap to cover your bald head, as he has a wonderful head of hair on him."

Bertie left the man at the bar and made his way back to the ship and called the mate into his cabin.

"There is no risk to you at all. If anything goes wrong you simply say that I took the passport and clothes without your permission, I am the one taking the risk, not you. He is willing to pay us well to get to Spain, it is easy money," Bertie explained.

The man handed over his spare clothes and his passport and Bertie gave him five hundred pesetas, as his share of the man's fee.

He put the clothes into an old bag and then walked into town where he had met the man earlier that day. No-one appeared at dusk, so Bertie went for a short walk round town and heard someone call him as he walked past a narrow alley.

"Capitan, Capitan, down here, it is me." He recognised the atrocious Spanish immediately and slowly walked down the alley.

His contact was lying on his side with blood still seeping from his arm and chest and dried blood covering his head.

"I think it was two German agents that caught me. I was buying the hat you suggested and they heard my Spanish and followed me. Lucky for me a couple of policemen were walking down the street, so they dumped me in here and ran off."

Bertie helped the man out of his blood stained clothes and tore his shirt into strips and bound up the wounds as best he could. He then helped him into the clothes he had brought with him and lifted him to his feet. With the hat in place and with his arm supporting his weight, the two men made it slowly back to the dock.

"What is wrong with your friend?" the dock policeman asked Bertie.

"This is the third time he has had too much to drink and tried to take on the world; but it did take three of those Nazis to put him down this time, so we can at least be proud of that. One of them must have pulled a knife on him, so I will have to stitch him up again and we should be sailing in an hour, who would be a Capitan, I ask you."

Bertie gave the policeman both passports and he studied the injured man carefully;

"I should really make a report of this but I hate paperwork, take him away Capitan and teach him how to behave," he said, handing the passports back.

"Thank you Capitan, you have probably just saved my life," the agent said to Bertie, as they made their way to the ship.

The Mate was looking out for them and clambered down to the dock as he saw Bertie approaching and between them they got the injured man aboard and put him into one of the smaller passenger cabins.

While the Mate got the ship moving and sailed it out of Lisbon harbour, Bertie and Brock got the newcomer undressed and then cleaned and dressed his wounds. Bertie gave him some morphine to kill the pain while he stitched up his arm and chest and left Brock to look after him. They arrived at Barcelona the next day and unloaded the cargo and let all the crew leave the ship. As luck would have it, Paco and Luca had come to greet the ship and discuss future possible contracts with Bertie and between the four of them, they managed to get the British agent off the ship and into Bertie's car without too much trouble.

Paco and Luca returned home and Bertie and Brock slowly drove up to Roses with the injured man.

"What's his name dad," Deborah asked, once he was safely installed in one of the bedrooms.

"I don't know Deborah, it's often safer to keep those sorts of details private, if you know what I mean. He is just a middle aged man, working for the British Secret Service, who got wounded in the service of his country and who has turned to us for assistance."

"He's not middle-aged Dad," she replied, "I would say he is about the same age as me. He has had his head partially shaved and he is wearing make-up, are you still quite sure you know who he is?"

Chapter 21
Red Rabbit

Bertie and Brock went into the bedroom where the wounded man lay, not knowing what to expect and found him sound asleep on the bed, almost exactly where they had left him. They took his clothes and shoes and carried them into the dining room and put them on the table.

"Apart from the shoes and underclothes, these are the clothes that belonged to the Mate, so I wouldn't expect to find anything here, but we will check anyway," Bertie said.

"What did you do with his own clothes Brock, they were in that bag?" Bertie asked.

"They are in the back of your car, I'll go and get them," Brock replied.

"There was some French coins in his trouser pocket along with a handkerchief, a Jack-knife, a door key and a torch battery. His shirt had been torn up by Bertie to make bandages, so there was not much of that left, but Bertie did notice that the label had been removed from the collar.

"He has a wallet in his coat dad, I'll go through it," Deborah offered.

"French money, Portuguese money, picture of a man, woman, boy and a girl, oh it says on the back 'Clacton - August 1921', looks like it was raining."

"That would be about right for Clacton," Bertie joked.

"Oh, I don't believe it, typical man," Deborah exclaimed, "three contraceptives in his wallet, what sort of a person have you brought home dad?"

Bertie walked round the table and took the wallet off his daughter and put the contents back inside.

"I have just about had enough of your histrionics Deborah, it's high time you started to grow up. I have absolutely no doubt that this is a very brave young man, who is risking everything for his country and does not need you to pass judgement on his morals. Contraceptives make excellent waterproof bags for carrying sensitive items through damp and even watery conditions, so just keep any future comments to yourself, is that understood?"

Deborah gulped and looked at Rosie for support, who spoke quietly to her,

"Your father is quite right Deborah, you really can be a bit silly sometimes, my dear."

Deborah left the room and went to her bedroom and as she lay on her bed, feeling very sorry for herself, she heard the wounded man next door let out a gasp of pain and as she dashed into the room, she saw him sitting up in bed, holding the blood stained bandage round his chest.

"Are you O.K.?" Deborah asked him, in a concerned voice.

"I think I must have pulled the dressing off the wound when I rolled over and it started bleeding again. It seems to have stopped again now, but I could do with a fresh dressing if you happen to have one. Can I ask you where I am and who you are, as I have no real memory of anything after Captain Chavez gave me the morphine."

"This is Captain Chavez's home and I am his daughter Deborah, so who are you and what's your name?"

"Sergeant-Navigator MacDonald Livingstone Forbes Smith of His Majesty's Royal Air Force, at your service Miss, but everyone calls me Mac. I don't suppose you are interested in hearing my R.A.F. Serial Number are you?"

"Not at this precise point in time," she said laughing, "I'll get you another dressing Mac, I won't be a minute," with which she skipped out of the room and into the bathroom and took another dressing from the cupboard. As she passed the dining room she called out,

"Dad, Mac is awake and needs another dressing for his chest; do you want to take a look at the wound or shall I just see to it?"

The three looked at each other and smiled and getting up from the table, trooped into the bedroom after Deborah. Introductions were made, hands shaken and thanks expressed for help and assistance given. Bertie checked the wound and found that the stitches were intact, but a large scab had been pulled off with the old dressing and it had started to bleed again. He cleaned the wound in the chest and the one in the arm and applied new dressings to both.

"Your arm wound is a long cut but it is not too deep Mac," Bertie informed him, "but the chest wound is a lot deeper and had it been an inch to the left, you and I would not be having this conversation. You are lucky to be alive."

"I realise that sir and I want you to know that I will always be in your debt for saving my life in Lisbon."

"You must be starving," said Rosie, "I will bring you something to eat and drink, so that you can start to build your strength up again young man."

"Thank you, I could eat a horse, it seems days since I had a good meal."

While Rosie prepared dinner, Brock cleaned all traces of blood from the car and after letting Mac go through his old clothes, burnt them on a bonfire in the yard, while Deborah just sat and chatted with her patient in his room. Bertie meanwhile, got on the radio to his contact and informed them that a package had been collected in Lisbon but had been damaged in transit and was in his home being mended.

The question came back, "How long will it take to fix Lisbon package and what were the markings and numbers on the said package?"

Bertie replied, "Package badly damaged will take at least a month to fix and markings were MLFS1914."

The reply came back, "Markings confirm that the package is authentic, please repair and keep us informed when ready."

Bertie informed everyone that London had confirmed Mac was the genuine article and that his presence should not be publicised, but if anyone should ask about him, they should say that he was just a labourer looking for work, who had badly cut himself on a saw he was using.

Rosie said that she wanted to get back to Benicarlo as Alice had not been too well before she left and wanted to go and see how she was feeling now.

Bertie drove her and Brock there the next day, leaving Deborah to look after Mac. When they arrived they found Alice in bed with Luca nursing her and asked if anyone had called a doctor for her.

"I don't need a doctor Bertie, it's just a bit of a fever," she told her son.

Bertie was not so sure and insisted on calling the doctor, who arrived an hour later. He said that she had a very high fever but was not certain what it was and would come back the next day to do some tests on her.

Bertie went next door to see Paco and to ask him if he might use the telephone to call Deborah.

"Your Gran is not at all well Deborah and I am going to stay here the night, will you be able to manage on your own?"

"Of course I will dad; Mac is still asleep most of the time. Give Gran my love and let me know how she is tomorrow."

Bertie sat up that night chatting with his mother about her life and all the good times and not so good times, that they had shared together.

"I have been so fortunate Bertie," she said, "your dad and his parents and I, got on so well together for all those years and we had such happy times together, especially while we were at Gravesend and I want you to know that you have been such a good son to me and we were all so proud of you, when you went to that Naval School and then passed your Mates Certificate. I was so sad after your dad died, but living with Deborah in London was so enjoyable and helped me through those difficult days, we had such times together, she and I."

Bertie smiled at the frail old lady and squeezed her hand as she continued;

"And then I came here to Spain and met Luca, he is such a nice man and we have been on some wonderful trips around Spain together, who would ever have thought that I would have found such happiness again?"

She looked up at her son and smiled as she said to him, "I know how much you loved your wife and no-one will ever take her place, but if you should get the chance to find someone else you care for Bertie, don't let it pass you by son."

"I won't mum and I want you to know what a terrific mother you have been and to know how much both Deborah and I love you. She asked me to give you her love, just now on the phone. I have always been loved and cared for and encouraged by you and dad and everything I have achieved is down to the pair of you."

By now they were both feeling chocked and the tears were streaming down both their cheeks. Bertie squeezed her hand and kissed her cheek and excused himself, so he could go to the bathroom, where he wept like a baby.

Luca had gone back into the room and was sitting by the bedside when Bertie had finally composed himself and after having a glass of wine, walked back into his mother's bedroom to bid her goodnight.

"She has gone Bertie," Luca said, "as I sat down next to her, she smiled at me and squeezed my hand and said 'thank you' and then 'goodbye' and closed her eyes and just peacefully passed away. Your mother was the sweetest, gentlest person I have ever known, I will miss her so much."

Rosie and Brock offered to stay with Mac, so that Deborah could attend her Granny's funeral. Bertie drove them up to Roses the next day and brought Deborah back down to Benicarlo the following day with him.

Alice was buried in the same graveyard as her grandson and daughter-in-law on Friday the 28th June 1940, which also happened to be the same day that Great Britain recognized that General Charles de Gaulle, had become the leader of the Free French.

The legalities in Spain were quite simple, as Alice was just a long term visitor and did not own any property there. Bertie wrote to the solicitor in Harwich with a copy of the death certificate and explained that neither he nor his daughter would be able to visit his offices, while the war was in progress, but to send any correspondence to his holiday home in Benicarlo.

It was agreed that Rosie and Brock would continue to live at Benicarlo until such time as they could travel to South Africa and then home to New Zealand. Deborah packed up her Gran's personal things and had them taken to their home in Roses and after allowing Rosie to take any items of clothing that she wanted for herself, gave the remainder of the useable items to the church and burned what was left.

Mac was up and about at the end of June, having regained his strength and partially recovered from his wounds, although his chest wound was still not properly healed. He was lying in bed one morning and noticed Deborah as she passed his open door, so wanting a glass of water; he called out to her;

"Debwah, Debwah, would you mind getting me a glass of water please?"

She came into his room with her hands on her hips and said to him;

"What did you just say to me Mac?"

"I asked you if you would be so kind as to get me a glass of water."

"No, you fool; before that. What did you call me?"

"I called your name," he said evasively.

"You can't sound your 'R's can you?" she said mockingly.

"You called me DebWah, didn't you? I thought once before you had a problem with your 'R's but didn't like to say anything. Say 'Red Rabbit runs riot'. Go on, I dare you."

"No. Anyway, it's rude to mock the afflicted. I had enough of that at school."

"Oh, go on Mac, just for me and I'll go and get you a glass of dad's best wine, even though you are quite capable of getting your own glass of water."

"We both know you will just laugh at me," Mac replied.

"Go on Mac. I pwomise I won't laugh at you," she said.

"See, you are doing it already! One condition then, if you laugh at me, you have to allow me to call you Debbie from now on."

"No way, my friend at school called her pet goldfish Debbie, but you can call me Debs, but only if I laugh, right!"

Mac got out of bed and took up a 'hoppy rabbit' pose, with his hands in front of him, sort of floppy like and his front top teeth over his bottom lip and bounced across the room to stop in front of her and looked up in a very appealing manner and said in a childish sort of voice;

"Wed, Wabbit, Wuns, Wiot!"

She tried biting down on her bottom lip and screwing up her face, but then he bounced round in a circle and said it again;

"Please miss but, Wed, Wabbit, Weally does Wun Wiot!"

The laugh came out so forceful and loud that it actually disturbed Bertie who was working outside in the garden, he informed her later. She laughed and laughed and just kept laughing and when he finally stood up and stopped bouncing around, she found herself with her arms round his neck, laughing on his shoulder.

At what point the laughing stopped and the kissing started is hard to say, but it was certainly a good ten minutes later before they emerged from the room, arm in arm, making their way to the kitchen for that glass of wine she had promised.

The first time Bertie heard Mac call his daughter Debs he waited for the eruption, but nothing came, so he assumed it had not registered with her, that her name had been vandalized by Mac.

By the third time, he realised that something had changed in their relationship and spoke with Deborah about it, after Mac had gone back to bed.

"What's going on between you two Deborah," he asked.

"Nothing," she replied.

"Don't lie to me Deborah. The last time a boy called you 'Debs', your Granny was called into school and had to speak to your teacher about the incident."

"I lost a bet dad, that's all. If I laughed at something I made him say, then he could call me Debs."

"Now I am intrigued, what did you make him say?" Bertie enquired and so the story was repeated, with her doing the impression of Mac hopping around the room and then saying,

"Please miss but, Wed, Wabbit, Weally does Wun Wiot!"

They both laughed loudly and heard Mac shout from his room,

"Hey Debs, are you two taking the Wabbit out of me?"

The friendship continued to grow stronger each day and each of them were dreading the day when Mac would be strong enough to continue with his mission and cause their separation.

Bertie did manage to get a few minutes alone with Mac a day or so later, when he reminded him that he was a guest under his roof and that he expected him to act like a gentleman in his relationship with Deborah.

"I have to confess sir that I have come to have very strong feeling for your daughter, but you have my word that nothing inappropriate has or will happen between us."

"Thank you Mac, I appreciate that. But on another subject, I have been asked to take you to Rialp on Wednesday of next week; they say it is important that you are in the hotel bar at 3:00pm, with a rucksack and your travelling things. I have been asked to make sure you are equipped to cross the Pyrenees into France, with the man who will meet you there. I suggest you say nothing to Deborah at the moment, we will just say that we are going on a trip to Rialp, is that clear?"

"Yes sir and thank you," Mac solemnly replied.

The next day was Thursday the 18th July 1940 and Bertie announced over breakfast that he fancied spending a few days up in the house at Rialp and asked Mac if he would like to accompany him.

"I would love to," Mac replied, "but if we are going to do any serious walking, I will need the proper equipment."

"I could take Mac into Barcelona dad, I wanted to do some shopping there anyway," Deborah offered.

"Well it would save me a trip and I did have some paperwork I wanted to do today. How do you feel about travelling on the back of a motorcycle, driven by a lunatic Mac?"

"Sounds like an offer I can't refuse; but I would, of course, prefer to be the driver," he replied.

"Not in a month of Sundays," Deborah retorted.

"Have you ever driven a motorcycle before then," Bertie enquired.

"Yes sir, I am the proud owner of a 250cc Francis Barnett Cruiser. It was very useful during my training and allowed me to get home from Lincoln during my weekends off, to see the family."

"250cc's, my Indian is almost 1,000cc's bigger. That is just a toy Mac and I certainly couldn't trust you to ride my Chief, no you can ride in the sidecar, you will be safe from harm there and not upset the balance of the bike either."

The leg pulling continued all through breakfast and at the end Bertie gave Mac enough money to purchase everything he would need, plus spares as well.

Deborah drove into Barcelona and accompanied Mac while he went round a number of second hand shops, buying anything that was serviceable and then he got her to take him to one or two high class Men's shops, for other personal items he preferred to buy new. He also bought some climbing gear, a mountain jacket and a brand new pair of boots and a tin of dubbin. He made a point of wearing the boots for three to four hours a day thereafter, until they were broken in.

It was then his turn to accompany Deborah to several Lady's shops, where she purchased a couple of dresses, a skirt and blouse and a thick coat for the bike. On one occasion he was sent off on an errand, while she went into a shop on her own. They found a nice restaurant where they enjoyed a meal together and took a slow ride back to Roses, arriving late in the evening to find that Bertie had already gone to bed.

They drank coffee, they kissed and cuddled on the settee and when Bertie awoke early the next day, he found them still there, stretched out on the settee, sound asleep in each other's arms.

"Oh Deborah, my little girl, I hope this is not going to end up with you having a broken heart," he said quietly.

Deborah had written to Annette as soon as it had been decided to go to Rialp and told her they would be arriving late Monday night, as Bertie had said that he needed to go to Barcelona on Sunday and get something from the ship, but would not return until Monday lunchtime. She said that it would be wonderful to see Annette again and that they planned to stay there for at least a week.

Bertie had also arranged to see Paco and Luca at the ship, as they needed to discuss the forthcoming voyage to South Africa.

"We know it could be dangerous Bertie, but we have been offered treble the normal fees for this trip and it would give your two friends Brock and Rosie a chance to head off back to New Zealand; but if you really don't want to do it, then we will understand. But you have after all, always been lucky, my friend," Paco finished with.

"All I am saying is that it is dangerous, but you are the owners of El Burro and if you are prepared to take the risk, then of course I will be the Capitan as normal. Just one thing though, if Brock and Rosie leave the ship at Cape Town, then I don't have a cook for the return journey and if this cargo is so valuable, I will not want to take on someone new that I don't know, for the return trip."

"We have already thought of that Bertie," said Paco, "Luca and I have decided to take one of the deluxe cabins and we will be passengers on the way out and I will be cook on the way back. How's that for a suggestion?"

"Just like old times, sounds good to me, if you two old codgers think you are still up to it!"

"Hey, we can still teach you a thing or two, young-un and while I think of it," said Luca, "we have arranged for the extra steel plates and shutters to be fitted to the bridge as you asked and I have also arranged for two heavy duty machine guns to be mounted either end of the ship. We expect that everything will be done by the middle of August, ready for our departure on the 19th of August."

"Just one more thing," Bertie said, "and please don't ask me why, but I need to take one of those Lee Enfield rifles and some ammunition with me today, so can you get a replacement Paco?"

"No problem my friend and have a good trip to Rialp and don't take any risks, this next voyage is important for us all and we need you in one piece."

Bertie arrived home about lunchtime and they had a light meal together, packed the car and headed off for Rialp. They stopped in Berga for afternoon refreshments and arrived in Rialp around seven pm. A message had been put under the door by one of the neighbours, saying that Annette would be arriving by bus on Tuesday, but not to wait in for her.

Deborah unpacked all the supplies she had brought with her but Bertie decided that they would eat in the local hotel that evening.

"Give me ten minutes to get over there and organize a table and make sure everything is safe," he told Mac, "you never know who you might bump into in this town."

Bertie went to the hotel and spoke with the manager, who was an old friend of Luca's, who assigned him a table in the corner and said that there was no-one present that he should worry about.

When Deborah and Mac arrived, they had a drink in the bar and ordered their meals. The manager called them to their table about twenty minutes later and told Bertie as they were walking across the room that a Frenchman had just arrived on foot, who was acting a bit suspicious.

"He is sitting over there to the right of the door; if you go to the toilet you will get a good look at him as you pass by the table," the manager suggested.

Everyone sat down and enjoyed their first course of soup and a roll and while they were waiting for the second course, Bertie excused himself and went to the toilet. He studied the man as he walked past and on his return he sat down at the man's table,

"Bonjour David, comment allez vous?" he asked.

The man stared at him, "Bertie is that really you, I was told to expect a Capitan Chavez, I had no idea it would be you, someone told me you were in Australia."

"It's good to see you my friend, come and join us at our table, I think I have someone with me that you have come to meet; I can't believe how much you resemble your father, the first time I met him; are he and your mother well?"

"I won't join you tonight Bertie, as I may have been followed here, are you stopping in the hotel?"

Bertie told him about the house and where it was located and suggested he join them there later.

"You kindly asked after my parents, Bertie," he said, "to be honest I don't know how they are as they were rounded up along with all the other Jews in Tarbes and shipped off to a camp in Germany or Poland or somewhere. I have tried to make enquiries about them, but with no luck as yet, so I don't know where they are, or even if they are alive or dead."

"I am so sorry for you David, but how did you manage to stay free?"

"I was away on business when it happened and since my wife is not a Jewess, she was left alone in our home and was able to warn me not to return to Tarbes; so I joined the Resistance and am a member of a cell in the hills near Saint-Girons. Our main duty apart from disrupting the German supply lines, is to smuggle Allied airmen across the border to Spain. I have one such man about twenty miles north of here, just outside of Esterri, but he is badly injured. A German plane was flying over our route and we had to dive for cover and he fell down a steep slope and has broken his leg. I have tied it up but he is in great pain, I have been wondering how to transport him, so you are a real answer to prayer. Would you be willing to come with me tonight and pick him up and bring him back to your house?"

"Of course, we will eat our meal and meet you at the house at nine thirty, see you later," with which Bertie returned to his table and simply said to Deborah and Mac, "It's quite safe, I have met the man before, he is one of us and will join us at the house later. Eat up, the food is getting cold."

They enjoyed their meal and Deborah and Mac flirted with each other and Bertie tried to pretend that nothing was the matter, but they could see that his brain was in over-drive. They walked back to the house and on the dot of 9:30pm they heard the back door open and someone come in. Bertie told them to get down on the floor and to be quiet and stood in a dark corner of the room with his Luger pointing at the doorway.

"Bertie it is I David, shout out where I thought you had been if it is safe."

"Australia, David, please come in," Bertie replied.

David entered the room carrying a sub-machine gun and smiled when he saw Bertie in the corner.

"Well we seem to agree my friend that we all need to be cautious," Bertie said, "this is my daughter Deborah and this is Mac, whom I presume you came to meet."

They shook hands and sat down and had a drink while they got to know each other a bit more.

"Since I was coming here to pick up Mac anyway, when the airman was passed on to us from the other cell, it was decided that I might as well bring him along with me, rather than have to hide him in the woods for several weeks," David explained.

"Oh Mac, you're going with David over the mountains to France, aren't you," Deborah exclaimed, "you deceived me both of you, how could you?" With which she left the room in tears and went to her own bedroom.

"David and I are going to pick up the injured airman Mac, you stay here and try and talk some sense into my daughter, will you?"

While Mac did his best to comfort Deborah and make her aware of his plans, Bertie got the car out of the basement garage and drove up to Esterri and collected the injured man who was well hidden in a barn. David knocked twice and waited a minute and then knocked twice again, but got no reaction from inside the barn. He opened the side door and called out the agreed 'Codeword' but again got no reaction,

"Something is not right Bertie, I will go in and take a look, you wait here. Give me your Luger and you take the machine gun and come in firing if I call you."

The barn was in darkness and David entered on his stomach and slithered across the floor to where a couple of milk churns were standing together, while Bertie knelt outside by the main door with the sub-machine gun cocked and ready.

Nothing moved in the barn so David proceeded to the place where he had left the airman and then called out;

"Come in Bertie, it is quite safe, the man has passed out; come and give me a hand to carry him to the car please."

Bertie went into the barn, propping the big door open and between them they lifted the man up and carefully carried him to the car and laid him on the back seat, just as he regained consciousness.

"It's O.K. you are with friends, lie still while we make you comfortable," Bertie informed the man. "There should be some rope in the boot along with a couple of blankets David, I think that we will need to tie him in place, or he will be falling off the seat on that bumpy road which will make his injury a lot worse" Bertie suggested.

David got the rope and using the blanket as padding, tied the man to the back seat, so he would not roll around. Bertie then drove very gingerly back to Rialp and parked the car in the basement. Mac had seen the car approaching and was there to help them lift the man out and get him upstairs.

Deborah had been busy preparing a bed for the airman and had some food and drink ready for them all, as well.

"He is in a bad way, we need to get a doctor to see him," said Bertie.

"I know where he lives as I was skiing with his daughter when we were here before, I will go and get him," Deborah said.

Although it was late, the doctor was still up and playing cards with some friends and was happy to accompany Deborah to the house. She started to try and make up a story as to who the man was, but the doctor stopped her.

"Young lady, I do not want to know who he is, or where he is from, or where he is going. He is injured and I will help him, so please tell me nothing."

The doctor examined the leg and living in a mountainous region, he was used to dealing with broken bones. He straightened the limb and aligned the bones and then tied the two legs together with splints to stop them moving around and gave the man a sedative.

"I will return after dinner tomorrow night to see how he is, but you really will need to get him to hospital to have that leg set properly in plaster," the doctor advised.

"Thank you doctor," said Bertie, passing him some pesetas to cover his fee, with a bit to spare, "we will see you tomorrow."

"You are most welcome Capitan Chavez, I bid you and your family a very good night," the doctor replied.

Annette arrived on Tuesday and immediately took charge of caring for the injured airman. His name was John and he was a pilot, a single man in his forties who could actually speak a little Spanish; so with Deborah acting as interpreter when they hit an impasse, the two seemed to understand each other and get on quite well together.

In the afternoon, Bertie and David took Mac up into the hills for a walk and to try out his gear and Bertie presented him with the 303 Lee Enfield and some ammunition, to have a few practice shots.

Annette cooked a fabulous final meal that Tuesday and they even managed to carry John through to join them. The doctor called a bit later and was pleased with his patient's progress, but warned about overdoing it, or of leaving it too long before visiting a hospital.

They had a leisurely day Wednesday, with another practice walk in the afternoon for Mac, but this time Deborah went instead of Bertie and David. After about an hour's walking, they stopped for a rest and sat together, looking out over the valley below.

"I have a present for you Mac," Deborah informed him, "I got it when we were in Barcelona, here this is for you, I hope you like it," with which she passed him a small package.

He took the package and kissed her on the lips and just sat looking into her face,

"Thank you my love but I am sorry, I don't have anything for you," he said sadly.

"It doesn't matter Mac, open your present."

He opened the package and found a beautiful old Swiss wrist watch inside and put it on his wrist.

"It's beautiful Debs, I lost my other watch in Lisbon. I don't know what to say."

"I thought a second-hand watch would be a lot safer than a new one, in case anyone stopped you. I got them to engrave 'WLDC' on the back, 'With Love from Deborah Chavez'. Oh Mac, I have never loved anyone like this before and I am so scared of losing you," she sobbed.

"Hush Deborah, don't cry. The watch is beautiful and here, I want you to have my Jack Knife. It has been with me since I was a kid, it was given to me by someone who loved me and now I give it to someone that I love."

They sat and chatted and walked a bit more, but eventually it was time to return to the house for their final dinner together.

The meal was a more sober affair that evening and after it was finished, Mac was allowed to say his goodbyes to Deborah in private, before he and David got into the car with Bertie, along with all their gear and were driven to the barn outside of Esterri, that they had visited on the Monday.

Bertie and Mac shook hands and hugged each other and wished each other good luck and a speedy end to the war and as David led Mac back across the Pyrenees to southern France and the horrors of war, Bertie drove back to Rialp and a distraught daughter.

"I don't know what to say to you Deborah, except life goes on and we each have to live it to the full," Bertie said softly. "You have heard Mac's story and he has been lucky, blessed, call it what you will, all through his life. We know that he and his parents are Christians, because he told us so and he firmly believes that someone has been watching out for him and protecting him throughout his life and he clearly believes that his protector will continue to watch over him and you will have to keep believing the same thing too."

"I know dad, thanks for reminding me. I just love him so much, I can't bear the thought of losing him."

They stayed in Rialp for two more days and started the drive back to Roses on the Saturday, accompanied by Annette, who seemed to have grown quite attached to John.

"Stop in Berga, Bertie; as I have a cousin who works at the little hospital there and we will be able to get John seen to, without anyone asking awkward questions," she suggested.

As it happened, the cousin who was a nurse, was on duty that day and immediately arranged for a doctor to see John right away. He confirmed that the doctor in Rialp, who he knew very well, had set his leg properly and that he appeared to be in good health with no complications. The cousin then put a plaster cast on John's leg and suggested that he be brought back to see her in six weeks time, to have it inspected.

"Do not worry Annette, there is no record of your visit or of your friend John, your secret is safe with me," she said, with a twinkle in her eye.

They arrived at their house around six and between them got John out of the car and into the house and installed him in the third bedroom, while Annette made up the put-u-up in Deborah's room,

"This is something new for me," said Deborah, "having a room-mate, I hope you don't snore Annette."

"Well this is a first for me too Deborah, so I guess we will both find out, won't we!"

That evening Bertie was on the radio to London and was told that they had a special message for him,

"Go on," he said, "I am ready, what is the message?"

"The message is 'Red Rabbit is safely in his burrow', I repeat, 'Red Rabbit is safely in his burrow'."

Chapter 22
A Cargo of Farm Machinery

For reasons that no-one would explain, the trip to South Africa was delayed by the mystery customer for two months. During that time Bertie and El Burro Volando II made several trips around the Mediterranean which covered the costs of the trips, but made no great profits for the owners, although the Capitan and crew made their normal trading profits.

In September Bertie drove John and Annette to Berga where Rosie's cousin removed the plaster cast and got a doctor to inspect the leg, while Annette and her cousin chatted in another room. The doctor joined them and they discussed the problem for ten minutes before she went back into the ward and spoke with John.

"The doctor has a concern John that the leg has not healed as fast as it should have and thinks it is best to put on another light-weight plaster and for you to come back in another month's time," she said.

"Is there something wrong with the leg, has it not been set properly," John asked, "I really do need to get back to England as soon as I can," he said.

"I know that John, but you need your leg to be strong and fit if you are to fly again, but if you want to ignore the doctor's advice, then that is your decision of course; I am sure that you know far better than the doctor does, of what your leg is able to withstand right now," with which she left the ward and went back outside to see the doctor and her cousin.

"Where has the doctor gone?" Annette asked.

"He said he wants nothing to do with this Annette, but agrees that a lightweight plaster for another couple of weeks will not do any harm, but a month is too long, the muscles will start to waste away. What did you just say to John?" her cousin asked.

"Mine to know and yours to wonder, my dear," Annette replied, "just put the plaster on his leg and say nothing else to him, understood!"

Bertie had been sitting in the Waiting Room while all this was going on, reading a newspaper and Annette came and sat down by his side and quietly said to him,

"I suppose you heard all of that Bertie?" she enquired.

"I certainly did, you little schemer. Trying to keep him here for as long as you can I suppose; don't worry, I won't say anything. Your secret is safe with me Annette."

"Thank you Bertie. I have never had a boyfriend before, let alone a man I love and who loves me back in return. I just don't want to let him go back to England again. What he did before, flying those bombers and getting shot down, was so dangerous, I am afraid of losing him."

"I understand that Annette, but two weeks at the most and then he comes back here and has it removed. He will still need another couple of weeks before his leg is strong again and he is able to travel back to England. John is a brave man and a patriot, he must never know what you have done or he will never trust you again, is that clear?"

When they all got back to Roses, Deborah announced that there had been a radio message for Bertie and that he was to make contact with London that evening. When he finally got through, he was surprised to find that Michael was on the London end, with a very short coded message and with the instruction that he was to maintain radio silence until he was otherwise notified.

When the message was de-coded, it read, 'Make no contact London compromised. Visit Rialp 6th each month. Take packages to Palma when ready.'

"Are we in danger dad?" Deborah asked him.

"No, Michael would have given me the coded command to leave immediately if he thought we were in danger. I suspect that our role of collecting people from Rialp is far more important than passing information about German shipping and he is just protecting his 'Spanish assets', that's all."

During the next trip to North Africa, Bertie was very pleased that the extra steel plates had been fitted to the bridge as they came under attack from pirates who were armed with light machine guns. Bertie decided not to display the heavy machine guns that were hidden under tarpaulins, but used the Mp38's and rifles to see the pirates off; the Mate proving to be a very good shot with the 303.

They all went back to Berga at the beginning of October and the plaster cast was finally removed from John's leg, which had become weak and thin in the last two months. He was given exercises to do each day and over the next couple of weeks grew fit and strong once more and talked excitedly about getting back to England and flying again and teaching the Bosch a lesson for shooting him down.

As it was close to the 6th of the month they decided to go up to Rialp and spend a few days there and see if David or any of his group made contact with them. Just before mid-night on Sunday the 6th October 1940, David came into the house accompanied by two British airmen. Bertie and Deborah allowed John to act as interpreter and maintained the image of a Spanish Sea Capitan and his daughter.

While the airmen were being taken into the house, Bertie got the car out and drove David back to Esterri and asked him if he knew any more about London having been compromised.

"No my friend, we got no more information than you, just to be here on the 6th if we had any packages to deliver," David informed him.

"I will probably be away for the next two months David, but Deborah has said she is prepared to come up here on her motorcycle to meet you, not that I am too keen on her doing that, if I am honest."

"I can understand that Bertie. We do have an alternative route, so I will only bring her someone if it is absolutely necessary, but I would still like her to come if you don't mind."

"How is Mac doing David?"

"He was only with us for a couple of weeks when he was ordered to make his way to Lyon and we have heard nothing since. Tell Deborah I am sorry and if I hear anything I will let her know."

"I will," said Bertie, "where do you want me to drop you?"

"This will do fine, thank you. You had better go back to Rialp now my friend and have a good time on your next voyage and I will hopefully see you again next year. I have now a most unpleasant task to perform. We suspected that one of our men was betraying us to the Germans and now we have the proof we needed and I have been instructed not to return with him. I don't suppose you have your Luger with you, do you?"

Bertie took the pistol out from under his car seat and gave it to David, who walked across to a ruined farmhouse where the other men were hiding. Two shots rang out and a few minutes later, David returned and passed the pistol to Bertie.

"He has given my men a lot of information about the Germans, such a shame he turned traitor, his mother and sisters do so much for the Resistance. We will bury him here and I will take the shell casings back with me to show he was shot by a German gun and he will be treated as a hero. Au revoir mon ami."

When Bertie returned to Rialp, Deborah was happily chatting in English, for she had discovered that one of the young airmen had worked for the same company as her in London and had recognised her and called her name, so there was no point in continuing the pretence.

He explained to Annette that it would be best if she said goodbye to John tonight, as there was not enough room in the car for them all to return to Roses and he would take her to Sort in the morning.

"Perhaps I can get the bus to Roses next week, some time," she suggested to him.

"By all means Annette, I am sure Deborah will enjoy the company as I will be away on a long voyage and John and these other two men, will be coming with me. In fact I would be most grateful if you did come and keep her company while I am away."

The next day John and Bertie drove Annette home to Sort and Bertie went into the local hotel for a coffee and a sandwich, to give the two of them time to say their farewells in private. John joined Bertie about forty minutes later and the two men returned to Rialp without a word passing between them for most of the journey.

As they reached the outskirts of Rialp John said, "While we are on our own Bertie, I want you to know that this is not just a wartime romance between me and Annette, but I have just left the woman that I will marry once this war is over, assuming we both survive it. I know she had me put in plaster for two weeks more than necessary, I heard enough of their conversation to make out what she was doing, but these last few weeks have been the best of my life and I want to thank you for making it all possible."

"You are most welcome John and I truly hope that you are able to fulfill your wish and to marry Annette one day."

"When will I be leaving for England and will you be taking the other two men as well?" John asked.

"We leave this coming Wednesday or Thursday and yes, they will come with us, but do not mention this to anyone else at the moment please."

Bertie drove to Barcelona on the Tuesday to meet with Luca and Paco to discuss the forthcoming trip and wondered how he was going to tell them about the need to call at Palma on the way.

"Just a slight change of plans Bertie, nothing for you to worry about," said Luca.

"Now you have got me worried," Bertie replied, "what has changed exactly?"

"We are not now going to Cape Town but to Port Elizabeth instead. Have you been there before?"

"Once or twice, I don't see any real problem in that. Do we know why they have changed ports?"

"The customer wants us to load manganese ore and has changed his supplier or something, that's all," Luca replied.

"There is another small change," Paco interjected, "it shouldn't add more than half a day to the journey time and it is a most lucrative additional contract for us."

"You're the boss Paco, what do you want me to do?"

"We have been asked to pick up some passengers in Palma who want to go to South Africa with us, there could be as many as twenty of them, we think."

"Does this mean that you two are no longer coming then?" Bertie enquired.

"Certainly not," Paco answered, "we have been looking forward to this trip for months; the passengers will just have to cram into the cabins and make do. That is what we told the customer and he understands that."

"Just one more final thing," Luca said hesitantly, "I have arranged to drop some cargo off at Lagos. I know you have bad memories of the place Bertie, but it was too good an offer to turn down."

"That was a long time ago Luca and that happened to Bertie Bannister, not Bertram Chavez. Do not worry my friend, I am not afraid to shoot to kill these days, when I have to."

"We thought you would say that," Luca responded, "this is going to be a most interesting and rewarding voyage, for all of us Bertie."

"Oh, just one more thing I wanted to tell you," Bertie said, "I have three packages to drop off at Palma which I will bring aboard with me on Wednesday evening and keep safely out of sight in my cabin. Since we will also have Rosie with us on this trip, I have assigned her one of the smaller cabins and with all of these extra passengers on board, she will come in most handy in the galley, helping Brock. I agree with you Luca, I think we are in for a most interesting voyage to South Africa."

Bertie arrived at the ship after dark on Wednesday evening and got the three men aboard and into his cabin without anyone spotting them. Luca and Paco were already aboard and had brought Brock and Rosie with them. The Mate was called into the Bridge and told about the passengers they would be picking up at Palma and to make sure that the cabins were neat and tidy and were free of all the crew's belongings.

"I am sorry Brock, but you and Rosie will have to manage in a standard cabin this time as we will need to put four of the other passengers in the deluxe suites and since Rosie has agreed to assist you in the galley, she will be on full wages for this trip," Bertie informed him.

They set sail on Thursday the 10th October 1940 at sunrise and arrived in Palma a few hours later. Bertie had been wondering how to deliver the three packages he had on board and who to deliver them to, when a customs officer came aboard and said he wanted to inspect the cargo. Bertie took him down to the rear hold where the man revealed his true identity as a British spy and informed Bertie that, 'The cockles in Cockermouth are truly excellent this year'

"Is that so," Bertie replied, "but I prefer 'Kendal Mint-cake'."

"How many airmen do you have on board with you captain?"

"Three, an older man and two younger men. The older man broke his leg in the escape from France and we have been waiting until it was properly mended and he was able to walk again before moving him," Bertie informed him. "The two younger men we picked up on Sunday and they are both very fit."

"You should have a large crate marked 'Melons' or such like, for unloading at Palma. It should have been the last thing you loaded at Barcelona."

"I see it," said Bertie, "it's over there."

The two men walked across to the crate.

"There should be a little doorway in the side, here it is and if I turn this knob here, the door should come open," the agent said. The door opened and the agent continued, "This crate actually contains equipment for the passengers you are picking up here, as well as a few melons on top, just in case anyone opened it. If you go and get the three men, I will start to unload the melons and the gear.

Bertie went up on deck and called Brock to the bridge and told him to quietly take the three men in his cabin to the rear hold and to put some melons he will find down there with the ship's supplies. He told the mate that they were unloading one crate and to get the hoist ready. Bertie then went down to the hold himself and when the crate was unloaded and the equipment safely secured, the three airmen went inside and strapped themselves to the wall of the crate. The covers over the hold were removed and the crate was lifted out of the ship onto the back of a small truck that had driven along the dock and stopped by the ship. The truck drove off with the three men in the crate, the covers were replaced over the hold and by early afternoon the ship was heading out of Palma on its way to South Africa.

The first stop was Freetown, Sierra Leone where Paco had bought his monkey all those years ago and he and Bertie went back to the same market where monkeys were still being sold, but this time Paco haggled for an African drum and Bertie purchased some uncut diamonds and a gold necklace. The ship loaded fresh supplies and fuel and after waiting an extra day for two passengers who went ashore to see the sights and did not return, Bertie finally left without them, after giving the officers at the local police station, details about them.

They arrived in Lagos in the middle of November where a further six passengers 'went missing' and all of the cargo from the forward hold was unloaded or moved to the rear hold and a cargo of tin was taken on board in its place.

Bertie warned the passengers and crew of the dangers of Lagos and instructed them to go in threes and to be armed and ready for action at all times. Once again Paco had a buyer for some rolls of silk but insisted that the buyer come to the ship and inspect them, which he did. They haggled for an hour or so and eventually agreed on a price that both seemed pleased with and an appropriate number of gold sovereigns were handed over and ten rolls of finest Italian silk were unloaded and carefully placed into a waiting car.

One crewman who ignored Bertie's orders and went out on his own, was severely beaten and robbed and was unable to work for a week, so had his pay docked accordingly.

Although Rosie was nervous about going ashore, eventually she and Brock with Paco and Luca booked a taxi and went on a ride around the town, stopping at a well known restaurant for dinner, which everyone enjoyed. She purchased a Zebra skin and a spear, for her living room wall in Auckland and Brock bought her an Ivory necklace and a carved elephant.

They replenished their fuel and food supplies once again and left Lagos a week after they had arrived there and steamed down the coast of West Africa, without incident and anchored in Port Elizabeth the first week of December.

The remaining passengers went ashore first, but told Bertie that they would be travelling back to Spain with him on the return leg of the journey. The remaining cargo in the stern hold was unloaded along with all the equipment which the passengers had brought with them. Paco and Luca went ashore to see their agent and were told that the cargo of manganese was not ready for them yet and that it would be at least another week or two, maybe even longer.

"What are we supposed to do for two weeks or more?" Paco asked the agent.

"Have you thought about a safari or hunting or something like that?" the agent enquired, but before Paco could answer him, he smiled and said,

"Look gentlemen, I do have some farm machinery that is urgently required in Beira in Mozambique, I can offer you excellent terms for this consignment and by the time you get back here, I am sure the manganese will be ready for loading."

"We might well have been interested in an extra trip to Beira," Luca informed the agent, "but we already have a cargo of tin loaded in the forward hold, what are we supposed to do with that?" he asked.

"I am sure I can find a buyer for the tin, if you are prepared to sell it here," the agent said, "and you can always get some more from Lagos on your return trip to Spain, if you wanted to."

Now since the tin had been bought speculatively by the two men, on the assumption that someone would want to buy it off them during a period of war, they agreed to sell it to the agent and to take the proposed cargo of machinery to Beira and bring a cargo of cotton and nuts back to Port Elizabeth.

Bertie agreed with the new arrangements and thought it was much better to keep the crew busy, than to have them kicking their heels in a strange port for weeks on end. Four of the passengers rejoined the ship on its voyage to Beira and accompanied the farm machinery that was unloaded there, on its long journey to wherever it was headed and a cargo of cotton and cashew nuts was loaded and made ready for the trip back to Port Elizabeth.

While all of this was going on, Luca and Paco opted to stay behind with Rosie and to try and find a passage for her and Brock back to New Zealand. They eventually succeeded in getting them a working passage on a liner heading for Australia, which left Cape Town at the end of January 1941 and after spending a further two weeks in Sydney, they finally arrived home in Auckland at the end of March.

While El Burro was docked at Beira, a man called at the shipping agents office and asked to speak with Capitan Chavez. He said he was staying at the local hotel and would be grateful if the Capitan would have dinner with him that evening at 8:00pm, as the man had a business proposition to discuss. The shipping agent duly notified Bertie of the invitation, but warned him that it had been rumoured that German and Italian secret agents had been seen in Beira and that he should go prepared for trouble.

He discussed the matter with the Mate and Brock and suggested that they both booked for dinner at 7:30pm at the same hotel and that they both went armed. The Mate informed Bertie that he owned two Beretta pistols, so it was agreed that he and Brock should take them and that Bertie would take his Luger.

They all went out and checked the hotel in the afternoon and Bertie called in to see the shipping agent on his way back to the ship and asked him to inform the mystery man that he would have dinner with him that evening and also asked the agent to reserve a table for the Mate and Brock at the same hotel restaurant.

When Bertie arrived at the hotel he called at Reception and asked if there was a message for him and was handed an envelope with his name on, which contained a note, saying that his host was seated at table seven and was waiting for him. He walked over and sat down at table seven where a middle aged woman was sitting on her own reading a book.

He did not know what to say to her and which language he should use, to say it in; but as he continued to look at her, he slowly realised that he had met this lady before, many years ago in Santiago, so he spoke to her in Spanish.

"Mrs. Michael, this is a surprise," Bertie said, "as he reached across the table and shook her hand."

"Capitan Chavez, how nice to see you again, you are well I trust?"

Bertie nodded, still in a state of surprise.

"I was very sorry to hear about your wife, please accept my condolences. I gather that the T.B. returned to strike at her again."

"Thank you, yes, that is correct. But at least we had another eleven years together, due to your efforts and her friends and family over there. I will always be most grateful to you for what you did for her. What happened in Santiago after we left?"

"They rounded up a few people and questioned them, but we had already sent Manuel and her cousin over the mountains to Bolivia and everyone assumed that Deborah was with them, so eventually they let the matter go and lost interest in her."

"Don't think me rude Mrs. Michael, but you do not appear to have aged a single day since last I saw you, amazing, quite amazing," Bertie commented.

"Not really Capitan Chavez, I was heavily disguised back then and I am wearing the same wig again today and Mr. Michael thought it would be of help if you recognised me; but he still asked me to inform you that 'The cockles in Cockermouth are truly excellent this year'."

"You know it sounds more ridiculous every time I say," Bertie replied, "but I prefer 'Kendal Mint-cake'."

The waiter arrived and took their order and brought them a bottle of white wine, which he left in the middle of the table. Bertie poured Mrs. Michael and himself a large glass of wine and they toasted each other's good health.

"I assume the two men at the table by the window, who have been staring at us for the last ten minutes, are with you?" she enquired.

"Yes, afraid so. I was told that Italian and German agents are here in town and since I had no idea who I was meeting, decided to play safe and bring some backup. I'll just give them the 'thumbs up' so they know everything is O.K." With which he turned round and indicated to the two men that everything was in order, so that they could relax and enjoy their meal.

"Well Mrs. Michael, do you have another name?" Bertie asked.

"Too many to remember Capitan, so Mrs. Michael will do fine. You must be wondering what I am doing here in Beira and why I wished to speak with you."

"I assume it has something to do with the cargo of manganese that I am going to pick up when I return to Port Elizabeth. I know it is used in the manufacture of armaments and I assume you are concerned where it is destined for; the answer to which question, I do not know."

"Very good Capitan, but we already know the answer to that; it is supposedly bound for Germany, your friend Luca has not been quite honest with you."

"I am sorry, but Spain is neutral in this war and as I understand it, trades with both sides of the conflict. There is nothing I can do about that, I wished there was!"

"I have obviously not made myself clear Capitan. That manganese is not going to the Germans. If we don't get it, then no-one is going to get it," she said emphatically.

"Are you threatening me and my very neutral ship Mrs. Michael?"

"Of course not, I would not dream of doing such a thing Capitan Chavez; but a magnetic mine can sink a neutral ship, just as well as it can sink an enemy ship. One more thing Mr. Bannister, let me remind you that you are still a British citizen, albeit you are working undercover as a Spanish sea captain; how long do you think the enemy would let you sail un-challenged if they knew the truth about you?"

"You really would do that wouldn't you, and next you are going to tell me that you would have me shot as a traitor, if I deliver this cargo of manganese to the Germans!"

She sat there looking at him and then smiled, nodded once, shrugged her shoulders and started to eat her main course of local game, which the waiter had just set before them.

They didn't talk much during the meal, which gave Bertie the opportunity to think over what she had been saying to him. When the waiter cleared the desert plates away, they both ordered coffee and she lit a cigarette and sat there waiting for him to say something.

"We both know I have no choice in the matter, so what do you want me to do, but please remember that I have two of the ship's owners with me and they have been good friends to me and I would not want to see them hurt over this," Bertie said.

"Luca and Paco have been good to you, but you also have made them and their family very rich; thanks in some measure to the protection we have always given to you. We know all about your trading and smuggling activities Capitan and have turned a blind eye to them, so make sure your friends understand that. Which side of the conflict do you think they really support, if they had to make a choice?"

"They hate the fascists and loathe the Germans in particular, they support the Allies, without a doubt."

"Good, that is what we thought too. The plan is very simple, you take the manganese across to Recife in Brazil and deliver it to an American ship you will find anchored there. You then come back here, pick up the original cargo and go back to Spain with it."

"I thought Brazil had its own manganese mines, so what's the catch Mrs. Michael, what is so special about this manganese?" he asked.

"The manganese itself is not special at all, but the steel boxes you will put at the bottom of the hold, before you load the manganese are special and the cargo you will be returning with, is very special indeed; a bit like the cargo you delivered here the other day. You can tell the owners that they will be very well rewarded for this extra voyage and will continue to enjoy the protection of the British Navy."

"Won't the enemy suspect something is up when we delay the trip even more and make a mysterious voyage across the Ocean to South America?"

"Possibly, but the Brazilian ambassador to South Africa has just been given some bad family news and is anxious to get home, so your agent has booked him and his wife into one of the deluxe cabins, for a one way trip to Rio de Janeiro, on your ship. He will have his own chef and steward travelling with him and I have booked two of my younger associates to travel with you as well."

"You seem to have thought of everything Mrs. Michael. What am I allowed to say to Luca and Paco and what happens if they want to come with me?"

"You can tell them everything I have said, apart from the small matter of the steel chests that will be loaded first. We have no problem with them travelling with you, if they want to, but it would be better if they stayed in South Africa."

When Bertie returned to Port Elizabeth, he had a very heated exchange with Luca and Paco in their hotel room, concerning the changed arrangements regarding the manganese and the trip to Brazil.

"You had no authority to change the arrangements without speaking to us first Bertie," Luca shouted at him, "we are the owners and it should have been our decision and not yours. We should sack you for this!"

"Go ahead Luca and see how far you get on your journey home without me, before a mysterious accident happens to you or you hit a magnetic mine," Bertie shouted back.

"Because of me and my connections, you and your family have become rich and have been protected from danger, so far in this war. A Capitan has the authority to make whatever decisions he feels are necessary to protect his ship and that is what I did."

"Bertie is quite right Luca and I have always wanted to visit Brazil," said Paco, "so I will go with him on this trip. I suggest you stay here in this nice hotel we have been staying in and that you just enjoy yourself for the few weeks we are away."

"Why are you taking his side Paco?" Luca thundered, "we are the owners, not him."

"Did your brother consult you on every decision he made when he was Capitan, Luca? Of course not and if we were not here, Bertie would not be having this conversation, we would just be getting a cable, telling us he was going to make some more money for us. If you do not want to stay here I will ask the agent to book you on the next ship that is going to Spain, that choice is yours, but the decision to go to Brazil has been made and we will honour it."

"Very well, you are right Paco" said Luca, "but I will speak with the agent and see if we can't find a shipment of coffee to bring back from Brazil, it would be worth a fortune in Europe right now."

"Only a few tons Luca, as I have already agreed to bring some American farm machinery back with me, did I not mention that already," Bertie said.

"No you did not and I am getting tired of this nonsense," Luca said solemnly, with which he left the room and went down to the bar.

"I will speak with him Bertie," Paco said, "I assume this is the same sort of machinery that you took to Beira with you and that you really had no choice in the matter?"

"I assume so," Bertie replied, "how did you know about that?"

"Let's just say that I have a nose for these things and I always want to know what is in the hold of a ship that I own or travel in. Of course we know who you are and what you have been doing my friend and we support you. Luca has just not been himself since your mother died, don't worry, he will be fine."

Bertie and the crew held a farewell party for Brock and Rosie and said their goodbyes before leaving for South America. The Brazilian ambassador and his wife were not the most agreeable of people and everyone was very relieved when they left the ship in Rio and El Burro made its way to Recife without them. The remaining passengers stayed on board and as one of them was a radio operator, Bertie had allowed him to use the radio on a regular basis, during the trip.

"Capitan Chavez, you are to tie up at that dock over there, behind that American warship and wait for further orders," the group's leader said to him as they entered the harbour at Recife.

Bertie did as he was told and waited at the dock for two days before the man came to see him again.

"Regrettably the freighter has been damaged en route and will not be here for another month, so it has been decided to unload the cargo now, onto that pier over there. I have been instructed to tell you that we will use our own men to unload it and you must give your men a couple of days shore leave."

Bertie moved the ship to the pier and after tying up told his men they had two days shore leave and gave them extra pay to spend, leaving just Bertie and Paco and Mrs. Michael's associates on the ship.

The following morning they started to unloaded the forward hold first and then the stern hold where the steel chests were located. As soon as the first chest was spotted, the unloading stopped and a party of American marines with shovels, went down into the hold and dug the chest clear and a net was lowered and it was lifted out and immediately taken to the American warship which had come alongside the El Burro. The same procedure was followed for the remainder of the chests and then the rest of the manganese was unloaded.

"So, did they tell you what they were putting in the chests Bertie?" Paco asked.

"No they didn't and I didn't ask Paco. I really have no idea, but I would guess gold or silver or something very valuable to give to the Americans."

"I would love to see inside one of those chests," Paco commented.

"They would shoot you stone dead if you did, just forget about them and what you have seen today my friend, it never happened."

Bertie had the holds swept clean by the marines before the cargo of 'farm machinery' was loaded. He and Paco were entertained by the captain and officers of the warship that evening and they left port early the following morning.

The crew returned to El Burro the following day, some the worse for wear and others escorted by weeping senoritas. Bertie ordered them to make sure the cargo was evenly loaded and secured and as Luca had managed to get the coffee transferred to Recife, it was loaded a couple of days later and packed around the machinery crates and the ship set sail the same evening for South Africa.

They arrived in Cape Town where the machinery was unloaded and then went on to Port Elizabeth where the new consignment of manganese was waiting for them. Luca had decided that he did not want to visit Lagos on the way home so both holds were filled to the brim with a combination of manganese and coffee.

They called in at Freetown on the way back for fuel and fresh supplies and were surprised when two of their original passengers, looking very much the worse for wear, re-joined the ship for the journey back to Barcelona.

They finally arrived home in April 1941 and when Luca sat down and finally worked out the profit for the voyage, he was able to tell the family that they had made more money in the last six months, than the previous three years put together.

Unfortunately, he was at a family celebration in honour of a recent addition to his great niece's family a few weeks later, when he had a massive heart attack and died.

Chapter 23
White Faced Chickens

During the next few weeks, some members of Luca's family came to the opinion that the delayed return trip from South Africa, had caused his heart attack and that Bertie was to blame for his demise. Paco told them that this was nonsense, but the moaning continued and in the end, the family decided that it was time for Bertie to go and that a younger family member, who had recently qualified for his Master's Certificate, be appointed as the new Capitan of El Burro, in his place.

"The El Burro belongs to the family Paco and I know you have argued in my favour, but to be honest, I have just had my sixty second birthday and am feeling tired myself after this last trip and would enjoy having a few months break, so why not give your nephew the chance to be Capitan while I am on holiday and see how he gets on. That way there will be no bad feelings towards him from the crew, since I have not been sacked, but am just taking a break."

"That is very noble of you my friend," Paco replied, "Luca would be horrified if he knew that they are using his death as an excuse to get rid of you like this. You have been so good for the family and I am truly sorry that they have reacted in this way against you, I am ashamed and deeply embarrassed."

"Thank you Paco, but there is no need for you to feel that way. Your friendship and that of Luca's, towards me and my family, has meant so much to me over the years that I trust that whatever happens with the captaincy of the ship, that our friendship will continue to be strong and warm," Bertie replied, and the two men shook hands and parted company.

"Let me get this straight dad," Deborah said to him, when he informed her of his conversation with Paco. "After all you have done for that ungrateful load of money grubbers, they sacked you!"

"Well I wouldn't have put it in quite those terms Deborah, but in essence yes, you are right, but only if it does not work out with the new man. He may well encounter a lot more difficulties than he is expecting. It has taken me many years to build up the contacts that I trade with and to develop a high level of trust with them and he will be starting from scratch. Just because he is Capitan of El Burro, does not mean he will get the same deals that I got. He is an unknown quantity and will have to earn his stripes, just as I did."

"So what are you going to do with yourself now and will it make any difference to us all, now that Greece has surrendered to the Germans?"

"Well actually I think it will Deborah, but more to the El Burro than to us as individuals. They might find themselves doing a lot more of their trade with Germany and its allies than they did before and as someone said to me quite recently, a magnetic mine cannot tell the difference between an enemy ship and a neutral ship, so they will have to be even more vigilant in the future. So yes, Greece surrendering may well make a significant difference to what they are able to do!"

"But what about you, dad, what do you have planned for yourself?"

"A good question Deborah. I am going to rest and do some fishing and simply enjoy life with my daughter for a while, so I am open to any suggestions you might care to make."

"I was going up to Rialp this Thursday, since Friday is the 6th of June and I have arranged to meet Annette there again, not that we have had anything to do since you went on your last trip. Why don't you come with me, now that you are unemployed, it's so beautiful there at this time of the year?" she suggested.

"I would love to come with you, we can take the walking gear and go up into the hills, has Annette heard from John since he went back to England?"

"She occasionally gets a letter from him, but he has to be careful what he says to her. He spent several weeks at some sort of centre for injured servicemen near Aylesbury, but is flying again now as an instructor, with just the occasional flight over enemy territory, so she is a lot happier than she was before, about his safety. Do you mind taking the car to Rialp, as I want to take the Indian in for a service, in fact we could go to Barcelona today if you wanted to."

Deborah wanted to do a bit of shopping in town, so Bertie drove down in the afternoon and met her around four thirty at the hotel they often used when staying overnight in Barcelona. They had a drink and something to eat and decided to drive down to Benicarlo to check the house was all right, now that Rosie and Brock were no longer using it and stay down for a few days.

Paco saw them arrive and invited them to have dinner with him, which they accepted.

"Good job we left some of our clothes and things here dad," Deborah remarked, "have you seen my hairbrush, the one with the silver handle, you brought me back from Italy that time?"

"Try the drawer, in the dresser, in the living room," Bertie shouted from the bathroom, "Rosie seemed to stuff everything in there, if she did not know where to put it."

"Got it!" she said. "Goodness dad, the drawer is full of un-opened letters for you and me and Gran, did you know they were here?"

"Ah, yes, she did tell me there was some mail, sort it out into piles and we will go through it before dinner."

They sorted the mail into piles and Deborah went through the cards and letters for her and Bertie started on the letters that were addressed to his mother.

"This is interesting Deborah, did your Gran mention that she had changed her mind about selling her house?"

"No, she never said anything to me dad; I thought she was selling it to give herself a small pension."

"So did I," Bertie replied, "but it appears she was able to manage on the housekeeping money I gave her and decided to rent the house to the new manager who was working for the Alderton's and just had the rent paid into her bank account in Harwich."

"So does that mean it's your house or our house or what?" Deborah enquired.

"Hold on, there should be a letter here from the solicitor, I am sure I saw one as I sorted them out, got it, let's see what he has to say."

Deborah walked over and stood behind her father as he read the letter from the solicitor about his mother's Will.

"O.K. well the nub of it is that I get the house and you get whatever is in her bank account, which appears to stand at five hundred and eighty seven pounds, sixteen shillings and ten pence. Goodness, she was a lot better off than I had imagined."

"Gran was an inspired household budget manager dad. I often went to the shops with her and she knew where to go for all the bargains and always haggled with the stallholders whenever she could."

"I am surprised that she did not leave the house to both of us though," Bertie remarked.

"Not really, she told me that she was surprised that I got Great Uncle Harry's flat and not you, so she obviously decided that this was the fair way to arrange matters and she was quite right. What do you think we should do now?"

"We will both write to the solicitor and tell him what we want him to do. You should instruct him to hold the money for your account and to transfer it to your old bank account in Harwich. I assume you kept it open as I suggested?"

"Yes dad."

"Good. I will write and tell him to continue to rent the property out and to pay the money I receive, into your account after taking out any costs or deductions."

"That's generous of you, thanks. Anyway it's time to go dad, Paco has just given us a call and we can finish this tomorrow."

They had a pleasant meal with Paco, who tactfully asked them what they had decided to do with the house, now that they were living at Roses.

"I don't really want to sell it Paco, not just for sentimental reasons, but for practical ones as well. Deborah and I need to have all our mail from England sent here, as we do not exist as 'the Bannister's' in Roses, but as 'the Chavez's'. Why do you ask, do you have anything in mind for it?" Bertie enquired.

"My niece and her husband would like to come and live here in Benicarlo and run a small fishing business with me, using the boat that Luca and I purchased. Now I think it is a wonderful idea and I get on well with my niece and her husband, but they have three small children and I could not have them living with me, the noise and mess, you understand!"

"I can well understand that Paco," Bertie replied, "so I guess you are suggesting that they come and live here, in my house; I see."

"What do you think about the idea?"

"As long as they looked after all our mail for us and we were able to stay with you when we came to visit, I don't see why we could not rent it them, at least until this awful war is over and I can become my old self again."

The next day they wrote to the solicitor in Harwich giving him their instructions, packed up a few of their clothes and moved them to Paco's spare room and agreed a price for renting the house to the niece and her husband. They filled the car with everything else they did not want to leave in the house and drove home to Roses.

Bertie went on the radio as usual and was surprised to find that London responded to his call sign and that they were happy to chat to him and reminded him to be in Rialp on the 6th in case there was a package waiting for him.

They drove up there on the Thursday and called for Annette on the way and arrived in the house around six p.m. They went across to the hotel for dinner, where Bertie had a drink and a chat with the manager, while Deborah and Annette caught up with each other's news.

"I haven't seen your French friend for many months now Capitan," the manager informed him, "but there seems to be a lot more Spanish military in the mountains these days, he is probably being very careful."

"Thank you for telling me that, I will be on my guard," Bertie said thoughtfully.

The next day the three discussed what they should do in light of the news about the increased military presence.

"There is a farm at Esterri that sells eggs and poultry and I could do with replacing two of my old chickens with some new ones, why not take a ride up there and use that as the reason for our visit if anyone should stop us," Annette suggested.

"Good idea Annette and there is a box in the workshop we could put them in," Bertie added, "you and I can drive up after lunch and leave Deborah here in town, in case David comes directly to Rialp as he did before."

The ladies had a walk around town in the morning and had a light lunch at the hotel and made a point of calling at the hardware shop and buying some chicken food, for the new birds they hoped to purchase later that day and mentioned this to the proprietor.

"If I remember correctly, Senora Garza has some excellent 'Clown' chickens on her farm and she may well be prepared to sell you a couple, if you tell her that I mentioned it to you," he informed Annette.

"Thank you, I will certainly do that," Annette replied.

As she and Deborah were walking back to the house, Deborah asked her,

"Did I hear correctly in the shop, about what he said to you, when he called them 'Clown' chickens?"

"They are a very old breed of Spanish chicken which are black apart from a white face, hence the reason they are called 'clowns'. They should lay about three or four eggs a week each and are excellent to eat. They will do me very nicely."

While they had been in town, Bertie had got the car out and had given it a good clean, inside and out and made a big show of putting the crate in the back. He had then gone into the workshop and thoroughly cleaned his Luger pistol and made sure it was full of ammunition.

He and Annette got into the car and slowly drove to Esterri, making a point of stopping and looking at the scenery on the way, giving the appearance of a couple of holidaymakers, going no-where in particular and with all the time in the world to get there. As they got close to Esterri they came upon two Spanish soldiers who waved them down and asked them what they were doing and where they were going.

Bertie had wound the window down, but before he could say a word, Annette leaned across him and launched into a tirade of accusations, complaints and comments, to one of the men whom she happened to recognise.

"What do you mean by stopping me like this? Do you know who I am? You wait till I next see your mother and tell her that she cannot have any more eggs because her son would not allow me to purchase fresh hens! I can't wait to see how she explains that to everyone else in Sort, who will also be going without their fresh eggs, thanks to her son!"

The other soldier stepped away from the car chuckling to himself and left his colleague to handle this irate lady on his own, who happened to be a neighbour to the other soldier's mother.

"I did not say that you cannot go any further Senorita Burra, I just said I needed to know why you wanted to go to Esterri, that is all," the young soldier explained. "I saw Senora Garza at her farm yesterday and I hope you are successful, I know how much my mother loves your fresh eggs, I am sorry for troubling you."

Bertie was dying to ask why the military were out in force and were stopping people, but decided not to interfere in the conversation, since they had been given the all clear to proceed. As they approached the barn where David and his men had hidden before, there was a sheep grazing at the roadside, so Bertie sounded his horn twice, slowed down as he went past the sheep and then continued along the road to the farm. They pulled up alongside the farmhouse and Annette got out of the car to see if anyone was home. She walked round to the rear of the house and found Senora Garza sitting in her garden, enjoying a glass of wine and a piece of homemade cake. Annette explained why she had come to see her and was told to fetch her friend from the car, which she did. Bertie joined the two ladies in the garden and ate his way through a huge slice of cake, while the whole matter of the chickens was discussed over a glass of wine.

Bertie limited himself to one glass of wine, but the ladies needed several more, while the merits of different breeds of chicken were discussed, along with feed mixes, chicken houses, sanitation and the annoying presence of the military.

"They refuse to tell us why they are here, but we think it has something to do with all the people coming across from France to escape the Germans," she said. "Poor souls, who can blame them; wanting to get away from that nightmare."

"Have you had any of them come here to you?" Annette asked innocently.

"Not directly," Senora Garza replied, "but my husband often leaves food and drink in the barn you passed down the road and it normally only stays there a few days. We know that it is not much, but we feel we are doing something to help them."

"That is most kind of you and your husband, Senora," Bertie said, "I am sure it is much appreciated."

In the end Annette picked three chickens to purchase, after carefully inspecting them all. She told Bertie that there was one for certain and two others she could not decide between, so to save further delays, he suggested that she take them both. She got them at a very good price after lengthy negotiations with the owner and was told that a few more would be ready for sale in a month or so.

Unfortunately, three birds in a crate was one too many and as the owner did not have a box she could lend to Annette, he finally suggested to her,

"I suppose we could put a blanket on the back seat and put the crate with two of the older birds in, on the seat and let the young bird just sit next to them and see how we get on." Which is what they decided to do.

When they got level with the barn, Bertie stopped the car and went round to the boot and took the other blanket out and laid it over the floor at the back, he then went over to the barn as if to relieve himself and waited round the corner of the barn, out of sight of the road, to see if anything happened.

"Psst, Burt, over here. It's me David. I saw you earlier when you hooted the horn and drove past, I knew you would be back for us later."

The two men shook hands and then David introduced his companion to Bertie,

"This is my wife, Esther. Esther, this is my old friend Burt, but he goes by the name of Capitan Chavez."

Bertie shook the woman's hand and could see that she was visibly shaking and that it was not from the cold.

"It has taken three days longer than usual to make the crossing, due to all the extra soldiers on both sides of the border now. Unfortunately, Esther has become suspected by the Germans of helping the Resistance and I wanted her to be somewhere safe and with someone who would look after her. You will understand how I feel, my friend."

"Of course I do, David. Are you coming with us along with Esther this time?"

"No, I have to go back to France, they need me and I have some new recruits to collect on the way. The dangers are ever present and I will operate much more efficiently if I am not worrying about the welfare of my wife. Will you be able to get her back safely to your house, with all these soldiers around?"

"As long as she does not mind sharing the back seat with a few chickens, she will be fine. I have Annette with me and she seems to know everyone around here."

"Before you go, I am afraid I have some bad news for your daughter, it concerns Mac. He was arrested by the Gestapo and taken to one of their interrogation centres for questioning. He knew so much about our organisation that we could not risk him being tortured and telling what he knew. We had to call in an air strike and the building received a direct hit and was completely destroyed."

"Were there no survivors at all?" Bertie asked.

"None that we could discover. There was also an ammunition store there in an outbuilding and when it went up, it caused a terrible fire and everything and everyone was burnt to a crisp. There was virtually nothing left, but on the arm of one of the corpses was a watch, which had also been destroyed, but there were four letters engraved on the back of it 'WLDC'. I know it was the watch that Deborah had given to Mac, because he had shown it to me as we walked together on our way into France."

"She will be devastated David, but thank you for telling me."

"Bertie, Bertie, get a move on, there are soldiers heading this way from the hillside opposite, we need to get going," Annette said, as she came running to where they were talking.

David said goodbye to his wife and disappeared across the field in the opposite direction to the soldiers. Esther was told to lie across the floor at the back of the car and was covered with a blanket and they then set off down the road, with the young chicken flapping around on the back seat.

When the two men who stopped them earlier in the day, realised who it was in the car and saw the chickens on the back seat, they just waved them through, rather than risk another tirade from the formidable Miss Burra.

It was agreed to take Annette and Esther and the chickens to Annette's house in Sort and for Bertie and Deborah to collect Esther in the morning and take her to Roses, giving Bertie the opportunity to break the bad news to Deborah about Mac.

She was not able to cry when she heard about Mac's death, she just became very silent and something inside her seemed to die.

"I knew it was too good to be true, I didn't deserve someone as nice as Mac, I knew it would not last dad, I have been waiting for this, ever since he left."

"Deborah, I am so sorry, war is such an evil thing, it takes the good along with the bad and Mac was one of the best men I have ever met."

"It's O.K. dad, what do they say about loving someone, 'it's better to have loved and lost, than never to have loved at all'. I am not so sure about that, though."

That was the last thing she ever said about Mac. She never wept for him, she never mentioned him ever again and neither did Bertie. The daughter he knew died that day and someone quite different took her place; someone hard and callous, where most humans were concerned, but gentle and caring when it came to animals and their welfare.

They picked up Esther the next day and drove her to Roses with them. Annette offered to come as well, but Deborah refused her offer, but did ask if she could take two of the chickens with them to start her own chicken coop back home. She bought herself a horse and had riding lessons and spent days on her own, riding on her horse or on her motorcycle, around the countryside.

When the 6th of July came round she did not want to go to Rialp with Bertie, but stayed behind with Esther, while Bertie went on his own. The same thing happened in August and September, but she did ask Bertie to bring three more chickens back with him to add to the two she already had. David did not appear again at Rialp and neither did anyone else.

Esther took over the running of the house from Deborah and slowly became stronger and more secure in herself. She told Bertie that she had been molested by a couple of German soldiers, who had told her that they knew her husband was with the Resistance and that they could arrest her, whenever they wanted to and that they would be back for her some time soon. The nightmares slowly receded as the weeks passed and she slept quite well most nights.

Towards the end of September Bertie got a radio message saying that German agents were hunting Esther in Spain and that he should take her to Gibraltar for her own safety and that he should stay away from Rialp until otherwise instructed. He did not say anything to Esther about this, although he did tell Deborah.

Bertie started to use his fishing boat again and persuaded Deborah and Esther to dress as men and to be his crew. After a few weeks they became quite proficient working together and started to bring home reasonable catches each night, which they sold locally.

"I would love to fish from Benicarlo again," he announced one night over dinner.

"Paco said we could stay with him whenever we wanted to, so why don't we go down there," Deborah suggested, "what do you think Esther, do you fancy seeing dad's old home."

"I like it here," she answered nervously, "but if you two want to go, then of course I will come with you, I would not want to stay here on my own."

"Good that's decided, we leave tomorrow, I will ring Paco and arrange the details. Esther you can travel with Deborah on the motorcycle or you can come with me in the boat. Your choice, but it will take me a few hours longer to get down there by sea!"

"If I go with Deborah, would it be possible to do some shopping in Barcelona, on the way?" she asked.

"That's fine by me," Deborah replied, "but we will need the sidecar to put our things in, so you will have to travel pillion, unless dad takes them with him in the boat, of course."

A neighbour agreed to look after the horse and chickens while they were away and they departed Roses the following day, Wednesday 1st October 1941. Bertie left before dawn and arrived in Barcelona in late afternoon and stayed at a small hotel by the beach, where he met up with Deborah and Esther after their shopping trip. They had a meal together at a local restaurant and were on their way again to Benicarlo the next day.

Paco was extremely pleased to see the two ladies and made them welcome and was waiting by the beach when Bertie finally arrived an hour after sunset.

"I was getting worried about you my friend, you must be tired, let me help you with the boat."

"Good to see you Paco, did Deborah and Esther arrive safely?"

"Yes and they are making dinner for us, well Esther is, Deborah went for a walk as soon as she arrived here. She seems different somehow, has something happened that I need to know about?"

Bertie told him about the death of Mac and how it had affected Deborah and then he explained about Esther and the need to get her to Gibraltar for her own safety.

"It is dangerous for you to go there Bertie, are you sure you can't take her to Palma as you did before?"

"I am absolutely certain. I will just have to take the risk; I owe that to her and her husband, in view of the risks they have taken for others."

"Then I will come with you and if we are successful, maybe I can talk you into becoming Capitan of El Burro once again."

"Why so? Has it not worked out with your new Capitan then?"

"So far we have lost money on every trip he has made and he has twice damaged the ship in getting in and out of different ports. The Mate resigned after the last trip and the rest of the crew are all threatening to leave as they have not made any extra money since you left and the British have been less than friendly towards us, on several occasions already."

"Hey, in case you are thinking I have said anything to them, let me tell you I haven't. But I did warn you that things were getting more dangerous, especially if the balance of your trade shifted towards the enemy."

"I know you did and I also warned the family of the increased risk. What do you say though, if I help you get Esther to Gibraltar, will you take over the El Burro again and let our new Capitan become your First Mate."

"It's a deal Paco, but don't say anything to Esther about it at the moment please, just in case we get delayed for any reason, one thing at a time."

"Agreed Bertie, I will say nothing to her. Deborah was busy when I left going through your mail, I was going to send it to you and then I got your telephone call so kept it for you.

But it is time to eat and you must be hungry, I hope this Esther is a good cook."

"There is a letter from the Letting Agent, saying that the house in Harwich will become vacant at the end of the year dad, would you mind if I went back to England and lived there again?" she said, as they chatted after dinner.

"No, if that is what you want Deborah, but can I ask you why?"

"Everyone I loved in Spain is dead, I don't want to be here any- more. I want to go home to England and do what I can to help beat the Germans."

"I see," he said sadly, "let me think about it a bit."

"There is nothing to think about, it's easy dad. Why not just take me to Gibraltar along with Esther. She can stay there and be safe and I can travel back to England on one of the Navy's ships. Surely your contacts would be able to arrange that for me, after all I have done for them."

"What was that you said Deborah, about me going to Gibraltar?" Esther asked.

"Thank you Deborah, but I will answer that question," Bertie said firmly.

"I have been told that there are German agents in Spain searching for anyone who has crossed over from France, so it has been decided that you would be a lot safer in Gibraltar than here, that is all Esther."

"Is that why we have all been out in the boat and why we have come here then," Esther asked.

"In part yes, but in part I love fishing and thought that you would both enjoy it too; which I believe you did."

"Yes I did, thank you. When do we leave?"

"Not for a day or two yet and then I will get Deborah to take you down to Malaga on her motorcycle, while I take the boat down by sea."

"And I will go with him, so we can do some fishing and not attract anyone's attention," said Paco.

"Can I take the Indian to England with me dad?"

"If we can get it on the boat and make it safe, I don't see why not Deborah."

The next day Bertie put some flowers on the family graves, but Deborah did not want to go with him. He and Paco discussed at length the best way to get everyone safely to Gibraltar and Paco informed the Burra family that Capitan Chavez was prepared to take over El Burro again, for which they were all very thankful.

In the end they stopped in Benicarlo for almost five weeks as Esther's nightmares had returned and Bertie waited until she was feeling secure again before they resumed their journey. They met up at Malaga on the 11th November 1941 and spent two days resting before they set out on the final leg of the journey to Gibraltar. On the 13th November 1941 the British aircraft carrier Ark Royal was sunk off Gibraltar by a U-boat and with all that was going on in the area, no-one took any notice of a thirty foot long fishing boat as it slowly made its way into the harbour the next day.

Bertie was taken to see the Garrison Commander where he briefly explained who he and the other people with him were and what they were doing in Gibraltar. He was passed to Military Intelligence who immediately radioed London to get verification of his story. They were all held in the garrison over night and the boat, motorcycle and catch of fish were impounded. Eventually Michael became available and spoke with Bertie and the officer in charge who had been handling matters in Gibraltar. Everything was explained to the officer, who then made arrangements to find accommodation and work for Esther, for as long as she required it and for getting Deborah and her motorcycle shipped across the sea to England.

By Christmas 1941 Deborah was living on her own in the house at Harwich, having acquired some second hand furniture and bed linen and had secured a job working in the accounts department at Alderton's warehouses, where her mother and grandparents had worked before her. Esther was working as a radio operator for Military Intelligence in Gibraltar and Bertie, having taken his fishing boat back to Roses, with Paco's help, was once more Capitan of El Burro Volando II and was starting to make a profit again for the family and the crew.

Chapter 24
El Burro to the Rescue

When Annette heard that Deborah had gone back to England, she offered to keep house for Bertie in Roses. She said that she had such happy memories of the time she spent there with John, that she just liked being there as it reminded her of him. She told Bertie that he had been injured again on a bombing raid over Germany when his aircraft had been hit by flak, but he told her that although it was not serious, it did mean that his flying days were well and truly over.

"I am truly sorry to hear that he has been hurt again Bertie," she said, "but I am also relieved to know that in the future, he will be a lot safer with a ground based job in England than flying dangerous missions over Germany. He still won't tell me what his injuries were though, which does worry me a bit."

"If it was serious Annette, he would not be working at all, so it is probably just something that affects his ability to fly a plane and I do not have any idea what that might be, so please don't ask me."

The war in North Africa severely restricted the movements and trading opportunities for El Burro during 1942 and the first half of 1943 but once Italy had surrendered to the Allies in early September, Bertie and Paco were able to arrange many lucrative contracts, ferrying equipment and some injured men from Tripoli and Tunisia across the Mediterranean Sea to Salerno in Italy. Although there was some risk to their 'neutral' position, Bertie always carried out these voyages at night with the ship's name covered over and flying a British Flag. In view of his detailed knowledge of the Mediterranean Sea, he often led a small convoy of boats on these missions and only once was one of the ships attacked by a 'U' boat, before an accompanying destroyer was able to chase it away.

During the last four months of 1943 Paco was able to arrange for a second trip to Port Elizabeth to collect a cargo of manganese ore for delivery to Southampton and offered to come along and act as cook for the passengers and crew of El Burro. Annette laughed when she heard this and said that whilst his cooking was adequate for the crew, she did not think it would be adequate for fare paying passengers and offered to come along herself to fulfill that role.

"Annette, I have to tell you that there is a war going on still and whilst we have been extremely lucky so far on all of our ventures, there is still a very significant element of danger to this particular voyage."

"I know Bertie, but you said you were going to Southampton in England and it would give me the chance to leave the ship there and to go and visit my John in Lincoln. If you didn't mind, that is."

"Of course I don't mind Annette, but we will only be in Southampton a few days and if you were not back when we departed, I would have to leave you behind. Do you understand what I am saying to you?"

"Oh I certainly do Bertie and thank you so much." With which she threw her arms round his neck and gave him a big hug.

They called at the usual places for supplies and to trade, on the way to South Africa and were pleased to find that the cargo was ready and waiting this time, with no special requests or threats to worry about. All the passengers left the ship and only two, a husband and wife returning to England, had booked for the return journey, so Annette was allotted one of the deluxe cabins in appreciation of her hard work, a gesture which was much appreciated by her.

Bertie had a few days to spare in South Africa, so he and Paco took Annette into Cape Town and showed her the sights and some of the places they had visited before and helped her to invest her hard earned wages in a very attractive diamond ring and necklace and a gold watch for John.

Annette had written to John saying that she hoped to be in Southampton at the end of December and that she would let him know which hotel she was staying in as soon as she arrived there and John had managed to agree with his Commanding Officer that he could take leave, as soon as he heard from Annette, assuming that there was nothing urgent in progress, at the base.

The ship arrived in Southampton on Friday the 17th December 1943 and Bertie, Paco and Annette were able to get adjoining rooms at the Star Hotel on the High Street. Paco and Annette both spoke a little bit of English, but Bertie did all the bookings and ordering of food for them all, to save any misunderstandings among the hotel staff.

John arrived by train late Sunday night and was delighted to see Annette and having invited Bertie and Paco to come into Annette's room for a glass of champagne, that he had brought with him, did no more than drop down onto one knee and proposed to her.

"My wonderful, darling Annette," he said, "you are the only woman I have ever truly loved; will you do me the profound honour of marrying me and becoming my wife?"

"Oh John," she answered, with both her hands held to her face in surprise, "I would love to marry you and become your wife, for you too are the only man I have ever loved and I never want to be parted from you ever again." With which the happy couple embraced and the two friends offered their sincere congratulations.

Deborah arrived on the Monday and took over Annette's room, since she had gone up to Richmond with John in the morning, to meet his parents and sisters.

"That's nice for her," said Deborah, when Bertie told her about Annette and John, "I'm glad someone is happy. So what was so wrong with him that he couldn't fly anymore?"

"He had gone deaf in one ear and his left eye had been damaged by the flack, so it was just too unsafe for him to fly again."

"So how is life in Harwich, this time round?" he asked.

"I would say that it is just about as boring as last time round, maybe more so. I went up to London the other week, the devastation is unimaginable! My old flat took a hit and is gone, along with half the street it was on, it will take years for London to recover from this war."

"Does that mean you would like to come back to Spain with me? I can't imagine Annette will be coming back, now that she has become engaged to John."

"Of course it doesn't mean that, why would you even think it? I told you I didn't want to be there anymore. I might be bored in Harwich but at least I feel I am doing something useful here, not just hiding myself in safe old neutral Spain, out of harm's way, like some people I know."

The implication of what his daughter had just said to him, pierced him through and through;

"Are you calling me a coward Deborah?" he asked.

"Your words not mine dad."

"I think you had better go back to Harwich as soon as you can, you and I have nothing more to say to each other. I can't believe what you just said to me, my own daughter, you disgust me!"

"The feeling is mutual dad. Suit yourself, but it was you who called me and asked me to come and see you, not the other way round, remember!"

There was no kiss goodbye, no embrace, she picked up her suitcase which was lying on the bed, walked to the station and got the next train back to London and then out to Harwich. She had no more contact with her father for the remainder of the war.

Bertie and Paco left on El Burro the following Thursday, the 23rd December, without Annette and arrived back in Barcelona on Christmas Day. Paco never asked what had passed between Bertie and his daughter, but recognised the look of sadness in his eyes, that had not been there before. Bertie never mentioned Deborah again and Paco had the good sense not to ask about her.

In February Bertie received a letter from Annette announcing that She and John were to marry in Richmond on Saturday the 22nd of April 1944 and asked if he would be prepared to give her away, assuming he was able to make the journey. He discussed it with Paco, but they both decided it was not going to be possible to be in Richmond at that time, in view of the current schedule for El Burro, so he sent a note back thanking her for the invitation but saying he would not be able to get there for that date.

The wedding was a most joyful affair and the happy couple had a two day honeymoon in Oxford, before going back to R.A.F. married quarters in Lincoln. As her English improved, Annette began to make friends among the wives of the other officers in the camp, but she always felt cold and damp in Lincolnshire and badly missed the sunshine and warmth of Spain.

They were chatting by the fire, one chilly evening in late November when Annette raised the question of moving back to Spain, once the war was over.

"It has to end sometime John, it cannot go on forever. Some of the wives think the war could all be over by this time next year," she informed him.

"I know that is what they are saying Annette, but we just don't know, do we?"

"Couldn't you just speak with Deborah and see if she would consider selling her house in Roses to us. What can be the harm in that?"

"If her father is not speaking with her any more, what chance will we have? She is jealous of you because you have me and she has lost Mac. She didn't even have the good manners to reply to the Wedding Invitation."

"I know that is how it looks, but she is not really jealous of me, she is just hurting because she has lost the man she loved; she was an entirely different person while Mac was around."

"Well even if you are right, what sort of job would I be able to do in Spain, how would I earn a living and support us?"

"The house and garden have enough land to support us and we could take in holiday guests if we converted the stables to guest accommodation. You could learn how to fish and best of all, you will be able to paint again. Just think John, how wonderful that would be."

"You make it sound wonderful Annette and I am willing to give it a try, I know how much you miss Spain and the sunshine. Let's wait till next year when things should be a bit clearer regarding the end of the war and then we will go to Harwich and see her and speak with her face to face; that is the best way to do it, in my opinion."

It was in fact April 1945 before they made contact with Deborah and were able to travel to Harwich to see her.

"It's so good to see you again Deborah," said Annette as she and John sat down on the settee after giving her old friend a hug and a kiss.

"John has been so busy these last few months that we have not had a chance to come and see you. How have you been keeping?"

"Good, thank you Annette and I am sorry that I did not reply to your wedding invitation, it was rude of me, but belated congratulations and I hope you will both have a long and happy marriage together."

"Thank you," John replied, "we appreciate that, don't we Annette?"

"We do indeed John, thank you. Do you intend staying in Harwich, once the war is over?" Annette enquired.

"Goodness no, I loathe the place, I can't wait to get back to London again, I really miss the buzz of the big city, although it is looking very sad and devastated at the moment."

They chatted for a while and then had a walk down by the river and when they got back to the house, Deborah could see that there was something troubling Annette.

"Are you alright Annette, it looks like something is bothering you?" Deborah said.

"I'll come straight to the point," John said on his wife's behalf, "we were wondering if you would consider selling us your house in Roses? Annette can't wait to return to Spain as soon as hostilities end and we would like to make Roses our home."

"Well my dad lives there at the moment, as he is still renting out his house in Benicarlo to Paco's niece, as far as I know and this house here belongs to him, so it is all pretty complex and would need to be properly sorted out between us, but I would be happy to sell my house in Roses to you Annette. It's such a shame I can't have my old flat in London back again, I just loved living there before the war, it was great for work and the exhibitions and of course all the shows in the West End."

"I may be able to help you there Deborah. My grandparents used to own a shop in Fulham with a flat above it and although they sold the shop off when they retired, they kept the flat and we all used to stay in it when we were up in town, before the war spoiled everything for everyone. They have a tenant in there at the moment, but we think she will move back up north, once the war is over. If I give you the address, you can check it out when next you are in London."

"Sounds promising and Fulham is not too far from where I used to live, so yes I will certainly do that John."

Meanwhile in Spain, Bertie had persuaded Paco that they should do what they can to assist the Allies, as he believed the ultimate victory would be theirs, even if it took another year or so to complete. With the exception of carrying combat troops, Bertie continued to help where he could, regardless of the risks to himself and his ship. He was on the radio to London in November 1944 when he was informed that David and several of his comrades had been arrested by the Vichy police in France and taken to Marseille for questioning.

"When the war is almost over, why would the Vichy police arrest them now?" Bertie asked.

"Because they know the names of those who collaborated with the Germans and who were responsible for rounding up the Jews and sending them to their death," Michael replied.

"Surely they will already be dead then!" Bertie suggested.

"We don't believe so, not yet anyway. We think they will hold a trial with trumped up charges and then have them executed, so that there can be no come-back after the war."

"I see," said Bertie, "so what can I do to help them Michael?"

"We have a company of marine commandos at Toulon, ready to go and mount a rescue attempt, but they are being monitored and the moment the Vichy police know they are heading for Marseille, they will indeed execute David and the others. We have arranged for a troop transporter to leave with them on Wednesday evening, ostensibly heading for Rome, but we would like you to meet it, ten miles off Toulon and transfer the men and their equipment to your ship and then take the commandos to Marseille, so that they can launch a surprise attack."

"I guess we owe David and the others that much at least," Bertie said, "I can leave Barcelona tomorrow lunch time and be at the rendezvous point round about 3:00a.m. will that do?"

"Thank you Bertie, I knew I could rely on you," Michael said, "good luck my friend."

Bertie was not sure what Paco would say about the venture and did not want another confrontation with the Burra family, so he did not ask his permission for this trip. Without a cargo to load and unload, he did not need a full crew, so he drove to Barcelona and spoke with half a dozen of the men he knew he could rely on, plus he invited a couple of retired skippers to make up the remainder of the crew, who he knew would be sympathetic to the cause and left harbour just after mid-day. He was completely honest with the men about the risks involved, but they all agreed that they could not stand by and let these brave men die.

They met up with the troop transporter at the appointed time and transferred two dozen men plus their guns and other equipment to the ship and arrived at Marseille around dawn. As they tied up alongside an empty dock the local police arrived and demanded to know what was going on. Bertie invited them aboard, where they were quickly overpowered by the commandos, who interrogated them and discovered where the Vichy police were holding David and the others. Several soldiers exchanged uniforms with the policemen who were tied up and put in the rear hold and the covers replaced over them. The commandos, their transport and weapons were quickly unloaded and with the police car leading the way, the party headed for the Vichy H.Q.

The guard at the dock gate made the mistake of raising his weapon at the convoy and was shot dead for his trouble, with one of the commandos taking his place at the guard post. No one seemed to take too much notice of a police car leading a convoy of Allied soldiers and when they drove into the police compound they were not challenged or threatened at all. The commandos swarmed into the police station and soon found the prisoners, chained together in the cells. David and several others showed signs that they had already been tortured and had missing teeth and damaged hands, feet and limbs to prove it.

The opposition soon evaporated and it was reported afterwards, that those who were responsible for the torture had feared retribution and had shot themselves in the head and one or two others who had tried to resist the commandos, had been shot dead as well. Fortunately the commandos did not sustain any serious injuries, but two men were treated for flesh wounds.

As David was unable to walk un-aided, they offered to take him to hospital, but when he found out that a Capitan Chavez on El Burro Volando II had ferried the commandos to Marseille, he asked to be taken to the ship and to be allowed to travel back to Spain with Bertie and his crew. The other freed men opted to remain in France and return to their families.

A sergeant and two men drove David to the ship and helped him aboard, where Bertie greeted him and got a chair for him to sit on, while he had something to eat and drink. As the commandos were escorting the three captured policemen from the hold, David suddenly lunged at Bertie, pulled the Luger from his belt, where he had put it earlier and pointed it at one of the men under escort.

David and the policeman exchanged words, shouting at each other in French and when David flicked the safety lock off, it became apparent what was going to happen next. The sergeant moved quickly and knocked the gun upwards and the bullet passed over the man's head and before David had the chance to fire again, it was wrestled out of his grip.

"What on earth are you doing David?" Bertie asked him.

"This is the man who arrested my parents and had them sent to the Concentration camp," David explained, "he deserves to die."

"How can you be so sure it was him?" Bertie asked. "You told me you were away on business at the time."

"Esther saw him and another man snooping round the house a few hours beforehand and his role was confirmed to me by the man I executed at Rialp. He named this man as the ring-leader of the group. What makes it even worse, is that he used to work for my father in the shop when he was younger and when we were all gone away, he took it over and gave it to his brother to run for him. He is far worse than the Germans were, he betrayed his own friends and neighbours and stole their goods and belongings."

"If you would care to make a statement to that effect sir," the sergeant said, "I will take it with me and give it to the proper authorities. This man will certainly pay for his crimes, but in a proper court of law, not here, at your hands."

The statement was written out and signed by David and the sergeant asked Bertie and another of the old skippers to witness it. The commandos took the prisoners away and as there were no passengers or cargo that needed to go back to Barcelona, Bertie decided it would be better for David if he was to take him directly to Gibraltar, to be with his wife once again.

While they were on their way there, Bertie managed to make radio contact with the Military Intelligence officer he had dealt with before and to tell him that he was on his way with David and to let Esther know, so that she could be ready for her injured husband. Bertie made contact again when they were just a couple of hours away from port and were given precise details of where they should anchor in the harbour.

Before the ship had come to a standstill, a Navy launch had come alongside and the Intelligence Officer, accompanied by Esther and four sailors had come aboard.

"Capitan Chavez, I have to inform you that the Spanish authorities have already lodged a complaint about you taking the ship without the owner's permission and using it to assist the Allies in their war effort," the officer informed him.

"Oh really," said Bertie, "so what happens now?"

"We have of course denied any knowledge of any of this and have told them that whatever you did had nothing whatsoever to do with us. I am sorry sir, but officially we cannot help you; unofficially, we will apply all the pressure we can to assist you and once the war is over, I am sure they will have very short memories about all of this."

"Let's hope you are right Lieutenant, let's hope you are right! I would like to speak with David and Esther privately before they leave please."

"Of course sir and may I say in confidence, how much we have all admired your bravery and patriotism throughout the entire period of the war and how sorry we are to leave you in this mess. You have supported us every time we have asked you to and I personally feel saddened, that when a time has come that you need us to support you, we have refused to help you."

"Thank you Lieutenant, the fortunes of war, I guess!"

Bertie went to his cabin where he found David and Esther holding hands and crying and just being together.

"Esther has just told me what the officer said to you Burt, I don't know what to say, my friend! You saved my life and the lives of my friends, you saved Esther for me and now you will probably go to prison as a reward. I am so sorry; can't you just stay here with us in Gibraltar and quietly return to England some time?"

"I knew the risks I was taking, just like you did David, you have nothing to feel sorry about. I have to go back to make sure the rest of the crew come to no harm, but one of the old timers with me has an idea as to what we should say, so I am not expecting a severe sentence, just a slap on the wrist or a fine maybe."

"I do hope you are right," said Esther, "I like it here and would like to stay and start over again, but we will have to get David fit and well before we are able to do that."

"Maybe this will help you get started again," Bertie said, as he handed an old haversack over to David. "I know you lost everything you owned in France and I might well have everything of mine confiscated, that the authorities find on this ship, when I get back to Barcelona; so think of this as an investment, in all of our futures."

David opened the haversack and gasped, "Bertie, this is worth a small fortune are you sure you want to give us all of this to look after?"

"I would far rather you had it than the Spanish authorities," he answered back.

"Then we will treat it is an investment in our new jewellery business and we will hold it for you until you are able to come and collect it yourself. You are now a third share partner in the new 'Joseph's Jewellery and Antiques' business," David replied.

There was a knock at the door and the officer called out, "Time to go ashore folks, leaving in two minutes."

While Esther was in the bathroom, Bertie took the Luger from his belt and put it in the haversack saying,

"You take this with you David, as you never know what will happen next. The war is not over yet and you still need to be constantly on your guard, so good luck my friend."

Bertie had retained enough of his personal wealth, to pay all the men the standard wage for the trip, so that they could all say that as far as they knew it was a proper, approved voyage and that they had been paid accordingly.

When they returned to Barcelona the police were waiting for them and arrested Bertie the moment he stepped ashore. For two days they questioned him but he acted sick and deaf and pretended that he could not understand their questions. In the end Paco was brought in to speak with him, to see if he could get any sense out of him.

"I know this is just an act Bertie and I am sorry to see you in gaol like this, but taking the ship on a commando raid is beyond anything that even I would have agreed to, you could all have been killed and the ship sunk into the bargain."

Bertie looked him in the eye and said quietly,

"Paco, that is precisely why I did not discuss it with you. Remember that woman, Esther, that you helped me take to Gibraltar, it was her husband and some other Resistance leaders, that the Vichy police were torturing at Marseille. I could not stand by and do nothing and this was the best chance they had for escape and it worked Paco and El Burro was not damaged in the process; I just owe you for the fuel we used on the journey, that's all."

"But why didn't you tell me all this, I would have come with you Bertie."

"I did not want to involve you Paco, as Spain is a neutral in this War and I knew all this would happen once the authorities found out about it."

"I see," he said, "what can I do to help you get out of this mess?"

"Well first of all, the British are denying there was any commando raid in Marseille and therefore, know nothing about El Burro being involved in one. Old Pedro, who came with me, has told me that a massive stock of vintage Wines and Brandy has been found in Marseille and he is getting one of his relatives to acquire some for him, but to backdate all the paperwork to ten days ago. Once he has confirmed to me, that he has the papers, I will tell the world that we went to Marseille to collect the shipment before the Allies found it and claimed it for themselves."

"Very clever, so what do I tell the police?"

"Say nothing at the moment and that I am still not well and can't remember anything that happened. Then go and visit Pedro and ask if the paperwork is all in place and to confirm that the shipment is ready to be picked up. Once you know that it is ready, tell me and I will miraculously get better and remember what happened."

The following day Paco and Pedro came into the police station and spoke with Bertie and confirmed that the deal had been set up and the cargo and paperwork were all in place. They then informed the officer in charge that Bertie seemed a lot better and had got over his temporary amnesia, caused by a blow on the head from one of the soldiers at Marseille.

"So you see officer, there was no time to discuss the deal with the owners, as we had been told that the cargo was ready to be transported to the dock but that the allies would be landing troops and equipment there, for most of the following week."

"If that is the case, why did you not radio the owners once you were on your way, tell me that Capitan Chavez?" the officer replied.

"The war might almost be over, but there are still German warships in the Mediterranean Sea, so I considered it unwise to disclose this information. Besides which, I did not want the allies to find out about the cargo of vintage wine, or they would have taken all of it and we would have had nothing."

"So you arrive at Marseille and then what happens?"

"We went to the dock where Pedro's agent had the first part of the cargo stored, but unfortunately a British ship tied up behind us and as the troops disembarked they spotted the wine and decided to help themselves. I went ashore to speak with one of the officers who seemed to be in charge and told him that it was my cargo and his men were stealing it. He laughed in my face and told me to make a formal complaint to the Garrison Commander at Gibraltar. I stupidly tried to grab his arm to stop him leaving and he hit me in the chest as he pushed past me. I fell backwards over a crate and hit my head as I fell, which has given me these bouts of sickness and memory loss, which I have had ever since."

"I don't believe a word of this Capitan Chavez. Do you have any proof of this story that you have just told me?"

"I believe my old friend Pedro, who is sitting outside of your office has the paperwork with him, if you will excuse me a moment."

Bertie walked outside, spoke with Pedro who gave him the paperwork he needed, which he then gave to the officer when he went back into his office.

The officer inspected it and smiled as he passed it back to Bertie.

"So when are you now planning to get the cargo and bring it back to Barcelona, Capitan Chavez?"

"As soon as you release me and the owners agree to the trip, we will return to Marseille for the rest of the cargo."

"Just one more thing," the officer said, "do tell me what the Garrison Commander said when you made your official complaint to him?"

"He said it was a most unfortunate incident and he would look into the matter and speak with the Officer involved and if it proved to be true, that we would receive compensation."

"Really! Well when you come back to Barcelona from Marseille, I intend to be there to inspect the cargo and when you hear from the Garrison Commander, I want to see the letter. Is that clear Capitan Chavez?"

"Absolutely officer and I gather from Paco, that the Burra family have withdrawn all charges against me, now that they understand my reasons for the trip; so I assume I am free to go now?"

Bertie drove back to Roses and just slept for almost forty eight hours. Once he was awake he radioed Michael in London and told him what had been happening and how the British had deserted him to the mercies of the Spanish police.

"I don't want your sympathy Michael, I want a letter to me, from the Garrison Commander saying that he has investigated the matter and that he apologises for the incident and encloses a bank draft which is enough to cover the wages for the crew, the fuel we used and the lost profit for the trip."

"I'll do what I can Bertie, but there is a war on you know."

"I know that very well Michael, I have been fighting it for just as long as you and the other desk wallers in Whitehall, or wherever you are based now. My crew and I put our very lives on the line for you and I expect you to deliver for me this time, is that understood?" With which he ended his broadcast.

They eventually went back to Marseille in January and picked up the cargo of vintage wines, brandy, port and sherry, which they took back to Barcelona. The police officer was there to meet them when they docked and was presented with a fine old bottle of brandy for his efforts. Paco and Pedro found lots of willing buyers for the cargo, which eventually made a handsome profit for all involved.

Bertie never did get his letter from the Garrison Commander, but a large sum of money was transferred to his Spanish Bank account, which covered all the costs he had previously discussed with Michael plus a little extra for himself.

David wrote to say that he had virtually recovered from his wounds and that he and Esther had decided to remain in Gibraltar and were negotiating to purchase a shop with an apartment over it, in order to have proper premises for their new Jewellery and Antique business.

Bertie drove down to Benicarlo in May to visit Paco and his other friends and was with them on Tuesday the 8th May 1945 when Victory in Europe (V-E Day) was declared.

Chapter 25
New Beginnings

It took just over another three months and the deaths of thousands of more people, before the Japanese surrendered on the 14th August 1945. The war was finally over and Captain Bertie Bannister once again appeared on the scene and Capitan Bertram Chavez mysteriously disappeared.

The new Capitan of El Burro Volando II, actually took over the job in July and Bertie returned to England to see his daughter and to sort out his affairs.

"I am really sorry dad, for what I said to you at Southampton," were Deborah's first words to her father when he entered the house in Harwich. "I knew they were not true, but I was hurting so badly and I felt so alone, here on my own-"

"You don't need to say any more Deborah," Bertie interrupted, "I know you did not mean what you said, so let's just forget you ever said it and never mention it again, O.K.?"

They sat down and had a cup of tea and got to know each other again as they talked about their lives and their hopes for the future.

"I don't quite know how to tell you this dad, but I have sold the house in Roses to John and Annette," she informed him. Bertie looked surprised, but said nothing.

"Annette did say that she would be quite happy for you to live there with them, if you wanted to, but I am not sure it would be a good idea."

"I would agree with you there, she can be a bit tetchy about things sometimes, if they are not done her way. The house at Roses was yours, to do with as you wished Deborah and probably like you, it contains as many bad memories as good ones for me. I think you have made a good decision, for both of our sakes."

"Thanks dad. The other part of the deal with John and Annette, is that I get to have his grandparents flat in Fulham and it is not too far from where my old flat used to be. The old lady who was their tenant has moved back up north to live with her daughter, so it is now legally mine and I was hoping to move in at the end of August, which means that I won't need your house here in Harwich anymore."

"What about your job in the warehouse, what are you going to do about that?"

"I contacted my old company in London and they have offered me the position of assistant manager of the Household Insurance Department, which is where I first started working for them, so I have already resigned from my job here."

"My word, you have been busy, congratulations Deborah that is great news, well done," with which he gave his daughter a kiss and a big hug.

"The flat does have two bedrooms dad, if you wanted to live with me in London, you are most welcome to stay with me," she offered.

"Well it might be nice to come up to London occasionally and see a show with you, but I dislike big cities as much as you love them, so thanks, but no thanks."

"So what do you plan to do now?" she asked. "Will you get your house back in Benicarlo and live there, or live here in Harwich, or maybe you will retire to the country and write your memoirs. You certainly have a lot of interesting stories to tell!"

"I am not sure what to do, to tell you the truth, but like you, I do not want to live here in Harwich. This was your grandparents home, it was never really mine, I just had a room in the attic, The house we lived in at Gravesend is what I think of as my childhood home, but I have no desire to live there again either."

"Will you take me to see that house some time, and show me where you found the watch that really started your whole seafaring career?" Deborah asked.

"Yes, certainly I will, assuming the German bombs did not destroy it."

"So you know where you don't want to live, but that still does not answer the question of where you do want to be?"

"Very True. I suppose that I could live in Benicarlo again, but I would want to be out in a boat fishing or trading, but at sixty six, I think I am getting too old for that life and would not want to just play at it, like a lot of the old skippers do. No, your idea of a place in the English countryside is actually quite a good one and you're right, I do have some interesting yarns I could write down."

"That's great dad, I was really worried about telling you that I was evicting you from Roses; do you have any thoughts as to which part of the country you would like to settle in?"

"I am ashamed to admit that I do not know England that well and only visited Scotland once, when I was buying my Buckie Steam Drifter. When I was a young man, I went with a friend to visit his family in Aylesbury, Buckinghamshire and was really taken with the area round about there, so I might just start looking over that way and see what I can find."

"Didn't Rosie say that her ancestors were from that part of the country, as well?" said Deborah.

John was discharged from the Royal Air Force on the 31st March 1946 and he and Annette had all their things packed and were on a ship to Barcelona, ten days later. Bertie had already returned to Spain and he drove his car down to the port to meet them when they arrived. He then drove them to

Roses after arranging for their cases and trunks to follow by lorry, a few days later. Having deposited them in their new house and helped them to un-pack and get straight, he used the same packing cases to ship his and Deborah's things back to England, a couple of weeks after that.

He had arranged with Paco and his niece for them to carry on renting his house for at least a couple of years while he got himself settled in England. It also meant that if he could not settle there, he had somewhere to return to and would not have to build yet another house in Benicarlo to live in.

John had expressed interest in buying Bertie's car, the Renault Juvaquatre, but he was a bit short of cash, so since Bertie did not relish the idea of driving a 'left hand drive' car in England, he told him that he could borrow it, provided he kept it properly serviced, until he had sufficient funds to purchase it from him.

He went to the bank and closed his various bank accounts in the names of Bannister and Chavez and had the funds transferred to his bank account in England. His remaining 'nest egg' of the gold, money and jewellery that he had stashed away in his house in Benicarlo was removed from its 'hidey-hole' and carefully hidden about his person and in his luggage for his trip back to England. He declared his duty free allowance of brandy and tobacco and then calmly walked through the customs barrier at Dover without being stopped and searched.

Bertie returned to Harwich in early June and immediately spoke to an Estate Agent about selling the house and then spent a couple of weeks with Deborah in her flat, painting and decorating, while she was at work. Their short time together in her flat, firmly convinced both of them that they needed their own 'space and place' and never spoke of sharing a house again.

In mid June he travelled to Buckinghamshire and went to see an Estate Agent in Aylesbury that he had telephoned a few days earlier.

"Mr. Bannister, nice to meet you," the manager said to him, "I have details of five houses that I think might interest you, all in good positions and in an excellent state of repair, just as you specified."

"That sounds hopeful," Bertie replied, "shall we get started?"

"Just before we do," the Agent said, "may I ask if you have had any offers yet, for the house you are selling in Harwich?"

"I am pleased to report, that two days ago, a couple from London were shown round the house and went straight back to see my agent and made an offer for it, which I have since accepted."

"That is wonderful news, do you know if they have a property to sell first?"

"Apparently not, my agent tells me they are cash buyers and can Complete as soon as all the paperwork is in place, which is really good news."

"It certainly is Mr. Bannister, so let me show you what we have here."

It took Bertie less than ten minutes to realise that not one of the houses that the agent showed him, was suitable for his needs. Two houses were priced well over his budget, one was next to a Sewage Works, one was on a main road with heavy lorries going past all day and night and one was in the middle of Aylesbury, right next to the shops.

"Is that it? I did say to you on the telephone, a small cottage, in a rural location, by a river or a lake if possible. The only one of these which comes close to what I specified is the one by the sewage works, if you can call that a lake! Are there any other agents in this part of town that I can visit?" he asked, standing up and heading for the door.

"Perhaps Mr. Bannister might be interested in that little cottage in the clearing in the woods, just outside Upper Style," the receptionist suggested to the manager, "it is in a beautiful position and he may be happy to carry out the renovations that are needed."

"What little cottage is that?" asked Bertie.

"It is an estate cottage and has been empty since the War started," the manager replied, "it is not in a very good state of repair Mr. Bannister and it does not even have a bathroom. To be quite honest with you, I did not think you would be interested in it, considering the amount of work that needs to be done."

"Do you have any details that I could look at please?" Bertie asked.

The receptionist passed the details across to Bertie, who studied them with interest. "No bathroom but it has electricity, mains water and an inside toilet with a septic tank I see. Leasehold then, with fifty three years to run, well that should see me out all right. Can we go and see it, my daughter has been telling me that I need a new project to immerse myself in?"

The road from Aylesbury to Oxford went first through Lower Style and then passed through Upper Style, which was a small village with a population of about three hundred. At the edge of town was a big church surrounded by well kept gardens, where they turned right up a dirt track, passing a large house on their left and after about a quarter of a mile, the manager pulled off the road and stopped by an old bridle path that led into the wood.

"I hope you don't mind mud Mr. Bannister, this path does not get a lot of use and can get a bit boggy, I am afraid. Please follow me and mind where you tread, it's about a five minute walk down here."

They emerged from the wood into a large clearing with a cottage squarely situated in the middle of it. A boundary wall seemed to circle the cottage, but it had got broken down in places and stones were lying everywhere. An old gate sat in the middle of the front wall and looked like it had not seen a coat of varnish for decades and a wide gravel path, overgrown with weeds, went from the gate and led up to the solid wooden front door, which was in the middle of the cottage. An outbuilding of some description had been added to the left hand side of the cottage and the roof of the whole structure was covered in thatch, with the occasional bird flying in and out of it.

The estate agent remained silent and waited for his client to berate him for wasting his time, but to his surprise, he turned to him and said, "This is just what I had in mind, I really like it. It is certainly in need of some renovations and is going to take me a couple of years to get it how I want it, but as I said earlier, I need a new project and this will suit me fine."

"I can't tell you how relieved I am Mr. Bannister, I was secretly cursing my receptionist for mentioning the property to you. Shall we go inside?"

They went into the cottage and climbed the stairs and looked out of the upstairs windows and Bertie was delighted to discover that he could see the lake that belonged to the estate, from both bedrooms. Although the inside was dilapidated and the walls needed repairing and a coat of paint, they seemed to be sound, with no serious cracks in them and there did not appear to be any woodworm in the house and the water pressure from the tap in the outbuilding seemed good, but the sink in the kitchen was cracked and the cupboards were filthy and broken.

They went back to the Estate Agent's office in Aylesbury after the inspection, where Bertie made an official offer for the property and when he telephoned the manager the next day, he was delighted to find that his offer had been accepted, subject to a proper survey being carried out, on his behalf.

On Wednesday the 7th August 1946 the sale of the house in Harwich was completed and on Tuesday the 13th August 1946 Bertie became the proud owner of the old woodman's cottage on the Manor Estate in Upper Style, which from then on became known as 'Bertie's Cottage' to all the locals.

Deborah loved the cottage and often drove the Indian down for the weekend to give her dad a helping hand with the renovations. She had removed the sidecar from the motorcycle so that she could take the bike through the back gate of the garden attached to the flat and leave it there under a tarpaulin, when she was not using it.

As luck would have it, another cottage in the village was having its thatched roof repaired just after he moved in, so Bertie spoke to the two men who were doing it and they came round to take a look. They gave him an estimate which he accepted and they were able to work on it for him, during the last couple of weeks of September.

The old kitchen range was about done for and Deborah had told him about a new wood burning cooker, called a Rayburn Number 1, which she had seen at an exhibition in London. He made enquiries about the Rayburn and eventually ordered one with the seventeen gallon side tank, to provide his hot water; having agreed with the Estate Manager of the Manor, that he could have free access to all the dead branches he found in the woods around his cottage.

While the roof was being repaired and the kitchen was out of commission, Bertie stayed at the village pub, The Stag and became good friends with the landlord and his wife, Del and Sheila.

He spent Christmas 1946 with Deborah in Fulham and paid a visit to Michael and Anne Callard who were still living in London.

"Your friend David was a mine of information Bertie," Michael informed him, "no wonder the Vichy police wanted him dead and I am so sorry we left you in the lurch like we did, but I assume that the cash we sent you covered all of your expenses."

"It did, thank you Michael and no hard feelings on my part, I would have helped David to escape, whatever it might have cost me. Is he going to be allowed to remain in Gibraltar?"

"For as long as he wants to Bertie and I gather that you assisted him and his wife in setting up a new business there. Jewellery and antiques I have been told."

"I don't believe it," Bertie exclaimed, "is there anything your lot does not find out about people, what happened to privacy and being left alone to live your own life as you want to?"

"If those days ever existed, they have certainly gone now, my friend. But you have done your bit for your country and my parting gift to you when I retire is that I will remove your name and address from the records, if I can."

"Thank you Michael I appreciate that, but don't get me wrong, it has been both exciting and rewarding working with you and without your assistance I would never have managed to get Deborah out of Santiago. So I will always be in your debt for that."

"Have you thought of what you might do once the work on the cottage has been completed?" Anne enquired.

"I expect it to take me another fifteen or sixteen months and to be quite honest, I really don't know after that. There are some old friends in Australia and New Zealand that I would like to catch up with, so maybe a cruise will be on the cards, who knows? But I hope the two of you will come and visit me when you have a bit more spare time on your hands."

During 1947 Bertie replaced the rotten window frames in the bedrooms and repaired the ones downstairs and replaced all the broken panes of glass. He painted the whole house inside and out after repairing the cracked and broken plaster. He was assisted by a local man called Tom Small. He was an ex-soldier who was invalided out of the army in 1943 and had a mean and vicious temper, but worked well and got on with Bertie, right from the start, apart from one thing that is.

"I can't call you Bertie, it sounds a bit 'lardy dah', to put it bluntly," Tom said, when they were introduced by Del at the pub one night.

"O.K. Tom, my full name is Robert, so call me Robert then, if you find Bertie too hard to say."

"Look no offence meant, err Robert, but would you mind if I just called you Burt?"

"Not at all Tom. One of the bravest men I have ever known and a very dear friend, calls me Burt, so please feel free and let's drink to a long and happy friendship."

"To friendship," Tom replied, as he drank his beer.

"So we agree, a shilling an hour for forty hours a week and if you need some extra help, your son, young Tom, is willing to provide it at sixpence an hour and you can start on Monday morning, that is excellent news," Bertie said.

Tom and Bertie proved to be a formidable team and worked really well together and when an extra pair of hands were required, Tom's son could be relied on to assist the older men. In fact Bertie quite liked the young man and got him started on clearing the weeds from the garden and re-seeding the lawn and pruning the trees and shrubs, when he was not needed to help with the other jobs.

"Mr. Bannister, have you got a minute, come and see what I have found," young Tom called out one day, while pruning some badly overgrown rhododendron bushes in the back garden.

"What have you found there, son?" Bertie asked.

"I think it must have been a pond at some time, but is filled with muck and rubbish now, do you want me to clean it out for you?"

"Why not, it would be good to have a pond in my garden; I might even make a model of one of the ships I used to skipper, to sail on it."

The pond was cleaned out, repaired and filled with water and a few goldfish were added later and Bertie made a model of the Buckie Steam Drifter he once owned, to sit there in the middle of the pond, with a fishing net stowed at the rear, waiting to go over the side.

He was walking home from the village one day, carrying a couple of bags of groceries he had purchased from the village store and was approaching the large house on the left, which went by the name of Millstone House and was being very careful where he trod as it had been raining for a couple of days and the track had got very muddy; when suddenly the black Morris Eight, driven by one of the women who lived at the house, went flying past him, spraying him with muddy water and almost knocking him over and turned into the drive and stopped in front of the house.

As he got level with the gate, the woman was getting something out of the boot, so he shouted out to her;

"Hey you, you almost killed me with that car, why don't you slow down and drive a bit more carefully on these narrow tracks, you are a menace on the road!"

"What's wrong with you, you old fool? You can see the conditions out there, if I went slowly I would get bogged down and never get going again, you should have been on the other side of the track anyway," with which, Mrs. Black carried her package into the house and left Bertie to waddle home, in his wet clothes and carrying his soggy shopping.

On another occasion, Bertie was leaving the Post Office, having posted a parcel to Deborah and purchased a newspaper, which he was reading with interest and did not happen to notice that a woman was trying to get into the shop at the same time as he was trying to leave it, when they collided together in the doorway. Before he had time to apologise, the woman, who happened to be the Cook at Millstone House, immediately berated him for his rudeness and bad manners and ended up by saying,

"And do you always treat ladies this way, when leaving the village shop?"

To which he replied, "I have absolutely no idea madam, when I meet one I will let you know!" With which he left the shop and also left her standing there in the middle of the floor, slowly turning red, as everyone else stared at her, trying to stifle their laughter.

He was chatting to his new friend Geoff, who was the vicar at Upper Style, one day, when he mentioned these two incidents to him and asked what his view was of the ladies at Millstone House.

"The only one I can really claim to know is Mrs. Duffy-Smythe who is a most charming lady and as you know Bertie, is a regular member of the congregation here. She is an author and quite successful I believe, although I have not read any of her books myself. She also has a sister living with her, a Mrs. Black, who I suspect is the person you encountered in the driving incident. We do not have a lot to do with her, but Mildred seems to go out of her way to avoid her, which is most unusual for my wife.

The older lady you met was their cook and everyone seems to call her that, I have never known anyone to use her name. We find her quite pleasant, but she keeps herself to herself and only attends church for Christmas, Easter and Harvest Thanksgiving as a rule."

"Interesting, I will do my best to follow Mildred's example and avoid them all in the future. I hear on the grapevine that we have a new district nurse in town Geoff, have you met her yet?"

"I have not only met her, but recruited her into our choir. She is a Scots lass from Inverness; very pretty with a most beautiful voice, she will be a real asset to the village, in my opinion."

"I look forward to meeting her, perhaps I can get her and my daughter Deborah to become friends. One of the reasons she does not visit very often, is because she does not know anyone here and before you ask, no she will not come to church with me."

"Are you going to your daughter's for Christmas again this year Bertie?"

"No, I am visiting an old crewmate in Spain this year. Paco and I first sailed together over forty years ago and he has invited me over there to spend the winter with him, so I will be leaving here in late November and arrive back at the beginning of March."

"Lucky you, Mildred has always wanted to go to Spain, maybe one day. So will the work on the house stop while you are away?"

"To be honest there is not a lot left to do. Tom and I have finished the inside and he and his son will paint the outside for me, while I am away and finish off the garden wall and gate and hopefully do a few other jobs outside that need some attention."

"So what happens if anything goes wrong and he needs to contact you and how will you pay him his wages each week?"

"I was going to ask my good friend the vicar, if Tom could use his telephone to call me in Spain, if he had a problem and also if he would be willing to hold some cash for me and pay Tom and his son their wages each week and any other expenses they might incur. Would you mind doing that for me Geoff?"

"No of course not Bertie, assuming you can trust Tom not to try and cheat you."

"Oh he's a bit rough Geoff, but he is totally trustworthy, is there anything I can bring you or Mildred back from Spain with me, by way of a thank you present?"

Bertie went to Spain for the winter and returned at the beginning of March 1948 to find that all the jobs around the house were completed and that Tom was now working at the local Brickworks and doing odd-jobs for people at the weekends and that young Tom had kept working on the garden and given the grass its first cut of the year.

Deborah came down to visit her father, but was not interested in meeting the new District Nurse, or anyone else for that matter, as she was now heavily involved with the R.S.P.C.A. and was attending lectures and carrying out voluntary work, whenever she had a spare moment.

"So, how was Spain dad, anything exciting happen?" she asked.

"Not really, but it was great, I had a good time thank you Deborah. Paco's niece has asked to buy the house off me and I told her I would think about it."

"I was going to ask you what you were going to do next, now that the cottage is finished and I have to say, it looks really great. Would you want to go back to Spain, permanently?"

"No, is the honest answer, but I do need something new to do. I met up with some of the old skippers that I knew and frankly I found it a bit depressing, each trying to outdo the other with their stories, which everyone has heard countless times before anyway."

"I suppose you could sell the cottage and start again somewhere else, or what about visiting Rosie and Brock in New Zealand? I saw the Christmas card they sent you and they said that they would love to see you again."

"I have considered that and also visiting Shep and his wife and another friend in Australia, perhaps I will book something for next autumn and winter, but that is enough about me, tell me what you have been up to while I was away and congratulations on being promoted to manager at work, well done."

He busied himself during March with sorting out his shed, in the style that Rosie's first husband had used in New Zealand, as Tom and his son, had left in a bit of a mess. He planted a whole lot of new flowers in the garden and arranged a wooden seat he had purchased, in a corner at the back of the garden, overlooking the pond, where he could sit and snooze and read.

He was in the Post Office during the last week of March, having bought some stamps and a news paper when he noticed Cook walking towards the shop. He did no more, but open the door wide and bowed gracefully as she swept into the shop, totally ignoring his gesture. He went out chuckling to himself and wondering what comment she was going to make about him to the other customers.

It was a few days later on Tuesday the 6th April 1948, when boredom was beginning to set in and he was in the back garden, sitting on the bench and reading for the umpteenth time 'He would be a Gentleman' by Samuel Lover, the book given to him at Folkestone all those years ago, when he heard someone knocking loudly on the door and then the voice of a young man calling out, "Anyone at home!"

"I'm round the back, come round the back," he shouted out.

A young man in his late twenties, carrying an old axe walked round the corner of the house and stopped by the edge of the lawn and was obviously trying to locate Bertie's whereabouts.

"I am over here son, to your left and forward fifty feet."

The man followed Bertie's instructions and then spotted him sitting on the bench in the corner, hidden by the mass of flowers and bushes.

"Good afternoon sir, I hope I'm not disturbing you, would you be Bertie by any chance, I don't know the surname I'm afraid."

"Goodness me, the last time someone called me sir, I was a skipper of my own boat, but all I skipper now is that model on the pond, but yes I am Bertie and who might you be young man?"

"Digger Smith at your service, I have been taken on at Millstone House for a few days to do some odd jobs and was wondering if you could help me with this," he said, lifting the axe for Bertie's inspection.

"That my boy, has had its day, I will be pleased to help you bury it, get me a spade from the shed," he replied, pointing across the garden.

"Well actually I was hoping you might be able to help me sharpen it, it's all I have to chop up some wood for the fire, before we all freeze to death over there."

Bertie put the book down on the bench and walked towards Digger, he held out his hand and the two men shook hands and smiled at each other, as they each recognised a kindred spirit.

"I was working in the shed this morning, so I'm afraid it's a bit untidy at the moment, but somewhere in there I do have a small grindstone."

As Digger looked in the shed door, he noticed a few shavings on the floor and a couple of chisels on the bench, apart from that it was immaculate.

"If you think this is untidy, you should see the garage over at Millstone, this is a palace compared to what I had over there, to start with."

"Flattery will get you everywhere, my young friend, pass me down that red and gold box on the second shelf, will you please."

The box was duly passed down and opened and a small hand grindstone wrapped in an oily cloth was taken out. Bertie clamped it to a piece of wood, which he then clamped in his large woodworking vice.

"Have you by any chance used a grindstone before Digger?"

"No never," said Digger, "I have not had much experience with these sorts of tools, but I am pretty good with engines, not that that's relevant right now."

"I look back on my time, working with engines, with great pleasure Digger, as I am sure you do." Bertie said, warming to the young man. "There is something very satisfying in fixing an engine and seeing it burst into life. Now if you will turn the handle on the grindstone, I will hold the axe and we will see what we can do."

As the axe slowly responded to the grindstone, there was complete silence between them, apart from the occasional cursing by Bertie when he caught his finger on the edge of the moving stone.

"It isn't brilliant, but it's a lot better than it was. We sometimes get a travelling knife sharpener through here and he has a big grindstone which is what this axe really needs, if I see him I will ask him to call, but I do know that last time he was here, he had a run in with your Mrs. Black, not that that is a difficult thing to achieve, if you will excuse me saying so."

"Feel free, my own sentiments precisely," Digger remarked, as the two men studied their handiwork.

"Thirsty work eh, do you fancy a beer Digger?" Bertie asked, glad for a bit of male company.

"That's a big improvement, thank you," said Digger, as he tested the edge of the axe with his thumb; "do you mind if I call you Bertie?"

"Of course I don't mind; just don't call me 'late for lunch'."

"I would love a drink thanks, but nothing alcoholic for me, a cup of tea would do fine. Do you think I could use your bathroom Bertie, I'm busting a gut at the moment."

"That is completely out of the question," he replied in a stern voice, then paused for effect and continued, "mainly because I don't have one. But you can use my toilet which is the green door on the end. I'll put the kettle on."

The green door opened on to a room with a large sink, with a single tap and a smaller door leading to the WC. After washing his hands, Digger started to walk round the garden admiring the colours and their incredible neatness, not a weed in sight!

"Tea up Digger," called Bertie, "I'll take it over to my seat. No need to rush, we will let it brew a bit first."

The tour completed, Digger wandered over and sat down. "What are you reading?"

"Oh this is a very old novel called 'He would be a Gentleman' by Samuel Lover, "I must have read it twenty times over the years, it's a great story, you can borrow it when I have finished, if you like."

"Thanks, I would like to, but I'm not sure how long I will be staying at Millstone House. There is enough work to keep me going for weeks, but I had a run in with Mrs. Black yesterday and I am certain that she would throw me out today if she could."

"I presume you are cutting up logs and splitting them with the axe, what state is the saw in, as it's very dangerous to use a rusty saw, it might just break on you? You can borrow mine tonight if you wish and get yourself a new blade for your own one tomorrow. The Ironmonger's in the village stocks blades, if I remember correctly."

"Well if you don't mind, I will do just that and return your saw tomorrow; it will give me an excuse to escape the women for an hour or so."

The two men nattered for a bit longer and then Digger spotted the model boat on the pond,

"What sort of boat is that Bertie, I haven't seen one like that before?"

"It's called a Buckie Steam Drifter and it is the boat I used in the Mediterranean Sea during the First World War."

"How interesting, do you still have it tucked away somewhere?"

"Unfortunately not. It was in fact blown up by the British Navy at a place called Saranda in 1917."

"My goodness, that sounds fascinating, I would love to hear about it some time," Digger said.

"And I would be delighted to tell you my friend, my daughter has been urging me to sit down and write my memoirs, but I am not so sure, so it would be a good test to try out a story or two on you and see how quickly I can bore the pants off you."

"Sounds a great offer Bertie and I can't wait to meet this daughter of yours as well, she sounds delightful, but I guess I had better get back to Millstone House and start producing some firewood, before Cook refuses to feed me and Mrs. Black issues my discharge papers."

"Not a problem my young friend, you go and do what you have to do and try and keep those particular ladies happy, my story can wait for another day."

Epilogue

Take pride in all you seek to do,
And always do your best;
For others may be counting
That they're safe to take their rest.
For you have said, "I'll see to that."
And your word is good and true,
For you are known to be the one,
Whose errors are but few.
So don't begrudge the extra mile
That sometimes you must tread;
Take care in all the little things,
So no-one needs to dread.
Be proud of all you ever do
And don't skimp or cheat or mar;
And never spoil the ship my friend,
To save just a ha'porth of tar.

26th March 2011 LS

Lightning Source UK Ltd.
Milton Keynes UK
178176UK00003B/6/P